"The fabulous Joan Overfield leaps into glory with a splendiferous foray into time-travel the way you always wanted it to be. [In *The Door Ajar*] Ms. Overfield has gifted us with a magnificent triumph of the heart, a surefire classic every romance fan will read over and over again."—*Romantic Times*

\* \* \*

# FUTURE PROMISE

"Miranda?" Alec lay a gentle hand on her arm. "What's wrong?"

"One hundred and eighty-four years," she whispered brokenly, tears spilling over to rain down her cheeks. "It's gone, Alec. It's all gone."

As if they had been waiting for only that, emotions so powerful that they literally took away her breath, erupted inside of her, engulfing her in a tidal wave of grief and sorrow. She gave a keening cry, turning instinctively toward the only sense of security she had found in this overwhelming new time.

"Everyone I ever knew or ever loved is dead," she sobbed, clinging to Alec's shoulder. "I'm alone, I'm all alone."

Alec tightened his arms about her, his own eyes burning as he listened to her anguish. He wanted to tell her that he knew how she felt, that he'd also lost everything, but the words wouldn't come. He could only hold her tighter, choking back his own howls of despair, as he listened to the pain pouring out of her.

"My husband is dead, and I was never his wife!" she cried, her whole body shaking with delayed reaction. "What will I do? What will happen to me? Oh God, I'm so afraid!"

"Shhh, it's all right now, it's all right," Alec whispered roughly, his hand shaking as he smoothed back her hair from her forehead. "I'll keep you safe, I promise you."

# ZEBRA'S REGENCY ROMANCES
# DAZZLE AND DELIGHT

**A BEGUILING INTRIGUE** (4441, $3.99)
by Olivia Sumner

Pretty as a picture Justine Riggs cared nothing for propriety. She dressed as a boy, sat on her horse like a jockey, and pondered the stars like a scientist. But when she tried to best the handsome Quenton Fletcher, Marquess of Devon, by proving that she was the better equestrian, he would try to prove Justine's antics were pure folly. The game he had in mind was seduction—never imagining that he might lose his heart in the process!

**AN INCONVENIENT ENGAGEMENT** (4442, $3.99)
by Joy Reed

Rebecca Wentworth was furious when she saw her betrothed waltzing with another. So she decides to make him jealous by flirting with the handsomest man at the ball, John Collinwood, Earl of Stanford. The "wicked" nobleman knew exactly what the enticing miss was up to—and he was only too happy to play along. But as Rebecca gazed into his magnificent eyes, her errant fiancé was soon utterly forgotten!

**SCANDAL'S LADY** (4472, $3.99)
by Mary Kingsley

Cassandra was shocked to learn that the new Earl of Lynton was her childhood friend, Nicholas St. John. After years at sea and mixed feelings Nicholas had come home to take the family title. And although Cassandra knew her place as a governess, she could not help the thrill that went through her each time he was near. Nicholas was pleased to find that his old friend Cassandra was his new next door neighbor, but after being near her, he wondered if mere friendship would be enough . . .

**HIS LORDSHIP'S REWARD** (4473, $3.99)
by Carola Dunn

As the daughter of a seasoned soldier, Fanny Ingram was accustomed to the vagaries of military life and cared not a whit about matters of rank and social standing. So she certainly never foresaw her *tendre* for handsome Viscount Roworth of Kent with whom she was forced to share lodgings, while he carried out his clandestine activities on behalf of the British Army. And though good sense told Roworth to keep his distance, he couldn't stop from taking Fanny in his arms for a kiss that made all hearts equal!

*Available wherever paperbacks are sold, or order direct from the Publisher. Send cover price plus 50¢ per copy for mailing and handling to Penguin USA, P.O. Box 999, c/o Dept. 17109, Bergenfield, NJ 07621. Residents of New York and Tennessee must include sales tax. DO NOT SEND CASH.*

# Joan Overfield

# The Door Ajar

**ZEBRA BOOKS**
**KENSINGTON PUBLISHING CORP.**

ZEBRA BOOKS are published by

Kensington Publishing Corp.
850 Third Avenue
New York, NY 10022

Copyright © 1995 by Joan Overfield

All rights reserved. No part of this book may be reproduced in any form or by any means without the prior written consent of the Publisher, excepting brief quotes used in reviews.

If you purchased this book without a cover, you should be aware that this book is stolen property. It was reported as "unsold and destroyed" to the Publisher and neither the Author nor the Publisher has received any payment for this "stripped book."

Zebra and the Z logo Reg. U.S. Pat. & TM Off.

First Printing: November, 1995

Printed in the United States of America

*To Donna Cummings, my good friend and a fellow believer in Arconians. Here's the time-travel I vowed I'd never write. But absolutely no pirates!!!*

This book is also lovingly dedicated to the memory of
Ann Katherine Esparza. 1953-1995

"She should have died hereafter.
There should have been time for such a word."
                                        —Wm. Shakespeare

And so we must keep apart,
You there, and I here.
With just the door ajar,
That oceans are. . . .
                    —*Emily Dickinson*

# *Prologue*

*London, 1666*

They were coming for him. Aylwyn Murrdoc, wizard of the black arts, did not need the use of his seeing glass to tell him that. Word had reached him that his protégé, Jonathan, had been seized by the witch-hunters, and he knew it would take but a few hours on the rack to make the pitiful wretch tell all. It sorrowed him to think he could have chosen so poorly for the Master, but he accepted philosophically that there was little even he could do to alter the past. And in any event, 'twas the future that held his interest now. The future; beneath his neatly trimmed beard, his lips twisted in a sardonic smile.

Safe in his secret room, especially designed to ancient specifications, Aylwyn worked feverishly to finish his spell. Hiding in time was a practice many of his kind engaged in, but it was not without its inherent risks. One had to be prudent; weighing the dangers of the future against the dangers of the present. He would use the spell only as a last resort; waiting until the witch-hunters actually made an attempt to seize him before unleashing the awesome power he had at his command. He needed but a few hours, and—

"Master Murrdoc! Master Murrdoc!" The frantic pounding on the door shattered Aylwyn's reverie, and for a brief moment he feared he had already waited too long. Hastily tucking his book in its hiding place, he crossed the floor and unbolted the door. His manservant stood on the threshold, and the terror evident on his plain features did little to ease Aylwyn's fears.

"What is it, man?" he demanded, his cultured voice rough with fear. "Has someone come to see me?"

"No, master, but—"

"Then why are you here?" Aylwyn interrupted, relief all but making him giddy. "Have I not told you I am never to be disturbed whilst I am in my private chambers? Fool! Be gone with you!" And he started to close the door.

"But, master, we must flee!" The manservant was near tears, dancing from one foot to the other. "The fire is being carried on the wind! All of London is ablaze, and if we do not leave now, we will most surely perish!"

*Fire!* Aylwyn went pale with terror. Of all the elements, it was the one he feared most. It was the reason he was so determined to flee before the witch-hunters got their foul hands on him. It was not death he feared, but rather death by burning, for all knew the flames could take not only a witch's life, but his immortal powers as well.

"How can this be?" he demanded hoarsely, certain he could already smell the stench of smoke. "I was told the fire was not expected to burn so far."

" 'Tis the wind, it carries the burning embers and starts fires anew," the manservant explained impatiently. "Houses on the next street have already had their roofs set ablaze; that is why we must leave. Now," he added, when Aylwyn still did not move.

Aylwyn cast an anguished look over his shoulder, torn between his fear of the rapidly approaching flames, and his fear of the witch-hunters. "Take what gold and money you can carry," he instructed the servant, thinking quickly. "Make your way to my brother's home, and wait for me there. I must see to my books."

"But, master—"

"Do it, dolt!" Aylwyn snapped, sending the man a dark scowl. "I shall join you when I can, now go!" And he slammed the door.

Behind it he could hear the sounds of shouts and running footsteps, but he closed his mind to the noise. Returning to his table, he retrieved the instruments of power from their hiding place and began the incantation. It took all of his concentration and skill, and when he was finished, the room was glowing with a pale greenish light. He stood in that light, eyes closing with pleasure as he felt the energy he had unleashed snapping around him. He had but to make use of the medallion about his throat, and he would vanish; going beyond the witch-hunters' ability to claim him.

For a moment he was tempted to do just that; reasoning that if he disappeared now, it would be assumed he had died in the fire. He even began chanting in the old tongue, exulting in the increase of power all around him. He could hear the hum, feel it burning his flesh with its white flames, and the sensation frightened him. He dropped his hands at once, taking a hasty step backward. None of his studies had indicated that passing through the barrier of time should hurt, and he feared he had made a miscalculation. When he returned, he would have to study his notes again and, if necessary, recast the spell.

The smell of smoke grew even stronger as Aylwyn hurried to secure his precious books. He also hid anything to do with the Craft, knowing all would be lost should they be discovered. He was about to leave, when he remembered his medallion. It had been placed about his neck the day he was declared High Warlock, and it was the source of his great power; without it he would be as helpless as any foolish mortal. He pulled the medallion out from beneath his jacket, and after a moment's consideration, he decided to hide it somewhere in the room as well.

He had just concealed it and was about to leave, when once again someone began pounding on the door. "The roof is ablaze!" he heard one of the servants scream. "Hurry, master, hurry!"

Aylwyn needed no more urging. He flung open the door, almost knocking the elderly man to the ground in his haste to be gone. He dashed down the narrow stairs, the acrid smoke stinging his nose and his eyes. In his fevered mind he could hear the crackle of the greedy flames as they devoured his home, and terror rose up like bile to choke him. He could not burn, he thought desperately, his fingers clawing at the heavy wooden door as he struggled to open it. Finally the door opened and he gave a grateful sob, dashing out into the streets and into a scene that came straight from his most fearsome nightmare.

The narrow street was choked with wagons and people, all fleeing the high wall of hellish fire that was advancing inexorably toward them. Smoke and ash made the day as night, and to the east the sky was lit with a terrible glow. Above the shouts and noise, he could hear the screams of horses driven half-mad by the smell of smoke, and it fed the panic that was robbing him of his ability to reason. Crazed with fear he threw himself into the crowd, shoving people out of his way in his desperate desire to reach safety.

His ears were deaf to everything, and he did not hear the warning someone shouted as the burning building to his left suddenly collapsed, sending flaming bricks and timber spilling on to the crowded streets. The others around him, more alert to the danger, retreated in time, but Aylwyn kept running, not aware of the danger until the very last second. He glanced up in horror, the scream of despair he uttered disappearing as the flaming wall fell upon him, engulfing him in fire and the death he had feared most.

Days later, his brother returned to the house, and upon discovering the secret room with its evil signs painted on the floor and walls, ordered it walled up before the church should learn of its existence. All of the servants who had worked for Aylwyn took a sacred vow never to speak of the room, and his brother sold the house as quickly as he could. Years became centuries as the room remained hidden behind brick and mortar, the power trapped inside humming as it waited . . .

# One

*London, June, 1811*

The small, Jacobean-styled house on Curzon Street was not at all what Miss Miranda Winthrop had been expecting. Granted, Stephen had warned her that the house was old-fashioned and sadly in want of refurbishing, but she'd assumed he was merely being modest, as was his custom. But gazing up at the dilapidated house with its soot-blackened bricks and its broken window panes, Miranda found she was perilously close to tears. *This* was to be her new home?

"You're disappointed, aren't you?" Stephen Hallforth, the seventh earl of Harrington, asked quietly, his blue eyes cool as he studied Miranda's face. "I am sorry."

Miranda's cheeks flushed with dismay at the note of censure in Stephen's deep voice. She knew his considerable pride was already stung by the fact that she was far wealthier than he, and the last thing she wanted was for him to think she had found even the slightest fault in the house he had recently inherited. Pushing the discontentment from her mind, she lifted her face to his, a bright smile pinned to her lips.

"Nonsense, Stephen," she said firmly, laying a shy hand on his muscular arm. "I am not in least disappointed. I am simply," she hesitated, searching for the correct adjective, "surprised," she concluded, deciding that was as close to the truth as she dared stray. "The house is a great deal older than the other homes on this street, is it not?"

"By a hundred years, at least," Stephen responded, his clipped tone making it obvious her blithe explanation had failed to convince him. "It was built shortly before the Great Fire, and it was one of the few structures in the area to have escaped serious damage. The houses on either side were completely destroyed."

"Ah, that would explain their newer appearance," Miranda said with a nod, eager to convince him of her delight. "Well, shall we go in, then? I am anxious to see my new home."

Instead of complying, Stephen remained where he was, his expression dark as he continued staring down at her. "Miranda, if you feel the house will not suit, then kindly say so. I am sure we shall be able to find something else. In a more fashionable part of town, perhaps?"

Miranda nervously tucked a stray blond curl beneath her stylish bonnet. This wasn't the first time Stephen had hinted she was overly concerned with appearances, and it hurt that he should think so little of her. They might be engaged to be wed, but in reality, they were all but strangers to one other. Once they were married, she was certain she would be able to convince him that she wasn't an encroaching, grasping Cit like her annoying step-papa.

She raised her chin higher, holding her temper in check with considerable effort. "I have already said I was but surprised by the house's age," she said, her green eyes filled with pride as she met his hooded gaze. "Now, do let us go inside, the wind is most sharp," and with that she took a determined step forward, leaving him no choice but to accompany her.

There was no butler to answer the door, but the apron-clad workman who admitted them seemed efficient enough.

"Mind yer step, me lord, me lady," he warned with a broken-toothed grin. "These old floors be in need of shoring up. Watch where ye put yer feet, else ye're like to find yerself in the cellars with the rats."

"Rats?" Despite her desire to appear enthralled with the house, Miranda could not keep her voice from quavering.

"Big as pups," the workman elaborated, his grin widening. "Not that ye need to be worryin', me lady. I brought me two terriers with me, and they'll see to the vermin, I promise ye."

Their voices drew the attention of the small staff already in residence, and the flustered housekeeper was soon making her bows to them. She began apologizing profusely for not greeting them, and she might have continued in this same vein forever had Miranda not gently, but firmly, interrupted her.

"Calm yourself, Mrs. Finch," she said, giving the older woman a warm smile. "It is of no moment. And in any case, it is his lordship and I who ought to be tendering our apologies to you. It was quite bad of us to pop in on you without so much as a word of warning."

The apology had its desired effect, and the older woman relaxed with a gusty sigh. "It *were* a bit of a shock," she conceded, venturing a small frown of disapproval on her new mistress. "Had I known you was expected, I would have had a fine tea waiting for you."

"It is my fault," Miranda said, doing her best to look penitent. "We were driving through Green Park, and as we were so close, I couldn't resist stopping in for a look. I do hope we haven't inconvenienced you and the staff overly much?"

"Not at all, Miss," the housekeeper assured her, looking pleased by her employer's graciousness. "And if you'll but give me a half hour, I promise to have a proper tea prepared for you."

Miranda replied that a cup of tea was just what she needed, and after watching the housekeeper depart in a rustle of starched skirts, Stephen took her arm once again.

"Neatly done, my dear," he said, leading her around a burly man who was busy scraping fading wallpaper from the wall. "However, in the future, might I advise you not be so quick to apologize? It never does to make one's servants feel as if they have the upper hand. It tends to makes them lazy."

A small prick of resentment stabbed Miranda at his implica-

tion that she did not know how to deal with a staff. She had
been handling servants since she was a child, and she'd learned
that kindness was usually the quickest route to efficient service.
She was strongly tempted to tell him just that, but as usual, she
was far too shy to say anything so bold. Perhaps after they were
wed she would lose her awe of him, but until then, she was
determined to keep such thoughts to herself.

To her surprise, Stephen led her into one of the rooms located
off the dusty hallway and carefully closed the door. Uncertain
what to expect, she couldn't help but jump when he pulled her
into his arms; his touch was gentle as he raised her face to his.

"I am sorry, Miranda," he said softly, stroking her cheek with
a gloved finger. "That was a dreadfully snappish thing for me
to say. I did not mean to imply that you would not know how
to run a household, I promise you. I have every faith you will
be an exemplary wife. I suppose it is because I am somewhat
embarrassed at having brought you to such a hovel," he added,
casting a disparaging glance at the scarred floors and crumbling
plaster. "Believe me, had I known things were so bad as this, I
should never have suggested we move in here after we are wed."

Miranda's anger melted at his sincere apology, and at his un-
expected touch. They had been engaged for the better part of
five months, and this was one of the few times he had touched
her in anything approaching a personal manner. She was beginning to fear he regretted their engagement, and the fact he was
holding her so easily gave her hope for the marriage that was
less than two weeks away. Feeling greatly daring, she raised her
hand to brush a strand of light brown hair from his forehead.

"I admit it is not quite what I expected," she said softly, her
eyes glowing as she touched his face. "But I am sure in time I
shall come to adore it."

"Are you certain?" He still looked worried. "As you can see,
it is a devil of a mess, and I fear it will take a fortune to set it
to rights."

His distress made her smile. "That is my concern," she reminded him sternly. "Did you not agree that restoring the house would be my wedding gift to you?"

The frown vanished, replaced by a rueful grin. "So I did, my sweet," he said, the rare endearment making her heart race with delight. "But that was before I knew what a pesthole the place had become. I fear you have gotten the worst end of the bargain, madam."

Her smile wavered at his mention of the marriage settlement he and her stepfather had made. He had called it a bargain also, making it sound as if she had purchased Stephen from a stall on market day. The comment had stung, but she'd attributed it to Elias's grasping nature. Now she could not help but wonder if that was how Stephen himself viewed the matter.

The depressing thought plagued her for the rest of the tour, making it difficult for her to feign enthusiasm for her new home. Like most houses of the period, the rooms were small and dark, and had little to recommend them. She did like the latticed windows with their diamond-shaped panes, and she and the housekeeper had an earnest discussion as to which window treatment would show the windows to their best advantage.

They had just decided upon sheer drapes with a Roman valance, when a loud crash sounded from the floor above them. They ran out into the hall and saw Stephen dashing up the stairs, but when Miranda would have followed, he called out a warning.

"Stay where you are, my dear," he said, casting a stern frown over his shoulder. "It may be dangerous."

Several anxious minutes passed, and then there was another crash, followed by excited shouting. Miranda was wondering if the entire house was about to come falling down about their ears, when Stephen leaned over the railing, a smear of white dust adorning his cheek.

"Come and see what we have found!" he called out, his voice filled with boyish delight. "I vow, I have never seen the like!" This was too much for Miranda's curiosity, and she picked up her skirts and hurried up the narrow staircase. Stephen was waiting for her, and he led her down the dark hall where a group of workmen were gathered around a gaping hole that had been punched in the wall.

"We just knocked down the wall, and there it were," a man with a large hammer cradled in his beefy hands said, looking wide-eyed as a lad. "I thought were one o' them priest holes at first, but it were too big."

"What is it?" Miranda demanded, standing on the tips of her toes so that she could see over the men's heads.

"A hidden room," Stephen said, placing his arm about her waist and guiding her around the men. "From the looks of things, it must have been closed up for over a century!"

Miranda ventured forward cautiously, peering into the dim room with increasing uneasiness. The closer she got to the room, the more uneasy she became, and when Stephen began urging her inside, she dug in her heels with surprising strength.

"Why, my dear, what is it?" he asked, his hand tightening comfortingly about her waist. "Surely you are not afraid? It is quite safe, I assure you."

Miranda flushed, feeling much like a foolish schoolgirl. "Certainly I am not afraid," she denied, although she wouldn't take another step forward. "It is just that it is so very dark inside. If there was a hole in the floor, I should fall right through it."

Stephen ordered two of the workmen to light their torches, and had another man fetch a brace of candles from the housekeeper. Soon the room was bright as midday, but the sight that greeted their eyes did little to ease the fear eating at Miranda's soul. If anything, it made her more apprehensive than ever.

The room was oddly shaped, with five walls instead of four, and those walls were decorated with faded symbols she'd never seen before. There seemed to be no evidence of either door or an outside window, and the lack of such things struck her as highly odd. Both the floor and the few pieces of furniture that remained were shrouded with thick dust, and a strange-looking mirror hung on the far wall, its glassy surface dulled by decades of grime. She took a cautious step forward, and the moment she crossed the threshold, she felt a burning tingle that made her jerk back with a cry of alarm.

"I—I do not wish to go in there!" she exclaimed, her heart hammering as she turned to Stephen. "Please, my lord, take me downstairs at once!"

"Of course, Miranda," he said, his tone solicitous as he slid a gentle arm about her waist. "Poor child, you are trembling!" he added, clearly alarmed at her shivering. "I am sorry. I should never have insisted you see the room, if I knew it was going to frighten you so!"

Miranda was too upset to respond, but allowed him to guide her downstairs where the housekeeper was waiting with tea and soothing words of comfort. By the time she had finished her second cup, she was beginning to feel more like herself, and with the return of self came an acute sense of embarrassment. She cast Stephen a shy look, her cheeks pinking at the worried expression on his face.

"I must apologize, sir," she said, unconsciously squaring her shoulders as she met his somber blue eyes. "I hadn't meant to act so missish. I'm not usually so chicken-hearted," she added with a rueful laugh, and was relieved when he smiled in return.

"I know you are not," he said in a gentle voice, setting his cup to one side and leaning forward to capture her hand in his. "And again, I am sincerely sorry for upsetting you." He gave her a long look, his touch comforting as he continued cradling her hand in his.

"What is it that frightened you?" he asked, the tone of his voice making it obvious he was genuinely curious. "Did you think the room was haunted?"

"Oh no!" she exclaimed, horrified he should think her so foolish. "I do not believe in spirits!"

"Then what, dearest?" he pressed, his dark brown eyebrows meeting over his nose. "What did you fear about the room?"

Miranda paused, searching for some rational explanation for her behavior. She had sensed something, she admitted silently, something very strong, and very evil, but upon her life she could think of no word that would describe the sensation. She knit her brows together, certain that if she thought hard enough, the explanation would come to her.

*Power.* She blinked as the word seemed to leap into her mind, but she realized that was precisely what she had felt. Raw, savage power, like that which lingered in the air after a thunder storm. Power that was potent and malevolent; power that had waited over a hundred years to be unleashed . . . In the next moment she was shaking her head, her logical mind rejecting such dramatic absurdity. When Stephen spoke her name in concern, she lifted her head and gave him another smile.

"It is nothing, my lord," she said at last. "Upon reflection I am sure 'tis naught but a sudden case of bridal nerves. I shall be fine, I promise you."

"Are you certain?" He looked far from convinced. "If the room truly bothers you, we can have it walled up again."

Miranda opened her mouth to agree, but quickly closed it again, realizing that if she did that, he would know the room had affected her sensibilities. She thought quickly, then managed a credible laugh. "There is no reason to do that," she said, forcing a cheerful note into her voice. "As I said, 'tis nothing more serious than the jitters, and I daresay that by the time we move in, I shall be quite over my foolishness."

He gave her another incisive stare before releasing her hand. "As you wish," he said, retrieving his cup of tea as he leaned back in his chair.

"However, I should like it left untouched . . . until we decide what to do with it, that is," she added hastily. "With so much to be done is such a short time, I should rather concentrate on the main rooms of the house first. It is less than a fortnight until our marriage, you know."

Stephen nodded coolly, his expression enigmatic as he met her eyes. "Yes," he agreed, his voice curiously devoid of emotion, as he took a sip of tea. "So it is."

* * *

"Will there be anything else, my lady?" the young maid asked, her eyes filled with curiosity as she studied Miranda.

"No, Mary, that is all, thank you," Miranda said, gazing at her reflection with trepidation. It was her wedding night, and she was waiting nervously for her new husband to come to her.

"Then I shall bid you good night," the maid said, dropping a curtsey as she backed toward the door. "I shall just put out the candle, and—"

"No!" Miranda interrupted, heart pounding with heady anticipation. "Leave it lit, and—and the rest as well."

The maid raised an eyebrow, but she was obviously too well trained to question her mistress. She merely curtsied again and departed, closing the door behind her.

Left alone, Miranda allowed herself to relax, her shoulders slumping as she turned back to the cheval glass. She was dressed in a revealing peignoir of virginal white, lavishly trimmed with ribbons and lace. Her blond hair had been brushed until it gleamed, and it fell about her shoulders in soft waves, framing a face that was far too pale. Her hand shook slightly as she dipped her rabbit's paw in the jar of rouge, adding a touch of color to her cheeks. It seemed to help, although her green eyes were still too dark and too wide for her liking.

She had a vague idea of what to expect, and the notion of Stephen making love to her filled her with a confusing whirl of emotions. It would hurt, that much she knew, but she had also heard it whispered that it could be pleasurable, if a man was but gentle. Stephen had always treated her with gentleness and consideration, but they were married now, and she had observed that a man's behavior often changed once a woman became his property. Only look at the way her stepfather had treated her and her mama, once he'd had the wealthy widow safely under his thumb . . .

A shudder shook her slender frame, and she resolutely pushed the memory from her mind. No, she told herself, picking up a bottle of perfume and dabbing a bit of the soft rose scent to her wrists. This was her wedding night, and she refused to let Elias ruin it for her as he had ruined everything else. At least he was powerless to hurt her now, she mused, the realization making her smile. As Stephen's wife, she was free at last from her step-father's greedy, thieving ways.

A discreet glance at the clock on her dressing table showed that it had been almost an hour since she had retired to her rooms to prepare herself. Surely Stephen would be arriving any moment now. The thought drove her to her feet, and she cast a nervous glance at the silk-draped bed, wondering if it would be better if she was already abed when Stephen joined her. She decided it would, and after shedding her filmy robe, she climbed onto the bed and under the covers.

Time seemed to slow to a crawl as she waited, but still Stephen did not come. To distract herself she occupied her mind by study-ing her bedchamber, noting the miraculous changes that had occurred since the first time she'd visited the house. She'd been back several times since then, watching with pleasure as her new home slowly took shape. Upon reflection she decided to accent the house's age, rather than trying to bring it up to current fash-ion. By mixing new styles with old she had achieved a look that was both elegant and welcoming, and she had the added pleasure of knowing Stephen approved of her efforts.

She'd also given the hidden room a wide berth, although she had noted that the hole in the wall had been patched and a secret door found. It had been cut into the wall so cleverly, a person could be standing right beside it and never see it; at least that was what she heard one of the footmen tell a maid. It had been cleaned, but other than that it had been left untouched, and she knew that sooner or later she would have no choice but to come to some sort of decision as to what she should do with it. She knew she had no intention of ever venturing inside again, but she could always have it redone to suit Stephen. A study, perhaps, she mused, recalling a bookshelf along one wall, or even a gam-ing room, although she did not think Stephen was a gamester.

More time passed, and Miranda grew increasingly agitated as Stephen did not appear. Perhaps he wasn't coming, she worried, nibbling on her bottom lip with consternation. Maybe he thought to give her time to know him before seeking his husbandly rights, and although she knew she should be grateful for his kindness, she couldn't help but feel disappointed. Disappointed and hurt, she admitted, her gaze sliding to the door that connected her room to the sitting room she shared with Stephen.

Before her good sense could caution her, she slipped out of the bed and tiptoed over to the door. Drawing a steady breath for courage, she opened the door and peeked into the darkened sitting room. A shaft of light from Stephen's bedchamber was visible beneath his door, and after assuring herself her conduct wasn't in the least unseemly, she closed her door and crept stealthily across the Aubusson carpet. She'd almost reached the door when the sound of voices brought her to a startled halt. Good heavens! she realized in shock, Stephen had a visitor!

She stood in frozen uncertainty, until her curiosity got the better of her. Taking care not to be heard, she made her way to his door, lightly resting her hand on the brass handle as she strained to hear what was being said.

". . . her stepfather," she heard the disgust in Stephen's voice. "He wanted the papers giving him control over the money signed on the very steps of the church! How the devil do you think that would have looked?"

"Not good, I imagine," she heard a familiar voice respond with a wry chuckle. "Well, however hard the old boy might have wrangled, I do not see that you are in any position to quibble. He settled fifty thousand pounds on you for taking the chit off his hands, did he not?"

Miranda stiffened in shock. Fifty thousand pounds! Her stepfather had told her the sum settled on Stephen was less than half that amount! And what did he mean about giving Elias control over her money? That made no sense at all. Then she realized that Stephen was speaking, and she pressed her ear against the door, straining to catch the words.

"I know that," Stephen's voice was heavy with resignation, "and that is not the issue. It is just . . . oh, devil take it! I *like*

Miranda, I truly do, and I feel as if I am deceiving her in the cruelest way possible."

"You are being too hard on yourself." The other man sounded bored. "From what you have said, your sweet wife is no green miss, and is awake to all accounts. Surely she must realize this is no love match."

The callous remark made her press her fist to her mouth to hold back a cry of pain. She'd always known Stephen didn't love her, but until this very moment it hadn't occurred to her that he meant to use her; use her as her stepfather had tried to use her. The searing agony was almost more than she could bear, but she couldn't move. She could only stand there in silence, listening as every dream she'd ever held was smashed to pieces.

"Circumstances may have forced me into a marriage of convenience, but I still have enough honor not to have wooed her with promises I can not keep," she could hear the grim pride in Stephen's voice. "I have told her that I care for her, that I respect her, and that is the truth."

"Then why all the handwringing and gnashing of teeth?" The man was laughing now. "Your bride awaits you, and if you are in no mind to do your duty, I should be more than delighted to take your place. I have always thought her a comely wench."

Miranda couldn't bear to hear another word. The paralysis holding her broke at last, and she stumbled back from the door, fighting back a sob. She would flee, she decided, unmindful of the tears streaming down her face. She would find some place to hide, and the first thing tomorrow she would seek an annulment.

She dashed back into her own room, and was trying to decide on how best to carry out her plan, when she heard the sound of a door closing. Seconds later she heard footsteps on the stairs and realized Stephen's mysterious caller had taken his leave. The thought that her husband would soon be joining her to "do his duty," was enough to send her out into the hall in search of a place to hide. She'd seek sanctuary in the servants' quarters, she thought, reasoning Stephen's considerable pride would keep him from seeking her there.

She turned toward the hall, and hadn't taken but a few steps, when she saw the door to the hidden room standing open. A faint greenish white glow seemed to be coming from inside, and even as she was wondering how the door came to be open, she was realizing that it was the perfect solution to her problems. Stephen knew how afraid she was of the room, and it was the last place he would think to look for her. It also occurred to her that the room might have a secret passage of some kind, and that thought was enough to overcome her terror. She hurried into the room, releasing an unconscious sigh when she felt no repeat of the painful sensation she'd experienced when she'd first entered the room.

After securing the door, she turned to study her refuge, and was surprised to see that the glow she had noted seemed to come from the room itself, rather than from any kind of flame. The phenomenon puzzled her, but she had too much on her mind at the moment to care. Remembering her thoughts about the possibility of a secret passage, she crossed the room, noting as she did so, the strange figures painted on the wood floor. A five-pointed star in a circle lying crookedly on its side caught her interest, but as with the glow, she quickly put it from her mind.

She spent several minutes running her fingers along the walls looking for access to the passage, but all to no avail. She was beginning to think she had made an error, when the wall suddenly opened with a rusty-sounding groan. She leapt back, but instead of the passage she had been expecting to find, there was only a row of shelves filled with books and other artifacts. Curious, she picked up several of the items, wondering how long they had been hidden there, and why they weren't coated with dust. A gleam of metal caught her attention, and she picked up a medallion, noting with a detached sense of calm that it was also a five-pointed star with symbols carved in the middle.

The medallion fascinated her, and unaware of what she was doing, she slipped it over her head. The moment the metal came in contact with her flesh, the room grew bright with the greenish light, and a low hum seemed to come from the very walls. She noted these oddities as if from a great distance, her limbs heavy with lethargy as she walked to stand in the center of the star painted on the floor. She had to run, she thought, her mind growing hazy. She had to hide. It was her only chance . . .

"Miranda?" She heard Stephen's voice from the hall. "Miranda, where are you?"

The sound of her name broke the spell that seemed to be holding her, but when she tried to step out of the circle, she found she couldn't move. She tried again, but to her horror her feet refused to obey the command of her mind. She could hear Stephen moving down the hall, opening and closing doors as he called out to her. In seconds he would find her, and then all would be lost.

Suddenly the room exploded with light, and with a cry she raised her arms to shield her eyes from the brightness. She could feel a terrible burning engulf her, and thought she must surely be dying. She screamed again, and her last thought as the hellish light swallowed her was that she was dying without ever knowing what it was to love and be loved.

# Two

*London, The Present*

"I mean it, Alec. I've put up with your nonsense for the past eighteen months, but this is enough!" Cara Bramwell Marsdale exclaimed, light brown eyes sparkling with fury as she glared at her disheveled older brother. "If you think you're moving into that house, you're out of your bloody mind!"

Alec Bramwell gave her a cold look, plainly unimpressed by her fiery outburst. He thrust his hand through his thick, black hair, raising a pint of lager to his lips to take a sip. "My life, my decision," he said, his voice edged with a hard note of warning that would have had most men taking a step back. But, as usual, it had no effect on his brattish sister.

"My brother, my worry," she said, pointing an accusatory finger at him. "You know you're in no condition to deal with things just yet. Why not sell the house as is and be done with it? Robert said you've been offered a good price for it."

Alec's golden-colored eyes narrowed at the mention of his sister's partner and his long-time friend. "Robert is a nosey old woman!" he snapped, setting down his glass of beer and leaning forward to pierce her with a fierce look. "And I'm not selling Jane's house."

The fire died in Cara's eyes, and she reached out to cover her brother's hand with her own. "Jane is dead, Alec," she said softly, the compassion she showed the rape victims she dealt with on a daily basis evident in her glowing eyes. "I know how much you loved her, but you must accept the fact that she is gone, and that she's never coming back."

Alec didn't speak at first, his jaw clenching with the effort not to howl out his rage and pain. He felt like shouting that he knew Jane was dead, that he'd accepted months ago that he had lost her. God, how could he help but accept it, when he had been the one to respond to the bomb blast? When he had been the one to identify what was left of her when they dug her out of the rubble? The image was burned indelibly on his mind, and even now, months later, he could remember every horrifying detail of what he had seen . . .

"Alec," Cara's voice cut into his anguished memories, and he raised his eyes to find her watching with obvious concern. He pushed back his response to the love he could feel emanating from her, and twisted his lips in a bitter smile.

"Still afraid I'll stick my head in an oven, little sister?" he asked, freeing his hand from her urgent grip and picking up his glass of lager. "Or do you think I'll lock myself in a room and eat my own gun? Well, you can relax, the guvenor took my weapon as soon as we confirmed Jane's ID."

Cara remembered that, and remembered also it had taken three strong officers to disarm Alec and hold him still while the emergency doctors gave him a sedative. She'd been on duty herself, and they had sent a car to pick her up. She'd heard Alec's screams when she got to hospital, and her first thought was that he'd been hurt. Then the sister had told her about Jane, and she knew the source of her brother's terrible pain.

"I can't talk you out of this, then?" she asked at last, accepting the inevitable with a tired sigh.

"Not a chance."

"I didn't know you fancied yourself a handyman," Cara drawled after a few moments. "What do you intend doing?"

"Knock down a few walls, patch up the plaster, maybe sand the floor in the parlor," Alec replied, remembering painfully how he and Jane had planned each project. "Nothing very difficult."

Cara was silent a long moment, and then an impish grin lifted the corners of her lips. "You'll probably end up nailing your feet to the floor," she said smugly, every inch the annoying little sister. "You always were bloody useless, when it came to using your hands."

His own lips twitched in response. "I'll learn," he said mildly. "And you say bloody too much."

"It's so I won't say something worse," Cara returned calmly. "On the streets one hears filth so often it becomes appallingly easy to use it oneself." She fell silent again, moving her glass of wine from one hand to the other.

"Paul left some of his tools behind when he moved out," she said carefully, not meeting his eyes. "I was going to sell them, but I suppose I could give them to you . . . for a price."

Alec stiffened warily. "What price?"

She met his gaze then. "I want you to talk to your counselor . . . no, wait," she added, when she saw his mouth open in automatic protest. "I want you to tell her what you're planning, and if she agrees, the tools are yours. All right?"

Alec leaned back against the wooden booth and muttered a dark expletive beneath his breath. After several seconds he gave his sister a long-suffering look. "God, you're a bossy bitch."

Cara grinned, understanding that he was going to be sensible . . . for a change. "I know," she said, lifting her glass in a mocking salute. "Robert is always telling me it's part of my charm."

"Robert's a happily married man."

"Which makes him the perfect partner for a divorcée such as myself. Now, will you talk to your counselor?"

He pretended to consider the matter. "Is there a screwdriver in those tools?"

"Power-driven with interchangeable heads."

"All right," he said with a decisive nod. "But," he added warningly, "regardless of what the doctor says, I'm moving into the house, and nothing you say is going to change that."

* * *

The next three days passed quickly for Alec. To placate Cara he'd gone to the department therapist he'd been seeing since Jane's death, and to his relief she heartily endorsed his decision. A closure, she called it, adding that it was an important step in his recovery. Of course, she thought he was refurbishing the house so that he could sell it, and he hadn't the slightest compunction about deceiving her. Whatever it took, that was his motto.

Several of his old mates from SO 13, the elite Counter-Terrorism Squad at Scotland Yard, helped him move out of the small bedsetter he'd been living in for the past eighteen months and into the house. Since he had only his clothes and stereo equipment, the move didn't take long, and after wishing him the best, they left. He knew they realized he was still uncomfortable around them, and he was grateful for their understanding.

Following his return from administrative leave, he'd been re-assigned to another unit, but he hoped to be back at his *real* job within the week. He'd just passed the last of the extensive psychological testing ordered by his commanding officer, and he was expecting the call any day now.

He spent his first morning in the house cleaning and settling into one of the bedrooms. He'd lived there with Jane prior to her death, but he couldn't bear to enter the room they had shared. Cara had wanted to clear out Jane's clothes and other personal belongings, but he'd threatened to break her arms if she tried. He'd been drunk at the time, but he must have been damned convincing because his sister had never broached the matter again. Later, he told himself, steeling himself for the pain he knew he would have to face. He would deal with it later.

After restoring the house to some semblance of order, he went to some of the nearby shops and bought enough groceries to keep himself from starving. He thought about buying something more potent as well, but his rehabilitation process had made him painfully aware of the crutch alcohol had become for him. He put the beer back and bought some fruit juice instead.

At that point he checked to see what jobs demanded his immediate attention. He was on the first floor, checking the wall for insect damage and dry rot, when he suddenly stopped. Odd, he mused, his brow furrowing as he ran his hand over the cool plaster; this section wasn't plumb with the rest of the wall. It was at least two inches off, and such carelessness seemed out of place, given the good condition of the rest of the house. That meant, he reasoned, that this discrepancy was deliberate, and was not the result of shoddy workmanship.

Curious, he picked up the hammer and gave the wall a light tap. It sounded solid to him, and so he gave the wall on the other side of the hall a tap as well, his head cocked to one side as he listened for any difference. Yes, he thought, his heart beginning to race with excitement, there was a definite difference in the sounds.

He sat back on his heels, the hammer dangling from his fingers as he gazed at the wall that had first caught his notice. He knew from what Jane had told him, that the house had been remodeled many times in its three-hundred-year history, and he reasoned it was more than likely that a room could have been enclosed. There were three rooms on each side of the narrow hall, but that didn't mean that at one point of time there might have been more. He glanced down at his hammer, and then shrugged. What the hell, he thought, rising to his feet and walking over to stand in front of the wall. In for a penny, in for a pound.

It took several strong swings, but he managed to break through the thin layer of plaster and board that had been placed over the original wall. That wall was also covered with white plaster, but something in its style reminded him of the walls in an old inn where he and Jane had stayed while visiting Rye. That inn dated back to the Elizabethan period, and the thought that this wall was just as old was doubly intriguing. He picked up the hammer again and resumed his enthusiastic swinging, until he broke through to empty space.

At last, he thought, setting down the hammer with a relieved sigh and picking up his portable work light. He shone it through the hole, and was delighted to see that he was right. There *was* a hidden room, and that knowledge was all it took to have him picking up his hammer again. This time he didn't stop until he had knocked out a space big enough to step through.

The room was small and dark, and the musty smell inside made his nose wrinkle in disgust. Place smells like a bleeding tomb, he thought, slowly swinging the light around as he studied the room. There were no paintings hanging on the walls, but he thought he could see something still visible through the dust and grime of uncounted years. He stepped closer, holding the light up for a better look, as he ran his finger over the five-pointed star that had been painted there. No wonder the room had been walled up, he decided, lowering the torch to his side. Apparently one of the house's previous owners had engaged in an interesting and dangerous hobby.

His curiosity piqued, he began examining the room more thoroughly, his well-trained mind registering everything with increasing excitement. The first thing he noted was that the room was five-sided, and that almost every wall had a satanic symbol of some kind painted on its surface. He knelt down on one knee in the center of the room, brushing aside the dirt and dust to uncover a blood red pentagram with a yellow center that had been painted on the floor. There was some writing beside one of the star's arms, and he was bending closer to examine it, when he heard the chime of the doorbell.

He ignored it at first, but when the bell was followed by incessant pounding, he rose to his feet with a muttered curse. He knew of only one person obnoxious enough to keep beating on a locked door. Swearing even more creatively, he stalked down the stairs and threw open the door to his little sister.

"What the hell do you want?" he snapped, hands on his hips as he glared down at Cara.

"And hello to you, too, brother dearest," she responded coolly, her chin jutting forward as she studied his disheveled condition. "What on earth have you been doing?" she asked, brushing past him. "You look like a vagrant!"

The memory of what he'd found melted Alec's hostility, and he grabbed her hand in his. "Come upstairs," he said, already dragging her toward the staircase. "I've something to show you. You're not going to believe what I found!"

"If it's a body, I'm not interested. I spent all morning attending a postmortem, and I've had my fill of death, thank you," Cara warned, although she was relieved by his excitement. It had been months since she'd seen Alec excited about anything.

Alec tossed her a boyish grin over his shoulder. "There's no body," he promised, his amber eyes dancing. "Or at least, if there is, I haven't found it yet."

"Well, that's certainly encouraging," Cara grumbled as he continued dragging her down the hall. "But I still don't see what—" She stopped, her eyes widening when she saw the hole he had knocked in the wall. "Oh my God!"

"I told you," Alec said with a laugh, dropping her hand and stepping through the hole. "Wait until you see what's on the other side!" he called back, his voice echoing hollowly.

Cara stood as if rooted to the threadbare carpet, a sudden uneasiness making her wish for the weapon she sometimes carried when on special duty. She hadn't been this nervous since responding to her first homicide scene, and it took all of her willpower not to plead with Alec to come out of there before it was too late. She edged closer, craning her neck so she could get a better look at the hole and what lay just beyond it. What she saw had her jaw dropping in disbelief.

"Is that a room?" she demanded, curiosity overcoming caution.

He moved to the center of the room and picked up the work light. "Come closer and see," he taunted, his lips curving in a nasty smile. "Unless you're afraid."

Cara glared at him, knowing he was manipulating her, but unable to resist. She'd fought her way up the ranks to become one of the youngest inspectors in Scotland Yard's history, and she hadn't achieved her goal by backing away from a challenge. Drawing a deep breath, she stepped through the shattered wall.

"You think you're so bloody clever," she muttered, heart hammering as she glanced uneasily about her. There was something about the room that had her senses screaming an urgent warning, and the pentagrams she could see on the walls only added to her uneasiness. She took another step forward when a hot flash of pain sent her stumbling back with a startled cry.

"What is it?" Alec turned around from the wall he had been examining, a look of concern on his face.

"Something shocked me!" Cara exclaimed, the fear she'd been feeling increasing in volume. This time she didn't try ignoring the sensation, but began backing out of the room.

"I'm getting out of here," she said, not caring what he thought. "And if you've a brain left, you'll do the same."

Alec stared after her in shock. "Cara, what the—" His protest ended in a blistering curse when she disappeared through the hole. He heard her footsteps on the stairs and bent down to switch off the light. "Oh hell," he grumbled, and then thundered down the stairs after her. He found her standing in the drawing room, her arms wrapped defensively about her as she gazed out the window.

"Want to tell me what that was all about?" he asked, his tone softening slightly as he lay a comforting hand on her shoulder. "I've never seen you act like this."

"That's because I've never felt like this before," Cara replied, shuddering at the memory. "God, it was just too weird. What kind of place *is* that?"

"Damned if I know," Alec admitted, his interest in his discovery temporarily replacing his concern for his sister. "But I'm fairly certain it must have something to do with black magic. Wonder if the lab boys in SO 7 would like to pop in for a peek. They're the experts on satanic rituals, aren't they?"

Cara heard his interest, and it was enough to make her put aside her own fears. She'd willingly face armed members of the PIRA, if it brought Alec back to life. "Sergeant Flemming's your man," she said, doing her best to share his enthusiasm. "He helped us on the Watchton case, and he knows all about witch-craft and satanism."

Alec nodded thoughtfully. "Maybe I'll give him a call," he promised, then cocked his head to one side to study his sister. "Was there any particular reason you stopped by?" he asked, his dark brows gathering in a suspicious scowl.

Cara immediately assumed an innocent expression, knowing he would toss her out on her ear if he even guessed she'd been checking up on him. "I thought we could pop over to Shepherd's Market for something to eat," she said, meeting his gaze without so much as flinching. "I've been working all morning, and I'm starving. I'm also buying," she added this last with a defensive lift of her chin, the tone in her voice daring him to object.

For a moment she thought he would see through her ruse and hurl her offer back in her face, but after a tense moment he gave a negligent shrug. "I'll get my coat," he said, turning toward the hall closet.

"Wait!" she exclaimed, grabbing his arm and casting a nervous glance at the ceiling. "You're . . . you're not going to go off and leave that place open, are you?"

"Of course, I am," he replied, frowning at her in annoyance. "What do you expect me to do, patch the hole back up and forget the room exists?"

"I would."

To her surprise he actually grinned. "That's because you keep reading Stephen King novels," he said, reaching out to give the end of her nose a teasing pinch. "It never fails to amaze me, how someone who makes her living as a police inspector can scare herself silly reading those damned things."

Cara flushed with anger and embarrassment. "And it never fails to amaze *me* that someone who trained with the SAS couldn't operate a gas cooker if his life depended on it," she responded, batting his hand away with a scowl. "That's really why I stopped by. Left to your own devices, you'd soon starve to death."

Less than half an hour later, they were sitting in a dimly lit restaurant eating spaghetti and sharing a bottle of burgundy. Cara had recovered from whatever had upset her, and she soon had Alec chuckling with her wicked description of her chief inspector's many peccadillos.

"You're making that up," he accused at one point, eyes sparkling as he pictured the prim little man Cara described with gleeful disrespect. "No one is that odd."

"Word of honor," she intoned, one hand held up as if she were swearing an oath. "Kittrick won't allow cell phones in the squadroom because he insists they emit radio waves which . . . ahem . . . interfere with a man's ability to perform his marital duties." She mimicked her supervisor's prim tones so accurately, that Alec threw back his head and roared with laughter.

"What does he think they'll do to *you?*" he asked once he'd stopped laughing.

"He hasn't said," Cara said, folding her hands on the table and doing her best to look demure. "But then I'm almost certain he doesn't believe I'm really one of the squad. I daresay he thinks I'm there to operate the tea cart."

"God, what a pompous ass he sounds," Alec murmured with a rueful shake of his head. "Jane would have kicked him in the—" He halted abruptly, the laughter dying in his eyes.

There was an uncomfortable silence, and then Cara leaned forward to cover his hand with her own. "Yes, she would have," she said, her voice soft. "It's all right to talk about Jane," she added, when he remained silent. "She was a wonderful person, and she deserves to be remembered."

Alec flinched at the pain that tore through him at the mention of Jane's name. He hated it when anyone spoke of her in the past tense, because it made her death that much more real to him, that much more final. He picked up his glass of wine, his face tight with agony as he met his sister's worried gaze.

"Quite the therapist, aren't you?" he sneered, taking a deep sip of wine. "I wonder if this is how you talk to rape victims, and if you have any idea how condescending you sound?"

Cara jerked her head back, her eyes bright with tears she

refused to let fall. "And I wonder if you have any idea what a bastard you can be," she said, only the trembling of her lips betraying how deeply his words had cut.

Alec bit back an angry curse, his cheeks flushing with shame. He lowered his gaze to the table, struggling to control the emotions raging inside him. "I'm sorry," he apologized roughly, "It's just I . . . I . . ." his voice trailed off, and when he raised his eyes, they were bleak with desolation. "I miss Jane, Cara," he confessed brokenly. "I miss her so damn much."

The tears Cara had refused to let fall in anger, now flowed in empathy for her brother's pain. She leaned over the rickety table, her fingers tightening on his. "Oh, Alec, I—" The rest of her words were lost by the raucous beeping of her pager.

"Oh, bloody hell," she exclaimed, unsnapping the pager from her belt. "I'll have to call in." She excused herself and returned a few minutes later, a grim look on her face.

"I'm afraid I have to report to hospital," she said, signaling for the bill as she took her seat. "I'm sorry."

"It's all right." Alec had been a cop too long to be upset by the abrupt end to their night. "But why do you have to report in? I thought this was your free night."

"It was," Cara pulled out her credit card and handed it to the hovering server. "But I'm angling for a promotion to homicide, and so I agreed to be on call for the next few weeks."

Alec's lips twitched in amusement. "Brown-noser," he accused, sprawling back in his chair and toasting her with his glass of wine.

"Layabout," she returned in kind. "Just wait until you're back on the job, and haven't a moment to call your own." She pulled on her coat, her eyes worried as they studied his face. "Are you certain you're going to be all right?" she asked quietly. "I could stop by after I'm finished."

Alec paused a moment, vaguely surprised to discover he wanted to say yes. He almost did just that, but in the end his pride rose to the fore, and he shook his head. "I'll be fine," he said, scraping up a smile for her benefit. "Your call could take hours, and I'll probably be in bed long before you've finished."

After making him promise to call her the next afternoon, Cara hurried out the door, leaving Alec to finish his meal in brooding silence. He also finished the bottle of wine, and the warm glow left him feeling so mellow, he ordered a half-bottle as well. By the time he drained it, he was lost in a pleasant fog. Refusing the barman's offer to fetch him a taxi, he left the restaurant and weaved his way home. Fortunately he only had a few blocks to go, and he was soon on his doorstep, fumbling with his keys.

Once inside he managed to throw the bolt, and then stumbled his way up the stairs. He'd almost reached his room when an odd glow caught his eye. He staggered to a halt, blinking at the light radiating from the secret room. What the hell, he thought, trying to force his befuddled mind to function. It took him several seconds, but he finally concluded that he must have left his work light on when Cara had raced out of the room. The temptation to ignore the light and go to bed was strong, but he wasn't so drunk not to realize the danger of fire, should the lamp overheat. Cursing inventively he tottered across the hall, and with only a little difficulty managed to climb through the hole he had knocked in the wall a few hours earlier.

If the room had seemed ominous during the day, it was doubly so at night. The pentagrams painted on the walls seemed far more vivid, as if they'd been freshly painted, and the glow that had caught his attention flooded the room with an unholy light. It seemed to be coming from the walls themselves, a fact which in his inebriated state, struck him as merely interesting. It was too bad Jane wasn't here, he mused, a sad smile touching his lips. There was nothing she'd liked better than a good mystery, and she wouldn't have rested until she'd discovered the source of the strange glow.

The thought sent the familiar shaft of pain shooting through him, and for a moment it was more than he could bear. He closed his eyes, dropping to his knees as he struggled against the overwhelming sense of grief washing over him. How was he supposed to survive? he wondered bleakly, drawing in a shuddering breath. How was he supposed to survive when the only thing that had made his life worth living had been cruelly ripped from him?

As he knelt there he felt a sudden burst of heat, and an odd humming filled his ears. Even though his eyes were closed, he could sense the flash of bright light that exploded in the room, and he instinctively raised his arms to shield his face. The light seemed to go on forever, but when it finally faded, he cautiously lowered his arms and glanced around him.

The room was still glowing, although not quite as brightly as before, and his ears were still buzzing from the hum. He shook his head and rose awkwardly to his feet, deciding that he'd had enough of the place for one night. Maybe Cara was right, he concluded, turning toward the door. Maybe there was something dangerous about the room, and he should just wall it back up and forget all about it. He'd almost reached the hole when something made him stop, and as if against his will, he turned slowly around to stare at the center of the room.

At first he could see nothing out of the unusual, and he was about to turn around again when a flash of white made him glance down at the floor where he had found the pentagram. His jaw dropped in disbelief at the woman he saw lying there, her long blond hair spilling over the filmy white silk of her peignoir.

At first he refused to believe the evidence of his own eyes, certain there had to be some logical explanation for what he was seeing. Then he thought of all the wine he'd drunk and gave a relieved sigh. Of course, he was seeing things, he assured himself, pleased at his own cleverness. He was as smashed as a soccer fan, and although he'd never suffered from d.t.'s before, it didn't mean he couldn't be having them now. He'd just close his eyes and count to ten, and when he opened them again, the woman would be gone. What the hell? It worked on the monsters he'd been convinced lived beneath his bed when he was six.

He counted twice, just to be certain, and when he was finished, he carefully pried open one eye and glanced down.

"Shit!" The curse tore from his lips when he saw the woman still lying on the dusty floor, her legs curled to one side and both hands palms up at her side. It was the sight of those palms, so helpless and fragile-looking, that broke the paralysis holding him. Even drunk on his tail, he was too good of a cop to turn his back on anyone in need.

He took a cautious step forward, until the toes of his scarred workboots were almost touching the woman's shoulder. Standing this close to her he could feel the warmth emanating from her body, and the tactile sensation was almost enough to sober him. If she was a hallucination, he thought, dropping awkwardly on one knee beside her, then she was a damned good one. His hand hovered uncertainly in the air before he lowered it to her shoulder, and he jumped slightly when he felt warm, living flesh beneath his sweaty palm. So much for her being a figment of his imagination, he thought, giving her a gentle shake.

"Madam?" He said, half-fearing, half-praying she would vanish beneath his touch. "Madam, are you all right?"

When she didn't stir he rested his fingers against her neck, measuring her pulse with the training that was second nature even now. Fast but steady, he decided, also noting that her respiration seemed good. He dropped his gaze to her chest, and was stunned by the sensual jolt his body gave when he saw her nipples beneath the soft silk. The power of his response angered him, and he snatched back his hand as if he'd been burned.

Perhaps she was an illusion after all, he brooded, thrusting an unsteady hand through his hair. She had to be. He loved Jane too much to feel sexual attraction toward another woman. He rocked back on his haunches and was trying to decide what to do when the woman gave a low moan and started moving. Instantly he was all cop again.

"Madam, I'm an officer," he said, forcing his voice to sound reassuring as he gave her another shake. "Are you ill?"

She moaned again, moving her head restlessly, as if fighting her way to consciousness. Alec brushed aside the strands of bright blond hair that had fallen across her face, and the stunning perfection of her features made the breath catch in his throat. Even as he was absorbing the impact her beauty had on him, her thick lashes fluttered, and a pair of dazed green eyes stared into his in obvious confusion.

That it was difficult for him to find his voice added to his anger, and his tone was clipped as he spoke.

"I'm Inspector Alec Bramwell with the Metropolitan Police Force," he said, his eyes narrowing as he met her gaze, "and I want to know how the hell you got into my house."

# Three

The voice seemed to come from a great distance, and it took every ounce of will Miranda possessed to concentrate. Her whole body felt as if a hundred heavy woolen blankets had been piled upon it, and her head throbbed as if from a terrible fever. Still, the voice persisted, and unable to resist its call, she forced her eyes to open. A man was bent over her, and she frowned up at him in bewilderment.

"Stephen?"

The man's brows gathered in a dark scowl, and she wondered if perhaps she'd been a trifle forward. Stephen was an earl, after all, she could not fault him for disapproving of her familiar use of his name. She licked lips that were unbearably dry and tried again.

"My lord, what has happened? Where am I?" She realized as she spoke the words that she had no idea as to her location, and the very notion struck her as decidedly shocking. She'd never suffered from the vapors before, and she hoped she hadn't given Stephen a horror of her. Her stepfather had been quite insistent when he'd informed her that she was to accept his lordship's offer, and she could imagine his anger if Stephen was to suddenly cry off. Her stepfather . . . her eyes clouded in confusion at the pain and anger she felt when she linked Stephen and Elias in the same thought. What on earth . . .

"Don't you dare black out on me!" The man above her gave her an angry shake, sending a shock of pain shooting through her. "Answer my question, damn it! How'd you get in here?"

The man's rough touch as well as his crude speech shocked Miranda into full wakefulness, and she realized she was staring into the face of a virtual stranger. The man's hair was as black as night, falling to his shoulders in dark curly waves, and eyes as gold and piercing as a hawk's glittered down at her from a face that was darkly savage. There was more gold, this in the shape of a circlet, dangling from his ear, and she reached the horrifying conclusion that he was one of the gypsies she had been warned of for most of her life. This was the first time she had ever met one of the wretches in person, but it was quite obvious from this man's behavior that their villainy had not been overstated. She began struggling, doing her best to wrench herself free from his bruising grip.

"Release me at once, you scoundrel!" she cried, her nose wrinkling at the smell of spirits she could detect on his clothing. "His lordship shall see you swing if you but touch me!" She managed to bring up her hand, and knew a moment of fierce pleasure when she landed a solid blow on his tanned cheek.

"Ouch!" The man jerked his head back, and there was another struggle as he managed to capture both her hands in his. He leaned over her, his hard body pressing against hers so firmly that a fresh wave of terror washed over Miranda. My dear heaven, she thought, fighting against the black mists swirling in her head, was he going to rape her?

"What's wrong with you?" the man was demanding, seeming more annoyed than crazed by lust. "Didn't you hear me? I'm a police officer. I won't hurt you; all right?"

Miranda had no notion what a police officer might be, but she gave a jerky nod, praying it would help win her freedom. If the blackguard did mean to violate her, she decided, her chin firming with resolve, then she would make it as difficult for him as possible.

"That's better," the man lifted his body from hers, but still kept a firm grip on her hands. "Let's start again, shall we? I'm Alec Bramwell. Want to tell me who you are, and how you managed to beam yourself into this room?"

His confusing words were making her head ring, but Miranda was determined to give him the answers he sought. If she could but keep him talking long enough, help would most surely arrive, and then she would be free. Now, what was it he wanted to know? Ah yes, her name. Her name . . . Miranda's brows knitted in confusion.

"Oh come on, honey," the man gave her hands a gentle shake. "Don't try that old amnesia bit on me. You know who you are."

"Of course, I know who I am!" Miranda retorted, her heart beginning to pound as memories spun through her head. She could see herself standing at the altar at St. George's, as she pledged her life to Stephen. See the wedding breakfast Elias had held in their honor, and the sparkle of the champagne in the crystal goblets, as their guests raised toast after toast to them. And she could see herself in her peignoir, waiting in bed for a groom who did not come . . .

"Well?" Another shake. "Come on, blondie, I'm waiting."

The impatience in her captor's voice broke Miranda's reverie, and she brought her chin up in haughty anger. "I am Lady Miranda Hallforth, the countess of Harrington, and I demand you release me this very moment!"

The man's features went blank with shock, and then, to Miranda's fury, he threw back his head and gave a roar of laughter. "A countess?" he said, his eyes dancing in obvious derision. "Now I know I've lost my bleeding mind."

"Don't you dare speak to me in that odious manner, you . . . you thief!" Miranda's fear was lost in her outrage. She had never considered herself to be above her fellow man, but she was cursed if she would allow a common cutpurse to make sport of her. "If you do not leave this house this very moment, my husband shall see you shipped to Van Diemen's Land!" She added this final threat with a toss of her head, recalling that her steppapa had said thieves feared transportation to penal colonies far more than the gibbet.

To her fury he seemed more amused than cowed by her words. "Right, and next you're going to be saying it's off with my head," he chuckled, but to her relief he released her hands, pushing himself up as he stood above her.

Miranda was not about to remain sprawled in the dust, and managed with only a little difficulty to struggle to her feet. "Don't be absurd," she snapped, fighting back the nausea and dizziness that threatened to overwhelm her. "This isn't France."

"And it's not Disneyland, either," the man replied, weaving on his feet and suddenly looking the worse for drink. "Look, I'm not in any mood for this. If you're here to rip me off, help yourself. The VCR and CD player are in the parlor, but I'd appreciate it if you left the silver tray. It belonged to my grand-mother."

Although seconds before she would have rejoiced at his de-parture, Miranda found herself clinging to his arm. "Wait," she pleaded, not certain why she should feel so bereft and alone. "Where are you going?"

"Why, off to bed, your royal majesty," he said, staggering as he attempted a bow. "Care to join me?" When her face flamed red, he looked smugly pleased with himself. "Didn't think so."

Miranda ignored the crude jibe. "Where is Stephen?" she demanded, focusing her thoughts on her husband. Had this mocking stranger already murdered him? she wondered wildly. Was that why Stephen hadn't come to her bed? The very possi-bility made her tremble with fear and anger. "What have you done with him?" she cried, her hands tightening on the sleeve of his jacket. "Answer me, or I shall summon the Watch!"

He freed himself from her grip with a negligent shrug. "Sum-mon whomever you like, princess," he said, turning toward the door without so much as a backward glance. "I'm out of here."

"But I demand that you—"

He whirled around at her words, staggering slightly, and for a moment it looked as if he would collapse in an ignoble heap. At the last moment he managed to catch himself, and when he'd regained his footing, he sent her a burning glare. "Look," he said, his words slurring, "I don't give a damn if you're real, or if I'm imagining this whole ridiculous conversation. I'm going

to bed. Whomever or whatever you are, you can go to hell." And
with that he turned and made his way through the gaping hole
in the far wall.

Miranda stared at the hole in bewilderment, struggling for a
memory that seemed vitally important. She had been with
Stephen when the workman knocked the hole in the wall, she
remembered, her head beginning to swim as exhaustion threatened to swamp her. But hadn't it been patched? She seemed to
recall something about a door . . . she tried to concentrate, but
the memory would not come.

She stood in the center of the room for several minutes, growing more weary and confused with each passing second. When
she felt as if she was about to swoon again, she decided it might
be best to go in search of assistance. Surely Mr. Bramwell, if
indeed that was his name, would be gone by now, and she could
ring for the servants. The thought of servants suddenly seemed
vastly reassuring, and she forced herself to cross the room and
crawl through the hole.

On the other side of the hole she found herself facing a dark
hallway. Scolding herself for not bringing a candle with her, she
placed her hand against the wall and began carefully making her
way down the hall. She hadn't taken but a few steps, when her
hand encountered a small lever built in the wall, and when she
moved it, the hallway exploded with light.

Miranda gave a sharp cry and dropped to her knees, her arms
lifted to cradle her head. It was just like before, she thought
wildly, trembling with fear at the memory of a flash of light and
a searing pain. She waited several seconds, and when there was
no repeat of the terrible pain, she cautiously lowered her arms
and glanced about her.

The hallway was far different than she remembered, she realized dully, her heart racing with terror. She *knew* she was in
the house on Curzon Street, and yet nothing was as it should
be. She tried to concentrate, to think of her next step, but she
seemed unable to focus her spinning thoughts. Bed, she thought,
blinking her heavy eyes as she stared at a closed door. She would

go to bed, and doubtlessly in the morning this would all be as a dream to her. Perhaps she was already dreaming, she mused, and heaved a soft sigh. Yes, that was the answer, this was all a dream.

Using the wall as a brace, she pushed herself to her feet and weaved toward the door. It seemed stuck at first, but she managed to shove it open, staggering as she fell into the room. With the light from the hall she could make out the shadowy shape of a bed, and she made for it with a sob of relief.

The bed was wide and soft, if somewhat dusty, and as she crawled beneath the covers, Miranda made a mental note to speak with the housekeeper. The maids must be given better instruction, she decided, and then in a heartbeat she fell into a black and dreamless sleep.

She hurt. The thought penetrated the mists filling Miranda's heads and she snuggled deeper into the pillows. She was so tired, and she wanted to sleep forever. She was almost certain she and Stephen had no plans for that day, and that meant she could be as lazy as she—Stephen!

In a flash it all came back to her. Her wedding, her wedding night, and the hurtful, hateful words she had heard the unknown man speak. *"He settled fifty thousand pounds on you for taking the chit off his hands, did he not?"*

Miranda's eyes flew open and she sat up with a startled cry, her fist pressed to her mouth. Stephen had married her for her money. The realization hurt more than she believed could be possible, and she felt as betrayed as if she'd discovered him with another woman. Why hadn't he told her? she wondered, blinking back scalding tears. Oh, she'd known he didn't love her. She didn't love him, if it came to that, but she had liked him, respected him, yet all the while he had been using her.

Well, there was nothing to be done about it now, she decided, pushing a weary hand through the heavy fall of her hair. She and Stephen were legally wed, and even though she had toyed with the thought of annulment last night, she knew she had no choice but to accept her fate. Once she reached that conclusion, she realized she was famished, and she began looking about her for a rope pull to summon the maid.

What sort of room was this? she thought, confusion mounting as she took in the details of her new room. And what sort of staff did Stephen employ, that would allow a room to fall into such a disheveled state? Clearly her first task as the new countess of Harrington would be to give her servants a stern lecture as to their duties, she decided, throwing back her covers and rising from her bed to better inspect her quarters.

The dust she had noted from her bed covered the floor and furniture, including a few pieces of furniture she could not recognize. One piece especially caught her notice—a large square box with a dark grayish piece of glass—and she bent down to peer at it. If it was a mirror, she decided after a moment, it wasn't a very good one. She could scarce see her own reflection in the dusty glass.

She spent the next several minutes exploring the room, and each item she found added to her growing agitation. In addition to the odd furniture there was a bewildering collection of clothing in the drawers and in the small room she recognized as a closet, and none of the garments she discovered could be considered even remotely respectable. Where the devil was she?

When she thought she would go mad if she did not find some answers to the list of questions that grew longer with each passing second, Miranda decided to go in search of those answers herself. Another search of the room uncovered an ugly robe of some fuzzy pink material which, although it was quite hideous, was surprisingly comfortable. She belted the robe about her and then tiptoed across the room to the door. She pressed her ear to it, and when she was certain no one was lurking outside, she inched it open and peered cautiously about her.

As it had the night before, the hall glowed with light, although it seemed fainter now. She decided it must be the new gaslight everyone was talking about, and silently conceded it was far more efficient than mere candlelight. If she wasn't in her own home, she would have to speak with Stephen about having it installed in their house.

Making her way toward the stairs, she noted more strange items of furniture and some paintings on the wall that were unlike anything she had ever seen before. They were startlingly lifelike, and she could not help but admire the artist's skill at the incredible detail in each picture. She stopped at the sight of one of them—a portrait of the wild gypsy she remembered from last night. At least she thought it was him. His hair was shorter and he was dressed in a neat blue uniform, a blue and white checkered hat set firmly on his dark curls.

There were several other pictures featuring the man, some showing him in another uniform, this one an ugly blend of green and brown, his face smeared with soot and dirt. He was glaring out from the canvas, a deadly-looking rifle cradled in his hands, and she shivered at the aura of menace emanating from him. Another picture showed him laughing, his arm draped about a lovely woman with auburn hair. He looked years younger, and she wondered if the lady was his mistress. Certainly no man, even a disreputable gypsy, would allow his wife to be painted in such a scandalously short gown.

She was studying another portrait, when she heard the sound of a door creaking open. She whirled around, a scream catching in her throat when the flesh and blood man whose images she had been studying stepped out into the hall. Her horrified eyes travelled down a tanned chest dusted with black curly hair, and came to rest on a pair of bold blue smallclothes that were the most indecent thing she could ever have imagined. A soft gasp escaped from her lips, and she clapped a hand over her mouth.

The sound brought the man's head up, and he blinked at her in sleepy confusion. His eyes widened, and then he closed them again, uttering a curse as he shoved a hand through his dark curls.

"Oh, hell," he said, sounding thoroughly disgusted with the situation. "You're real."

Miranda could think of nothing to say. The hallway was dipping and spinning about her, and her last thought as she crum-
pled to the floor, was that for someone who never swooned, she
seemed to be doing a great deal of it lately.

"Damn!"
The exclamation burst from Alec's lips as he rushed toward
the stricken woman. He remembered her from last night, but
he'd convinced himself she was part of some wild, improbable
fantasy. His therapist had warned him there would be side effects
once he began accepting Jane's death, but she'd neglected to
inform him those side effects would be stunning blondes with
upper-crust accents and delusions of royalty. Oh well. He knelt
beside the woman, relieved to see she'd only fainted . . . again.

He'd have to call 9-9-9, he decided, but perhaps not just yet.
The emergency call would bring more than medical assistance
once it was realized he was an officer, and he wasn't certain he
was up to explaining the woman's presence in his house to the
responding units. He especially didn't know what he'd do if it
turned out the woman was an illusion, and vanished the moment
the ambulance pulled up in front of the house. They'd likely haul
*him* away, he admitted, his lips curling in derision.

He was debating whether or not to give Cara an urgent call,
when the blonde gave a soft sigh and opened her eyes. This time
there was no confusion, but he did detect a glimmer of fear in
the misty green depths of her eyes, and he immediately set out
to reassure her.

"We meet again, Lady Miranda," he said, deciding it was best
to humor her for the moment. "Are you all right? Or are you
going to faint on me again?"

Miranda didn't know what shocked her more, that he should
speak her name so casually, or that he should be so indifferent
as to his unclothed state. Perhaps he was still jug-bitten and was
unaware of the fact, she thought, then blushed as she wondered
how best to apprise him of the situation.

"I shan't faint, sir," she managed, albeit in a shaky voice, her eyes fixed firmly on a point well past his bare shoulder. "However, I should prefer it if you would be so kind as to cover yourself. This is most improper."

"What?" Alec's brows wrinkled in confusion at her stilted speech.

Miranda's flush deepened, but she refused to dissemble. "You are unclothed, sir," she said in a tight voice. "Please don your garments before a servant catches us, and my reputation is destroyed beyond all hopes of repair."

Alec stared at her, torn between irritation and amusement. "You *are* joking, aren't you?" he asked, wondering who she thought she was fooling with her Queen Victoria imitation.

"Please."

The quiet desperation in her voice made Alec curse beneath his breath. Much as he disliked the thought of leaving her until he had more information, he realized he had no other choice. In the event he decided to take her in, he didn't want to give her room to lay a morals charge against him.

"Look," he said, sitting back on his heels and eyeing her warily, "if I leave you to get dressed, will you give me your word you won't beam out again?"

"Sir?" Miranda blinked at the unfamiliar term.

"Split," he amended, then when she still looked confused he gave a sigh. "Leave the house."

She bristled in indignation at the very suggestion. "Like this?" she said, indicating her attire with a wave of her hand. "I should hardly think so, sir. I am scarce in the habit of appearing in public in *déshabille*."

The sight of the ratty pink robe made the blood drain from Alec's face. "Where did you get that?" he demanded, his voice hoarse with pain as he recognized Jane's favorite robe.

"From the clothes press in the bedchamber," Miranda replied, wondering if she'd offended him somehow. He had gone quite pale, and the light had faded from his amber-colored eyes.

He looked as if he meant to say something, but at the last

moment he clamped his mouth shut, his expression hard and remote as he rose to his feet.

"Go downstairs and wait for me," he ordered in a clipped voice. "And don't even think about trying to sneak out. I'll only catch you, and when I do, I'll have you in lock-up so fast it'll make your pretty head swim." And with that he was gone, leaving Miranda to glare at his unclothed back.

Well, of all the ill-mannered oafs! she fumed, wishing she could leave before he could stop her. It would almost be worth the scandal she would court should she dash outside in her night clothes, and he could hardly give chase, considering the way *he* was dressed. She allowed the tempting thought to linger, and then pushed it from her mind. Of course, she wouldn't leave, she told herself, rising to her feet with a sigh. How could she? She wasn't even certain where she was.

The realization was sobering, and she found herself brooding over the matter as she made her way down the narrow staircase. She was still uncertain whether she was in Stephen's London home or at another location entirely, but regardless of where she might be, she could not understand why Stephen did not come for her. Surely if she had been kidnapped, as she was beginning to suspect was the case, he would make every attempt to rescue her. Unless, she decided, her heart sinking with despair, he had something to do with that kidnapping.

She'd just reached the bottom of the stairs and was trying to decide which way to go, when she heard a noise from the top of the steps. She turned just as Mr. Bramwell started down the stairway.

"I hope this meets with your ladyship's approval," he said, pulling a sweater over his head as he clattered his way down. She'd noted he'd also donned a pair of tight-fitting blue breeches, and she wondered how he had managed to dress so quickly. In the next moment she was dismissing the fact as unimportant. Now that he was properly attired, she was determined to learn what she could of her location, and once she had learned that, she would decide how best to affect her escape.

She recalled his threat to have her locked up, and repressed a shudder. If she had any hope of escaping, she knew she'd have to do everything within her power to avoid that possibility. "Am I to be your prisoner then, sir?" she asked quietly, praying he would be taken in by her submissive behavior.

The question brought Alec up short, and he eyed the blonde cautiously, as he finished fastening the belt about his waist. "At the moment, no," he said, his gaze resting on her strained expression. He heard the fear in her voice, and again, the cop in him overcame his irritation. He swallowed his impatience and stepped forward to lay a gentle hand on her elbow.

"I only want to know who you are and how you got into my house," he said, guiding her into the room he had set aside as the parlor. "After that, you're free to go."

The room he led her to was crowded with a jumble of boxes and shrouded furniture, and Miranda could not help but cringe. If she was being held prisoner in an abandoned house, it would make her escape that much more difficult.

Alec saw the look of gentle disgust on her face, and his willingness to treat her with kid gloves wavered. "You'll have to pardon the dust," he said, his tone derisive. "I've just moved in, and I haven't had time to hire a maid. Sit down."

Miranda accepted his explanation in silent relief. Servants were notoriously susceptible to bribes, and once he did employ a maid, she was fairly certain she would be able to convince the girl to help her. In the meanwhile, she had to first discover where she was being held.

"You keep saying 'your house,' " she said carefully, settling the folds of the robe about her as she sat on the chair he had indicated. "Am I to take it I am no longer in London?"

Alec's eyebrows rose at the question. "Of course, you are, where'd you think you were?"

"I see," Miranda took care to hide her excitement. "Precisely where in London am I?" she added, praying she wasn't in some dreadful quarter where she would be in more danger on the street than she was in the empty house.

"Mayfair," Alec snapped, deciding he'd had enough of the interrogation. He was the cop here, he reminded himself grimly, and it was about time he got to the bottom of things. Suppressing the good manners his mother had despaired of ever teaching him, he leaned forward and captured her hand in his.

"Just cut the crap, all right?" he began, ruthlessly ignoring her start of fear. "I've a busy day ahead of me, and I'm not in the mood for twenty questions. Now, once more, who are you, and what are you doing here?"

Before she could answer, his phone gave a commanding warble. He was tempted to ignore it, but he was on call-up duty, and knew he had no other choice. Pinning her with a stern look he rose to his feet. "Stay here," he ordered, then crossed the room to scoop up his cordless phone.

"Bramwell," he snapped into the receiver, and then his expression grew dark. "No, this isn't the Floral Shop! You've rung the wrong number!" And he disconnected the caller with an angry flip of his finger. He turned around to renew his demands for an explanation, and was stunned by the expression on his guest's face.

"What . . . what is that?" Miranda demanded, pointing a shaky finger at the white object he had tossed on the table.

"What?" Alec frowned in confusion.

"That thing you were talking into," Miranda said, trembling with fear. She didn't know why the device frightened her, but it did. It reminded her of her reaction to the hidden room, and she had to fight against the waves of panic rising in her.

Understanding dawned, and Alec gave a derisive laugh. "The phone? Oh come on, princess, don't try telling me you've never seen a cordless phone! Try pulling the other leg, sweetheart, it has bells on it."

"I don't care what you believe!" Miranda cried, too upset to prevaricate. "I've not seen one before! And do not presume to use that familiar tone with me!" she added, rising to her feet in an angry rush. "I shan't tolerate it!"

" 'Shan't tolerate it?' " Alec repeated in disbelief. "Lady, what's the matter with you? This isn't the bleeding Victorian Age, you know! Where the hell have you been living? A convent?"

"Certainly not!" Miranda bristled at his mocking question. "I'm hardly a Papist!"

"A . . ." His voice trailed off, and he realized she wasn't acting. Maybe he should have called 9-9-9 after all, he decided. The woman was obviously in need of help, and she'd be better off in official custody until her family could be found.

"All right," he said, steeling himself for her reply, "we'll play this your way. You say you're Lady Miranda Hallforth, right? And you're a countess?"

"The countess of Harrington," Miranda agreed, not trusting his affable demeanor for a moment. He was up to something, she was certain of it, and she moved to one side so that she could make a dash for it if need be.

He countered her movement with a shift of his lean body. "The countess of Harrington, got it. Now, care to tell me what year it is?"

"The year?" His query made her frown in bewilderment. "Don't be absurd, sir, it is the year of our Lord, 1811."

Alec gave her a disbelieving look, and then slowly shook his head. "Lady Miranda," he said, his lips curving in a rueful smile, "I'm afraid you're in for a bit of a surprise."

The feeling of terror she had been feeling turned Miranda's blood to ice. "Are you trying to tell me I am wrong?" she demanded, her legs trembling so violently she feared they would not hold her.

"By about one hundred and eighty years," he replied, folding his arms over his chest and meeting her stunned gaze. "So, your ladyship, unless you're going to try to convince me you're Sleeping Beauty, you'd better explain what the hell you're doing in my house in London, 1995. And whatever your explanation, it had best be damned good, because as of this moment, I don't believe a bloody word you're saying."

# *Four*

Miranda stared at him incredulously. "You're mad," she whispered, her voice shaking with fear. "It is 1811. I *know* it is 1811."

He shook his head. "It's 1995. June 7th, to be exact," he said, his manner gentle but firm as he helped her to the settee.

"No, no, you're trying to confuse me," Miranda collapsed on the soft cushions, her hands clasped together to hide their trembling. He sounded so calm, so reasonable, she felt her confidence waver.

He opened his mouth as if to argue, then abruptly closed it again. "All right," he said, kneeling before her until their eyes were level. "Let's say you're right, and it is 1811. How do you explain that?" He indicated the strange white contraption with a jerk of his head. "Did they have telephones back then?"

Miranda eyed the device with loathing. "I . . ." she bit her lip and then glanced down at her hands. "No," she admitted brokenly, "I have never seen anything of the like. What . . . what does it do?"

He hesitated a moment, his brows knitting in thought. "It's a communication device," he said at last. "You use it to speak to people who are a great distance away."

Miranda considered that, frantically searching for some way to disprove his insane explanation. Then it came to her, and she raised her head to give him a smug smile. "How do I know you were speaking with someone?" she asked, relief spreading through her as she realized she had solved the mystery. "I heard no other voice. You could have been pretending."

Her cool reasoning seemed to take him by surprise. "That's true," he agreed, eyeing her with respect. He drummed his fingers on his knee, and then reached behind him to grab the device from the table.

"What are you doing?" she demanded, as he punched a series of buttons on the base.

"Calling my sister," he replied in that same calm tone. "I don't think she's home, but at least we'll reach her answering—" his voice broke off and he handed the thing to Miranda. "Here, I want you to listen to this."

She accepted it gingerly, holding it to her ear as she had seen him do. When she heard the disembodied voice speak, it was all she could do not to cry out in alarm.

"We can't talk right now," she heard the woman say. "Leave your name, your number, and the time you called, and we'll ring you back when we bloody well feel like it. Alec, if this is you, call me at SO7, I'll be there for the rest of the day."

The device fell from her fingers, and she regarded him with horror. "You're trying to bewitch me," she accused, glaring at him as if he were the devil incarnate. "I've never believed in such nonsense, but it is the only possible explanation."

Her use of the word bewitch made him jerk, and a thoughtful expression stole across his handsome face. He ran a hand over his neck and gave a weary sigh as he rose to his feet.

"I want you to go back upstairs and get dressed," he said, speaking slowly as if not to frighten her. "I promise I won't hurt you, but I need to get you some help. You can see that, can't you?" he added when she caught her breath in an audible gasp. "You need help."

*Help.* Miranda clung to the word with desperation. If she could get him to take her outside, surely she could manage to get away, she thought, her mind racing with plans.

"Perhaps you are right," she said, rising to her feet as well and moving away from him. "If you will excuse me, I believe

I shall do as you ask. I will be down momentarily." And with that she turned and fled from the room as if all the hounds in hell were chasing her.

She dashed out into the hallway, and was about to run up the stairs when she saw the front door. She hesitated only a moment before running over to it, her fingers fumbling with the lock. Her breath was coming out in ragged gasps as she pushed open the heavy door, and stumbled out on to the front steps.

She hadn't taken a full step when she slammed to a halt, her eyes widening in stupefaction at the street before her. Gone was the world she knew, and in its place was a scene so unlike anything she had ever imagined that she froze in horror. The street was thick with carriages that roared past the house in a rush of sound, carriages that had no horses pulling them. She stared at this amazing sight, and a terror greater than anything she had ever experienced exploded inside her. Slamming the door shut she fell to the floor, her arms covering her head as she gave a piercing scream.

"Miranda!" Her captor was at her side in less than a moment, his tone gentle as he took her in his arms. "What is it?"

In answer she gestured wildly toward the door, unable to speak for the horror rioting inside her.

"It's all right," he soothed, running a rough hand over her hair. "I won't let anything harm you. You're safe."

Miranda could only shake her head, and burrow her face against the front of his sweater. "It's true," she whispered, uncontrollable tremors wracking her as she recalled the chaotic scene she had witnessed when she'd opened the door. "My God, it's true!"

"What's true?" he asked, tilting her face up to his and searching her expression with worried eyes.

She gave a shuddering sigh, scarce believing her own words even as she spoke them. "Everything you said. It is not 1811, it is 1995, and I have no notion how I got here."

\* \* \*

Twenty minutes later Miranda sat in the kitchen with the man she knew as Alec, nursing cups of coffee as he gently coaxed her story from her. A story so wildly improbable that she was beginning to suspect they would surely be clapped into Bedlam, did this time possess such institutions. She, for telling such a wild tale, and he, because, God help them both, he appeared to accept every word of it.

"And you say it was after you put this around your neck that you disappeared?" he said, frowning down at the pendant cradled in the palm of his hand.

Miranda nodded weakly. She'd forgotten all about the necklace until she'd begun speaking, and then she'd reached beneath her robe and pulled it out to show him. When he'd asked to see it she'd surrendered it gladly, feeling a giddy sense of relief when she'd placed it in his waiting hand.

"I . . . I found it hidden in the wall," she said, struggling to comprehend the incredible truth. "There were other items there as well, books and things, but something made me slip it about my neck. The moment I did, the room began burning with a terrible light, there was a flash, and then I was here."

Alec turned the pentagram over, tracing the points of the star with a thoughtful finger. "Heaven and earth," he murmured.

"I beg your pardon?"

"Shakespeare," he explained, raising his head to give her a reassuring smile. " 'There are more things in heaven and earth than are dreamt of in your philosophy.' "

His remark surprised Miranda. "You know Shakespeare, sir?"

"Let's just say I've heard of him," Alec replied with a smile.

"This is all so fantastic," Miranda said suddenly, rubbing her arms as the enormity of her situation struck her anew. "How could one hundred and eighty-four years vanish in the wink of an eye? 'Tis impossible!"

Alec eyed her with wry resignation. "I'd like to agree, but your presence here would seem to indicate otherwise," he drawled, his amber-colored eyes dancing with amusement." In the meanwhile, we'd better start making plans."

"What sort of plans?" Miranda was instantly wary.

"How we shall explain you, for one thing," he replied, the laughter fading from his eyes. "You'll need documentation of some kind, and—" His words were interrupted by another trill from the telephone. He rose to his feet and stalked over to the counter to pick it up.

"If that's another wrong number, I won't be responsible for my actions," he grumbled, snatching up the receiver with marked impatience. "Bramwell!" he snapped, and then his expression hardened into a harsh mask.

"Are you certain?" he asked, listening several more minutes before sighing. "No, if it is the Red Coalition, it's no joke," he said, squeezing his eyes shut and pinching the bridge of his nose. "Those bastards never joke. Evacuate and secure the scene, and I'll be there when I can. What? Yes, you'd better send a car, I'll be expecting it." And with that he hung up the phone, his jaw clenching as he stared off into space.

He looked so somber that Miranda could not help but be alarmed. "Is something wrong?" she asked nervously. She couldn't imagine what catastrophes this new world held, but she did not doubt but that something terrible had occurred. She had never seen a man look so implacable . . .

At first she didn't think he would tell her, but after a few moments he gave another sigh. "I have to go in," he said, his golden eyes dark as he met her gaze. "I told you I'm a police officer; it's rather like being a soldier, and I've just been called in to duty. I can't refuse."

Duty and obligation were things she understood all too well, and even though she quailed at the thought of being left alone, she knew she would say nothing to dissuade him. "Of course," she said softly, her shoulders straightening with unconscious pride as she faced him. "Shall I wait for you here?"

"Lord, yes," he said, pushing himself away from the wall and crossing the room to stand before her. "I don't want you to even think about going outside," he warned her sternly. "You'd get smashed flat by a lorry before you got two blocks from here. Is that understood?"

"Perfectly, Mr. Bramwell," Miranda answered coolly, trying not to bristle at the arrogance in his voice. She knew he was only thinking of her safety, but that didn't mean she appreciated being addressed as if she were a simpleminded child. Then she thought about his orders, and gave him a puzzled frown. "What is a lorry?"

Alec lifted his eyes heavenward. "I rest my case," he muttered, pulling his sweater over his head as he moved toward the doorway. "Wait here, I'll be right back."

Miranda raised an eyebrow at the imperious command, but did as he instructed. While he was gone, she entertained herself by peeking into cupboards and opening and closing doors. The large white cupboard that held a variety of cold liquids and food particularly intrigued her, and she made a mental note to ask him what it was. She was peering at a square box on the counter and trying to discern its function, when she heard him coming down the stairs. She turned just as he strode into the room, and the sight of him made her jaw drop in amazement.

In the short time he had been gone, he had managed to bathe and shave, and he looked nothing like the disreputable creature she had met last night. He was in fact quite handsome, and the fact that she noticed such a thing left her feeling decidedly disconcerted. That discomfiture increased when he came to an abrupt halt, his brows meeting in a displeased scowl.

"What's the matter?" he demanded, his hand going to the narrow cravat knotted at his throat. "Don't men wear ties where you're from?"

Miranda flushed at having been caught gaping at him like a schoolgirl. "If you are referring to your cravat, indeed they do, Mr. Bramwell," she said, hiding her embarrassment behind a show of hauteur. "It is just that I am surprised you are not in uniform. You did say you were a soldier, did you not?"

"A sort of soldier," he corrected, "and I only wear my uniform under duress. That's one of the reasons I wanted to be an inspector, we only dress in our blues on special occasions."

"I see," Miranda replied, grateful he seemed willing to accept her response. Just to be certain, she thought it might be prudent to give him a nudge in the proper direction. She'd already noted he was overly fond of issuing orders, and decided she would oblige him.

"Have you any other instructions for me?" she asked, her tone unconsciously challenging as she faced him.

He studied her several seconds before answering. "Actually, I have," he said slowly. "I want you to give me your word you won't go into the secret room until I get back."

Miranda wasn't sure what she'd been expecting, but it wasn't that. She blinked at him in mystification. "What?"

"Stay out of the secret room," he repeated, stepping forward to grasp her by the shoulders. "We haven't any idea how it works, or even *if* it will work again, but do you really want to find out by being zapped to God knows where, or more importantly, God knows *when?*"

Miranda didn't have to think twice before replying. "No," she said, closing her eyes and shuddering at the memory of the burning pain that had consumed her. "No, I would die sooner than face that again."

"Then don't go in there," he said, squeezing her shoulders comfortingly before taking a step back.

Miranda nodded mutely, deciding the danger the room possessed was far greater than anything this terrifying time could pose. She was trying to think of something to say when she heard a shrill sound from the streets, and Mr. Bramwell turned toward the door.

"Make sure the door is locked, and don't let anyone in but me," he said, talking rapidly as he walked out into the hallway. "If you get hungry, help yourself to whatever's in the fridge, but don't try using the stove. I don't want to come home and find you've burned the place to the ground."

Miranda's pride simmered at the hint that she was not to be

trusted. "Anything else, sir?" she asked, wondering if all men in this time were so impossibly arrogant.

He paused, a rare grin lighting his eyes at her waspish tones. "Yes," he said, his hand on the door handle, "I want you to watch the television while I'm gone. I figure it'll either scare the hell out of you, or keep you entertained until I'm back." And then he was gone, ignoring her strangled cry of exasperation.

It took Miranda over an hour to discover which of the perplexing items in the house was the television. She'd toyed with everything until she'd flicked a switch on the square black box sitting in the parlor, and the glass had leapt to life with light and sound. She'd have endured torture before admitting to her smug host that she had indeed been terrified, but once she discerned the people in the box could neither see nor hear her, she had soon lost interest.

The books and newspapers she found were another matter, and she spent another two hours eagerly learning all she could of the strange new world in which she now found herself. Most of it was incomprehensible to her, but she was able to understand enough to realize things hadn't changed all that much. The world was still full of squabbles and wars, politics were as tangled a mess as ever, and the current Prince of Wales was as unable to get along with his wife as was Prinny.

At least this Princess of Wales was prettier, she thought, studying a black and white painting of the slender blonde who was waving to some unknown person. She also noted this princess had two sons, and she was relieved the secession was secured. How nice to know all the worry over Princess Charlotte was for naught, she mused, setting the paper aside with a sigh. It was evident she had made a good marriage, and had provided the heirs the crown so desperately needed.

Thoughts of weddings and heirs drove the smile from her lips, as a sudden realization struck her. Good heavens! she thought, the papers sliding to the floor as she sat up. She was a widow! Unless he had managed to live to a very old age indeed, Stephen would have died well over a century ago. The notion left her bereft of feeling, and she could only stare off into space as she struggled to accept the idea of Stephen's death. How odd, she mused, to be a widow before ever having been a wife.

The rest of the morning passed quickly; nearing noon, Miranda's stomach began rumbling. The thought of preparing her own meal was daunting, but given that her only other alternative was starvation, she overcame her trepidation and began poking about in the cold cupboard. Inside she found some meat and cheese, and a selection of fruit that had her mouth watering. She also found a red and blue tin similar to one she'd seen on the television, so she knew it contained a beverage. It took her several minutes to open it, but she had to admit 'twas delicious. Rather like champagne, she decided, with its bubbles and fizz.

After enjoying her nuncheon, she decided it was time to dress and went back upstairs to search for something proper to wear. The clothespress was filled with a variety of garments, but she had a great deal of difficulty imagining herself in any of them. The blue cloth breeches were discarded as being too scandalous, but in the end she found a gown whose length didn't leave her blushing in shame. She also found several items she thought were undergarments, although she was hanged if she could discern their function.

Once she was dressed she retired to the bathroom, and the things she found in there had her wide-eyed with wonder. Evidently this new time had much to recommend it, she thought, turning spigots on and off and operating the water closet with childish delight. A peek in the mirrored chest on the wall revealed a great deal of masculine paraphernalia that intrigued her more than she dared admit. It also drove home a fact she had managed to ignore until that very moment; she was sharing a house with a man who was not her husband.

The blood drained from her face as she slowly closed the cupboard's door. She would be branded a fallen woman if anyone learned she had passed the night under his roof. At least, she amended, her brows gathering in a frown, in *her* time she would be considered quite ruined. In this strange time and place, who knew what the conventions might be?

What she really needed, she decided, making her way back down the stairs, was to talk to other people and learn for herself what was proper and what was not. She trusted Mr. Bramwell to a point, but in the event that she was playing fast and loose with her reputation, she would as lief discover that now before placing herself beyond the pale.

The prospect was as tempting as it was terrifying, and for a moment she was bitterly torn. She knew Mr. Bramwell had told her to remain inside, but she didn't see how he could object to her having a quick look about. She had only his word that the world she had glimpsed was dangerous. Would it not be wisest to discern the truth of that for herself, rather than meekly accept his dictum?

The more she thought of it, the more she decided she had the right of it. She had always prided herself on behaving as a lady should, but Mr. Bramwell was neither her husband nor her father, and he had no right to order her about. And, an insidious voice whispered in her ear, if she were very clever and very careful, there was no reason why he should learn of it. She would walk no further than the corner, and return at once. What could it possibly hurt?

Could she do it? she wondered, casting a nervous glance at the bolted door. Then she thought of the wondrous new world that lay on the other side of that door, and wondered how she could not. To remain inside would be rather like going to the theatre and then sitting with her back to the stage for the entire performance. It made no sense, and she had always regarded herself as a sensible creature.

Her decision made, she dashed back upstairs and grabbed the pelisse she had spied earlier. It was covered with some shiny material and fastened she knew not how, but she reasoned it would keep her warm enough. She quickly slipped it on and started down the stairs, and had almost reached the bottom, when she heard the distinctive jingling of the telephone device.

She walked into the kitchen, listening to the shrill sound and nervously chewing her lip. The plethora of instructions Mr. Bramwell had issued had not included what to do if the telephone sounded, and she was uncertain what she should do. Then she remembered he had said it was used so people could communicate with each other from great distances, and she wondered if he might be attempting to communicate with her. The possibility was enough to have her picking up the telephone and holding it to her ear, as she had seen him do.

"Bramwell." She barked in to it, imitating the way her host had behaved. There was a scratchy silence, and then she heard a puzzled female voice.

"Alec?"

Miranda had no idea how to respond, but it seemed incredibly rude to say nothing, and so after a brief pause she said, "Mr. Bramwell is not in residence at the moment. Would you care to leave a message?"

There was another silence, and then the woman demanded, "Who the bloody hell is this?"

That a female should speak so vulgarly shocked Miranda, but at the moment she was more concerned with how to explain her presence in a bachelor's establishment. "I am the maid, madam," she replied, thinking quickly. "May I be of assistance?"

"The maid?" The woman sounded more suspicious than ever. "When did he hire you?"

"This is my first day, madam," Miranda said in what she hoped was a suitably servile tone. "And if you will forgive my saying so, there is a great deal to be done. The house is in a terrible state of disarray."

"It's an unholy mess from the little I saw of it," came the grumbled reply. "Well, did my brother say where he was going or when he would be back?"

"I believe he was called in to duty, and he did not say when he would return. He only said I was not to burn the house to the ground in his absence," Miranda didn't know what made her add that, but when she heard the woman give a soft chuckle, she knew she had said precisely the right thing.

"That sounds like Alec, all right," the woman said, the distrust vanishing from her voice. "Well, I'll let you get back to work, then. Just tell him Cara called, and that I'll be dropping by to-night."

"Very good, madam," Miranda said, setting the phone back on the counter with an incredible sense of triumph. She had done it! she thought, excitement racing through her. Perhaps this new world wouldn't prove so difficult after all. She savored her victory another moment and then walked out of the kitchen, her head held high as she opened the front door and walked out of the house and into the twentieth century.

THE DOOR AJAR

# Five

It was a scene straight from the bowels of hell. The swirling lights of emergency vehicles cast their unholy glow on the rain-swept streets, and crowds of rescue personnel could be seen swarming into the shattered ruins of what had once been a sedate office building.

"Christ, would you look at that!" The young officer who had driven him to the scene gave a low whistle as he viewed the carnage. "The whole bloody place is gone!"

Alec said nothing, his face grim as he stepped out of the car. The call-up marked his official return to duty, but he wished the situation hadn't been quite so dramatic. He hoped Dickerson had followed his instructions and got everyone out, otherwise they'd be picking up pieces of victims for the next several hours. Alec was leaning against the side of the car, gazing at the still-smoldering pile of bricks and twisted timber, when a dark-clad man with a black ski mask pulled over his head walked up to him.

"Lovely sight, isn't it?" the man said, blue eyes sharp as he studied Alec's face.

"I've seen worse," Alec replied, his tone even as he met his old SAS commander's gaze. "So've you."

Lieutenant Major Keller shrugged his massive shoulders, then turned back to survey the bombed-out building. "I suppose," he said, his deep voice tight with cold anger. "But it still makes me sick to my stomach."

Alec gave a jerky nod, trying not to remember what he had

found the last time he'd entered a bombing site. "Casualties?" he asked, reaching deep inside him for the control he knew he would need.

"Some, not as many as there could have been. We got ample warning . . . this time," Keller answered, maintaining a casual pose even while keeping a sharp eye on the crowd of curiosity-seekers being kept at bay by the police barricades. Terrorists sometimes returned to the scene of the crime; not only to gloat at the destruction they had wrought, but to spy on the investigators pouring over whatever evidence they could find.

Alec nodded, keeping his own vigil as well. "I heard that," he said, thinking of the scattered bits of intelligence he had received on the wild ride to the site. "Not like the Coalition to give a warning; maybe they're developing a humanitarian side in their old age."

Keller gave a snort, thinking of the hardened terrorist organization who had redefined the meaning of terrorism following the collapse of the Soviet Bloc. "Not bloody likely," he said derisively. "In fact, it's so unlike our old comrades that we're beginning to wonder if they're being set up to take the fall for someone else. Our Belfast friends, perhaps."

Alec digested the information in silence before replying. "Did the call come through the Samaritans?" he asked, knowing that was usually how the IRA issued their warnings.

Keller shook his head. "Bastard called one of the offices; got a secretary, who, thank God, kept her wits about her and got everyone out. That's her over there talking to Spencer." He nodded in the direction of a dazed-looking blonde, who was in deep conversation with a plump officer.

Alec recognized the officer, and decided to interview the woman himself. Spencer was a good cop, but he was also appallingly old-fashioned, and he tended to treat female witnesses with a mixture of courtesy and condescension. Alec doubted his notes would be of any use.

"So, what's the SAS's role in all this?" he drawled, not taking his gaze from the blonde. "Just happen to be passing by, and thought you'd stop and say hallo?"

There was a tense silence before Keller answered. "We're making sure our Belfast friends aren't involved," he said with obvious reluctance. "We've a painfully negotiated cease-fire underway just now, and we want to make sure we don't have some crazy bugger running around carrying out his own agenda. I don't need to tell you what that would mean."

Alec didn't bother answering. He didn't have to. Every officer in London, whether he was involved in counter-terrorism or not, knew that the failure of the cease-fire would mean a resumption of the bombing campaign that had already wreaked its bloody havoc on the country. It was something any man, himself included, would give his life to prevent.

"There's more."

The quiet note of warning brought Alec's head snapping up, his eyes narrowing as he studied Keller's hooded face. "What is it?" he asked, steeling himself as if for a blow.

"Preliminary recon indicates the suspects used the same kind of explosive here as they did at King's Road," Keller said, his blue eyes expressionless as they met Alec's gaze. "I thought you should know."

Alec didn't speak at first, lost in the horror of his memories. He remembered the carnage the explosion had wrought, the bodies blown apart by the force of the powerful explosive the terrorists had concocted, and then he remembered catching a glimpse of a familiar-looking coat peeking out of a pile of still-burning rubble . . .

"Sergeant?"

The use of his old rank snapped Alec out of his dark daze, and he gave Keller a jerky nod. "I'll pass it on to the lads," he said, turning his thoughts to the present. "Any signs the bombers left any surprise packages behind?"

Keller understood. Alec was asking about booby traps. Again he shook his head. "SU swept the area before letting the rescue squad in; it's clean."

Alec noted the constable had finished interviewing the blonde, and without a word of goodbye to Keller, he pushed himself away from the car and started forward. The sight of another man, obviously an officer, wanting to talk to her, made the woman's black-tinted lips thin in impatience.

"Not another copper," she said, thrusting a shaking hand through her tumbled curls. "How many of you are there?"

"Not enough, apparently," Alec said coldly, his eyes flicking over her shoulder to where the building was still smoldering. "I'm Inspector Bramwell with Scotland Yard, and I need to speak with you."

The woman gave a guilty flinch, but resolutely stood her ground. "So long as you don't call me dearie and pat my hand, I suppose I can answer your questions," she said, her gaze meeting his. "What is it you want to know?"

Alec admired her courage as he flipped open his notebook. "Everything you told the other officer," he said, "including the things you were too annoyed or embarrassed to tell him."

The blonde took a deep breath, and then told Alec all she could remember of the call. As she talked he made copious notes, jotting down bits of information he hoped he would be able to use later. While she was talking he heard the rescuers give two long blasts on the whistles they wore about their necks, and knew it meant bodies had been found. The stakes had just been anteed to murder, and the icy feeling in the pit of his stomach grew even worse.

"Is that it?" he asked when she'd finished. There had been four other long blasts, bringing the number of victims to three, and he prayed that would be the last of them. "Is there anything else you remember? What about background noise? Was there anything to indicate where the call might have originated? Street noise, or music, anything like that?"

The blonde took a jerky puff from the cigarette Alec had borrowed from another officer. "I've been trained, you know," she said, a note of irritation creeping into her voice as she blew out a plume of smoke. "I know what to listen for, and it's like I said, the caller was female, German or Austrian, I think, judging from her accent, and she said that she was from the Red Coalition, and that a bomb had been planted in the building and to get everyone out. There was no noise of any kind in the background, and after she'd delivered the message, she hung up."

Alec felt a warning tingle at the back of his neck. "After she delivered the message," he repeated carefully, not wishing to frighten her. "That seems an odd way of putting it. How do you mean that?"

She gave him a baffled look. "Well, that's what she was doing, wasn't it?" she said, taking another deep drag. "She said a bomb had been planted—"

"And that's how she put it?" Alec interrupted, his senses beginning to hum with excitement. "A bomb had been planted? Not that they themselves had planted it?"

"No!" The blonde threw the cigarette on the ground, her willingness to cooperate vanishing. "Look," she said, tears beginning to pool in her heavily lined eyes, "I've told you what was said, I even wrote it down and gave it to that other officer! I don't see why I have to keep going over and over it with you!" Her mouth trembled, and she suddenly looked quite young. "I want to go home, my mum will be worried starkers!"

Alec knew he had pressed hard enough and backed away immediately. "That's fine, Melanie," he said, stealing a covert glance at his notes for her name. "You've been wonderfully helpful, thank you. Just go over to that car over there, and an officer will see you home. All right?"

She rubbed her nose with the back of her hand. "All right," she said, her voice trembling as reaction finally set in. "Was anyone hurt? Did they all get out in time?"

Alec thought of the whistle blasts and shook his head. "It's still too early to tell," he lied, deciding it wouldn't hurt to keep her in ignorance another few hours. "And be sure you leave your address with the sergeant, so our chaplain can call on you."

Melanie's eyes grew wide. "Oh, I don't need a priest," she assured him anxiously. "I'm Buddhist!"

Alec smiled slightly. "Our chaplain's a very democratic fellow," he replied gently. "He's just someone to talk to, really, and you've had a terrible shock. You need to talk this out with professionals, and he can see that you get the proper help."

His smile did much to reassure the younger woman, and she started to turn away. She'd taken but a few steps when she suddenly stopped and turned around.

"Inspector Bramwell?" she said, flushing slightly. "I've just remembered something. It may be nothing but . . ."

"What is it?" he asked, hurrying to her side.

Her flush increased, and a faintly flustered look stole into her eyes. "Well, this is going to sound dreadfully silly, but it was the woman's voice . . . she . . . she sounded embarrassed."

"Embarrassed?" Alec repeated, his eyebrows climbing in surprise.

Melanie gave a quick nod. "It wasn't so much what she said," she said, her confidence increasing when she saw he was really listening. "It was the way she said it. Almost . . . I don't know, apologetic, like she was a neighbor calling to make amends because her dog had dug up the flowers. I got the feeling she was even sorry. Does . . . does that help?" she studied him worriedly.

Alec was quiet a long moment as he considered the possible ramifications of what he had just learned. "Yes, Melanie," he said quietly, "it helps a great deal."


Miranda's first thought upon venturing out of the house was that she had made a terrible mistake. She even turned around, only to discover that the door had closed and locked behind her, trapping her outside. At first she hovered uncertainly on the doorstep, her heart pounding with a heady mixture of terror and excitement as she tried to decide what to do.

In the end her common sense overcame her trepidation, and she told herself the only sensible thing to do was to go for a short walk. She had no idea how long Mr. Bramwell's mission might detain him, and she reasoned she could hardly stand on the doorstep like a tradesman seeking entry without attracting attention. Her mind made up, she took a deep breath and stepped off the front steps.

Her overwhelming impression of this new time was the noise and the incredible speed with which everything moved. The horseless carriages she knew to be cars, but she couldn't decide which of the fearsome objects were the lorries her surly host had warned her about. The press of people and especially the clothes they wore also caught her notice, and it was all she could do not to gape at them like the greenest chit from the country.

She was shocked to note that many of the women wore trousers, and then was more shocked still to see others wearing skirts so short they made her jaw drop. If it came to choosing between the two fashions, she decided she preferred trousers. The thought of baring her legs to the stares of strangers was not something she could contemplate with anything approaching equanimity.

At first she stayed on Curzon Street, walking up one side and down the other as she slowly took in her surroundings. A few buildings were familiar to her, and she took comfort in their solid presence. Chesterfield Street angled off to the right, and on impulse she wandered down the tiny, narrow street, studying the buildings with the blue plaques denoting their famous former residents. She smiled at one bolted to the side of a cream-colored building, thinking how puffed up Brummel would be if he knew his modest home would be preserved for the ages.

She soon returned to Curzon Street, and walked until she came back to Clarges Street. Stephen's home sat near the corner, and she knew she could either go there and sit demurely on the steps and await Mr. Bramwell's return, or she could continue exploring. She glanced at the shuttered, abandoned-looking house, and then down the twisting street that in the past had led to Picadilly and the center of London. A lifetime of always doing what was right and proper warred with her newfound sense of rebellion, and promptly lost. Making sure the street was free of cars, she dashed across it and started resolutely toward Picadilly.

If Curzon Street had stunned her, the sight of Picadilly left her incapable of thought. Never in her wildest dreams could she have imagined such a cacophony of sight and sound, and for a moment all she could do was stand and stare in wonder. Cars and huge red conveyances, some as big as houses, whizzed past her at frightening speeds, and everywhere she looked, she could see people of every hue and description. It was like something out of a dream, and she had never been more enchanted.

She saw a thick mass of people standing at the corner, and when they started to cross the street, she decided to follow. She hadn't taken but a few steps, when there was a terrifying blast of noise to her left. Fear made her freeze in her tracks, and then she was suddenly grabbed from behind and jerked back on the curb, just as a black car whizzed past her with a shriek of brakes.

"The damned fool!" The man who had pulled her out of harm's way was glaring after the car, his hand still closed protectively about her arm. "He might have killed you!"

Miranda found speech quite beyond her. She could only stand and tremble, thinking somewhat dazedly that if that was one of the lorries Mr. Bramwell had mentioned, then he had been right to caution her against them.

"Are you all right, miss?" The man must have felt her trembling, because he was gazing down at her, his light blue eyes filled with concern.

Miranda drew a shaky breath. "I . . . I . . . am fine, sir, th-thank you," she stammered, forcing the words past her chattering teeth. She realized how close she had come to dying, and the realization left her on the verge of collapse.

"Blasted taxis think they own the streets," the man said, his voice soothing as he continued to study her. "I got his number, if you'd like to ring the company and report him."

"No, that—that will not be necessary," Miranda assured him, struggling to regain her composure. She finally managed to scrape up a smile, albeit a shaky one, which she offered her rescuer. "And to be fair, the fault was more mine than it was the driver's. I fear I was not paying proper attention."

"Well, if you're certain," the hesitation in his voice made it plain he was far from convinced. The crowd was beginning to surge impatiently about them, and a particularly strong shove would have sent Miranda tumbling had the man not had a firm hold on her arm. He helped steady her, and the next time the crowd pushed forward, he let the momentum carry them across the street. When they'd safely reached the other side he turned to her, his pale blue eyes anxious as they studied her face.

"Listen," he began, his tone diffident, "I don't want you to think this is a pickup, because it's not, but you really look shaken. There's a restaurant just inside the door here, will you let me buy you a cup of coffee or something?"

He sounded so sincere, so anxious to please, that Miranda felt her natural reluctance fading. In *her* day, of course, she'd never have considered his invitation for a moment, but as circumstances had so dramatically illustrated, she was no longer in her day. She flicked his face a searching glance before reaching her decision.

"A cup of tea sounds lovely, sir," she said, shyly lowering her lashes. "Thank you."

An oddly relieved look flashed across his face and was gone, he took hold of her arm and led her through the shop's double doors. Inside was a bewildering assortment of food and other items, and Miranda did her best not to gawk as he guided her past the many tempting displays.

"Is this your first time at Fortnum's?" he asked solicitously, smiling as she stopped to examine a glass cabinet filled with cheese. "A bit overwhelming, isn't it?"

"A bit," Miranda agreed hollowly, her eyes as wide as a child's at a Christmas pantomime.

To her relief he asked no more questions, but led her up a wide staircase where a line of people were waiting to be seated. Several minutes later they were seated at a damask-covered table, and at her nod, he ordered a serving of tea. As soon as the server had left, her rescuer gave her a charming smile and said, "I suppose the first thing I should do is introduce myself," he said, offering her his hand. "I'm Professor Geoffrey Kingston, I teach economics at London University."

Miranda hesitated, unsure how to respond. She still did not know what the rules were in this new time, and she had no desire to put herself beyond the pale. Thinking carefully, she decided she had no choice but to follow his lead. "I am Miss Miranda Winthrop," she said at last, reluctant to give her proper title. "And I am very much in your debt, Professor Kingston."

"Geoffrey, please," he said, giving her another smile. "Are you from London, Miranda?"

Good heavens, how was she to answer *that?* Miranda wondered, fighting the urge to break into hysterical laughter. "I was born in London," she temporized, thinking it was as close to the truth as she dared stray. "But I have been away for several years."

"Really?" He looked intrigued. "Do you find it much changed from what you remember?"

"In some ways," Miranda agreed, her lips curving at the irony of her reply. "Yet in others, it is much the same.

They continued chatting idly, and by the time the tea was delivered, Miranda had all but recovered from her fright. She found Professor Kingston to be quite charming, if a trifle inquisitive, and she could not help but compare his polished manners to those of her churlish host. The professor was obviously a gentleman, she decided, while Mr. Bramwell was sadly in want of refining. The knowledge amused her for some reason, and she was considering the matter when her gaze happened to stray to the large clock mounted on the wall.

"Gracious, it cannot be so late as that!" she exclaimed, horrified to discover more than an hour had passed. "I must be going! If Mr. Bramwell has returned, he will be furious to find me gone!"

The professor signaled for the server to bring the bill. "Is Mr. Bramwell your employer?" he asked, giving her a curious look.

Miranda had to think a moment before answering. "No," she said, recalling how she had stretched the truth to explain her unusual situation, "as I explained, I am staying with friends until

I can settle my affairs, and he is my host. I fear he is most strict in his notions," she added, hoping the professor would think Mr. Bramwell an older man.

"He sounds like a real Hitler," Professor Kingston said as he tossed a handful of money on the table. "Well, I suppose we should get you home before he sends you to a concentration camp. Do you need a taxi, or did you come by the tube?"

Miranda blinked at him, lost in confusion. "The tube?"

"The underground," he explained, and then when she continued to look puzzled, he gave a slight smile. "Judging by your accent, I suppose I shouldn't be surprised you don't know what the tube is," he added, a sarcastic edge Miranda could not like stealing into his voice. "Did your limo drop you off?"

Miranda did not know what a limo was either, but she was not about to share her ignorance with him. Instead she brought her chin up, her eyes frosting over with displeasure as she met his gaze. "As it happens, sir, I walked to Picadilly," she said, every inch the haughty countess. "And I assure you, I need no help returning to my house."

For a moment she didn't think he meant to speak, but then he gave her a sheepish smile. "I really put my foot in it, didn't I?" he asked, ducking his head in obvious embarrassment. "I'm sorry, I shouldn't have said that."

"No, you should not have," she agreed, although she relented enough to send him a cool smile.

"I'm sorry," he said again, his hand on her back as he guided her through the maze of tables. "Chock it up to my parents. They were hippies in the sixties, and I'm afraid some of their antiestablishment views rubbed off on me. I hope I haven't offended you?"

Considering she hadn't understood most of what he had said, Miranda thought there was little danger of that. If she was ever to comprehend this new time, she would have to take pains to learn the language. Either that, she decided with a rueful smile, or she would have to hire an interpreter as her step-papa had done when he had gone to Italy.

Professor Kingston escorted Miranda out of the store, hovering uncertainly at her side as they waited to cross the street. "Are you certain you'll be all right?" he asked, shifting from one foot to another as he gazed down at her. "I could walk you home, maybe explain what happened to your host. He could hardly be angry at you if he knew—"

"No!" Miranda interrupted, wincing at how Mr. Bramwell would gloat if he'd learned of her near-fatal encounter with the taxi. "That is," she added when she saw the professor's puzzled expression, "I don't wish to worry him. He is possessed of a rather excitable disposition, you see."

Professor Kingston gave her another of his odd, searching looks before slowly nodding. "Yes," he said, "I do. Well, good-bye then, Miranda, enjoy your visit to London," and with that he melted away into the bustling crowds.

Miranda stared after him, and then dismissed his behavior as yet another puzzling aspect of the new world in which she found herself. Paying close attention to traffic this time, she managed to cross the street without incident. The temptation to continue exploring was strong, but she resisted it, fearing she may have already tarried too long. She only hoped she arrived home ahead of Mr. Bramwell, although how she would explain her presence on his doorstep, she knew not. She would just have to think of something, she decided, ignoring the way her heart pounded with trepidation.

It took her less than fifteen minutes to reach the house, and for a few moments she stood on the street gazing up at it. It looked smaller and somehow abandoned-looking, she mused, her eyes misting with tears. She remembered Mr. Bramwell had mentioned that he'd just moved into the house, and she wondered how long it had sat empty. Months, if the dust in the bedchamber was any indication, she decided as she started up the steps with a sigh. It was fortunate she hadn't materialized in the room sooner, else she may have found herself in very dire straits indeed.

When she reached the door she stared at it with a frown,

wondering if there was a way she could possibly force it open.
She gave the handle an experimental rattle, and then leapt back
with a terrified shriek, when it suddenly flew open and she found
herself face-to-face with her furious host. They regarded each
other a brief moment, and then he reached out and grabbed her
hand, pulling her inside before she could utter a single word of
protest. He slammed the door behind her, his eyes sparkling like
molten gold as he glared down at her.

"Where the bloody hell have you been?"

# *Six*

There was a moment of stunned silence as Alec and Lady Miranda exchanged furious glares. When he'd returned home to find her gone, his first thought was that he'd imagined the whole damned thing. *A time-traveller,* for God's sake. But when he'd forced himself to go into the room he had shared with Jane, he'd discovered Miranda's white negligee lying neatly on the bed. Seeing it assured him he hadn't lost his mind, which relieved him more than he dared admit, but it still didn't explain what had happened to her.

Had the mysterious forces that deposited her in the hidden room yanked her back again? he'd wondered. Or was there a simpler, more sinister reason behind her disappearance? Given her terrified reaction when she'd opened the front door, he was fairly certain she'd never voluntarily leave the house, which meant she must have been taken against her will. Even though there was no sign of a struggle, he'd been toying with the idea of calling it in, when he'd glanced out to see her walking calmly up the steps. Now she was standing before him looking as haughty and disapproving as the queen, and he could cheerfully have throttled her.

"Well?" he barked, when she remained silent. "I'm waiting. Want to tell me where you've been for the past hour?"

Rather than bursting into tears, as she knew he expected, Miranda gave him a look that could have frozen lava. "Is this how people in this time greet one another?" she asked coolly, jerking her arm out of his grasp. "If so, I fear manners have deteriorated even further than I surmised."

Alec flushed in anger and embarrassment. "Don't take that lady-of-the-manor tone with me!" he snapped, furious she was managing to turn the tables on him. "I thought I told you to stay in the damned house. What the hell do you mean by disobeying me?"

Miranda, who had always considered herself the most placid of ladies, gave serious thought to kicking him in the shins as hard as she could. Only the certainty he would doubtlessly reciprocate kept her from acting on the impulse, and she contented herself with a scornful glare instead.

"A woman, Mr. Bramwell, might reasonably be expected to obey a husband or a father," she informed him in her iciest tones, "but as you are neither, I can see no reason why I should follow your dictums. Now," she added when he opened his mouth in protest, "if you are quite finished ringing a peal over my head, I should like to retire to my rooms. It has been a rather eventful day." She gave him a mocking smile that made his jaw clench with fury.

For a moment Alec was tempted to put his fist through a wall, but in the end he managed to get himself under control. One of the first lessons he'd learned as an SAS recruit was the need to master his emotions, and he was damned if he'd let some misty-eyed blonde turn him inside out again.

"Look," he began, making a conscious effort to rein in his temper, "I didn't ask you to stay—"

"Ordered," she corrected, her gaze holding his defiantly. "You *ordered* me to stay."

"I didn't *ask* you to stay inside out of sheer spite," he continued, ignoring her interruption. "You haven't the slightest conception how dangerous it is out there, and I was only trying to keep you safe. If you thought I was a little harsh, I'm sorry, but I was only thinking of you. Can't you accept that?"

Miranda considered his question several seconds before replying. "Perhaps," she allowed, "had you done me the courtesy of explaining your reasons, rather than barking out commands like . . . a . . . . a . . ." she struggled to remember the name the professor had called him. "A Hitler," she concluded, feeling vastly pleased with herself.

To her delight his jaw dropped, then snapped shut as a tide of dark red washed over his high cheekbones. "What the devil do you know about Hitler?" he demanded, looking more furious than ever.

"I heard his name in passing, and understood him to be a most autocratic fellow," she answered, exulting in his obvious discomfiture. " 'Twould seem I had the right of it."

Alec clenched his fists until he could all but feel the bones popping. "I was worried," he said tightly, anger and frustration boiling up in him. "I've been back for almost an hour, and when I couldn't find you, I thought something had happened."

Miranda was taken aback by his stilted confession. She couldn't remember the last time anyone had shown concern for her well-being, and for a moment she wasn't sure how to respond. She realized she'd been behaving like a perfect shrew, and a sense of contrition washed over her.

"I never meant to cause you concern, and for that I am sorry," she said quietly, dropping her gaze as she turned away. "I only meant to go for a short walk, but somehow time seemed to slip away from me. An apparent problem with me of late," she added, discovering a heretofore undiscovered gift for irony.

Her apology as well as her weak attempt at a joke defused the last of Alec's temper. He'd never been one to hold a grudge, and he decided that if she could be so magnanimous, then so could he. "That's all right," he said, offering her a placating smile. "And I'm sorry for jumping down your throat the moment you walked in the door. But as I said, I was worried about you."

She turned at that, intrigued by his admission. "What did you think had happened to me?" she asked curiously.

"Considering the way you materialized out of thin air, how the he—how the devil was I supposed to know?" he asked, mak-

ing a belated attempt to clean up his language. "For all I knew,
you'd gone back to wherever—whenever you came from."

"Eighteen-eleven," she reminded him, still scarcely able to
believe the incredible truth of what had happened.

"Eighteen-eleven," he agreed, then shook his head with a
rusty laugh. "God, will you listen to us?" he asked, giving her
a whimsical smile. "You do realize that if you aren't a time-
traveller, the pair of us are mad as hatters?"

Her lips twitched in reluctant humor. "If such is the case, sir,
I hope your society is kinder to lunatics than they were in my
day. I've no desire to end my days in Bedlam."

"Nor do I," he agreed, remembering a film he had seen on
nineteenth-century insane asylums. "And for God's sake, will
you please call me Alec? Hearing you call me 'sir' or Mr. Bramwell makes me feel like my own grandfather."

Miranda remembered the easy way the professor had used her
given name, and gave him a probing look. "Do all men and
women address each other so familiarly?" she asked, anxious to
learn the truth. "In my time it would have been considered fast."

He hid a grin at her old-fashioned remark. "Not in this time,"
he said, thinking that if she learned precisely how loose things
had become, she'd probably faint with horror. "These days almost everyone calls each other by their Christian names, and no
one thinks a thing about it."

"I see," she said awkwardly, her cheeks pinking as she recalled discovering his grooming items in the upstairs cupboard.
"And do they reside under the same roof without benefit of a
proper chaperon?"

It took him several seconds to catch her meaning. "Live together, do you mean?" he asked, then felt a twinge of remorse
when her face grew bright red. "All the time," he added quickly,
hoping to reassure her. "But you can relax. We're not living
together, at least, not in the accepted sense of the word."

Her cheeks now grew a deathly white. "What is the accepted
sense of the word?" she asked, swallowing nervously.

Alec found himself wishing Cara was there to help explain

things to Miranda. Talking things out was really more her forte than it was his, and he sensed he was making a sad hash of it. When Miranda repeated her question, he sent her a frustrated scowl. "What do you think it means?" he grumbled, feeling like a sex pervert at one of the peek shows in Soho.

Miranda's green eyes pooled with tears. "That is what I thought," she said, her head drooping with shame. "People will think I am your mistress."

The sight of those tears made Alec blanch. "Damn it, Miranda, no one thinks about such rot these days!" he exclaimed, gesturing helplessly. "So long as it keeps out of the papers and off the television, most people could care less!"

"*I* care!" she cried, placing her fist over her heart. "Perhaps you can view such things with indifference, but I can not. I am a married woman, and I have my reputation to think of! In my eyes, if I remain with you, I am ruined!"

There was a short, charged silence that was broken by a sudden knock at the door. Alec ignored it at first, but when the doorbell began ringing as well, he knew he had no choice but to answer. He glanced out the small diamond-shaped window in the door, and muttered a frustrated curse beneath his breath.

"Blast it, it's Cara!" he said, forgetting that only seconds earlier he'd been wishing for his sister's company. "What's she doing here?"

Miranda gave a guilty start. "I . . . I forgot to tell you," she admitted, unsure if she welcomed or feared the interruption, "but she called on the telephone machine and said she would be coming by this evening."

Alec paused, his hand on the door's handle. "*You* answered the phone?" he asked, shooting her a stunned look.

"I thought perhaps it was you attempting to communicate with me," she explained, hoping she hadn't broken some odd social convention. "I—I told her I was the maid," she added when he kept staring at her.

"The maid?" Alec repeated, then cursed again as the doorbell sounded impatiently. He tore open the door and glared at his

sister, who was standing on the doorstep with a knowing smirk
on her lips. "What do you want?" he demanded, his tone of
voice as belligerent as the scowl on his face.

Cara raised an eyebrow mockingly, her light brown eyes dancing with amusement. "Interrupting something, am I?" she
drawled, her gaze flicking past her brother's broad shoulder to
rest on the beautiful blonde she could see cowering behind him.
Intrigued, she brushed her way past Alec as if he wasn't there.

"Hello," she said, her manner deliberately friendly as she gave
the unknown woman a warm smile. "Are you the woman I spoke
with earlier? The maid?"

"Don't be an ass, Cara, you know damned well she's not the
maid," Alec retorted, slamming the door shut.

Cara's glance strayed to the parlor, where piles of boxes could
be seen lying in cluttered heaps. "Well, if she was, luv, I was
going to suggest you give her the sack," she said, then turned
to offer her hand to the blonde who was regarding her with
wide-eyed wonder.

"Don't you hate it when people talk about you as if you're
not there?" she asked, still smiling. "I'm Cara Marsdale, this
beast's sister, and you are . . . ?"

Miranda stared at the other woman's hand, uncertain what to
do. But years of having manners drilled in her by a succession
of governesses was too strong to overcome, and she accepted
the proffered hand with a shy smile. "I am Miss Miranda Winthrop," she said, once again neglecting to give her title. And in
truth, she admitted with a sudden flash of sadness, she had no
real claim to it. She might have been Stephen's bride, but she
had never been his wife, and now she never would.

Cara heard the cultured elegance in the other woman's soft
voice, and her gaze grew even more curious. "And are you going
to tell me what you're doing arguing with my brother in the
middle of his foyer, Miss Miranda Winthrop," she asked, sweetly,
"or are you going to let me guess?"

Without realizing the significance of his actions, Alec moved
to stand protectively beside Miranda. "Guess all you like, you

obnoxious brat," he informed Cara with a formidable glare, "you'll never come close in a million years."

Cara raised both eyebrows at that. "Oh?"

Alec blew out his breath with a gusty sigh. "Oh, to hell with it," he said, thrusting a hand through his hair and exchanging glances with Miranda. She gave a jerky nod, and he turned back to Cara, who was regarding them both with unabashed curiosity.

"You might as well come inside," he said, gesturing to the parlor. "Miranda and I have a little story to tell you . . ."

"You're both going to sit there, calm as you please, and ask me to believe that Miranda is a time-traveller?" Cara asked when they'd finished their story. "From the Regency?"

Alex folded his arms across his chest, feeling both foolish and defensive at the shock on Cara's face. He knew the truth defied credulity, but that didn't mean his sister had to look at him like he was a prime candidate for a mental ward. "Yes," he said, thrusting his jean-clad legs out in front of him and giving her a dark scowl, "that's precisely what we're asking."

Cara shook her head. "Alec, I want to believe you, but—"

"I realize how fantastical this must sound," Miranda interrupted, eager to convince Alec's sister of the truth, "but that is precisely what happened. I—I do not know how, or why, but one moment I was there, in the past, and the next . . ."

"And the next you were here," Cara finished for her, finally, incredibly, accepting their tale. "Good lord, you must have thought you were having some sort of nightmare!"

Miranda nodded, grateful for the other woman's understanding. "I had no notion what might have happened," she admitted, shuddering as she recalled her fear and confusion upon waking. "The two of you seem quite comfortable with the notion of travelling through time, but I had never even heard of such a thing!"

"Yes, I can imagine it must have been disconcerting," Cara agreed, her gaze flicking toward her brother. "And to think the first thing you saw was this lout bending over you. Poor child. What you must have thought!"

An imp of mischief brought a sparkle to Miranda's eyes at the memory of the scowling, disheveled man she had first seen. "Actually," she admitted, a smile curving her lips, "I thought he was a Gypsy, who'd broken into the house and was going to rob us all. He already smelled as if he'd discovered the wine cellar."

Cara burst into delighted laughter, and a moment later Miranda joined in. Alec gave them both menacing looks as they finally subsided into breathless giggles. "If you've quite finished laughing, do you think we might get back to the matter at hand?" he asked between clenched teeth.

Cara grinned at him, every inch the obnoxious younger sister. "Certainly, darling," she informed him sweetly. "Er . . . what *is* the matter at hand?"

"Her," Alec jerked his head in Miranda's direction, "and more precisely, what I am supposed to do with her. I can't just wall her back up, you know."

"No, I suppose not," Cara's amusement vanished abruptly. She turned to Miranda, who was also looking solemn. "Have you tried accessing the time-whatever and going back?"

Miranda reluctantly shook her head. "No," she admitted with a sigh. "Mr. Bramwell . . . Alec, asked me not to attempt it on my own, and—and I must admit to having my own reservations."

That seemed to startle Cara, and she gave her an incredulous look. "Why? Don't you *want* to go back?" she asked curiously.

Miranda thought of Stephen and his betrayal of her and blushed unhappily. "Of course," she said, threading her fingers together and refusing to gaze at either Cara or Alec. "But I have been thinking, and what if I do not return to my time? What if I return to a time when the room is still walled up, and the house abandoned? I should starve."

The grim thought made Cara blanch. "I hadn't thought of that," she admitted, shuddering with horror, "but you're right, of course, that is a possibility."

"Also, the passage through time was quite painful," Miranda added, the searing pain she had experienced fresh in her mind. "I don't think I should care to experience it again, unless I had no other choice."

"I've also decided it's too dangerous," Alec interjected firmly, deciding he'd remained silent long enough. "Remember the pentagrams on the floor and walls?" he reminded his sister with a frown. "If some kind of black magic is involved, I don't think we should be mucking with it. For now, I want Miranda to stay out of that damned room."

"Miranda? What about *you?*" Cara was quick to pick up on his telling omission. "I didn't like the way that place felt, and I think you should stay out of it as well. Unless you want to end up like the Count of Monte Cristo?" she gave him a challenging glare.

He dismissed her concerns with an indifferent shrug. "I should be safe enough," he said, thinking he didn't give a damn if he got zapped back into the past or not. "Besides, I want to see if those books and other things Miranda saw are still there. They might give us some clues as to what we're dealing with."

They continued arguing back and forth, and listening to them squabble gave Miranda the urge to become more assertive in the discussion. For all his autocratic ways, she noted that Alec actually listened to his sister, even deferring to her at one point, and he also seemed to give credence to her opinions when she offered them. She remembered how her stepfather had coldly ignored her objections the few times she'd dared speak up, and even Stephen often brushed her comments aside when her ideas did not coincide with his own. Were all men of this time like him? she wondered. If so, it would explain why his sister was so outspoken and independent.

"That reminds me," Cara said suddenly, drawing Miranda out of her reverie. "What happened to the pendant you were wearing? I'm willing to bet it's the key to all this."

"It's in my desk at work," Alec said, speaking before Miranda had the chance to open her mouth. "Until we've a better idea what we're dealing with, I don't want it in the house."

Cara accepted his decision with a nod. "Then you're stuck here," she said, her chin cradled on her hand as she studied Miranda's face. "How do you feel about that?"

Miranda shrugged helplessly, feeling suddenly very lost and alone. "I really do not see that it matters how I feel," she said, blinking back tears. "I can not go back to my time, and so I must accept this time. There is nothing else to be done."

Alec saw the tears on her lashes and felt a shard of empathy pierce the protective shell he had built around his emotions. When he'd finally accepted that he wasn't going to kill himself, he'd felt much the same way—a stranger trapped in a life and a world not of his choosing. No wonder Miranda had gone off on her own, he decided, wincing as he remembered the way he'd raged at her. She hadn't been purposefully defying him, she'd been running. As he'd been running since the day Jane had died . . .

"Well, I don't know about the two of you," Cara said suddenly, her voice determinedly bright, "but all this talk of time-travel has made me famished. Why don't we go some place for a pizza?"

"Pizza?" Miranda frowned over the unfamiliar word.

Cara gave another laugh, leaning forward to squeeze her hand. "Miranda, my sweet," she said, brown eyes sparkling, "do you ever have a lot to learn about the twentieth century!"

Pizza, Miranda was pleased to discover, was a delectable concoction of melted cheese, spicy meats, and an exotic sauce. Once she'd recovered from the shock of learning it was eaten with one's hands rather than using cutlery she'd tucked into it with delicate greed, devouring several pieces beneath Cara's approving gaze. "We'll make a modern woman of you yet," she told Miranda, taking a sip of foamy lager. "Are you sure you wouldn't like a glass of ale or some wine? Women are allowed to drink in public these days, you know."

Miranda's gaze strayed to a nearby table where several other women were boisterously enjoying their own meal and glasses of wine. "I realize that," she said dryly, noting that the bolder of the ladies was eyeing Alec with lascivious interest. "But I prefer my cola, thank you. It is most delicious."

"God, what it must have been like before junk food," Cara mumbled around a mouthful of pizza, "I'd have starved!"

The rest of the meal passed quickly, as Miranda overcame her reticence and began quizzing the spirited Cara about life in the latter part of the twentieth century. She was shocked to learn that the other woman was also a police officer, and had recently been promoted to the rank of inspector. But it was learning she had her own flat in St. Johns Wood that rendered Miranda speechless.

"Then it is permissible for a female to set up her own establishment?" she asked, when she finally regained use of her voice. "Without a risk of scandal?"

"Certainly!" Cara said, obviously amused by Miranda's reaction. "These are the nineteen nineties, and women can do whatever they bloody like! Of course," she added with a shrug, "living on one's own can be frightfully expensive, which is why most women have flatmates to help share costs."

A glimmer of a plan danced in Miranda's mind. "Do you have a . . . er . . . flatmate?" she asked, toying with her paper napkin.

"Me? No," Cara took another sip of lager. "When my husband and I divorced, I took a lump settlement, so money's not a problem; thank God."

Miranda choked on her sip of cola. "You are *divorced?* " she gasped, staring at Cara in dismay.

Alec, who had been content to sit quietly and let Cara handle the conversation, sat forward at the expression on Miranda's face. "You don't need to look at my sister as if she's some sort of harlot!" he snapped, brows meeting over his nose as he glared at Miranda. "Divorce is perfectly acceptable these days."

Miranda flushed brightly, more distressed at having offended Cara than at the lashing tone in Alec's voice. She spared him a haughty look before turning to Cara. "I did not mean to give offense, ma'am," she said in a quiet voice. "It is just that in my time, divorces required an act of Parliament and were very difficult to obtain. I certainly did not mean to imply you were a . . . a harlot," she stumbled over the word.

"It's all right," Cara assured her, accepting her apology with an understanding smile. "Lord knows the mistakes *I'd* make if I got zapped back to your era. I'd probably end up in the Tower!" And she laughed over the image.

The uncomfortable moment passed, for the women at least, and they soon resumed their easy conversation. Alec, however, was far from mollified, and settled back in his chair to sip his beer and brood. He knew he was being an ass, but Miranda's prim and proper manner was beginning to get to him. He knew it wasn't her fault, that she was only behaving as she'd been taught, but he was tired of feeling like an uneducated oaf every time he was around her. She had only to lift an elegant eyebrow in that snooty way of hers, and he was spoiling for a fight.

Watching her, he couldn't help but compare her to Jane, and a fresh wave of pain washed over him. Although she hadn't been quite as beautiful as Miranda, Jane had been blunt, determined, and possessed of a drive to succeed that had often left him shaking his head in admiration. But when they were alone together, the tough cop became a very sexy woman, who— His thoughts slammed to a halt and he rose abruptly to his feet.

"Alec?" Cara was gazing up at him worriedly.

"I have to use the toilet," he said, his jaw clenching as he pushed back his chair and walked away from the table without another word.

Cara watched him go, her eyes filled with her own pain. She picked up her glass and took a shaky sip. "Damn," she muttered, blinking rapidly to keep the tears in her eyes from falling.

"What is it? Is something wrong with Mr. Bramwell?" Miranda asked, her gaze following Alec as he disappeared in the smoky air of the small restaurant Cara had selected.

Cara bit her lip, feeling an uncustomary indecision. In addition to being a huge pain in the arse, her brother was almost fanatically obsessive about his privacy, and she knew he'd hit the roof if he discovered she'd told Miranda about Jane; about the bombing and its terrible aftermath. But on the other hand, she reasoned, it was hardly fair to Miranda to leave her in the dark. She weighed her options before reaching a swift decision.

"Did you ever wonder where the clothes you're wearing came from?" she asked, keeping her tone light as she met Miranda's gaze. "Unless you think my macho brother is a drag queen," she added, unable to resist the temptation to tease just a little.

Miranda blinked in surprise. "I . . . I suppose I did wonder," she admitted, trying to recall her exact thoughts when she'd first discovered the clothing hanging in the wardrobe. She gave Cara a curious look as she considered the implications of the question. "They are not yours, then?"

Cara shook her head. "They belonged to Jane," she said, choosing each word with the greatest care. "She . . . she was Alec's fiancée, but she died about a year and a half ago. He's still not over it."

Miranda's heart softened at once. "I see," she said softly, remembering the portrait of the smiling, auburn-haired woman on the upstairs wall. So she and the brooding Mr. Bramwell had more in common than she first suspected, she thought, toying with her glass. He had lost his fiancée to the power of death, while she had lost a husband to the even more powerful force of time. It should have made them friends, but somehow she doubted that would be the case.

"She and Alec were living together when she died," Cara continued, eager to tell her as much as she could before Alec's return. "Afterwards I wanted to get rid of her things, but he wouldn't let me. Now it looks as if it's a blessing I didn't," she added, eyes gleaming with laughter as she took in the borrowed dress and jacket Miranda was wearing.

Miranda managed a weak smile in return. "Considering what I was wearing when I appeared in this time, I would agree," she said, her smile fading as she considered something Cara had said.

Ever sensitive to the moods of others, Cara gently patted her hand. "What is it?" she asked, her gaze seeking Miranda's. "You can ask me anything."

Miranda took a deep breath and willed herself not to blush. "Do . . . do men and women often live together?"

Cara looked puzzled by the question. "All the time."

"Even . . ." Miranda swallowed uncomfortably, "even if they are not lovers?"

Finally Cara understood the source of Miranda's nervousness. "You're talking about the situation between you and Alec, aren't you?" she asked softly.

Miranda bobbed her head in affirmation and repeated the argument she and Alec had been having prior to Cara's arrival. "He has said it doesn't matter," she concluded, looking troubled, "but I can not like it. In my day a good reputation was among a woman's most precious possessions, and I have no desire to risk mine in this time. Can you understand that?"

Reluctantly Cara could, and she gave a heavy sigh. "Your day sounds bloody awful," she grumbled, drumming her fingers on the table's scarred wood top. "All that obsession with propriety would drive me mad. However, if you're thinking they'll stone you at the crossroads for sharing a house with Alec, you're wrong. People really *don't* care, Miranda, and if someone is crass enough to mention the matter, just tell them you're his tenant or something. Better yet, tell them to go to hell."

"Tenant?" Miranda ignored the last part of Cara's suggestion.

"Sure, tell them he's subletting a room to you," Cara said, expanding on her idea. "It's done all the time; especially in this part of London. No one will think a thing about it."

Miranda remained silent as she considered Cara's advice. The idea of lying distressed her, but then she realized she could scarce tell anyone the truth. From what Alec had said, claiming to be a time-traveller would be as dangerous now as it was in 1811. And although she would die sooner than admit it, she really didn't wish to leave the house. It was her only contact with all that was familiar, and for the moment at least, she felt safest there. Relieved that she had finally resolved the matter, she settled back in her chair, eyeing Cara thoughtfully. Now there was just one thing that troubled her.

"Cara?"

"Hmm?" Cara was searching the smoky darkness for any sign of her brother.

"What is a drag queen?"

The question brought Cara's gaze snapping back to Miranda, and she gave a slow grin. "I've said it before, but I'll say it again," she drawled, "you have a lot to learn about the twentieth century, my dear. Now listen carefully, Auntie Cara is about to give you a history lesson . . ."

# *Seven*

By the time a grim-faced Alec returned to the table, Miranda was wide-eyed and speechless at all Cara had told her. When he curtly suggested they leave, she was more than happy to comply, and they were soon walking down the rain-swept sidewalk toward Curzon Street. They'd reached the house and Alec was fumbling with the key, when Cara laid a restraining hand on his arm.

"I heard what happened at the Docklands," she said, her gaze searching the harsh planes of his face revealed by the pale yellow security light. "You'll be going in tomorrow, then?"

Alec hesitated a moment before answering. "The forensic team at SO 7 should have the prelims done," he said, striving for the professional cool he knew his sister would expect. "I'll look over the results in the morning, and then re-interview a few witnesses. It shouldn't take long."

Cara touched his cheek. "Are you all right?"

He jerked his head back, scowling down at her. "I'm fine," he snarled, annoyed that she still thought him unstable. "You know the captain would never have let me resume my duties, if he didn't think I could handle it."

Cara had been a little sister too long to be intimidated by his black mood. "I didn't ask if you could handle it," she returned, glowering up at him. "I asked if you were all right."

Alec's anger evaporated as he accepted her concern. "I'm fine," he repeated, this time with a slight smile. "I'll admit to some bad moments, but . . ." he shrugged, then met her gaze, his eyes dark with determination. "I'm going to get them, Cara," he vowed in a soft voice, "I'm going to nail them to the wall."

Cara started to answer, then realized that Miranda was watching them, a puzzled look on her face. "Sorry," she apologized, not wishing her to feel excluded. "Cop talk; an occupational hazard, I'm afraid."

"That's all right," Miranda said, not having the slightest clue what they were talking about. She wondered what an SO 7 might be, and if it had anything to do with Cara and Alec's occupations. She rather suspected it did, and then she wondered if such work was as dangerous as she feared it would be.

"Well, it looks as if you'll be left to your own devices, Miranda," Cara was regarding her with a friendly smile. "Why don't I come by in the morning and give you the Cook's tour?"

"That sounds lovely," Miranda responded, although she was curious why Cara would think she'd be interested in a cook's tour of the city. What could be so interesting about marketplaces?

Alec's scowl returned. "I was planning on taking the afternoon off to show Miranda about," he grumbled, feeling decidedly left out. "London's changed a great deal in two hundred years. I'm sure there's much she'll find fascinating."

"Historical sites, you mean," Cara said, rolling her eyes in disgust. "Well, you can drag poor Miranda wherever you please, but *I* intend showing her the really important places."

"Like what?" he demanded indignantly.

"The shops, of course," Cara replied, leaning past him to give Miranda a quick grin. "Good night, luv, I'll ring you tomorrow around nine o' clock." She waved to Alec, and then hurried to the small car parked in front of the house. The car gave a bleating sound and then disappeared into the rainy night, its glowing red lights reminding Miranda of a demon's eyes.

"Do you own one of those . . . those things?" she asked Alec, nodding after the car.

He hid a quick grin at the trepidation in her cultured voice. "As a matter of fact, I do," he said, opening the front door before turning to face her. "I keep it garaged not far from here. Why? Do want to go for a drive?"

Miranda watched another car go whizzing past and gave a heavy sigh. "Only if I must," she said, quivering at the thought of riding inside one of the beasts. "They seem to go very fast."

Alec placed his hand into the small of her back. "We'll wait until later, then," he promised, guiding her inside. "When you're ready, we'll drive down to Kent. How does that sound?"

Miranda thought it sounded awful, but she managed a non-committal nod. A delicate brass lamp with a mauve glass shade had been left burning on a table beside the stairs, and it cast a warm, intimate glow about the entryway. Her gaze strayed to the lamp, mentally comparing the misty light to the flickering illumination offered by a candle's flame. Inexplicably, she felt her eyes fill with tears.

"Miranda?" Alec laid a gentle hand on her arm. "What's wrong?"

"One hundred and eighty-four years," she whispered brokenly, tears spilling over to rain down her cheeks. "It's gone, Alec. It's all gone."

As if they had been waiting for only that, emotions so powerful they literally took away her breath erupted inside of her, engulfing her in a tidal wave of grief and sorrow. She gave a keening cry, turning instinctively toward the only sense of security she had found in this overwhelming new time.

"Everyone I ever knew or ever loved is dead," she sobbed, clinging to Alec's shoulder. "I'm alone, I'm all alone."

Alec tightened his arms about her, his own eyes burning as he listened to her anguish. He wanted to tell her that he knew how she felt, that he'd also lost everything, but the words wouldn't come. He could only hold her tighter, choking back his own howls of despair as he listened to the pain pouring out of her.

"My husband is dead, and I was never his wife!" she cried, her whole body shaking with delayed reaction. "What will I do? What will happen to me? Oh God, I'm so afraid!"

"Shhh, it's all right now, it's all right," Alec whispered roughly, his hand shaking as he smoothed back her hair from her forehead. "I'll keep you safe, I promise you."

Miranda could only shake her head, too disconsolate to find any comfort in a world so unlike anything she had ever known. Even when she'd been walking about the streets, her dazed eyes taking in sights her rational mind couldn't begin to fathom, she'd wanted to believe this was all some sort of fantastical dream. But now she knew it to be horribly real, and for the briefest of moments, that reality was more than she could bear. Even death would have been preferable to this, she thought, another sob racking her as she surrendered to her wild grief.

Alec continued holding her, recognizing the futility of the comfort he had tried to offer. He more than anyone knew how such attempts at consolation hurt more than they ever helped, and he only hoped Miranda wouldn't become so hysterical he'd be forced to call Cara for help. But at last her sobs quieted and the tremors shaking her slender body lessened, and she seemed content to stand where she was; holding him even as he was holding her. Eventually he felt her stiffen, and he quickly dropped his arms.

"Better now?" he asked, his anxious gaze searching her face as he took a cautious step back.

She nodded, her cheeks flushed from her tears. "Yes, I am, th-thank you," she stammered, her embarrassment painfully obvious in the way she refused to let her eyes meet his. This sudden shyness was so different from the proud defiance she'd displayed earlier that afternoon, that he slipped his hand beneath her chin and gently raised her face to his.

"After what you've been through?" he asked, his expression chiding. "My God, Miranda, it's a bloody wonder you didn't throw back your head and bay at the moon!"

She gave a reluctant chuckle and wiped a shaking hand over her cheeks. "I hope I am not so lacking in control as that!" she said, sniffing delicately and wishing for a handkerchief. "I feel foolish enough as it is, I assure you. What a watering pot you must think me," she added with a weak attempt at humor.

To her surprise he took her words seriously, his amber-colored eyes darkening as he continued studying her. "I think you a very brave woman, who is handling the incredible with more grace than I could ever muster," he said quietly. "I don't even want to imagine how I would react were our situations reversed."

She studied his lean, handsome face, trying to envision him in a cravat and the high-collared jackets Stephen favored. The image conjured brought a rueful smile to her lips. "You couldn't wear this, to be sure," she said, reaching up and shyly touching the gold circlet dangling from his ear. "I fear it would cause a most dreadful scandal."

Considering the reactions of some of the more conservative members of the force when nonuniformed male officers were allowed to wear earrings, Alec couldn't help but grin in response. "I'd be taken for a gypsy, would I?"

Her smile deepened as the last of her pain faded to a dull and distant ache. "At the very least," she assured him, her eyes twinkling in laughter. "More likely they would think you a brigand, and order you clapped in gaol for the public good!"

The idea of himself as a lawless pirate appealed to Alec's vanity, and he was about to give an answering quip, when he became aware of Miranda's hand resting against his neck. Her palm was soft and warm against his flesh, and he could smell the delicate scent of lavender and roses clinging to her golden hair. He felt his body harden, and the involuntary response filled him with a sick sense of guilt. Except for Cara, it was the first time a woman had touched him since he and Jane had last made love, and he felt as if he'd just betrayed her very memory.

Sensing his sudden withdrawal Miranda raised her eyes to his, and the turbulent emotions she saw reflected there brought her to a belated awareness that they were all but embracing. Blushing in distress, she dropped her hand and took a hasty step backward.

"I suppose I should go up to bed," she said, her gaze fixed

on the toes of her shoes. "As I remarked earlier, it has been a rather eventful day."

Alec stared at the top of her head, his hands clenched at his sides as he fought for control. "I'll probably be gone when you get up," he said, his voice strained. "If you need anything, ask Cara, she'll know how to have me paged."

Miranda nodded, hearing the dismissal in his voice. Tempting as it was to turn and flee, there was more she wished to say, and she raised her chin until she was gazing into his face once more. "Cara told me about your fiancée," she said quietly, "and I am very sorry. If you would prefer that I stay in another room, I quite understand."

Her words made Alec flinch, and a blistering oath burned on his lips. Thoughts of Jane tormented him, but above all he remembered her unstinting generosity. She would want Miranda to have whatever she needed, he realized bleakly, and forced himself to swallow the bitter words he'd been about to utter.

"There's no need for that," he said in a stiff voice. "Feel free to stay where you are; it makes no difference to me."

His offhanded reply was hardly the reassurance she had been seeking, but Miranda decided it would suffice for the moment. In the event she decided to remain in the house, she could always move into another room. Pleased with her decision, she bade him good night a second time and moved toward the stairs. She'd just started up them, when she heard Alec call her name.

"Yes?" She cast him a wary glance over her shoulder.

"I just wanted you to know that if there's anything you need to borrow, you can take whatever you like from the closet," he said, his strained voice letting her know the effort the words caused him. "Jane . . . Jane would have wanted me to help you."

Despite her own concerns, Miranda's heart was touched by his obvious pain. "Your Jane sounds a lovely person," she said softly. "I wish I might have met her."

For a moment she didn't think he was going to reply, but then he finally spoke. "I wish you might have met her as well," he said, his face reflecting no emotion as he turned toward the parlor. "Good night, Miranda, I'll see you tomorrow."

The next three days passed in a frightening whirlwind, as Alec and Cara introduced Miranda to the modern world. The size of the shops, especially Harrods, left Miranda speechless with shock, and she couldn't get enough of strolling down the crowded aisles and gawking at the many items being offered for sale. Despite her objections, Cara insisted upon buying Miranda some new clothing, seeming to sense her reluctance to continue wearing Jane's things. She even bought her a pair of shoes she called hightops, and Miranda thought the cloth shoes quite the most comfortable things she had ever worn.

Cara also introduced her to the wonders of the tube, the underground transportation system that had served London for the better part of a century. At first the crowds and the incredible speed at which the cars moved terrified Miranda, but she soon grew to accept them, marvelling at the experience of moving between St. Paul's and Mayfair in a matter of minutes.

Her excursions with Alec were of a more scholarly nature, as he took her to a variety of museums and libraries, some of which dated back to her time. The Wellington Museum just outside of Hyde Park especially interested her, and she wept with relief to learn that Napoleon would eventually be defeated. She wept even harder when she learned at what terrible cost that victory would be achieved.

Some four days after her journey through time, she was in the kitchen attempting to master the microwave machine, when Alec arrived home unexpectedly. When he saw her hovering in front of the machine, he gave her a curious look.

"What are you doing?" he asked, setting the sack he had brought in with him on the counter.

"Making certain I do not burn the quiche," she replied, not taking her eyes from the glass door. "I fear cooking for oneself even in this day is not as easy as one may first suppose."

He gazed past her to the dustbin where the charred remains of two other packages could be seen. "I see," he said, and Miranda could hear the laughter in his voice. She turned her head and gave him a withering look.

"I shouldn't be so smug were I you, sir," she informed him with a haughty sniff. "Cara has already warned me that your cooking skills are even more uncertain than mine."

He leaned against the counter, his arms folded across his chest as he grinned at her. "Cara's one to talk," he remarked dryly, looking more relaxed than she had ever seen him. "She gave her poor husband food poisoning the first time she tried cooking him supper."

"It was the chicken that was at fault," Miranda said, defending her friend loyally. "She warned me I must always take care to wash—" Her voice broke off as the microwave gave a loud ding. She opened the door and took out her dinner, a smile of triumph on her lips as she showed it to Alec.

"I did it!" she crowed, green eyes dancing with pride. "My very first meal!"

Her childlike delight in her accomplishment made Alec's grin widen. Experiencing his world through Miranda's eyes had given him a renewed sense of awe in all that had been accomplished in the past two hundred years, and he was now about to introduce her to one of the greatest wonders of them all.

"Well done, Julia Child," he congratulated her. "After you've finished feasting on your quiche, I want you to come into my study. There's something I want to show you."

"What?" She had peeled back the film from the tray and was sniffing her meal appreciatively.

"You'll see," he said, and then picked up the sack from the counter, leaving her to enjoy her quiche in private. In his study he booted up his computer, and then removed from the sack the books he'd just purchased. The man at the bookshop had assured him the manuals were so simple a child could comprehend them, and as he leafed through them, he hoped they wouldn't prove too difficult for Miranda. Although that shouldn't be a problem, he mused, thinking how she'd already mastered the VCR, the CD player, and now apparently the microwave.

He inserted the tutorial disks and brought up the beginner program, his heart giving a quick lurch as he remembered the frustrating hours he'd spent on the terminal, while Jane tried to teach him how to use the damned thing.

"Honestly, Bramwell, you are hopeless," she'd teased, laughing while he'd muttered threats and curses at the monitor. "It's a machine, not a suspect you can terrorize into cooperating. Just read the screen, and do what it tells you!"

That had precipitated one of their arguments which ended in a bout of lovemaking, and he could still hear her bright, clear laughter as he'd tumbled her off the swivel chair and on to the rug. The memory made him smile, a smile that quickly turned to a frown, as he realized with a start that for the first time since her death, he'd been able to think of Jane without the crushing painful loss. He was brooding over what that might mean when Miranda tapped on the door.

"What is it you wished to show me?" she asked, and then her eyes widened when she saw him at the computer. "You have the computer machine on!" she exclaimed, taking an eager step forward. "Cara showed it to me, but she said I wasn't to touch it without your permission."

"Consider this permission granted, then," he said, rising from the chair and gesturing for her to take his place. "And in the future, Miranda, it isn't necessary that you tack on the word machine to everything. We already know it's a machine."

Accustomed now to his lectures, Miranda felt no more than a sting of indignation at his admonishment. "Very well," she said, her attention already focused on the glowing screen in front of her. "What is the purpose of a computer?"

Her interest and her intelligence pleased Alec, and he launched into a brief, concise explanation of a computer and its many uses. When he finished, Miranda was regarding the screen with a look that bordered on adoration.

"And I can call any machine anywhere in the world, and it

will give me whatever information I desire?" she asked, touching the screen with a fingertip. "How wonderful!"

"So long as it has a modem and your systems are compatible," he said, leaning over her and tapping a few keys to start the program. "But before you learn to go on-line, you have to learn the basics. We'll start here."

He spent the next two hours going over the program and manuals with her, and once he was certain she wouldn't crash his hard drive, he left her to her own devices. Now that she was safely occupied, he was anxious to have another go at the hidden room. He'd already been in there twice before, but so far he hadn't managed to find the secret compartment Miranda had described to him. Today, he was determined to succeed.

Picking up his work light, he crawled through the hole, consciously leaving himself open to any "vibrations," such as Miranda and Cara had experienced. He waited, his breath tightly held, but he didn't feel so much as a tingle. Oh well, he gave a philosophical shrug, maybe it was a woman thing.

Once in the room he began walking around, copying the pentagrams and other symbols in the notebook he'd brought with him for that purpose. Flemming in Forensics was already pressing him for more information, and his eagerness to learn more had piqued Alec's own curiosity. Not that it needed piquing, he admitted ruefully. Miranda and the mystery behind her amazing journey was occupying his thoughts almost as much as the bombing of J and L Enterprises that had killed four people.

For a moment he allowed thoughts of his job to steal into his mind. The investigation was going amazingly smooth, but it was also going nowhere. Tests of the scene and on the bodies of the victims showed the explosive agent to be a form of plastique known to be favored by the Red Coalition, but oddly they had claimed no responsibility for the attack. And both wings of the IRA had been vociferous in proclaiming their innocence; an innocence his friends in the SAS had verified as genuine.

So, he thought, running his hand over the far wall in search of the hidden compartment, if neither terrorist group was behind the bombing, then who was? The damned building hadn't exploded on its own, that much was certain. And why had that particular company been targeted? There was always *some* justification, however off base, for an attack, but neither Scotland Yard nor Interpol had found any explanation for the explosion. And how was this bombing connected to the bombing that had killed Jane? These were all questions, he thought grimly, for which he would some day have the answers. And when he did . . . he cut the thought off, refusing to consider what he'd do once Jane's killers were in custody.

He was going over the wall a second time, when the panel he was touching suddenly slid open. Inside were the items Miranda had described, and a few more she had not. He picked up a dagger fashioned out of obsidian, and after giving it a cursory examination, he turned his attention to the leather-bound volumes on the shelves. A quick glance inside revealed pages covered with more enigmatic symbols, and he decided to show it to Keller. His old CO had been a master at cryptology, and it would be interesting to see what he discovered.

He found a wand, something that looked like a goatskin, and a black mirror that was an exact miniature of the one hanging on the wall. He couldn't discern a purpose behind any of the items, and after another few minutes of poking, he decided he'd learned enough for one day. He was in the process of returning some of the items to their hiding place, when he felt a sudden tingle on his back. What the hell, he thought, then turned around, his jaw dropping as he saw the room filling with the yellowish green light he remembered all too well.

*Miranda!* He began backing out of the room, the items at his feet completely forgotten. By the time he reached the hole in the wall, the room was pulsating with light, and a hum that sounded like the roar of the sea vibrated the walls. He squirmed through the hole with more speed than finesse, shouting Miranda's named as he dashed down the hall.

"What is it?" she poked her head out of the study door, her

expression going from curious to concerned as he ran toward her.

"Outside! Now!" he bellowed, grabbing her roughly by the arm and dragging her toward the stairs.

"What has happened?" she demanded as she struggled to keep up with him. "Alec, what's wrong?"

Alec didn't bother replying, his only thought to get her as far from the room and its terrifying power as possible. Explanations and even gentleness were unimportant compared to his desperation to save her. He continued dragging her down the stairs, pausing only to snatch his jacket from the newel post before shoving her out the door. It was only when the door had slammed behind them that the panic clawing at him diminished enough to let him relax. If he'd ever had any doubt about Miranda's story, he'd just had those doubts dispelled; in spades, he added silently, drawing in a deep breath of smoggy air.

"Alec?" Miranda was glowering up at him, clearly more exasperated than frightened by his behavior. "What on earth is wrong with you? I was just getting ready to print a document!"

The querulous demand following his bout of terror made Alec's temper flare to life, and all thoughts of offering her comfort vanished in a white hot flash. "Well, pardon me, your ladyship, for saving your bleeding life!" he snarled, hands fisted on his hips as he returned her glare. "I was examining the secret compartment you told me about, when the room started glowing and humming like an old TV set. I thought I'd better get you out of there before it zapped you into the great beyond, but perhaps I was mistaken. Feel free to go back inside, if you want." He flipped a mocking hand toward the locked door.

Her gaze followed his gesture, her cheeks paling as the importance of his words sank in. "Th-the room was glowing?" she stammered, her voice shaking as she took a hasty step backward.

Alec's temper cooled at her obvious fear. "I think we'll be safe out here," he said quietly, his outburst making him feel like an ill-mannered child. "But, just to be certain, why don't we go for a beer or something?"

She hesitated, then gave a jerky nod, and he dropped his arm across her shoulder as he led her to a nearby pub. He ordered a cola for her and some lager for himself, before returning to the wooden booth where he had stashed her. She looked so small and afraid that another wave of shame washed over him. *Terrific crisis technique, Bramwell,* he thought bitterly, castigating himself for his lack of finesse. Had he spoken to a witness or a victim like that, he'd probably have found himself demoted to constable in short order.

"Are you all right?" he asked, pushing the glass of cola toward her as he slid into the booth.

She raised her head, her green eyes meeting his as she dredged up a shaky smile. "Do you know how heartily sick I am of being asked that question?" she asked, reaching out to cup her glass with hands that weren't quite steady. "I am beginning to feel like some simpering schoolgirl, given to endless bouts of the vapors. But thank you, I am fine."

He smiled at her wry words. "I've never seen a case of the vapors," he said, following her lead and keeping his tone deliberately light. "What do they look like?"

She remembered a particular girl from her boarding school, who had been an expert at the art. "Endless tears, heart-wrenching wails, and the occasional swoon thrown in for dramatic affect," she said, also recalling she'd privately regarded the other girl as a perfect ninnyhammer.

"Sounds like a bunch of men watching a football game," Alec joked, and then grew somber. "What do you think we should do?"

Miranda's expression altered as she realized he wasn't talking about the vapors. "I suppose you are right, and it would be best that we stay out of the house for now," she said, her gaze dropping to the scarred tabletop. "The magic or whatever it is that propels the time-travel device is uncertain at best, and as you say, heaven only knows where or when it may send us."

Grateful she was being far more mature about the incident than he had been, Alec leaned back in his booth and concentrated on remembering all that had transpired in the hidden room. Calling upon his training as an inspector and a member of the SAS, he sifted through his emotions and impressions, putting them in order before reaching what seemed to him a logical conclusion.

"It *is* magic," he said at last, recalling the flash of wonder he'd felt when he'd turned around to find himself confronting a power he could never have imagined. "But all magic has its explanations, and if we can figure out what those explanations are, we'll have all the answers we need."

"And what then?" Miranda asked, nervously passing her glass from one hand to the other.

He glanced up at that, his brows meeting over his nose. "Then we'll send you back, of course," he said, looking puzzled. "Isn't that what you want?"

At first Miranda didn't answer, as a myriad of emotions swirled through her. She had convinced herself that the past was as lost to her as surely as if she had died, and she was finally coming to terms with her new life here. She was even beginning to accept the wonders that were commonplace in this time of miracles. But, her conscience argued sternly, if she *could* go back, shouldn't she? What was her duty? The moment she asked herself that, she knew what her answer would be.

"Yes," she said, a calm she hadn't felt since running into the secret room settling over her. "I want to go back very much."

Her cool certainty made Alec blink. "Then that's what we'll do," he said decisively, refusing to acknowledge the twinge of disappointment he felt. "But until we're dead certain we can control that magical force, I want you to stay out of the room."

Recalling she had already given her word on this point, Miranda flashed him a haughty glare. "I am hardly a fool, sir," she informed him icily, furious that he would dare question her honor. "I have no desire to put myself in needless danger, I assure you. And if you will but remember, I have already given you my promise not to go near that accursed place."

Her snootiness made Alec's lips quirk in perverse satisfaction. "You also gave me your word you'd stay in the house," he reminded her with a mocking drawl. "So you'll forgive me, princess, if I'm not exactly reassured by your promises."

Miranda's face flamed with fury. "I have already explained—"

"And so have I," he interrupted, leaning forward to capture her hand in his. "Stay out of the room, Miranda, I mean it. Now, do we understand each other?"

Resentment against his arrogant high-handedness simmered in Miranda as she met his burning golden gaze. "Oh, yes, Mr. Bramwell," she returned, using his proper name as if it were an epithet. "We understand each other perfectly well."

# *Eight*

The day following her confrontation with Alec, Miranda was laboring over the computer, when Alec returned from the Yard and demanded she join him for lunch. He was dressed in a crisp blue uniform, like the one she had seen in the picture, and when she questioned him about it, Alec gave a disgusted snort.

"Career Day," he grumbled, as he led Miranda to a table in the fast-food restaurant where they were dining. "Twice yearly they troop in all these bloody adolescents, and we're supposed to spend the next three hours convincing them they want to join the Force. God spare me."

He made the whole process sound as pleasant as a visit to the toothdrawers, and Miranda shot him a confused glance. "But I thought you liked being an officer," she said, tucking into her chips hungrily. Alec had introduced her to the fried potatoes her second day in the present, and after pizza, they were her favorite food in this new time.

"I *love* being an officer—an inspector, really—but I *hate* Career Day," he clarified, stuffing a chip into his mouth with a grim sigh. "First, they make us put on these bloody uniforms, which is ridiculous because inspectors don't even wear uniforms, except for special duty." Or to attend funerals, he suddenly thought, remembering the long line of uniformed men and women who had walked solemnly after the hearse bearing Jane's body. He shook off the painful memory and took a sip of his drink.

"As if that wasn't bad enough, they make us give these peppy little speeches about how rewarding a career in Law Enforcement can be. And do you know the first question one of the girls asked me?" He batted his lashes furiously, his voice going up several octaves. "Are all the blokes as good-looking as you?"

Miranda hid a quick grin at Alec's performance. "Yes, I can see where you would find that most vexing," she said, hiding her grin behind her straw as she took a noisy sip of cola.

He glowered at her. "Easy for you to snicker," he muttered, reaching for another chip. "You didn't spend the morning with the future leaders of society. Now *there's* a depressing thought." He gave another sigh and leaned back against the plastic booth.

"So, how are you getting on?" he asked, unwrapping his hamburger and taking a bite. "Have you thought about what we discussed last night? About your going back?"

Miranda hesitated only a moment, and then she was confessing everything in a rush. When she finished describing her fears and her ambiguous feelings about returning to her own time, he was looking surprisingly somber.

"I hadn't thought of it like that," he said slowly, drumming his fingers on the tabletop and frowning. "That one's place in time might be construed a duty, but I daresay you're right. And that raises a host of interesting questions, doesn't it?"

"What sort of questions?" Miranda asked, fascinated by his logical approach to the situation.

"Questions such as were you destined to come forward in time, in which case, remaining *here* would be your duty. Or is your presence here some sort of cosmic accident, that was never supposed to happen? And if that is the case, what happened after you disappeared?" he mused, his brown eyes glowing with excitement as he raised them to meet her gaze. "My God, Miranda, do you know what this could mean?"

Miranda was quiet, mulling over the puzzle she had just been presented. Her step-papa had always derided what he called her unfeminine intelligence, but at the moment she felt the greatest dullard to ever draw breath. What difference could her presence make in either time? she wondered. Surely what had happened was meant to happen. Unless . . . unless her being here now changed what was supposed to happen. She gave a soft gasp and placed her hand over her mouth.

"It means history itself could be affected!" he exclaimed, as if divining her thoughts. "Who knows what was changed when you came forward? You might have had a son who would have been a brilliant prime minister, or even led England into a disastrous war . . . everything could be totally different!"

"But what should I do?" Miranda cried, her food forgotten as she stared at Alec. "How will I know if I am fated to stay here, or to go back to my own time?"

Alec felt a familiar excitement shoot through him. It was the same way he felt when taking on a new case, and he decided to treat Miranda's dilemma in just that light. He leaned forward in the booth, his manner coolly professional as he pulled out his notebook and pen from his coat pocket.

"First we need to discover what happened after you vanished," he said briskly, giving his pen a click. "You said your husband was an earl, so that would make you . . . what? A countess?"

"The countess of Harrington," Miranda verified, trying to remain as calm as he was.

"Right, and wealthy in the bargain," Alec murmured, scribbling furiously. "I can't imagine a countess disappearing without there being a scandal. How long were the two of you married?"

Miranda squirmed uncomfortably on the hard plastic bench. She had told both Alec and Cara her tale several times, but there was always one vital part that she had left out . . . until now.

"Miranda?" He was frowning at her. "How long were you married to—what's his name again?"

"Stephen Hallforth, the seventh earl of Harrington," Miranda answered, her gaze fixed firmly on her hands. "And as for how long we had been married, I—I fear I disappeared on what would have been our wedding night."

"On your—" The pen dropped from Alec's fingers, and he gave Miranda an incredulous stare. "You're kidding!" he exclaimed in disbelief. "Your *wedding* night?"

Miranda gave a miserable nod, and soon the whole story came

spilling out of her, including her discovery of her step-papa's and Stephen's perfidy. When she finished speaking she was dabbing tears from her eyes, and Alec was looking as if he wanted to smash something over someone's head.

"The bastard! The rotten bastard!" he raged, golden eyes sparkling with fury. "He married you for your money!"

Miranda gave a loud sniff, her chest aching as she relived the terrible pain of discovering she had been used. "But you mustn't blame Stephen," she said, shredding a paper napkin with trembling fingers. "Such things were commonplace in my day, and had he been honest with me, I suppose I should not have cared so much. I had always been courted for my inheritance, and knew it was all I had to give a man. But—but I thought Stephen genuinely liked me, genuinely cared, and all the time . . ." Her voice quavered and she was unable to continue.

"And all the time he was conniving with your snake of a stepfather to rip you off," Alec concluded with obvious contempt. "Well, you may not blame him, but I sure as hell do. If he needed money so badly, why didn't he just go out and get a job?"

Miranda was shocked to the tips of her toes by his querulous demand. "He was a gentleman!

"A gentleman?" Alec gave a loud snort. "And I suppose by that you mean the world would have ended if he'd sullied his hands with anything approaching common labor! My God, what a useless, disgusting lot these aristocrats must have been. Marx was right; they deserved to be lined up against a wall and shot."

"Oh, but Stephen wasn't like that!" Miranda protested, horrified by his vehemence. "He may not have held a position as do you and Cara, but he worked very hard! He was a diligent landlord, and he took his duties in the House of Lords quite seriously. He rarely missed a debating session."

"He sounds like a real prince," Alec muttered sarcastically, and then gave a sudden start. "Good lord, Miranda," he said, staring at her in disbelief, "were you in love with this guy?"

Having already confessed everything else, Miranda could see no reason why she should not confess all. "No," she admitted, her eyes not meeting his. "I liked him, admired him, and I thought we could have a decent marriage. And, of course, he was most handsome," she added, blushing as she recalled how she used to dream about his kisses.

Alec was staring at her in confusion, trying to comprehend what she was saying. "Let me get this straight," he said, gesturing expressively. "You didn't love him, he didn't love you. Right?" When Miranda nodded, he blew out a noisy sigh. "So why'd you get married? I mean," he added, when Miranda would have spoken, "I know he married you for the money, but why did you marry him? What was in it for you?"

Miranda hesitated, more aware than ever of the differences that separated their two worlds. It was more than a matter of years, she realized wearily. It was a matter of perspectives, and morals, and so many other things she doubted she would ever make him understand.

"My day is not like yours," she said at last, searching for the words that would convince him. "We do not marry for frivolous reasons such as love, or—or even sexual attraction," she added, recalling a show she had seen on the television where a group of women had sat around talking about things that had made her jaw drop in disbelief. "We marry for position, or wealth, or for the good of the family. Love has very little to do with it."

"Then why were you so upset, when you found out Stephen had plotted with your stepfather?" Alec demanded, determined to understand what she was saying. "Why did it matter so much?"

Miranda could only shake her head. "I don't know," she confessed softly, "I only know that when I heard him talking to his friend, something inside of me exploded in pain. I had to get away; that's why I ran into the hidden room in the first place." She tilted her head to one side as a sudden thought struck her. "Do you think the room bewitched me?"

Alec's brows gathered in a scowl as he considered that. "It's possible," he conceded thoughtfully, "given all the satanic crap I found in there. Well, that's it, then. You're not stepping a foot in that house, until I get that hole patched."

His concern for her safety touched Miranda, but she wasn't convinced he was right. "But if we discover I belong in the past, won't we need the room and its magic?" she protested.

He waved away her objections with an impatient hand. "I can always knock out another hole in the damned wall," he said in the decisive voice she was beginning to recognize. "I'll take you by Cara's and—damn!" He broke off impatiently as the pager clipped to his belt began to beep raucously. He unclipped it, and after listening to it a moment, he slid out of the booth.

"I'll be right back," he said tersely, a cold, remote look sliding over his face. "Don't move."

Miranda watched him make his way to the front of the restaurant, where a phone was anchored to the wall. He made a quick call, and when he came back he was chillingly formal.

"I have to go in," he said, his eyes moving over her in a manner that made her feel as if she'd been dismissed. "Dispatch is sending a second car to take you to Cara's. I want you to wait there until I call you."

Miranda swallowed uneasily. "A car?"

Alec nodded, his mind already on his work. "Here's the key to Cara's," he said, taking a key from his ring and handing it to her. "She's on duty at the moment, but I'll leave her a message, so she'll know to expect you. If all goes well, she should be home by five or five-thirty."

"Alec, I should really prefer it if—"

"I'm probably going to be all night," he went on as if she hadn't spoken, "so you might as well crash on her divan. When it's safe to come home, I'll call. All right?" He finally looked at her.

Miranda paused, uncertain what she should do. She hated to be quarrelsome when it was obvious he was so distracted, but on the other hand, she had no intention of getting in one of those dreadful automobiles if she could avoid it.

"Miranda!"

She glanced up to find him glaring at her impatiently, and she gave him a reassuring smile. "I don't need a police car to take me to Cara's," she said calmly. "Just give me her address, and I'll take the tube instead."

His eyes narrowed in fury. "Damn it, I don't have time"—

"No, and I am sure neither do the other officers," she interrupted, her tone matching his for coolness. "You have already agreed that I should start learning my way about, and this is the perfect opportunity for me to do so. I promise I will go there straightaway, and I'll ring your office so you will know I have arrived. Okay?" she added the American word she had heard the other day, deciding it carried the condescension and impatience she wished to convey.

Alec thrust a hand through his hair, realizing irritably that she had a valid point. And at least she was accepting his decision to stay away from the house until he could fix the hole, he thought, rocking back on his heel and studying her face.

"How will you know which tube to take?" he asked suspiciously.

"I'll look on the map, and if necessary, I'll ask at the fare booth," she answered patiently. "Now, what is Cara's address?"

Alec glared down at her another moment, and then he realized he had no other choice. Short of ordering the responding constable to take her into custody, there was no way he could force her to do as he wished. And as she'd pointed out, the other officers had far more important things to do than act as taxi for a reluctant passenger. He plucked a napkin from the dispenser and scribbled Cara's address on it.

"Don't lose this," he ordered, handing it to her. "And if you *should* get lost, call 9-9-9. They'll help you."

"I won't get lost," she managed to keep the triumph out of her voice. "Now you'd better go, I'm sure your superiors must be needing you."

Alec hesitated. He could hear the approaching warble of an emergency siren and knew the car being sent for him was arriving. Frustration ate at him as he realized that he didn't want to leave. The realization so amazed him that he stepped away from the booth. "I'll call," he promised gruffly, and then turned and walked away without a backward glance.

It took Miranda a little over an hour to find Cara's flat, and after calling Alec's office as promised, she was unable to resist the urge to indulge in a bit of unabashed snooping. This was the first residence besides Alec's she had been in, and she was especially anxious to see how unmarried females lived in this time. She found many of the same machines that Alec kept in his house, and after several minutes of exploring, she retired to the front room to await Cara's return. Several hours passed, and just as she was growing concerned, Cara let herself in.

"Hello," she said, giving Miranda a quick smile as she shut and locked the door behind her. "Alec left a message saying to expect you. Did you have any trouble finding the place?"

"None at all," Miranda assured her, politically not mentioning that she'd twice boarded the wrong tube. "You have a lovely home," she added quickly, hoping Cara would accept her answer and not press for details as she was sure Alec would do.

"Thanks." Cara shed her coat as she talked. "I bought it after Paul and I called it quits, and I've been adding bits to it as I go along. That divan you're sitting on folds out into a bed, so you've a place to sleep if need be."

"Really?" Miranda ran her hand over the plump cushions. "It looks rather short, but I am certain I shall be comfortable."

Cara gave a fond laugh. "No, goose, the bed's *inside* the divan. I'll show you later, I promise, but now I must have a shower or I'll perish. There's wine in the fridge, if you're thirsty, so feel free to help yourself." And she walked into the other room, pulling her jumper over her head.

Miranda was sipping her glass of wine and watching the television when Cara returned, her slender body wrapped in a thick robe of emerald green velvet. Her dark brown hair was curling around her shoulders, and she looked far more feminine than Miranda had ever seen her. She must have been staring, because the other woman stopped, a dark eyebrow arching in amusement. "What? Have I grown another head or something? You're looking at me as if you've never seen me before in your life!"

Miranda felt an embarrassed flush steal across her cheeks, and hastily averted her eyes. "I am sorry," she said, feeling like a foolish chit. "I did not mean to stare, it is just . . ." she paused, trying to think of some plausible prevarication.

"Just what?" Cara pressed, her light brown eyes sparkling with interest as she reached for the glass of wine Miranda had poured for her. "Come on, luv, I shan't bite your head off, I promise you."

Miranda's shoulders relaxed slightly at the other woman's teasing words. "It is just you look so at ease," she said at last. "You always seem so busy, so . . ." she searched her memory for the word Alec used when describing his sister. "So focused. Alec says you are wired, whatever that may mean."

As Miranda expected, hearing her brother's observation brought a militant gleam to Cara's eyes. "Ha! He's a fine one to talk!" she muttered, throwing herself on to the divan beside Miranda. "The man's like a guided missile when he's on something. It would take a nuclear bomb to deflect him, once he's set a course."

Miranda thought of the adamant way he had refused to let her stay in the house until he deemed it safe. "Yes," she said in a soft voice, "he does seem rather determined at times."

"Determined? Try demented," Cara retorted, her bottom lip protruding in a childish pout that made her look years younger than the twenty-six Miranda knew her to be.

"Yes, I am sure he can be that as well," Miranda replied, secretly amused at the grudging affection Cara showed Alec.

Cara took another sip of wine and leaned her head back against the divan's flowered cushions. "Speaking of my dearest sibling, he left me a message asking me to let you stay here until he called. In fact," she added, slanting Miranda a speculative look, "he threatened me with bodily harm if I let you anywhere near the house. Want to tell me what's going on?"

Miranda gave her a disjointed account of all that had transpired, and by the time she was finished, Cara was all but quivering with excitement.

"The room was glowing?" she repeated, the glass of wine forgotten as she studied Miranda's face. "How extraordinary!"

"Your brother did not seem to think so," Miranda replied, remembering Alec's expression as he pulled her down the stairs. "And having experienced the room's power, I agree with him."

Cara remembered her own brush with whatever mysterious force lay behind the room's powerful secrets. "Yes, I'm sure you do," she said, her tone thoughtful. "And I must say, Alec's theory about history being altered is most intriguing. It raises all sorts of possibilities, doesn't it?"

"Perhaps," Miranda agreed, her head beginning to ache, "but I suppose there's no way we shall ever know."

Cara picked up her glass of wine and took a sip. "Isn't there?" she asked, her eyes taking on a thoughtful glow. "I agree with Alec. It isn't likely that a countess could just suddenly disappear without a fuss being made. What of your husband? Even if he didn't love you, wouldn't he have made some kind of effort to find you?"

"He would have left no stone unturned," Miranda said quietly, remembering Stephen's stern sense of duty. "Until he knew one way or another what had befallen me, I am sure he would never have given up looking."

"Well then, tomorrow morning we shall go to the library and start searching," Cara decisively. "They have old newspapers on file, and that is where we shall start. Now let's go eat, luv, I'm starving."

They shared a companionable dinner of curried chicken and rice, talking easily and watching television. At ten o'clock the national news came on, and the first story broadcast made Miranda's blood freeze with horror.

"For the second time in less than a week, central London was rocked by a powerful explosion," a somber-faced man intoned, his modulated voice revealing not the slightest trace of emotion. "Sources in the Metropolitan Police Department verify that as in the first bombing, the terrorist group known as the Red Coalition is believed to be responsible. We shall go now to the site of the deadly attack," and the screen switched to the smoking, twisted ruins of a building.

"At two-thirty this afternoon, the main offices of Holbrect International were leveled by a bomb, rumored to have been planted by members of the outlaw terrorist group calling themselves the Red Coalition," a blond woman said, her voice pitched above the wail of sirens in the background. "It was just after midday, and the offices were filled with workers and customers. Casualties are expected to run tragically high, with five confirmed dead at the scene, and at least fifteen additional victims transported to hospital in serious condition."

As the woman continued speaking the scene expanded, showing the destruction in graphic detail. A sobbing woman, her face awash with blood, was shown being led toward a waiting ambulance, while yellow-coated emergency workers frantically raced past with a stretcher bearing an unconscious man.

The blonde talked about other bombings, but Miranda's attention was caught by a set of broad shoulders. She leaned closer, her jaw dropping when a familiar face flickered on the screen.

"Cara, look!" she exclaimed. "That's Alec!"

"What the devil—" Cara also leaned forward, her expression going from puzzled to furious as she recognized her brother's features. "Those bloody idiots!" she cried, her hands clenching in fists as she stared at the screen. "They bloody well know they aren't supposed to air investigators' faces without permission!"

The scene shifted back to the lugubrious man at the start of the newscast, and he talked at length about statements from the Home Office and Buckingham Palace, before moving on to another story. Cara switched off the TV with an angry click, before shooting up from the divan to begin pacing the floor.

"I can't believe they were so sloppy as to show that!" she raged, her tone low and furious. "It's not against the law precisely, but they've never aired footage of SO 13's while on scene! It's not like he's a bobby walking a bloody beat!"

If Cara's tone of voice and expression had not betrayed her, a constant use of the word bloody would have been evidence of her agitation. Miranda noted she used the term only when upset, and she could think of only one reason why having Alec's face shown on the television should upset her so much.

"Is it dangerous for Alec to be seen?" she asked, her pulses beginning to race in fear.

"Not dangerous, but not safe either," Cara replied unhelpfully, still pacing. "There've been cases, in other countries, mind, of extremists taking out investigators, and the media and the Yard have always had this unspoken agreement about not airing footage of any officer actively participating in an investigation. If they need a quote, they're supposed to flash to a stand-up. That's what they're there for, for God's sake."

"A stand-up?" Miranda had been struggling to follow Cara's discourse, but this unfamiliar term had her stymied.

"A suit," Cara waved her hand. "You know, the press officer who gives the bastards all the lovely soundbites they want. Bolling is SO 13's stand-up, and the press are only supposed to show *his* face at these things."

Miranda remembered a round-faced gentlemen with white hair and somber blue eyes, who had described the bombing to the blond woman. "I think they already did," she said, and when she described the man she had seen, Cara gave a distracted nod.

"That's Colin," she said, thrusting a hand through her hair. "He took a bullet in the shoulder during the Oxford Street Siege. He really should have been cashiered out, but he became press officer instead. The higher-ups fawn over him, and the press like him because he's got a face like Father Christmas, and the viewers instinctively trust whatever nonsense he's spouting."

Which still did not explain why Cara was so upset, Miranda decided, chewing thoughtfully on her bottom lip. If she understood Cara's incomprehensible explanation, it was a mere violation of protocol to show Alec's face on television, and yet she had a feeling it was far more than that. And if it was more than that, her mind followed the thought to its logical conclusion, then the danger to Alec was more than a passing possibility. It was a dead certainty.

Her stomach gave an uncomfortable flutter at the thought of Alec being hurt, even—she swallowed as she recalled the pools of blood and shattered glass—even killed. He was the first person she had met in this new time, and although there were times when his arrogance drove her to distraction, the thought of anything happening to him was more than she could bear. He was so vital, so very much alive, that it seemed impossible he could be hurt.

The sobering prospect had a dampening effect on both ladies' spirits, and when Cara suggested it was time to retire for the evening, Miranda was only too happy to comply. Cara kept an extra toothbrush on hand, and after seeing to her toilet, Miranda donned the oversized shirt Cara gave her and returned to the front room to learn the secrets of the bed hidden in the divan.

They were just removing the cushions from the divan, when someone began pounding on Cara's front door. Given that it was well after eleven o'clock, Cara retrieved her baton from the umbrella stand, and after gesturing Miranda to stand back, she cautiously approached the door.

"Who is it?" she called out, her voice surprisingly authoritative.

"Alec! Who the hell do you think it is?" came the testy answer as the doorknob was rattled impatiently. "Now open the damned door!"

Cara peeked through the spy hole, and when she recognized her brother, she opened the door at once. "There's no need to kick the door in," she began grouchily. "I would have let—" Her voice broke off when Alec stumbled across the threshold, his rumpled hair and clothing and the smell of alcohol wafting from him telling her a story that was all too familiar.

She lowered the baton, her pretty face screwed up with fury as she glared at her disheveled, elder brother.

"Alec Leslie Bramwell!" she exclaimed, eyes flashing with indignation as she advanced on him. "You damned bugger! You're drunk!"

# Nine

Alec glared down at Cara, his eyes narrowing in fury. "I am not drunk," he denied, enunciating each word carefully. His gaze moved over her head to where Miranda was standing, and the sight of her was like taking a solid hit in the gut.

With her slender body revealed by a thin blue and white night-shirt and her blond hair tumbling past her shoulders in inviting disarray, she was the embodiment of every sweet, hot dream he had ever had. For a moment a thrill of potent desire shot through him, but even as he felt his body responding, he ruthlessly squashed the reaction. He pushed his way past Cara, swaying to a halt in front of Miranda.

"Ah, your ladyship," he said, staggering slightly as he attempted a sweeping bow. "So good to see you, your ladyship."

Her green eyes grew icy, and she raised her pointed chin a notch. "A pity the same can not be said of you," she said in the neat, precise tones that reminded him of a fussy schoolteacher. " 'Tis obvious you are much the worse for drink."

Her accusation brought his brows together in a resentful scowl. All right, he thought belligerently, maybe he *had* stopped for a few pints with the lads. So? He deserved it, didn't he? After the afternoon he'd had. After the things he'd seen . . . He shut the horrific images out of his mind.

"Oh, and I suppose your precious Stephen never had a single drink," he sneered, preferring the sharp slash of anger to the numbing despair that had engulfed him from the moment he'd received the call to report to the scene of the bombing.

"Stephen may have imbibed upon occasion," Miranda retorted coolly, "but I never saw him in his cups." Her dainty nose twitched a moment, and she added, "And from the smell of you, sir, I would say you have had more than a *few* drinks."

The insult made Alec see red. "Listen, sweetheart, I don't give a bloody damn what you—"

"Coffee," Cara interrupted, sending him stumbling toward the divan with a rough shove. "And give me any backchat, you lout, and I'm telling Mum!"

Alec shot his sister a bleary glare, knowing the obnoxious brat would make good on her threat. On the anniversary of Jane's death he'd stayed drunk for two solid days, and when he emerged from his alcoholic fog, he'd found his mother sitting at his bedside. Any notion he might have harbored that she was there to lend comfort were dispelled when she shoved him, fully dressed, into a freezing shower, and then forced him to drink a pot of the vilest coffee he'd ever tasted. When he was miserably sober, she had proceeded to pin his ears back with a blistering lecture he still remembered.

Defeated, he walked over to the divan, collapsing on it and sending both women burning looks. "God, are all women such bitches?" he asked of no one in particular.

"Only when they have to deal with idiot males like you," Cara muttered, jerking her head at Miranda. The two women disappeared into the small kitchen, and while they made coffee, he relaxed against the cushions, closing his eyes in exhaustion. Almost at once, the images he had tried so hard to block out came rushing in, sweeping him back into his own private hell.

The entire building was in flames when he arrived, and he and the other investigators were forced to stand back while the fire brigade fought the vicious blaze. In the end there wasn't much left, but he and his team had still pored over the smoking ruins, hoping to discover any small clue that would help them find the people responsible for the brutal carnage.

Four of the bodies were found almost at once, and his stomach had rolled at the smell of burned flesh. He was working in an area he believed to be the epicenter of the blast, carefully moving aside pieces of twisted metal, when he found the fifth body. A woman. He had frozen, a scream trapped in his throat as he gazed down at the pitiful form. For a moment he was back in that bombed-out department store, a howl of anguish tearing from him as he'd cradled Jane's body in his arms.

"Don't you dare pass out on me," Cara was standing over him, a cup of steaming coffee held in her hands. When she saw his eyes were open, she handed him the cup. "Here," she said, hovering over him as he took a cautious sip, "drink that, and then we'll see if you're sober enough to pour into a taxi."

"We?" He winced as the black liquid scalded his tongue. "Do you mean I actually have a say in the matter?"

"You? Of course not," Cara gave a regal sniff as she stepped back. "I was talking about Miranda and myself. *You're* in no shape to decide anything."

"And I wondered why Paul divorced you," Alec grumbled, taking another sip of coffee. The coffee—along with the ale he had drank—was making his stomach shimmy, and he sent a grim prayer heavenward that he wouldn't be sick all over Cara's new carpet. Knowing her, she'd make him clean it up afterward.

"How are things in your unit?" he asked Cara, ignoring Miranda for the moment. "I heard you got a break on the Stanton rape."

"We have a suspect under observation," Cara said after a moment's pause. "We're waiting for the magistrate's order to come through, and as soon as we have it, we'll be taking him in."

Alec nodded, happy to concentrate on anything other than his whirling head and twisting stomach. "I think the Arabs have the right of it," he said, aware the coffee was beginning to sober him. "Castrate the bastards; that should put an end to the problem once and for all."

"It would if rape was simply about sex," Cara argued, leaning forward. "But it's not about sex; it's about power and domination, and if you cut off a man's balls, he'll only—"

A choked sound from Miranda made both Alec and Cara

glance at her, and Cara instantly began apologizing. "I'm sorry, luv," she said, looking shame-faced. "Alec and I are so used to this sort of thing, we sometimes forget how it must sound to outsiders."

"Especially outsiders who make Queen Victoria look like a moral degenerate," Alec added, taking a perverse delight in her red cheeks. "What's wrong, my lady?" he added with a taunting smirk. "Didn't they have rapists in your day?"

Rather than blushing even more, Miranda met his mocking gaze with freezing composure. "I am ashamed to say they did," she said coolly, "but it was not a matter for polite discussion." She then turned her shoulder on him in a deliberate snub.

"What will happen to this creature when he is caught?" she asked Cara. "Will he be executed?"

"We no longer have the death penalty in the UK," Cara replied with a shake of her head. "I've always thought it a good thing, but now I'm not so certain. Things have become so violent, I sometimes think it might be the best answer—especially for lunatics like the Red Coalition."

Alec gave a slight jerk, but he didn't respond. He still hadn't made up his mind yet what he'd do when he caught the people behind the bombings. As an officer his duty was to take his prisoner alive, but as an SAS operative trained in antiterrorism, he'd learned his first lesson on the bloody streets of Belfast. The only good terrorist was a dead terrorist.

He continued drinking coffee, his stomach settling even as his head cleared. Miranda and Cara chatted casually about the difference between crime and punishment in her day and the present, but he made no effort to join them, preferring his own dark thoughts. He was about to suggest he leave, when the phone suddenly rang. Cara answered it on the second ring, and after listening for a few minutes, she hung up.

"That was Robert," she said, looking grim. "Our prime suspect just slit his wrists, and they're taking him to hospital now. It doesn't look good, and Robert says we'll have to hurry, if we're going to get a declaration from him."

Alec rose quickly to his feet. "I'll go with you," he said, ignoring the fact that his head began spinning the moment he stood.

Cara, en route to her room, paused to send him an incredulous look. "Smelling the way you do? Don't be an ass, Alec!" she said, then softened the harsh words with a gentle smile.

"Jefferson is going to be there, and you know there's nothing he'd like more than to report you for being under the influence. It's best you stay here. You take the divan, and Miranda can have my bed. I probably won't be home for hours."

Alec hesitated, suddenly aware that the last thing he wanted was to be alone with Miranda. "I was going to go home," he protested, forcing himself to sound in control. "You and Robert can drop me off on the way to hospital."

Cara sent him a level look. "Do you really want him to see you like this?" she asked, then pointed to the divan. "Sit."

Alec plopped back down, reasoning that it was useless to argue any further. He'd just wait until she was gone and then ring for a taxi, he decided, closing his eyes wearily.

Because of the urgency of the situation, Cara's partner remained in the car while she raced downstairs to meet him. Alec waited until he was sure they were gone, before rising to his feet a second time.

"Where are you going?" Miranda asked warily, her green eyes tracking his every movement.

"Ringing a taxi," he said, picking up the phone and piercing her with a challenging stare. "Up to stopping me?"

In answer she bent down and unplugged the phone. "Perhaps," she said, her lips curving in a mocking smile as she twirled the plug. "Cara said I was to see that you remained here, and that is precisely what I intend doing."

Outraged, he made a diving leap for the plug, and almost ended up face-first on the carpet for his pains. He didn't know what astounded him more, his own clumsiness, or the adroit way she had avoided him. He laid his hand against the wall to steady himself, his jaw clenching in fury as he glared at her. "Give that to me," he demanded, his voice low and deadly.

"No."

Her implacable reply made him slap his hand against the wall in frustration. "Damn it, Miranda, give me the bloody cord, or—"

"Or what?" she asked when he stopped abruptly.

His control snapped, unable to withstand the potent combination of alcohol, desire, and a despair so deep it burned clear to his soul. He straightened slowly, a wolfish smile stealing over his face. "Or I'll take you to bed," he said in a soft voice, his gaze holding hers as he advanced toward her, his intention all too obvious.

A look of alarm touched her face as she began backing away from him. "You're only trying to frighten me," she charged, her body tense as he continued his inexorable advance.

"Perhaps," he agreed, adroitly turning her own words against her. "Do I frighten you, Miranda?"

He saw her swallow, and then her chin came up again. "Of course not," she denied, albeit in a shaky voice. "I'm not in the least afraid of you."

He kept walking until he was standing in front of her, his body all but touching hers. He reached out a hand, capturing a strand of golden hair and wrapping it around his finger. "Do I excite you?" he asked, his voice low and husky as he caught the elusive scent of the cologne she favored.

Her cheeks grew red, and she batted his hand aside. "You flatter yourself!" she snapped, her eyes shooting green fire. "As if I would wish to be pawed by a drunken beast like you!"

Her words angered, but the anger was tempered by a hunger that burned even brighter. His arms closed about her, pulling her against his aching body. "You may not wish for my touch, princess," he sneered, resolutely closing his heart to the flash of panic in her eyes, "but you want it. You want it almost as much as I want you. I've wanted you until I'm mad with it, and tonight I intend doing something about it. I'm tired of going to bed alone," and his mouth closed on hers in a kiss that was both brutal and passionate.

She struggled furiously against the domination of his lips, her small hands ineffectually striking his chest. He ignored the blows, too lost in passion to pay them any mind. His embrace tightened, his body hungrily seeking hers even as his tongue demanded entrance to the hidden depths of her mouth.

"Open your mouth," he ordered hoarsely, nipping hungrily at her lips. "Didn't that cold fish you married teach you anything? Kiss me like a woman kisses her lover!"

Her lips parted, whether in shock or by design, and he was quick to press the advantage, deepening the kiss until he was lost in pleasure. She was sweeter than he had dared imagine, and the taste of her, the feel of her, drove out any thoughts of revenge or anger. He simply wanted, and his body trembled with the force of his desire.

"Miranda," he groaned her name against the soft flesh of her neck, his hand slipping down her body to gently cup her breast. "You are so beautiful, so sweet, I want to touch you everywhere."

The feel of her feminine softness beneath his palm made the blood pump hot and potent through Alec's veins. Sensations he hadn't allowed himself to feel in almost two years rioted inside him, making him shake with the force of his emotions. His lips returned to crush hers, his tongue plunging deep as he pressed her against his burgeoning erection.

When he heard her gasp and felt her tremble, he gave a soft laugh of satisfaction. His hand flew to the front of her prim nightshirt, making short work of the buttons as he slid his hand inside. He gave her breast a gentle caress, his thumb teasing the nipple as he flicked his tongue over her cheeks.

Tears.

Everything in Alec froze as the warm saltiness wetting her cheeks registered on his conscience. He slowly raised his head, his blazing passion turning to icy horror when he saw the tears staining her face. He stared at her a long moment, a feeling of intense self-loathing washing over him as reality set in with a deadly vengeance. He withdrew his hand, his fingers shaking as he refastened her buttons and gently pushed her from him. When he was certain she wouldn't collapse he walked over to the wall, his eyes closing as he laid his forehead against the cool plaster and began calling himself every foul name he could think of.

When he'd finished cursing everything and everyone, he opened his eyes and turned his head, his expression bleak as he studied her. "Are you okay?"

The lips he had abused only moments before trembled slightly as she took a shaky breath. "I . . . y-yes, I'm f-fine," she stammered, sounding so small and frightened that his stomach gave another nauseating plunge. He closed his eyes again and slammed his head against the wall hard enough to make his teeth rattle.

"God, Miranda," he said in a raw voice, grateful for the pain, and thinking it was no less than he deserved, "I don't think there are words to tell you how sorry I am."

"That's all right . . ." she began, and he interrupted with a curt movement of his head.

"No," he corrected bitterly, "no, it's not all right. It's *never* all right for a man to use sex as a weapon against a woman. If I hadn't stopped, I would have been no better than the scum Cara went to see." His lips twisted in a parody of a smile. "Maybe I should slit my wrists, too," he added, wondering if Cara had any razors in her medicine cupboard sharp enough to do a proper job of it.

He heard movement behind him, and realized she had walked up behind him. When he felt her tentative touch on his shoulder, it was all he could do not to flinch.

"You mustn't joke like that," she said, her voice so low and hesitant he could scarce hear it.

He gave a harsh laugh. "Who says I'm joking?"

"But—"

He uttered another blistering curse before opening his eyes

and turning around to meet her worried gaze. "Go to bed, Miranda," he said wearily, too heartsick to debate the matter. "We'll talk in the morning."

He could see relief as well as confusion reflected in her glorious eyes before she replied. "If you're certain," she said, backing slowly away. "I—I shall just say good night, then."

He understood the reason for her hesitancy, and dredged up a halfhearted grin. "Go," he said softly, "I promise not to do anything drastic in the meanwhile." He waited until she'd almost reached the door before calling out. "And Miranda?"

"Yes?" She glanced at him over her shoulder.

He nodded at the sturdy oak door separating the bedroom from the living area. "Lock the door."

Miranda lay awake hours after retiring, her troubled mind insisting upon reliving those moments in Alec's embrace. She kept remembering the feel of his arms, the warmth of his hands, and the taste of his mouth as he kissed her in a manner she blushed to recall. No other man, not even Stephen, had touched her like that, and what shamed and confused her most was that rather than being shocked or frightened by his actions, she had been aroused. She was a married woman, and the first man to bring her pleasure had not been her husband.

That was why she had wept, she admitted, shifting restlessly beneath her covers. Not because she was frightened, although she had been startled at first, but because rather than wanting to shove him away as a proper lady should have done, she'd wanted to pull him closer. She'd want to kiss and caress him as he was kissing and caressing her, and the admission filled her with mortification.

When she finally drifted into sleep, her dreams were restless and uneasy, and so at first she thought the sounds she was hearing were part of those dreams. A sharp cry had her bolting upright, the covers clutched to her chest as she tried to discover what had awakened her. She'd almost decided she'd been imagining things, when another cry sounded, and she realized they were coming from the front room where Alex was sleeping. She hesitated for less than a second before rolling off the bed and dashing over to unlock the door.

The front room was almost black, except for the light from the streets stealing around the partially closed drapes. She could scarce make out the dark shape of the divan, and she was debating whether or not to switch on a light, when Alec gave another piteous cry

"No! No! No! Jane!"

She leapt in alarm, a small shriek escaping her lips, and she almost knocked the lamp off the table in her haste to get it switched on. The room was instantly flooded with light, and it took her eyes several seconds to adjust to the brightness. When her vision cleared, she saw Alec on the divan, clearly caught in the toils of a terrible nightmare.

Her mind barely registered the fact that he was apparently unclothed, before she crept close enough to lay a cautious hand on his shoulder. "Alec?" she gave him a gentle shake. "Alec, wake up, you're dreaming."

He shot up off the divan, his gold eyes wild as he glanced about him. When he saw her squatting nervously beside the bed, he fell back against the sheets with a pungent oath, one arm flung protectively over his eyes. He lay like that several seconds, before lowering his arm with a heavy sigh.

"Was I screaming?" he asked, his deep voice rough with sleep.

Miranda was uncertain if the sounds he made qualified as a scream, and then shook her head. "No, not precisely," she said, amazed he could sound so calm when only seconds before he'd been writhing in horror.

"Well, thank God for that," he muttered, scrubbing a hand over his face before flashing her an enigmatic look. "Thanks for waking me, you can go back to bed now. I don't usually have the dreams twice in the same night."

"You've had these dreams before?" she asked curiously, ignoring the first part of his remarks.

Alec nodded, his expression growing bleak as he settled back against the pillows. He knew he should probably insist she leave, but somehow he couldn't bring himself to do so. He was used to dealing with the dream's aftermath on his own, but inexplicably he realized that this time he wanted to talk instead.

"They started right after Jane was killed," he said, his voice carefully neutral as he relived those black months of pain and despair. "The department's shrink called it post traumatic stress disorder, and assured me such dreams were normal, given the circumstances. She even said they'd eventually go away, but—" his one shoulder shrug was eloquent.

Miranda stared at his bare flesh, recalling the pictures she'd seen in the hallway of his house. Cara had confirmed that the pretty woman depicted in them was Alec's late fiancée, and had provided the amazing fact that she had been a police officer. She hastily averted her eyes, drawing on her courage before asking the question that had been plaguing her ever since Cara had first mentioned the other woman.

"Alec," she began carefully, "how did Jane die? I know she was an officer," she added when he gave a start, "but how did she die? Was it while she was on duty?"

Alec was quiet so long she thought he had no intention of answering, but then he gave a desolate laugh. "God, I wish it had been," he said, staring at the ceiling. "I was prepared for that. In our line of work, it's always a possibility, and you train yourself to accept it. England's not as bad as America, but officers do get killed, and so the knowledge it could happen is always there in the back of your head."

He fell quiet again, his expression distant, and Miranda knew he was lost in thought. "It was her off-duty day," he began again in the same, flat tone. "She'd inherited the house about three months before that, and we were living there while we worked on fixing it up. It would take years, we knew, but we thought it would be fun.

"I was at HQ, catching up on some paperwork and thinking about taking the afternoon off, when we got a call there'd been a bombing on King's Road at a department store. We got there just as the rescue brigade arrived, and because we knew casualties would be high, we went in before the area had been secured. I was digging through the rubble, when I saw a piece of cloth sticking out from beneath some timbers."

Miranda's stomach tightened in horror at his emotionless descriptions. "Oh Alec," she said softly, already knowing what he was about to say.

"It was a bright pink, and I remember thinking, 'Oh, Jane has a coat that color.' That was all, just one of those odd thoughts that flit in your mind at the most unlikely times. I gave a blast on my whistle to let the others know I'd found a possible victim, and I kept digging. You always hope for a live victim, that's how you're trained to think, and so I just kept digging, until I had her completely freed of the rubble."

"Alec," tears were streaming down Miranda's cheeks as she lay a hand on his arm. "I am so sorry . . ."

"They say I screamed, but I don't remember. All I can remember is holding her in my arms, and then there were all these hands snatching at me, pulling me away from her. I fought; one of my mates said I smashed his nose before they brought me down and got me strapped to a litter. I was taken to hospital, and they didn't release me for almost three days, and only then so I could attend the funeral."

"The Royal Family sent flowers, and the Prime Minister himself attended; at least," he added with another of those bitter smiles, "that's what I was told. I was drugged to the eyeballs, so my memory's not as clear as I'd like."

Miranda couldn't speak. She kept her hand on his arm as he continued talking, the story spilling out of him as if having told her this much, he had decided to tell her everything.

"Afterward I managed to get away from everyone, and I decided to go back to the house to get a few things. I walked into the parlor and saw the message light on the answering machine blinking. I don't know why I turned it on. Habit, I suppose. You see a red light blinking and you just answer it. The tape was full of phone messages, and so it had re-wound to the first message. It was from Jane."

*"Hello, ducks!"* He closed his eyes, remembering his anguish as he'd stood there in an empty house listening to her playful, lilting voice. *"Sorry I'm not there to greet you, but Royston's is having the most fantastic sale on curtain rods, and I've decided to pop down for a look. I'll see you when I get home, darling. I love you."*

"Curtain rods!" he exclaimed, tears burning his eyes as he glared at the ceiling. "She died for fucking curtain rods! That's what I couldn't take. That's what almost destroyed me. She wanted to buy some bloody curtain rods, and now she's dead. It was so useless," he added brokenly, a single tear wending down his cheek. "So damned useless."

Without thinking of the consequences, she leaned over him and gently brushed the tear from his face. She replaced it with a soft kiss, and then lay her hand on his cheek. "I wish I could say I understand how you feel," she said, her own voice trembling with emotion, "but I can't. I can't even begin to imagine what it's like to lose the one you love in so brutal a manner. And then to be the one to find her . . ." Her voice trailed off as a tremor shook her.

He reached up and covered her hand with his own, pressing it against his skin. "She wasn't burned," he said softly, turning his head until their eyes met. "The explosive used was a more sophisticated form of plastique, so there wasn't much fire in the blast zone. The doctors assured me she was probably killed instantly, and that helps. I couldn't have borne it if I'd thought she'd suffered."

Miranda could think of no response to that, and so an easy silence fell between them. She remained sitting beside the divan, her hand resting on Alec's cheek as she offered him what solace she could. After several minutes he gave a heavy sigh.

"What time is it?"

She squinted at the time flashing on the VCR. "Almost three o'clock," she said, sitting back on her heels.

He savored the feeling of her hand on his flesh before carefully lifting it from his cheek and lowering it to the divan. "It's late," he said, shifting away from her and fixing his eyes at a point over her head. "You should probably go back to bed. I'm sorry for disturbing you."

She watched him closely, her feeling of hurt turning to amusement as understanding dawned. "Alec, are you embarrassed?'

His head snapped around as he shot her an angry scowl. "Christ, yes!" he snarled, looking decidedly harassed.

"But why?" she demanded, fighting the urge to smile. "Surely not because you've had a nightmare?"

He sat up in bed, the sheets pooling at his waist as he struggled for the words that would explain his confusing tangle of emotions. "I was a basket case," he said grudgingly. "I was on medication and suicide watch for months afterward, and Cara would scarcely let me out of her sight. I *hated* being so weak, but there wasn't a damned thing I could do about it. It was like being on a jet that's going down. You want to make it stop, to make believe it's all a dream, but you can't. You know you're going to die, but all you can do is scream."

To his relief Miranda didn't pat his hand and offer nauseating platitudes, as everyone else had done. Instead she gave a thoughtful nod. "That's how I felt when I realized I'd passed through time," she said softly. "As if I were caught in some kind of bizarre dream. I remember thinking that if I could just wake up, everything would be all right." She gave him an impish smile and added, "I'm still waiting."

He returned her smile, the last of his pain fading as he flicked a stray curl back from her neck. "Thank you, Miranda."

"For what?" She was puzzled.

"For listening to me talk about Jane, for coming to help me when you thought I was in trouble. After I'd all but raped you, I wouldn't have blamed you if you'd left me to rot."

Miranda's cheeks grew a fiery red. "You didn't all but r—rape me," she denied, stumbling over the word. "And I already told you that I forgive you. You were drunk."

"I was an insufferable ass, and you should have kicked me in the balls," he said bluntly, refusing to cut himself the slightest slack. "I think if we're going to continue living together, you'd best have Cara teach you a few defensive moves. She has a brown belt in tai qwan do."

Miranda was torn between pleasure that his words indicated there might be more heated embraces, and confusion over his remarks about Cara. The confusion seemed the safest emotion to discuss, and so she slanted him a puzzled look.

"What is tai qwan do?" she asked, struggling to pronounce the word as he had done.

He gave her a piratical grin. "Something every modern woman should know," he said cheekily. "Just mind you don't get overconfident. Cara might have a brown belt, but I'm an instructor at the Yard."

Sensing he was bragging, she gave a sniff and scrambled awkwardly to her feet. "Mayhap 'tis you who should not grow overconfident," she informed him with a disdainful toss of the head. "The Bible warns that pride comes before a fall, does it not?"

He leaned back against the pillows, his expression insufferably smug as he folded his arms beneath his head. "So it does," he agreed, closing his eyes with a contented sigh. "Mind you turn out the light, will you? There's a love."

# Ten

The next morning over Miranda's vociferous objections, Alec returned to the house of Curzon Street to wall up the room. Her insistence that he at least retrieve the journals and other artifacts was also rejected, and after he'd left she turned to Cara with a scowl.

"Has he always been so insufferably arrogant?" she demanded, drinking the last of her cola. She'd become addicted to the beverage, and was delighted when Cara had thoughtfully stopped at the corner shop to buy her more.

"Alec?" Cara asked around a jaw-cracking yawn. "Lord, he was even worse. He was in the SAS for over five years and then he went straight to the academy so he naturally thought he was the most macho things on two legs. He was a real pig until he met Jane, but she mellowed him considerably, I can tell you."

Miranda's hand tightened on the red, white and blue can at the mention of Alec's fiancée. "Alec told me about Jane, about how she died," she said quietly. "It must have been terrible for him."

"It was bloody awful," Cara responded with her customary candor. "I was terrified he was going to waste himself, and then there was the drinking . . ." She shook her head and gave Miranda a curious look. "How did things go after I left, by the way? Did he get horribly obnoxious?"

Miranda willed herself not to blush. "A trifle," she said striving for indifference, "but he soon fell asleep."

"Passed out, you mean," Cara corrected, and then gave another yawn. "Although I must admit sleep sounds heavenly about now."

Miranda studied her worriedly, noting her drawn face and shadowed eyes. "Why don't you go to bed?" she suggested. "You needn't feel you have to stay up and keep me company."

Cara looked relieved. "Would you mind?" she asked. "I've been up for almost twenty-four hours, and I'm out on my feet."

"Of course not," Miranda assured her with a warm smile. "I'll just wait for Alec to come back, and perhaps play with your computer. I find them fascinating."

"Feel free," Cara was already on her feet and wandering toward the bedroom. "I'm on a computer network linked to the British Library, so explore away. Maybe you can find out what happened after you disappeared; that ought to be interesting. G'night," and she closed the door behind her.

It took Miranda the better part of an hour to figure out how to get the network on-line, but once she mastered that she was soon in the library files. A quick search revealed no mention of either Stephen or herself, and she was trying to figure how to get a human back on-line, when Alec returned, looking grim.

"Is there a problem?" Miranda asked, backing out of the program she was in. The first lesson she had been learned about computers was that they were even fussier than her step-papa's elderly housekeeper, and the last thing she wanted was to do anything to upset Cara's machine.

Alec thought of the urgent message waiting on his answering machine and gave a careless shrug. "Not really," he said, glancing around him with a frown. "Where's Cara?"

"In bed," Miranda replied, her attention focused on the computer's screen. "The poor lamb was about to drop. Why?"

He thrust a hand through his hair and bit back an impatient curse. He'd been hoping Cara would be available to keep an eye on Miranda, but now he'd have to improvise. "I need to go into the office for a few hours," he said, his tone harsher than he intended. "Do you want to stay here, or go back to the house?"

She raised her eyebrows at his answer. "Actually, I would like to go the British Library," she said, then hid a pleased smile when he gave a surprised start.

"The library?" he repeated, looking suspicious. "Whatever for?"

"Something Cara said," she replied, sending him an innocent smile. "Is there a reason why I should not be allowed to go?"

He was about to protest, then thought better of it. "None I can think of," he said, thinking aloud. "In fact, I suppose that's as good a place to stash you as any."

"*Stash* me?" She repeated the insulting remark indignantly.

He was already digging out his wallet. "Here's twenty pounds," he said, thrusting a handful of notes into her hand. "That should get you through the day. When you've finished, I want you to come back here rather than going to the house. The wall's not dry yet, and the fumes might make you ill."

"What fumes?" Miranda demanded, feeling rather like a child who'd just been sent off to play with a pat on the head.

"From the setting compound," Alec explained, waving his hand. "It can be toxic, but it should be safe by tonight. I'll meet you here around seven."

Miranda cast a dubious frown at him, certain he was up to something. "Very well," she said at last, deciding she would wait until later and then see if she could learn anything from Cara. "Will there be anything else?"

He thought a moment, then shook his head. "No, just try not to ride the tube after dark," he stopped at the sight of the smile playing about her lips. "Why?" he demanded suspiciously.

Her smile bloomed in all its glory. "No reason," she assured him sweetly. "It is just I can not remember the last time you left without issuing a list of commands for me to follow."

He bristled at her teasing words. "I don't issue commands!" he denied, resenting her implication that he was a petty tyrant.

To his fury she actually laughed, her green eyes sparkling as she rose to her feet. "We shall call them strong suggestions, then," she said, retrieving her purse from the desk's drawer before turning to face him. "Do you wish to remain here, or will you walk me to the tube stop?"

He glared at her again, sensing she was humoring him as one would an ill-mannered child. "Think you're clever, don't you?" he muttered, pausing long enough to write Cara a short note.

"Bloody clever," she replied, and then laughed again as his expression grew even more sour.


"Where the bloody devil have you been?" Commander Milsom barked out the moment Alec walked into the tactical room. "You were told to report almost two hours ago!"

Alec's eyebrow raised in amusement at his superior's querulous greeting. "I was told to report as soon as I could," he said, calmly shrugging off his jacket and draping it across the back of his chair. "This is the soonest I could manage."

"Spare us the comedy number, Bramwell," a lean man with cold eyes and an even colder expression said tersely. "Security Services has developed intelligence that a viable threat has been made against you, and it's been decided to upgrade you from Level Four to Level Three for your own protection. Now sit down."

Alec sat, doing his best to hide his shock. As a member of the SAS and SO 13, he was already considered a prime target for attack by disgruntled terrorists, but he'd never expected such a threat to be made; let alone for it to be taken seriously by the bloodless drones at A Squad. He leaned back in his chair and fixed the other man with a hard stare.

"What is the source of the intelligence? Was it an informant or an anonymous phone call?" he asked, thinking he'd decide for himself whether the threat was viable or nothing more than a lot of hot air.

The lean man's lips curled derisively. "An SAS man, and you can ask that?"

Alec's respect for his opponent went up a notch, even as his irritation increased. He'd have been suspicious as hell if the other man had been too forthcoming with information. Whoever he was, he was good. "The source of the threat, then?" he asked, mentally reviewing past cases. "The PIRA?" He'd brought a case against two members of the Provisional Wing of the IRA a few years back, and everyone knew the bastards had long memories.

The other man settled back in his chair, allowing a slight smile to cross his lips. "Ever hear of the Red Coalition?"

Alec's feet hit the floor with a thump as he sat up. "You're having me on," he said in disbelief, refusing to believe what he was hearing. "Why have they targeted me? That's not their MO."

A dismissive look from the man had Milsom rising to his feet, his fleshy face reddening as he slammed out of the room. Alec watched him go and then settled back in his chair, his manner purposefully casual as he flicked the other man an amused grin.

"Neat trick; don't suppose you'd care to teach it to me?"

The man's smile widened, and he dug out his ID and chucked it at Alec. "Christopher Deverham, Security Services, sorry for not introducing myself sooner."

Alec gave the ID card and shield a brief but thorough examination before tossing it back. "Going to answer my question?" he asked, his expression growing stern. "Why would the Red Coalition take it into their heads to come after me? I know they've been active lately, but that's a far cry from trying to take out a cop. Have they lost their bloody minds?"

Deverham hesitated a moment before answering. "That's the problem. One of them has."

"According to whom?" Alec asked, still not overly concerned. He'd always thought the majority of terrorists were crackpots, and this only confirmed his suspicions.

"Ursula Massendorf."

Had it been anyone other than a member of Security Services to say such a thing, Alec would have laughed in their face. "Ursula Massendorf?" he repeated incredulously. "But she's the leader of the Coalition!"

"Which is precisely why she's so anxious to get this matter resolved, as she puts it," Deverham said grimly. "It seems one of her associates has gone off his nut, and is acting without the group's permission. He's behind the bombings, not the Coalition, and they're more anxious than we are to get him off the streets."

Alec swore pungently. A rogue terrorist wasn't something he even wanted to think about. "Are they turning him in?" he asked, and then answered his own question. "No, of course not, if they were planning to do that there wouldn't be a threat."

"If I understood Fräulein Massendorf correctly, they have no intentions of handing him over to us," Deverham said with a humorless smile. "In fact, I believe they were getting ready to 'retire' the fellow when he went underground, taking half their arsenal with him. Unfortunately he's also their cooker, so unless they can find some sources in the Mid-East, they're pretty well toothless at the moment."

Alec digested the information in silence before asking, "What's the cooker's name?"

"Edward John Talbot. Ring any bells?"

Like most officers Alec carried a mental file in his head, and it took him only a few seconds to put a face to the name. "White male, thirties, brown and blue, degree in chemical engineering from Oxford, considered a sociopath with psychopathic tendencies," he said, and then frowned as he remembered something else. "Didn't I see a memo from Interpol that he was killed in a shoot-out in Lyons a few weeks back?"

"*Suspected* killed," Deverham corrected. "According to our Ms. Massendorf, the shoot-out was actually an ambush planned by the drug lord Talbot was free-lancing for—again without the group's permission—and the other gentleman apparently decided it was more cost-efficient to waste Talbot than to pay him. A costly mistake on their part, I might add."

"How do you mean?"

"The last two bombing targets were dummy corporations owned by a Mr. Lester Blackpool, the drug lord in question.

Apparently you're not the only one to displease Mr. Talbot, and given the success he's had against one of his targets, we've decided not to take any chances with you. Like it or not, Bramwell, we're on you".

An image of the victim he'd helped dig out of the smoldering rubble flashed in Alec's mind, filling him with deadly fury. "What about the King's Road bombing?" he asked, amazed he could sound so cool and in control, when there was a volcano of anger and rage exploding inside him. "Have they admitted to that?"

"No responsibility has been claimed, and it has nothing to do with these cases, as far as I can see," Deverham said, stroking his lip thoughtfully. "May I ask why you believe either Talbot or the Red Coalition may have been involved?"

"It was their MO: pyro-plastique explosives, two charges, both time-delayed, and no advance phone call to give warning," Alec said, rattling off the details of Jane's death emotionlessly. "It's them, all right. I can smell it, and by God, I'll see them pay for it."

Deverham looked uneasy for the first time since Alec walked in the room. "Look, Bramwell," he began cautiously, "I'm aware your fiancée was lost in that explosion, but—"

"Killed," Alec interrupted, his eyes blazing as they met his. "Jane was *killed*, damn it. So screw your polite euphemisms."

Deverham's eyes turned icy gray as he met Alec's glare. "I'm willing to cut you some slack," he cautioned softly, "but you're tacking rather close to the wind. Your fiancée was a member of this department, and although she wasn't on duty when she died, I have no intention of letting her death go unavenged. Those responsible will be caught and punished, I promise you that. Now, can we kindly get back to the matter at hand?"

Alec swallowed his anger, realizing the other man was right. "What proof does the Coalition have that Talbot will come after me?" he asked after a moment's pause. "Did he make threats?"

"He didn't have to. They found your address and a page from his diary, indicating he'd been stalking you," Deverham said, his

expression growing even grimmer as he jabbed a warning finger
at Alec. "And if you're thinking of shrugging this off, don't.
We've never lost an officer to a terrorist hit, and we're not about
to start with you. Is that understood, Inspector?"

Alec's jaw clenched, but he refrained from telling Deverham
where he could put his autocratic manner. "Perfectly," he said
coolly. "But what I was thinking was that the Coalition is being
suspiciously civic-minded for a group of terrorists. What's on?
Are they dealing for something? Amnesty, perhaps?"

"If they are, they can bloody well go to hell," Deverham said
so bluntly that Alec believed him at once. "Her majesty's gov-
ernment doesn't make deals with the likes of them."

"Have I permission to be armed?" Alec asked, addressing
what he saw as the most immediate concern. "I'm licensed; so's
my sister, Inspector Cara Marsdale."

"I've already received permission for you to be issued a side
arm," Deverham said, "but I'm not certain about your sister. The
threat is considered to be only against you."

"I want Cara armed, or guarded by an armed officer," Alec
insisted doggedly. "You and I both know that most terrorists,
even mad ones, always have back-ups to their primary targets.
I won't have Cara put at risk because of a tangle of red tape."

"I'll see to it at once." Deverham jotted down a note in the
leather book he'd pulled from his pocket. "What about your
parents? It's not customary, but I could assign them Level Four
protection, if you'd like."

Alec thought about his father, a former SAS man as well, and
grinned."Dad can take care of himself and my mother," he said
calmly. "But to be certain, I'll give him a call and explain the
situation. My mum has a sister in Calgary, Alberta, she's always
talking about visiting, now's as good a time as any."

"I'll call the RCMP and alert them." Another note was quickly
jotted down. "Is there anyone else you feel may be at risk because of you?"

Alec thought of Miranda, and paled. What the devil was he
supposed to do about her? he wondered wildly. If she was a

normal person he could have her shipped off to a safe house until this was all settled, but he doubted that would work in her case. She had no papers, no identification, and if Deverham got his bureaucratic little hands on her, he'd probably have her locked up as an undocumented alien. No, he decided, taking a deep breath, he couldn't risk her. He wouldn't.

"Bramwell?" The other man was frowning at him. "Is there anyone else you want listed? A girlfriend, perhaps? Your gram?"

"My gram died over five years ago," Alec replied coolly, folding his arms across his chest and striking an indifferent pose, "and I haven't got a girlfriend."

"Very well, then," Deverham continued with his note-taking. "We'll give you technical protection at your house, and assign an armed officer to accompany you when—"

"No."

The brusque interruption made Deverham look up in annoyance. "Look," he began testily, "I know you SAS types like to think of yourselves as invincible, but this isn't a beat-up march in the Brecons! Talbot's killed at least fifteen people by our count, and God knows how many others he may have done as well!"

"And I could take him out with two taps from my Browning FM before he could even blink," Alec said with deadly certainty. "You've seen my file, and you know I'm not bragging. I was the best shot in our regiment, and for us *SAS types,*" he flung the words back at Deverham, "that's saying one hell of a lot. I don't want or need some MPF recruit shagging me. If I need backup, I know where I can get it."

Deverham didn't pretend not to take his meaning. He set down his pen and studied Alec intently for several seconds. "Off record?" he asked at last.

Alec paused in suspicion, then gave a curt nod. "Off record."

"The police wish an arrest, and you are to do your best to accommodate them. But if you should be forced to deal with Talbot in a more permanent manner, other interested parties would prefer no identifiable body be found. Understood?"

Alec gave another nod, hiding his shock as he realized he'd just been sanctioned to kill. "Understood," he said softly, a feral smile touching his lips. *Finally,* he thought, his heart aching with fierce satisfaction. The revenge he had been seeking almost eighteen months was about to be his. All he needed to do was wait, and hope the price he would pay for his vengeance wouldn't be his life.

To Miranda's gentle disgust, the British Library with its many departments was nothing like the lending library she remembered from her day. It was huge, and so terribly stuffy it reminded her of a bishop's home she had once visited with her mother. Everyone seemed to know precisely what they were about, and she felt like a country bumpkin standing in the center of Charing Cross Road. Finally she glimpsed a sign that said *Information,* and she walked up to the bored-looking young man sitting behind the desk.

"Excuse me," she began politely, "but I'm looking for some information on a relation of mine who disappeared in the early 1800's. I was wondering if you have any newspapers from the period? I thought perhaps the *Times* would—"

"The exact date?" The young man interrupted, his expression of boredom and irritation increasing.

"June 17, 1811," Miranda provided, hiding her own irritation at the clerk's brusqueness.

The young man's fingers flew over the keyboard, tapping out a series of numbers that brought his screen humming to life. He pecked and typed for several more seconds, the silver cross dangling from his ear swinging from side to side as he worked. Suddenly he stopped, his sulky mouth protruding in a pout as he leaned forward to study the screen.

"Can't help you there," he said, sounding vaguely pleased about the fact. "They're switching those files from microfiche to CD-ROM, and they won't be available for a few more weeks. You'll have to check back."

"Oh." Miranda swallowed her disappointment. "Well, perhaps one of the other papers of the day——"

"We only have complete records of the *Times*," the clerk interrupted again, his gaze flicking past Miranda to the man standing behind her. "Unless your relation was important enough to have a book or article written about them, I'm afraid there's nothing I can do to help. Thank you."

Miranda knew she was being dismissed, and resolutely dug in her heels. She doubted that her disappearance would have been important enough to warrant a book, but she wasn't about to grant the officious clerk the satisfaction of sending her packing like an inopportune tradesman. Besides, as Alec had said, who knew how history might have been affected by her passage through time?

"Actually," she sent the clerk a sugary smile, "I seem to recall my great-aunt mentioning something about a book. Could you look it up, please?"

The clerk rolled his eyes to show he considered himself considerably ill used. "Name of the book or the person it was about?" he asked in tones of obvious resignation.

"Her name was Lady Miranda Hallforth, the countess of Harrington," Miranda replied, thinking how odd it was to refer to herself in the past tense.

More typing and clicking. "Nothing on her," the young man's voice fairly dripped with satisfaction. "As I said, you'll have to——" he broke off and frowned at the screen. "Do you know if her husband's name was Stephen?"

Miranda's heart began to race with hope. "Yes," she said, trying to hide her eagerness, "I believe it was."

"I have two entries about him," the clerk said, hitting another button and causing the printer at his elbow to begin spewing out paper. He ripped it off and handed it to her with a forced smile. "Also, if her husband was an earl, you might want to check one of the books on the peerage. I'm sure they'll be of some assistance. Third floor, in the rear. Thank you."

This time Miranda accepted her *congé,* satisfied at having

obtained something from the wretch. Really, she thought sourly, it was small wonder to her this time was in such a state. What was the world coming to, when one couldn't even get decent service from a clerk! In the next moment, she gave a philosophical shrug. Ah well, she supposed in the end it really was no matter, and at least now she had a place to begin her search.

She walked up the library's wide marble steps, studying the information printed on the paper the clerk had given her. The first book listed under Stephen's name was *Society's Tattle: Great Scandals of the Nineteenth Century,* and she was amused to think her disappearance may have caused a sensation amongst the *ton.* The other title, however, had her stopping, her brows gathering in a frown as she studied it. *Aristocracy on Trial.*

What on earth? She tried to imagine what Stephen might have done to result in his being brought to trial. Despite the fact he had married her for her fortune, he was one of the proudest men she had ever met, and she found it hard to believe he would do anything to bring disgrace on either himself or his name.

She was no closer to solving this puzzle when she was jostled from behind. She turned around, her apology dying as she recognized her rescuer from her first day in London. He seemed to recognize her at the same moment, and sent her a shy smile.

"Oh, hello," he said, shifting his pile of books from one arm to the other. "Nice to see you again."

"Good day, Professor," she nodded, somewhat embarrassed as she realized she couldn't recall his last name. She knew his given name was Geoffrey, but she wasn't about to call him that, regardless of what Alec and Cara had told her about the laxness of today's manners. "How are you?"

As if sensing her dilemma, he said, "It's all right, I can't remember your last name, either. Mine is Kingston, by the way, Geoffrey Kingston, and you are Miranda . . ."

"Winthrop," she provided, her reserve thawing as she offered him her hand. "We do seem to make a habit of running into each other in the oddest places, do we not?"

He shook her hand awkwardly, almost dropping several books

in the process. "Odd to you, perhaps," he said, reshuffling his load, "but this is all but my home away from home. Classes begin in a few weeks, and I'm preparing a new series of lectures on Marx. With the collapse of communism in Eastern Europe, I think it's time we re-thought his entire *Manifesto,* don't you agree?"

Miranda had a vague memory of communism and someone called Marx from one of the books Alec had her read. "It's always good to keep an open mind," she agreed, hoping her answer was noncommittal enough to satisfy him.

Apparently it did, for he gave an approving nod. "What brings you to the BL?" he asked curiously. "As I say, I spend a great deal of time here, and I can't recall seeing you before."

Miranda repeated her story about researching a distant relation, and he seemed quite interested. "I took honors in history, when I was an undergraduate," he said when she finished speaking. "I'd be more than happy to help you, if you'd like."

There was nothing Miranda would have liked more, but her gaze flicked to the books in his arms. "That would be very kind of you," she said politely, "but what of your own work? I shouldn't wish you to fall behind schedule because of me."

"Oh, it won't be a problem," he said quickly, his willingness to be of assistance reminding her of an eager schoolboy. "I'm a little ahead of schedule, and to be honest, I'd rather welcome a break from Marx. He was a dreadfully tiresome fellow, you know."

In the end Miranda accepted his offer of assistance, and they made their way to the library's top floor. They spent the next few hours poring over books and ancient documents, before finally uncovering anything about either Stephen or herself, and what she found had her staring at the page in disbelief.

"What is it?" Geoffrey—as he insisted she call him—asked, leaning over her shoulder to study what she was reading.

"It's—it's Stephen," she stammered, tears gathering in her eyes as the truth slowly sunk in. "He died a year after I—a year after my relation disappeared."

Geoffrey studied the date. "So he did," he agreed, then sent her a curious frown. "You seem rather upset by the fact. What difference does it make when he died? He'd have been dead long before now, anyway.

Tears spilled down Miranda's cheeks, as the reality of Stephen's death hit her like a hammer blow. "But he was so young," she whispered in a trembling voice, her heart breaking at the realization that she was truly a widow. "He wasn't even thirty-five. That is far too young to have died."

"Not back then," Geoffrey said with a shrug. "Disease was rampant in those days, and a simple cut could mean death. What does this mean?" He indicated a symbol beside Stephen's name.

Miranda stared at the mark, and felt a fresh flow of tears stinging her eyes. "It means the title died with the man," she said hollowly, recalling how seriously Stephen had taken his duty to the title, and how he worried because he had been the last of his line. "There was no heir to inherit."

"Oh." He gave her another thoughtful glance. "Listen, how about a break? The museum's just in the next building, and they have a wonderful cafeteria. No offense, but I think you could do with a cup of tea or something."

Miranda gave a miserable nod, and after returning the books to the librarian, they made their way to the main part of the complex. The short walk gave her time to compose herself, and by the time they reached the cafeteria, located in the basement of the museum, she was almost in control of her errant emotions.

"I am sorry for being so weepy," she said, sending him an apologetic smile as she stirred her tea. "But I have been working on this for so long, that I feel as if I know these people. I suppose that sounds dreadfully silly," she added, ducking her head in embarrassment.

"Not at all," he assured her, giving her hand an understanding squeeze. "I feel the same way when I'm doing my research. My students think I'm balmy for caring about something so dusty as Economics, but I find it fascinating."

What a thoroughly nice man, Miranda decided, appreciating

*Allow us to proposition you in a most provocative way.*

GET 4 REGENCY
ROMANCE NOVELS
*FREE*

An
$18.49
Value

**NO OBLIGATION TO
BUY ANYTHING, EVER.**

# PRESENTING AN IRRESISTIBLE OFFERING ON YOUR KIND OF ROMANCE.

## Receive 4 Zebra Regency Romance Novels (An $18.49 value) Free

Journey back to the romantic Regent Era with the world's finest romance authors. Zebra Regency Romance novels place you amongst the English *ton* of a distant past with witty dialogue, and stories of courtship so real, you feel that you're living them!

Experience it all through 4 FREE Zebra Regency Romance novels...yours just for the asking. When you join *the only book club dedicated to Regency Romance readers,* additional Regency Romances can be yours to preview FREE each month, with no obligation to buy anything, ever.

### Regency Subscribers Get First-Class Savings.

After your initial package of 4 FREE books, you'll begin to receive monthly shipments of new Zebra Regency titles. These all new novels will be delivered direct to your home as soon as they are published...sometimes even before the bookstores get them! Each monthly shipment of 4 books will be yours to examine for 10 days. Then, if you decide to keep the books, you'll pay the pre-ferred subscriber's price of just $3.65 per title. That's $14.60 for all 4 books...a savings of almost $4 off the publisher's price! What's more, $14.60 is your <u>total</u> price...there's no extra charge for shipping and handling.

### No Minimum Purchase, a Generous Return Privilege, and FREE Home Delivery! Plus a FREE Monthly Newsletter Filled With Author Interviews, Contests, and More!

We guarantee your satisfaction and you may return any shipment...for any rea-son...within 10 days and pay nothing that month. And if you want us to stop sending books, just say the word, you're under no obligation.

## Say Yes to 4 Free Books!

## COMPLETE AND RETURN THE ORDER CARD TO RECEIVE THIS $18.49 VALUE. ABSOLUTELY FREE.

*(If the certificate is missing below, write to: Zebra Home Subscription Service, Inc., 120 Brighton Road, P.O. Box 5214, Clifton, New Jersey 07015-5214*

## 4 FREE BOOKS

**Yes!** Please send me 4 Zebra Regency Romances without cost or obligation. I understand that each month thereafter I will be able to preview 4 new Regency Romances FREE for 10 days. Then, if I should decide to keep them, I will pay the money-saving preferred subscriber's price of just $14.60 for all 4...that's a savings of almost $4 off the publisher's price with no additional charge for shipping and handling. I may return any shipment within 10 days and owe nothing, and I may cancel this subscription at any time. My 4 FREE books will be mine to keep in any case.

Name _____

Address_____ Apt. _____

City _____ State _____ Zip _____

Telephone ( ) _____

Signature _____ RF1195
(If under 18, parent or guardian must sign.)

Terms and prices subject to change. Orders subject to acceptance by Zebra Home Subscription Service, Inc.

GET 4 REGENCY ROMANCE NOVELS FREE

An $18.49
value.
FREE!
No obligation
to buy
anything, ever.

ZEBRA HOME SUBSCRIPTION SERVICE, INC.

120 BRIGHTON ROAD

P.O. BOX 5214

CLIFTON, NEW JERSEY 07015-5214

AFFIX
STAMP
HERE

his efforts to put her at her ease. He was so kind and diffident, that she couldn't help but compare him to Alec. It was unlikely he would have been so understanding, she thought, and then dismissed the thought as unworthy . . . and untrue. He might not have demonstrated the professor's shy generosity, she admitted silently, but she knew he'd have done his best to reassure her.

"It's too bad those books you wanted weren't available," Geoffrey commented, taking a delicate bite of the egg and cheese sandwich he'd ordered. "You should have asked them to hold them for you when they're returned."

Miranda shifted uneasily on her seat. "I would have liked to," she admitted, remembering the awkward moment when the librarian had asked her for a card, "but I'm afraid I do not have a library card."

"Oh, that's no problem. Just stop at the desk and show them your ID, and they'll issue you one."

Miranda had no idea how to reply at first. "Unfortunately my purse was pinched last week," she said at last, borrowing some phrases she had heard from Cara. "I lost all my papers and had to cancel all my credit cards. It was a terrible hassle."

"I know what you mean," he agreed with a sympathetic smile. "Losing one's ID can be a dreadful pain."

"Well, I suppose I should be getting home," Miranda said, eager to be gone before he could ask her any other potentially awkward questions. "I'm under strict orders not to ride the tube after dark, so I had best get started."

"Ah yes, the oh-so-proper host," he commented, leaning back in his chair to study her. "I meant to ask if he was very angry about the other day. If so, I'd be happy to speak with him."

"Oh, no, there's no need for that!" Miranda said quickly, imagining Alec's reaction only all to well. He'd doubtlessly be furious she had dared speak with a stranger, and he'd probably follow up his tirade with a stern lecture about how dangerous things were in this time.

"That is," she amended hastily, "he was a bit miffed, but he soon got over it. You know how it is with the elderly," she added this last in a deliberate attempt to mislead him. She was still not yet ready to admit her unusual living arrangements to anyone, let alone a prim and proper professor of Economics.

"Wait," Geoffrey rose also, his napkin dangling awkwardly from his fingers as he stood, "before you go, I—I was wondering if you would care to have dinner with me. Nothing terribly fancy, mind," he added when he saw her hesitate, "I'm only a college professor. But I would very much like to see you again."

Miranda was both touched and thrilled as she realized he was asking her out on a date. The experience was so novel, she was almost tempted to say yes, but then she thought of Alec and the impossibility of explaining her odd circumstances.

"I would like that as well," she said with a gentle shake of her head, "but I'm afraid that isn't possible."

"Of course." She saw him swallow his disappointment and his pride. "I quite understand."

"But that doesn't mean we can not see each other again," she said quickly, her heart touched by his shy dignity. "I will still be doing my research, so perhaps we might meet here. If—if you still wish to help me, that is."

"I should like nothing better," he assured her so ardently that she could not help but blush. "Shall we say tomorrow, then? The same time and place?"

She was about to say yes, when she remembered Alec had said something about taking her to Brighton to show her Prinny's extravagant pavilion. "I am afraid I shall be out of town tomorrow," she said apologetically. "But perhaps we could meet in another few days? I could give you my telephone number, or perhaps you could give me yours?" she suggested, recalling Cara had said men and women often exchanged telephone numbers without the smallest hint of impropriety being attached to their actions.

"You had best give me yours," he said decisively. "I just moved into a new flat, and they haven't connected my service. You know how slow the BT can be," he added, rolling his eyes.

"Indeed I do," Miranda agreed, smiling as she thought how terribly impatient people were in this modern era. "It makes one wonder what people did before electricity, does it not?"

"I can't even imagine," Geoffrey said with a shudder. "It must have been awful."

Miranda suddenly thought of carriage rides at dawn and the sounds of a waltz echoing in a candlelit ballroom, and gave a wistful smile. "I daresay it had its advantages," she said, feeling another attack of weeping come over her as the enormity of all she had lost struck her anew. "Goodbye, Geoffrey, I shall look forward to hearing from you," she said quickly, snatching up her purse and rushing for the exit, praying she would make it to the streets without disgracing herself.

## Eleven

Alec and his sister were waiting when Miranda returned to Cara's. One look at his strained expression was enough to banish her own melancholy thoughts. "What is it?" she asked, setting her purse and packages on the hall table. "Has something happened?"

"In a manner of speaking." Alec's voice was heavy as he gestured toward the divan, "Sit down, Miranda, there's something we need to discuss with you."

Thoroughly alarmed, Miranda did as ordered, noting that Cara was sprawled in the leather club chair, her arms folded across her chest and a mutinous pout on her face. "All right," she said, once she was settled on the divan. "I am sitting. Will you please tell me what is wrong? You are frightening me."

She was uncertain what to expect, but whatever those expectations, they paled in comparison to the horrifying story Alec told in a cool voice devoid of any emotion. By the time he had finished speaking, Miranda was gaping at him in astonishment.

"Do you mean to say the authorities know where this fellow is, and they have made no move to arrest him?" she demanded in outrage. "How can this be?"

"Because they *don't* know where he is!" Alec returned with considerable irritation. "The bugger's gone to a bolt hole, and we've lost all track of him. To complicate matters, he's also running from the mob and his own people as well, so it's not likely we'll find him standing in the center of Piccadilly Circus waiting for a bus!"

Miranda sniffed and tossed her head at his churlish response. "I did not mean to imply you would," she said loftily. "I was merely expressing surprise he had yet to be apprehended."

"It isn't that easy," Alec began hotly, and then gave an exasperated sigh. "Why do I bother?" he asked, lifting his gaze to the ceiling as if in search of divine patience.

Miranda ignored him, mulling over something he had said. "You said you had been offered protection, does this mean the house will be guarded?" she asked, part of her blushing to think unseen eyes would be watching her and speculating on her relationship with Alec. The other part of her was more concerned with doing whatever was necessary to keep him safe, and told her modesty to go hang.

"A Squad handles threat containment," Alec replied mendaciously, not mentioning the battle he'd waged to keep his house from being placed under heavy watch. "They've hardened the physical security of the place by installing bars on the windows and burglar alarms, and they'll be doing periodic sweeps of the area to check for suspicious vehicles, so we should be safe enough. At least," he added, sliding a resentful glare in his sister's direction," *some* of us will be safe."

Cara shook back her dark hair and met his glare with a burning look of her own. "Don't even start," she warned in a tight voice. "I've already told you I won't move in with you and Miranda, and I've told you why. End of discussion."

Alec's jaw clenched in frustration, but much as he longed to ignore her objections, he grudgingly acknowledged those objections weren't without validity. Kettrick, her prissy supervisor, had disapproved of her from the start, and he was only waiting for some excuse to toss her off the squad. In a similar situation a male officer would be expected to tough it out, and that meant Cara couldn't . . . or rather, *wouldn't* run for protection. He gave her another glare and then sighed in defeat.

"I still say you're acting like an obstinate fool," he grumbled. "What makes you think people would assume you were staying with us for *your* safety? Couldn't you tell them you were helping me look after Miranda?"

Now it was Miranda who bristled. "I beg your pardon," she said frostily, "but I was unaware I required looking after. However," she added, turning her head and giving Cara a warm smile, "I do wish you would reconsider and stay with us. I shall worry about you here alone."

To Alec's amazement, Cara actually seemed to consider Miranda's invitation before shaking her head. "Thanks, luv, but I can look after myself," she said, her chin lifting with pride. "And now that I've been licensed to carry a weapon, I'll be even safer. And I needn't worry about a car bomb, either," she added with a flash of macabre humor. "Parking's impossible around here."

Alec saw the worry and confusion darkening Miranda's green eyes, and could have cheerfully throttled his chatty sister. He'd deliberately avoided mentioning the most serious threat—a car bomb—because he hadn't wanted to frighten her. She was nervous enough about cars as it was, and the last thing he wanted her to worry about was whether or not the car she was in was going to explode into flaming bits of debris. He shook off the violent image and gave both women a strained smile.

"Speaking of cars, I've decided we should take our trip to Brighton as planned," he began in a hearty voice that rang false even to his own ears. "I've arranged a day's holiday, and with the way things are going, we could do with a bit of fun."

"Sorry, but you'll have to carry on without me," Cara said with an apologetic shake of her head. "Our prime suspect's recovered enough to demand his solicitor, and we'll have to scramble like mad to keep his written confession from being tossed out as inadmissible."

"He wrote a confession?" Alec was temporarily diverted.

"Mmm. If the bloody rescue brigade had been less zealous rushing him to hospital, it would have been his suicide note," Cara replied, looking disgruntled. "But regardless of whatever legal tap-dancing his solicitor might do, Morrison will be going away for a very long time. In the note he copped to a homicide, and left directions guiding us to the body. Richard called a bit ago to say it had been exhumed, and we're waiting for an ID."

Miranda listened to their conversation in appalled silence, thinking she would never grow accustomed to the violence of this time. Her world might have had its problems, as Professor Kingston had pointed out earlier, but at least it didn't have mad bombers and murderous rapists lurking behind every bush. Compared to that, she thought sourly, pestilence and disease seemed tame!

Alec and Cara talked shop another few minutes, before Alec reached for his coat. "Well, if I can't talk you into moving in with me, do I at least have your word you'll be careful?" he asked, giving her nose a playful tweak. "No grandstanding?"

"Of course, you sot," she returned in kind, batting away his hand. "And mind you do the same; it's you this Talbot's after. That reminds me, when are Dad and Mum flying to Canada?"

Alec thought about the conversation he'd had with his parents prior to coming over to Cara's. "Monday morning," he said with a grin. "They'll be ringing you tonight to say goodbye. And I should warn you that Mum's new neighbor is a handsome bachelor with excellent prospects and a charming smile." He repeated his mother's glowing description with smug delight.

Cara rolled her eyes. "Spare me," she muttered, and then reached up to give Alec an impulsive hug. She also bestowed a similar hug on Miranda, drawing back to give her a quick grin. "Keep an eye on this oaf, won't you?" she ordered, her brandy-colored eyes dancing. "And if he gives you any trouble, you've my permission to bash him on the head with a cooking pot."

"I shall keep that in mind," Miranda promised, chuckling at the expression on Alec's face as she returned Cara's hug. She was still chuckling when she and Alec walked outside into the soft summer evening, his arm draped companionably about her shoulders. Halfway down the steps she suddenly stopped, eyes closing as she drew in a deep breath of air.

"What is it?" he asked, watching her curiously.

"Just comparing," she replied, opening her eyes with a sigh.

"Comparing what?" Without thinking he reached up and brushed back a strand of blond hair that had been blown across her cheek by the damp breeze. When she'd first come forward in time she'd kept her hair pinned back in a prim chignon, but lately she'd taken to wearing it down. He wondered if she knew how sexy she looked with those golden waves cascading about her face, and was annoyed with himself for having noticed.

"The smells," she said, answering his question with a half-smile. "Your London smells differently than mine."

Alec eyed a passing car that was belching out clouds of exhaust. "I'll bet," he muttered, taking her elbow as he guided her toward the curb.

"No, really," she insisted, hurrying to keep up with his longer stride. "My London reeked of smoke and filth and—" She stopped speaking when she saw him step out into the street and wave his hand. "What are you doing?"

"Getting us a taxi," he said, then nodded in satisfaction when one of the black cars screeched to a stop amid a chorus of horns. "Let's go," he said, dragging her toward the waiting cab.

Miranda panicked as she understood he meant for her to climb in the thing. "Alec, wait!" she protested, struggling valiantly to free herself. "I have no wish to ride in one of those things!"

"I know," he said unsympathetically, "but it's time you did. In you go."

"But Alec—"

He shoved her the rest of the way into the taxi, slamming the door behind him as he gave the driver his address. The car pulled away with another shriek of brakes, and he settled back against the leather seat to enjoy the ride to his house. After they'd gone a block or so, he glanced at Miranda and saw her huddling against the far door; her eyes were squeezed shut in fear.

"You can open your eyes," he said, trying very hard not to laugh at her reaction. "We're not going to die, you know."

"That is what you think," she muttered feelingly, warily opening one eye just as a speeding bus whizzed past them with inches to spare. She closed her eyes even tighter. "Oh, lord."

"Not to worry, madam," the driver called out cheerfully from the front seat. "I've the Knowledge, I have, and I've yet to lose a single passenger. Company docks you a day's wage for that," he added, winking at Alec in the mirror.

"How reassuring." Miranda knew he was teasing, but she could find little humor in the situation. She also knew she would have to become accustomed to travelling at such speeds, if she was ever to fit in to this time, but that did not mean she had to like it. She sucked in her breath as the taxi careened around the corner. "Talk to me," she ordered, grabbing Alec's hand in a death grip.

He did so, his lean fingers entwining with hers in a reassuring hold. "We should have an early start tomorrow," he said, lowering their joined hands to rest lightly on his thigh. "Brighton's not that far away, but I thought it might be fun to see something of the countryside as well. Would you like that?"

"I don't know," Miranda replied starkly, amazed they were still alive. "Will we be going this fast?"

"Maybe." Alec's lips curved in a wry smile. "Remind me never to take you to Germany. If this is how you react to London traffic, I shudder to think how you'd respond to the *Autobahn.*"

Miranda did not know what an Autobahn might be, but she did know when she was being made sport of. She opened her eyes and shot him a resentful glare. "And I should like to see how you would respond to some of the things I might be able to show you, were our situations reversed," she informed him in a tart tone. "You should not be so smug then, I promise you."

Her show of spirit delighted Alec, and he gave her hand a playful squeeze. "I'm sure you're right," he said, chuckling softly. "Now settle back and enjoy the ride, I give you my word you'll come to no harm."

To Miranda's amazement his patronizing words calmed her, and other than jumping a few times when another vehicle appeared to be rushing at them head-on, she managed to survive the ride to Curzon Street without making a complete cake of herself. She waited on the steps while Alec paid the driver, her gaze growing solemn as she noted the bars protecting the door and windows.

"I know it looks ugly," Alec's voice was subdued as he joined her, "but it need only be for a short while. Once Talbot's been taken out, we can take them down again."

"I realize that," Miranda said softly, feeling an inexplicable sadness creeping over her. "I was only thinking how little things have changed. Barred windows weren't unknown even in my time, and it is lowering to think that a society with the ability to put men on the moon should still be forced to rely on such crude methods to ensure their safety."

There seemed to be no answer to that and Alec unlocked the gated door, lecturing her as to its proper use as he did so. Once inside he showed her the panel bolted to the wall, punching in a series of numbers while an unseen bell sounded a warning. "Mind you always do this whenever you come back in," he commanded, demonstrating the sequence again. "If you don't, the alarm will be activated, and this place will be swarming with armed officers within minutes, and they won't be coming for tea."

He had her repeat the process several times before he was satisfied she could do it alone, and by the time they were done, Miranda's earlier melancholy had been replaced by irritation.

"I am not a complete idiot, you know," she said, sending him a scowl as she deactivated the beeping alarm.

"I didn't say you were," Alec replied, shrugging off his jacket and hanging it in the hall closet. He wore a leather brace under one arm, and when he turned to face her, he saw her studying him with wide eyes. He watched her for several seconds before speaking.

"If it frightens you, I can take it off," he said quietly, gesturing at the gun strapped to his side. "But I would prefer leaving it on, just in case. If something happens while we're inside, I may not have time to go searching for a weapon."

Miranda swallowed uncomfortably at his frank admission of the danger he was facing. "I'm not frightened," she denied. "Stephen often carried a pistol when we went out late at night. Footpads were everywhere, and other than the Charlies and the Bow Street Runners, there was no protection to speak of."

Alec eyed her for a long moment as a sudden thought occurred to him. "Do you know how to shoot?" he asked.

She started to shake her head and then hesitated. "I—I was shown once," she said, recalling a summer's afternoon long ago when one of her swains had let her hold his duelling pistol, "but I have never fired one." She eyed the black, square handle warily. "Will I need to learn?"

"It might be best," Alec said, refusing to think how his superiors would scream if they learned he'd armed a civilian. "In the event I'm killed, it may be up to you to save yourself. This," he patted the gun, "will at least give you a fighting chance at survival."

Miranda turned away, but not before he saw the tears in her eyes. He grabbed her by the shoulders, his fingers digging into her flesh as he whirled her around to face him.

"Blast it, Miranda, I'm not trying to frighten you!" he exclaimed, giving her a rough shake. "I'm trying to be realistic! I'm good; I'm vain enough to say I'm damned good, but I'm not immortal. I can be killed, and if I am, I don't want you placed at risk because of it!"

"I understand that!" Miranda's eyes sparkled with tears as she stared up into his face. "And I'm not frightened. It's just that I couldn't bear it if you were to die! I've already lost Stephen," she added brokenly, remembering her shock and pain when she'd seen the date of his death set down so matter-of-factly. "I don't want to lose you as well."

Alec's hands dropped to his sides at her stark admission. He took a stumbling step back, his head whirling as he gazed down at her. "How do you think I feel?" he asked in a guttural voice, the emotions tearing at him making him shake. "I don't want to care about you, damn it, but I do. And if something were to happen to you, and it was my fault, I—" he shook his head, unable to continue. "I couldn't take it," he said at last, his eyes full of hell as he gazed at her. "Not after Jane."

Tears blurred Miranda's vision as she reached up a shaking hand and laid it on his cheek. "I know," she said softly, her heart aching with the need to comfort. "I didn't wish to care for you either, but I could not seem to help myself. You've a certain rough charm about you, you know," she added teasingly, feeling greatly daring as she gave his cheek a playful pat.

Alec studied her, the anger and pain he'd been feeling replaced by an acute awareness of Miranda's beauty. His gaze fastened on her mouth, his body hardening as he remembered how incredibly sweet she had tasted. The erotic response stunned him, and he took a hasty step backward taking care to keep his face from reflecting the wayward direction of his thoughts.

"Come upstairs," he said, keeping his voice light as he offered her his hand. "I want to show you what I've done."

Miranda accepted his hand quietly, wondering if she'd gone mad. For a brief moment when he had been staring at her mouth, she had been certain he was going to kiss her again, and what bothered her most was that she could not say whether she was grateful he had controlled himself, or annoyed. That was what came from riding in those dreadful automobiles, she decided as she followed him up the narrow stairs. 'Twas obvious the wretched things had a most unfortunate effect upon the senses!

Up in the hallway she dutifully admired his patch work, kneeling as she brushed a wistful finger over the plaster. "I wish we might have learned more about the room," she said, sighing at the thought of all that mysterious power beyond the wall. "It seems a shame to hide it away like this."

Alec leaned a broad shoulder against the wall, his eyes never leaving her face. "Having second thoughts?" he asked, trying not to think what he would do if she said yes.

"No," she said, but he noted that she hesitated first. "It is just that I have been thinking, and it occurs to me that if the power is not a naturally occurring phenomenon, then it was created.

And if it was created, it ought to be possible to control it. Do you not agree?" She shot him a curious look.

Alec remembered the eerie glow that had filled the room, and shook his head. "Not me," he said firmly. "Our generation's opened enough Pandora's boxes as it is, and I'm not about to take the chance that whatever's in there might get out. We're best off letting it alone; believe me."

Miranda said nothing, but privately she could not help but wonder if Alec had been hasty in his actions. She remembered what she had learned of Stephen's death, and the feeling it had to do with her disappearance would not let her be. Was she responsible? she wondered. And if she was, what should she do about it? There seemed no way she would ever know for certain.

To Alec's relief Miranda's fear of cars eased once they left London traffic behind them. As they had all day before them and no real plans, he decided to take the longer route through Tunbridge Wells, and the expression on Miranda's face as they drove through the small town made him glad he had made the effort.

"Oh Alec," she exclaimed, eyes misting as they walked along the cobblestoned streets leading to the Pantiles. "It is almost as I remember it!"

"You've been here before, then?" he asked, feeling slightly miffed at the thought.

"My step-papa took us here when mother first took ill," she said, pausing to gaze in a bowed window. "It was closer to London than Bath, and far cheaper. Elias was always very frugal with Mama's money, except when it came to his own comforts, of course," she added, her lips twisting at the bitter memory.

They took tea at one of the many small shops lining the colonnaded walkway before walking back to the carpark, and to his relief she soon regained her earlier high spirits. They continued their leisurely drive through the Kent countryside, stopping whenever the whim took them, and by the time they reached Brighton, they were both relaxed and laughing.

"My good heavens, what is that?" Miranda demanded, pointing an accusatory finger at a building that was topped with an astonishing number of onion-shaped domes. "It is quite the most hideous-looking thing I have ever seen!"

Alec shot the building a teasing grin as they drove past. "That, dear countess, is your beloved prince's famous pavilion."

Miranda's jaw dropped in horrified astonishment. *"That* is what he will build as his great pleasure dome?" she exclaimed, turning her head to keep the structure in sight. "Good lord, the Whigs are right, the man is completely mad!"

"Wait until you see the inside," Alec was chuckling as he wheeled his car into a parking spot near the pier. "It looks like a cross between a very gaudy Chinese restaurant and an upper-class brothel. Our class visited it when I was in grammar school, and I remember getting my head whacked for laughing at a national treasure."

"It served you right," Miranda informed him with a prim sniff, and then frowned. "And how would you know what a brothel looks like?" she asked, bending a suspicious frown on him.

"I worked vice one term," he replied with an indifferent shrug, although he was secretly amused by her show of jealousy. "All in the line of duty, you know."

She gave another sniff, her nose held high as he draped his arm over her shoulder. Although the sun was shining, a strong breeze was blowing off the ocean, and Miranda was grateful she'd listened to Alec's admonishments and brought a sweater with her. Not that she intended confessing as much, of course. The man already held entirely too high an opinion of himself to suit her, and she was not about to add to his air of consequence by admitting he was right . . . again.

They queued up for the security check, and when it was their turn, Alec showed the portly man sitting behind the desk his badge. "I'm under special orders," he said, his voice low-pitched so as not to be overheard, "and I'm armed."

"I see." The man's pale blue eyes widened as he studied Alec in open curiosity. "No problem, then, Inspector," and he waved them through.

The inside of the pavilion was every bit as horrid as the outside, and Miranda was vocal in her disapproval of the decorative scheme. "It is quite the ugliest thing I have ever imagined," she said, shaking her head at the garish pink and blue wallpaper lining the wide halls. "I know his Royal Highness was renowned for his bad taste, but this surpasses even his assaults on culture at Carlton House!"

Alec grinned at her waspish tones. "I don't know," he drawled, cocking his head to one side as he studied the offending wallpaper. "I rather like it myself. How do you think it would look in the front parlor?"

"About as ghastly as it looks here," she retorted, shuddering at the thought. "And if you would dare hang such a monstrosity in your home, sir, then you are a braver man than I thought."

After leaving the pavilion they wandered through the twisting, narrow streets surrounding the area. There was a variety of shops and restaurants to be found, and when they came to a shop advertising history books, Miranda insisted they stop. She had the names of the books she was seeking tucked in her purse, and she was hoping to find a copy here.

The clerk didn't recognize either title, but he did have a collection of memoirs written by a Major Fitzburgh, and he assured her it was filled with gossip of the period. She glanced through it carefully, and was about to put it back on the shelf when a familiar name leapt off the page. The entry was dated 28 August 1833.

*"Read in the papers the other day that old Clutch-fist Elias Proctor has paid the debt of nature at long last. Nasty fellow. Always thought he had more to do with his stepdaughter's demise than he let on. Poor Harrington; I think of him still."*

Alec heard her gasp and hurried back to join her. "What is it?" he asked, glancing over her shoulder.

She indicated the passage with a trembling finger. "Demise, that means to die, doesn't it?" she asked, staring down at the yellowing page in confusion. "Does this mean I would have died if I stayed, or was it assumed I died when I disappeared?"

Alec took the book from her. "I don't know," he admitted, scanning ahead a few pages. "I can't find anything else. Do you want the book?"

"Please," she said, determined to read the whole thing from cover to cover the moment they got back to London. This was the first solid clue she had found, and she was anxious to discover all that she could.

They returned to the car in silence. It was late afternoon, and Alec was toying with the idea of driving along the ocean a bit before heading north. He unlocked the car door for Miranda, helping her inside before walking around to his own side. He was about to insert the key into the door, when he saw a piece of paper taped across the keyhole. The paper had one word scrawled across it.

*Boom.*

# Twelve

For a moment Alec was frozen with horror, then he was tearing around the car, yelling at Miranda, and tugging at the door. "Get out of there!" he shouted, shaking the handle and pounding the window with his fist. "God damn it, get out of there *now!*"

She unlocked the door, her expression incredulous as she stared up at him. "Alec? What—"

He bent down, unsnapping her seat belt and gathering her up in his arms. Her arms tightened around his neck instinctively as he turned, running for the low stone wall that separated the car park from the street. A small group of people were gaping at him, and Alec shouted out a warning to them as he dashed past.

"Car bomb! Get down!"

They didn't wait for an explanation, but immediately dove for cover. Miranda saw a man throw himself protectively over a small child seconds before Alec's full weight landed on her back, pressing her face-down into the gravel. Less than a moment later, a powerful explosion ripped the air, sending a shower of flaming debris down on the screaming people. She felt Alec flinch and heard his sharp gasp of pain, but when she tried to move, he pressed her down even harder.

"Don't move," he warned harshly. "There could be a second bomb." He raised his voice, shouting the same message to the others, and then he tucked her more securely beneath his body.

They waited for what seemed an eternity, and just as she was certain she would go mad, she felt him levering himself off of her. She cautiously turned her head, and the first thing she saw was the deadly-looking pistol clutched in his fist. She was still absorbing the sight when he carefully turned her over.

"Are you hurt?" he asked, his gaze searing a path over her face as he stared down at her.

"I . . ." She couldn't seem to think. Was she hurt? She took quick stock of her condition. "N-no," she stammered, gazing up at his grim face. "What about you?"

He didn't answer, but carefully set her to one side. "Stay here," he ordered, and then, taking care to stay low, he crawled over to the group of people who had been caught with them. "Scotland Yard!" she heard him call out. "Is anyone hurt?"

She could hear moans and cries, and unable to bear the suspense anymore, she cautiously raised her head and peered over the edge of the wall. The small car was completely engulfed in flames, and as she watched another small explosion sent a ball of fire shooting skyward. She winced and ducked her head, her body shaking as reaction began setting in. They could have died, she thought, trembling as the thought kept echoing in her mind. They could have died.

When the shaking subsided enough to be controlled, she thought about the others. Already she could hear the wail of approaching sirens, and the sound of them filled the air. Disregarding Alec's clipped orders, she crawled over to where he was huddled over a man who was bleeding from a deep gash in his back. He spared her a quick glare before turning his attention back to the groaning man.

"I thought I told you to stay over there," he said, pressing a shirt to the man's back. "You shouldn't be seeing this."

Miranda gazed around at the bleeding, dazed people lying on the gravel. "No one should be seeing this," she replied quietly, and then made her way to where a sobbing woman was cradling a limp child in her arms.

The next several minutes became a confusing whirl as an army of yellow-coated medics descended on them. Time lost any sense of meaning, and she watched the unfolding events as if from a great distance. She saw one medic take the child, while another dealt with the mother. She could hear sounds, but didn't know what they were, heard voices, but the words made no sense. It was only when she saw a medic turning his attention to Alec that the mists parted, and she darted forward with a sharp cry.

"It's no use your swearing at us, Officer," she heard the medic telling Alec in a stern voice, "you're going to hospital, and that's that."

"Alec!" She knocked the medic to one side, and clasped shaking hands to Alec's face. "Oh God, are you hurt?"

Alec saw the panic in her green eyes and silently condemned the hovering medic to hell. He brushed a tangle of blond hair back from her face, and dredged up a shaky smile. "I'm fine, sweetheart," he said, not aware of using the endearment. "It's just a precaution; that's all."

"It's just a possible fractured rib; that's all," the medic corrected, gently easing Miranda to one side. "And you'll need to have those burns tended as well."

"Burns!" Miranda scrambled around until she could see Alec's back. The thick leather jacket had melted around a gash, and she could see where his white sweater had burned away to show a patch of angry red skin. She bit her lip, recalling the way he'd thrown himself over her, and a rage greater than anything she had ever felt welled up inside of her.

"It was that Talbot, wasn't it?" she demanded, tears burning her eyes as she surged to her feet. "He did this to you!"

Alec flicked the medic a worried look; his thoughts turning toward the more prosaic matter of security. "Not now, Miranda," he cautioned with a shake of his head. "We'll talk about this late— Ow!" He broke off, a vicious curse peeling from his lips as he sent the medic a murderous scowl over his shoulder "What the bloody hell are you doing?"

"Preparing you for transfer," the medic said calmly, keeping the plaster pressed to the burn on Alec's back. "Now stop your complaining. Here's the litter."

Alec loudly protested being strapped face down on the litter, but his rescuers paid him no mind. They simply wheeled him away, and the last glimpse Miranda had of him was the outraged expression on his face as they slammed the doors of the ambulance closed. She watched it drive off, feeling a bubble of hysterical laughter rising in her throat. If only Cara had been here to see this, she thought, a tremor making her hands shake as she brushed back the hair from her face. Alec's little sister would probably have crowed with laughter to see her pompous brother wheeled off like a cranky baby in its pram.

"You too, miss," the medic was standing beside her, eyeing her with professional concern. "You don't appear to be hurt, but the doctors will need to check you over as well. Off you go now," and he turned her over to the others.

Miranda spent the next several hours being poked and prodded, and had matters not been so serious, she would have found the dazzling array of beeping machines to be quite fascinating. She answered the doctor's questions until she thought she would scream, and the moment they were finished with her, she was turned over to the police, where she began answering even more pointed questions.

No, she did not know how Inspector Bramwell knew the car was wired. No, she hadn't seen anyone following them on their drive from London. No, she had no identification; her purse had been in the car when it had exploded. This last was a bit of divine inspiration on her part, and she was congratulating herself on her cleverness, when one of the men asked her for her date of birth. Without thinking, she gave it to him.

"I beg your pardon?" He was blinking at her in astonishment.

"What?" She had already lost the thread of conversation, her thoughts centered on Alec. They would tell her only that he was in X-ray . . . whatever that was, and that he was doing as well as could be expected. She could see him soon, they assured her.

"Your date of birth," the officer repeated, gray eyes suspicious as they studied her face. "I asked you your date of birth, and you said April 11, 1787."

"Oh." She placed a hand to her head and tried to think. Mathematics had never been her strong suit, and at the moment adding and subtracting were beyond her meager abilities. "I'm twenty-four," she said at last, closing her eyes with an indifferent sigh. "Figure it out for yourself."

"1971," one of the other officers said, and she could hear the reprimand in his voice. "Ease off, Hooks. The doctor says she has a mild concussion."

The man called Hooks asked her several more questions, and Miranda was scarcely aware of what she said. She decided her answers must have made sense, because Hooks seemed satisfied with her responses. Finally they were closing their notebooks and nodding amongst themselves, apparently pleased with whatever she had told them. Now it was her turn to ask a few questions.

"How are the others?" she asked, fixing the oldest man with a stern look. "I saw a child was hurt. Will he be all right?"

The officer was happy to report that other than a mild concussion and a few cuts, the child was fine, and he was expected to be released tomorrow morning. Four other people including Alec had been injured seriously enough to require hospitalization, but thankfully none of the injuries were life-threatening. He was telling her about the injured man Alec had been tending, when a man with a black mask over his face walked in. The officers snapped to wary attention, but relaxed when the man spoke.

"SAS," he said coldly, but in a voice that brooked no opposition. "Unless you men have class-five security clearance, you are to leave."

The officers left, and Miranda noted they gave the man a wide berth, as if skirting something potentially dangerous. She waited until the others had gone before addressing the mask-clad man; her eyebrows arched in cool amusement.

"I really must learn more of this SAS," she said, refusing to let the stranger intimidate her as he had the others. "It must be an interesting organization to have such an effect on people."

Brilliant blue eyes stared at her from beneath the black wool.

"You don't know what the SAS is?" he asked, sounding even more suspicious than had Hooks when she'd given her birthdate.

"I know that Alec was a member," she replied, meeting his cool glare with equanimity. "And I know it has made him almost as top-lofty as you appear to be. What else do I need to know?"

Those blue eyes narrowed, and Miranda thought she saw an amused sparkle in them before the man spoke. "I'm Lieutenant Major Keller," he said, and she heard a decided note of laughter in his husky voice. "I was Bramwell's unit officer, and I'll be handling the inquiry. How are you feeling?"

Miranda considered his question before deciding to reply honestly. "Tired," she admitted, rolling her shoulders, "my head hurts, and I'm worried to death over Alec. No one will tell me anything other than he is 'as well as can be expected.' "

Now there was no mistaking the amusement in the sapphire eyes. "He's fine," he assured her gently. "He has a laceration on his back that required five stitches, first- and second-degree burns on his left shoulder, and a hairline fracture of his fifth posterior rib."

She paled at the litany of injuries. "You call that fine?" she asked in a weak voice.

"For a member of the SAS, it barely warrants a mention," Keller said, with the same casual arrogance she'd often heard in Alec's voice. "He must be getting slow, or he'd never have been hit. I'll have to give him bloody hell about it later."

Miranda blinked back tears, remembering how Alec had flinched when the debris had struck him. "He was trying to protect me," she said, her stomach twisting with an icy sickness. "If he hadn't done that, he would never have been hurt."

Keller remained silent a long moment. "I have to ask this," he said carefully, "both as Alec's friend and as an investigating officer. What is your connection to him?"

Lord, how to answer *that,* Miranda thought, too heartsick to dissemble. "Are you a police officer? Like Alec?" she asked at last, trying to find the words to explain herself to him. She'd hoped that he would say yes, as both Cara and Alec were officers, and they'd accepted her easily enough.

He shook his head. "I'm military, an Army officer, but we work with civilian authorities on cases involving terrorism," he said. "But you still haven't answered my question. Who are you precisely? And what have you to do with Alec?"

"What she has to do with me, you coldhearted bastard, is none of your damned business," Alec's voice sounded from the doorway, and Miranda turned to see him leaning against the doorjamb, his face pale with weariness and pain.

She hopped off the examining table and dashed to his side. "Are you hurt?" she demanded, wanting more than anything to throw herself against him, but too afraid she would cause him further pain if she did.

He must have read her thoughts, because he reached out his good arm and pulled her roughly against him. He bent his head and pressed a quick kiss on her forehead, before raising his eyes to meet Keller's implacable gaze.

"Will you take off that damned balaclava?" he demanded irritably. "You look like a bloody mugger."

Keller hesitated, then peeled off the black mask, revealing a face that was almost savagely handsome. "You never know who might be watching," he said coolly, focusing his attention on Alec. "Now, want to tell me what's going on?"

"What's going on is I have some maniac on my tail, and he just blew up my frigging car!" Alec snapped, furious that the authorities had seen fit to assign Rye to the case. He might have been able to finesse another officer, even an SAS man, but Ryerson Keller was as tough and tenacious as they came, and he could be like a bull dog, if he even suspected someone was being less than truthful with him.

"I knew that less than a minute after the bomb had detonated." Rye's voice was as cutting as the look he gave Alec. "Tell me what I don't know." He nodded at Miranda. "Tell me about her."

Alec hesitated, wishing there was some way he could spare Miranda; unfortunately he couldn't think of a damned thing. It was either tell Rye the truth and risk being locked in a neuro-logical unit for the next fortnight, or come up with some plausible explanation and hope like hell he bought it. It took him less than a moment to reach his decision.

"Who do you think she is?" he sneered, bending his head to press another kiss against Miranda's soft lips. "I'm a man, not a machine, and I'm entitled to some fun. Miranda is my live-in."

Keller's blue eyes narrowed intently as he studied Miranda's face. "You're living with Bramwell?" he asked in a soft voice.

Miranda's cheeks blushed a fiery red, but she resolutely met the other man's gaze. "Yes, I am," she said, feeling like the boldest strumpet in Covent Garden.

"Sleeping with him?"

The blunt question made her gasp, but before she could reply, Alec brought up his injured arm, enveloping her in a protective embrace. "Back off, Rye," he warned, his voice low and furious as he watched Keller. "I know you're just doing your job, but I won't warn you again. Leave her alone."

Rye didn't so much as blink. "You know better than that," he said, his tone every bit as hard as Alec's. "I want answers, and I mean to have them. Either here or at company headquarters; the decision is yours."

Alec glared at him for several seconds before turning to Miranda. "It's your choice," he said, searching her expression intently. "Do we tell him?"

Although she shuddered at the very thought of confessing all to the hard-faced stranger, Miranda knew it was her only option. She could feel the violent tension vibrating in Alec, and knew that if Keller persisted with his insulting questions, Alec would explode. The two might be friends, but she doubted that would matter in the end. And although she knew better than to admit it, she was deathly afraid Alec would be hurt. That was enough to decide her, and she gave a quick nod. He bestowed a reassuring hug on her and turned to Keller.

"Miranda's run away from her husband," he said coolly, ignoring her startled jerk. "He's very rich and very powerful, and she can't go back to him. Does that satisfy you?"

Keller absorbed the explanation in silence. "What is your husband's name?" he asked, addressing his question to Miranda.

"Stephen Hallforth," she answered, uncertain how much Alec wanted her to tell him. For the moment she was content to follow his lead, trusting him to keep her safe.

Keller shrugged. "Never heard of him."

"It's unlikely you should have done," Alec replied, picking each word with the care he usually devoted to defusing bombs. "He's not the type to draw the attention of the authorities, but he's dangerous nonetheless. If Miranda goes back to him, she'll die. It's that simple."

Rye's expression softened at the stark words, and he turned to Miranda. "Do you want to go back?" he asked gently.

Miranda thought about how impossible that now was, and she did not have to fake the tears that were burning her eyes. "I can't," she whispered brokenly, burying her face against Alec's chest. "I can't."

There was a long silence, and then Rye spoke to Alec. "What were you intending to do with her?" he asked, his voice tight with emotion. "We can lose her now so there's no official record of her having been interviewed, but what about later? She'll need ID, if she's to have anything approaching a normal life."

Alec relaxed as he realized Rye had accepted his story. He was also grateful his friend was approaching the matter with his usual cool logic, knowing it meant he could rely on both his discretion and his assistance. "I was hoping to contact some friends in Witness Relocation," he said, thinking of the tentative overtures he'd already made. "I know they usually don't handle this sort of thing, but they can bloody well try. I've pulled those buggers out of plenty of tight spots in the past, and the way I see it, they owe me."

"They owe me, too," Rye said, looking stern. "And the first chance I get, I'll start pulling in favors. Meanwhile, what about this business today? Was it your friend Talbot, do you think? Or is it one of your other admirers? You're such a popular lad."

Alec knew Rye was referring to their years in the SAS, when they had prices put on their heads by both the IRA and members of a pro-Palestinian group whose headquarters the SAS had destroyed in a lightning raid. "Talbot, I'm thinking," he answered slowly, forcing himself to view the attack in purely professional terms. "I know car bombs aren't the Coalition's usual method of assassination, but Talbot's gone freelance, so the old rules no longer apply where he's concerned."

Rye nodded in agreement. "Was it a genuine assassination attempt? Or was it just a head fu—"

"Rye!" Alec interrupted with an outraged scowl.

"Sorry." Rye sent Miranda a sheepish smile before continuing. "A head game?" he concluded diplomatically. "If that note hadn't been taped to your door, they'd be scraping what was left of you off the sand by now."

Miranda listened in mounting indignation as they debated the matter. She didn't know what outraged her more, that they could be so analytical about the vicious bombing, or that they seemed to have forgotten that both she and Alec had almost died. When they began talking about detonation points and electronic fields, she decided she'd had quite enough.

"I am sure the mother of that little boy will be vastly reassured to know the triggering device was set on microwave relay," she said waspishly, hands on her hips as she glared at both men. "But in the meanwhile, do you think we might get back to London? Poor Cara may have heard what happened, and she is certain to be frantic.

"I've already spoken to Cara," Alec replied, puzzled by her outburst. "She'll be dropping around tomorrow morning."

Miranda bit back a frustrated shriek. It never failed to amaze her how men who counted themselves as so intelligent could be so hopelessly thickheaded when it came to the simplest aspects of life. She tried again, her teeth clenched together to keep her from shrieking like a Billingsgate fishwife.

"I want to go home," she said, her voice tight. "Now."

The two men exchanged knowing looks that pushed her control to the breaking point. "I'll contact you tomorrow," Rye said to Alec, digging in to his pocket for a set of keys and chucking them to Alec. "Here, it's the Regimental car, so try not to get it blown up. You know how petty General Services can be."

Alec pocketed the keys deftly. "Do you mean I'm being allowed to drive myself?" he asked, more than a little surprised. It was SOP for a target to be driven everywhere, once a definite attempt had been made.

"I convinced them you had the—" Keller's eyes flicked in Miranda's direction, "stomach to drive back on your own. Just try not to notice the two cars shagging you. They like to think they're being discreet."

Alec merely grunted, accepting the fact that until Talbot had been neutralized, he'd have to become accustomed to having a tail. "What about Miranda?" he said, frowning as he realized his house would now be under constant watch. He supposed if worse came to worst, he could sneak her into Cara's flat, but at the moment he wanted her where he could keep an eye on her.

"I can control things at this end," Rye replied, looking thoughtful. "That won't stop your lads from making inquiries, mind, but I'm sure you'll be able to keep them in line."

Alec wondered how the devil he was supposed to do that, when he would be doing his best to keep from being relieved of duty by his edgy supervisor. At the very least he'd be reassigned to other cases, and he told himself he wouldn't fight it. He'd play along like a dutiful little boy, he decided, and the moment their backs were turned, he'd solve the case on his own. This was personal now, and he wasn't about to step aside for anyone.

They were almost at the door, when Alec spied the balaclava lying on a treatment tray. Since SAS soldiers engaged in counter-terrorism relied on anonymity to protect their lives, he snatched up the black cap and turned to Rye.

"You're forgetting your makeup, darling," he drawled, grin-

ning as he tossed the mask to Rye. "I wouldn't want you to go
out in public without your face on."

Stephen was waiting for her. Miranda whimpered softly, turning restlessly on her bed as the vague images in her dream slowly
took shape. It was their wedding night, and he was waiting in
his room, a smile of welcome on his lips as he held out his hand
to her. She drew nearer to him, heart pounding as she realized
she didn't want to go to him. He was her husband, yes, but he
wasn't the man she wanted, the man she really loved.

As if he was sensing her thoughts, the smile vanished from
Stephen's face, and the hand held out to hers was now imperious
in its command. She wanted to run, but she seemed helplessly
compelled to go forward, drawn toward her husband and the
marriage bed. As she neared the bed, Stephen began to change,
his handsome countenance melting hideously away until he re-
sembled a rotting corpse. His skeletal fingers were reaching for
her, clawing at her skin as he drew her nearer . . . nearer . . .

"Miranda, for God's sake, wake up!" Alec was shaking her,
his deep voice urgent as he called to her. "Wake up, damn it!"

"Alec!" Miranda's eyes flew open, and when she saw him
bending over her, she threw herself in his arms. "Oh God," she
sobbed, shaking with fear as she clung to his reassuring warmth.
"Oh God, oh God, oh God!"

Alec held her trembling body against his, trying to still his
wildly racing heart as he comforted her. "Shhh," he soothed,
running his hand through her tangled hair. "It's all right, darling.
Shhh . . ."

"It seemed so real!" Miranda cried, the horrifying details of
the nightmare making her shake. "But it was only a dream, thank
God, it was only a dream!"

Alec, who had his own experiences with screaming nightmares, understood precisely. Except in his case, he thought
grimly, he'd awakened to find the terrifying dream was a living
nightmare. The memory made him flinch, and he drew Miranda

closer, recalling how his heart had almost stopped at the sounds of her screams.

He'd been dozing fitfully, his body tense and battle-ready, when Miranda's screams had him leaping out of bed, the pistol from the bedside stand in his fist even as he was bursting through the door. The sight of Miranda twisting in her bedsheets as she fought off her nightmare had assured him she was in no physical danger, and he'd set the pistol on her table even as he was reaching for her.

"It was Stephen," Miranda said, knowing she was babbling, but needing to talk. "He was in his room, waiting for me, and I didn't want to go to him. Then he was a corpse, and—" she turned her head, pressing her face into his neck and inhaling the comforting scent of his cologne. "Just hold me, please."

Alec was more than happy to comply, even though holding her was putting an uncomfortable strain on his stitches. He'd have willingly endured torture, if it meant he could keep holding her like this. In the end, however, the pain became a little too persistent, and he shifted uncomfortably. Miranda felt his arms loosening, and tightened her hold.

"Don't leave!"

"I'm not," he assured her, dropping a gentle kiss on the top of her head as he turned carefully on his side, still holding her in his arms. "I'm just getting comfortable. My shoulder is giving me fits."

"Your shoulder!" she cried, her nightmare forgotten as she gazed down at him. "How are you feeling?" she demanded, tear-drenched eyes studying his face. "Are you in pain?"

Alec thought about that portion of his anatomy that was now in considerable pain, and becoming even more painful as his body responded mindlessly to her nearness. He shifted again, praying she was too much of an innocent to notice. "I'm fine," he managed, albeit through clenched teeth. "I'm just a bit . . . uh . . . stiff. I'll be all right by tomorrow."

Miranda shook her head, fresh tears falling as a new horror banished the last remnants of her nightmare. "You could have been killed," she said, her hands trembling as she cupped his face in her palms. "Don't take such chances, Alec," she implored, her fingers tracing lightly over his face as if she was committing it to memory. "Please. I should die if anything happened to you! I care about you so much!"

Alec felt his heartbeat accelerate at her impassioned words. "It's because of the explosion," he said slowly, his mind and body rioting as he realized how badly he wanted the desire he could feel vibrating from her to be real. "You're just saying that because we almost died this afternoon. It's a normal response; but it will pass."

Miranda stared down into his turbulent eyes, knowing the time for evasions and half-truths had passed. The knowledge that she could have lost him in less time than it takes to blink an eye banished her last, lingering doubts; and an odd peace stole over her as she reached a decision in her head that her heart had already reached days ago.

"It wasn't the bomb," she said quietly, her breath feathering over his lips as she pressed a soft kiss to his mouth. "And this feeling isn't going to pass, either."

"How—how do you know?" Alec demanded, sweat beading his brow as he fought the urge to take what she was so sweetly offering.

"Because I want you," she said simply, knowing a stronger declaration would have sent him scrambling for the door. "Why do you think I wept that night you kissed me?" she continued, brushing more kisses across his jaw. "It wasn't because I found your touch distasteful, it was because I liked it. And because I wanted you to go on touching me and never stop."

Alec needed no other encouragement. Even if it meant going straight to hell the moment it was over, he was going to make love to her. He closed his arms around her, pulling her down to him as his mouth took hers in a kiss of blazing passion.

# Thirteen

The touch of Alec's lips on hers sent pleasure shafting through Miranda, and she surrendered to the sweet sensations with a sigh. The strictures she'd been raised to believe in her entire life told her she was behaving like the veriest hussy, but she couldn't bring herself to care. She loved Alec, and nothing mattered but sharing that love with him. Tomorrow would be time enough for recriminations, she thought, burying her hands in his thick, soft hair. Tonight was only for them.

"Miranda, you are so sweet," he groaned, pressing frantic kisses down the line of her throat. "I've wanted to touch you like this since the moment I first saw you!"

The impassioned declaration thrilled her almost as much as the hot brush of his mouth over her sensitized flesh. She arched her neck, granting him even further access to her shoulders and the gentle slope of her breasts.

"When I first saw you lying on the floor, I thought I'd lost what was left of my mind," Alec said, his fingers shaking as he caressed her breasts through the soft silk of her nightgown. "You were so beautiful, I was certain you couldn't be real."

Miranda's lashes fluttered at the bold caress. "And I thought you were a g-gypsy," she stammered, her heartbeat quickening at his practiced touch. Stephen had never ventured beyond a few warm kisses, and now she was fiercely glad he hadn't cared enough about her to press for more. It seemed somehow right that Alec should be the first to show her passion.

She heard Alec give a soft chuckle as he playfully nipped her shoulder. "You threatened to have me arrested," he said, then stole her breath with an incredibly brazen caress. His hands were warm and sure as they gently cupped her aching breasts, his thumbs brushing over the crests until she was lost in a whirlwind of burning sensation.

He continued kissing and caressing her, gently stripping her nightgown from her without her being aware of it. Her hands were equally busy, learning the hair-dusted planes of his muscular chest with shy sensuality, and every time he groaned or sighed, she felt her passion accelerating. None of her girlish daydreaming prepared her for the hot reality of lovemaking, and she lost herself in its heady power.

Alec felt her surrender, and he took primitive satisfaction in knowing that Miranda wanted him every bit as much as he wanted her. Her breasts swelled in his hands as he stroked them ardently, unable to get enough of the feel of her. When he felt her nipples bead in response, he bent his head and took one in his mouth, teasing it with his tongue until she was writhing beneath him. She arched against him, pressing her feminine softness against his erection until he though he would go mad.

"Miranda!" His voice was urgent as he turned his head to press a kiss against her other breast. "You make my head swim!"

They kissed and stroked each other until Alec's body shook with the agonizing need for completion. But even as he felt the feathering approach of climax, he was drawing back, determined to please her completely before seeking his own release. Moving down her body, he trailed a line of kisses along her quivering flesh until his mouth was poised over her hidden depths. When his tongue flicked over her he felt her shatter, her hands clutching his hair as she gave a keening cry of delight.

He waited until her wild trembling had stopped, and then he gently slid a finger inside her, seeking the proof of virginity he was certain he would find. When he did, he raised his head and kissed her trembling mouth.

"I'll try to be gentle," he promised, taking her limp hand and lowering it to his hardness. "If you don't want this to go on, tell me now. In a few minutes, I may not be able to stop."

That he should show such control dazzled Miranda, almost as much as the passion he had just shown her. Knowing he cared more for her than for his own pleasures removed the last of her fears, and she smiled up at him with loving confidence.

"Don't stop," she implored, watching his eyes flare with desire as she closed her fingers around him. "Don't ever stop."

Alec lowered his head, his tongue thrusting demandingly into her mouth as he lifted her until her back was cradled by the mound of pillows. When she was positioned to his satisfaction, he kissed and teased her into a second climax, waiting until she was sobbing with passion before moving purposefully over her.

"Now, Miranda," he said, his voice tight as he settled into the cradle of her hips. "I'm going to take you now."

She was hot and sweet as he thrust into her, and he groaned in exquisite delight. He felt her innocence give way, and even as a red mist was coming over his eyes, he was watching her face for the slightest sign of discomfort. When there was none, he began moving, cautiously at first, and then deeper and faster, until they were both crying out from the wild glory of it.

He wanted it to last forever, but his body had been too long denied, and his climax slammed into him without warning. He cried out harshly, his body shuddering as satisfaction sweeter than anything he had ever known washed over him. When it was done, he collapsed on top of Miranda, too spent to move.

Miranda held him tightly, her quivering body absorbing the tremors that were shaking him. She buried a hand in his thick hair, her mind blank and a dazed smile on her face as she lay in blissful silence. They remained like that for several minutes, and just as she felt sleep stealing over her, Alec raised his head to gaze down at her.

"How are you?" he asked, his eyes darker than she had ever seen them as he studied her face. "I didn't hurt you, did I?"

She shook her head, brushing back the hair that had fallen

across his damp forehead. "No," she said softly, her eyes lambent with passion. "It was wonderful. *You* were wonderful."

To her delight, he actually flushed, ducking his head and averting his eyes like a schoolboy caught in mid-prank. "No, I wasn't," he said grimly, "I was rough. Worse, I was careless."

"Careless?" She was unable to resist the temptation to bury her hands in his thick hair. He really had the most marvelous hair, she thought dreamily, stroking her palms down his neck.

He reached up and caught one of her hands in his, his gaze holding hers as he stared down at her. "Birth control," he said bluntly, kissing her hand before lowering it to the sheets. "I was so far gone, I didn't give a thought to protecting you."

Miranda thought about that for a moment, searching the store of information she'd acquired on the twentieth century for a possible translation. Then she recalled something she'd seen on the television, and sent him a bright smile. "Condoms?"

Alec's eyes widened in amazement. "What do you know about condoms?" he demanded, his brows lowering in a suspicious scowl. "Has Cara been talking to you?"

"Of course not!" She gave his bare chest a playful slap. "I saw it on the television. I know all about safe sex, and AIDS, and unwanted pregnancies, and—"

He clapped his hand lightly over her mouth. "Those damned Conservatives in Parliament are right," he growled, glaring down at her. "TV is leading to the moral decay of our society. I see I shall have to vet the programs you've been watching!"

Miranda's eyes gleamed with laughter as she met his gaze, and he could feel her lips curving in a wicked smile. Unable to resist he bent his head, replacing his hand with his mouth and kissing her until they were both breathless with passion. When he raised his head again, her cheeks were delightfully flushed and her arms were locked around his neck.

Miranda could feel the desire humming through her, and the sensation left her feeling deliciously wanton. "Alec?" she moved her hips against his, her smile blooming when she felt his instant response.

"What?" Alec swallowed visibly.

She raised herself off the bed and brushed her lips over his chest. "Do you think we might be careless again?

"I'm glad you changed rooms," Alec said quietly, as he and Miranda lay in contented exhaustion. "It wouldn't have felt right if we'd made love in the bed I'd shared with Jane."

"I know," Miranda answered, mentally thanking whatever divine providence had prompted her to move into the guest room a few days after her arrival. This room wasn't so large as the other, but it was at least free of ghosts, and in the month she had been in this time, she had done her best to make it her own.

Alec drew a lazy circle on Miranda's bare shoulder with his fingertip, his body sated but his mind in a confusing whirl. Before meeting Jane, he'd been as randy as the next fellow, and although he'd always been careful to protect both himself and his partner, he'd never given one woman much thought while lying with another. But lying with Miranda he couldn't help but remember Jane and all the times they'd shared in bed. To his amazement, rather than the gut-wrenching guilt he'd been expecting, he felt only a vague sadness, a nostalgia for a time that had long since passed. It was a profound revelation.

He lifted his head from the pillows and leaned over Miranda. "Does it bother you, my talking about Jane?" he asked, cupping her chin and raising her face until he could read her eyes.

Miranda understood what asking that question must have cost him, and she knew that only the truth would serve between them. If they were to have any sort of future together, they would have to deal with Jane's memory. "A little," she answered truthfully, her hand stroking his cheek. "But I know you loved her, and I grieve that you lost her so tragically."

Alec remembered the horror, and his eyes grew dark. "It was hell," he said starkly. "I wanted to die, but I didn't have the guts to do anything about it. I thought I'd never get over it, but now . . ." he hesitated, as if uncertain he should continue.

"Now?" she pressed, holding her breath and trying not to hope, for fear of having those hopes dashed.

Alec blew out a long breath, his shoulders relaxing as a final acceptance stole over him. "Now I can say that while I still miss her, and I still grieve, I can think of her in the past and it doesn't hurt."

Miranda blinked back tears, wondering if Alec was aware how much he'd revealed with that quiet confession. For the first time since admitting her love, she began hoping it might some day be returned. All she needed was patience, she told herself, settling comfortably against his body. She had but to bide her time and pray that he had healed enough to love her.

The ringing of the phone shattered the early morning quiet, and Alec cursed roundly as he stumbled down the hall to answer it. "What?" he snarled, tucking the receiver between his shoulder and chin.

"This is Deverham," the security service officer's voice was equally clipped. "I'll expect to see you in my office in an hour." And he hung up before Alec could speak.

Alec glared at the receiver, giving serious thought to chucking it on the floor, before replacing it with another curse. Terrific, he thought sourly, thrusting an impatient hand through his tousled hair. What a perfect way to start the day. It was obvious Deverham was on a tear, and that he was probably in for a proper dressing down.

"Alec?" Miranda was standing in the doorway, the coverlet pressed protectively to her breast. "Is something wrong?"

He turned and glanced at her, taking a moment to appreciate her beauty before walking back to her. He stood in front of her, cupping her face between his hands and bending his head to drop a sizzling kiss on her lips. When he lifted his mouth, she had dropped the coverlet and was clinging to his neck with sweet abandon. He grinned down at her in masculine triumph. "Good morning," he drawled huskily.

"Good morning to you, too," she said, blushing at the sight of his bare body. She had kissed and caressed almost every inch of him last night, but she still found it embarrassing to look at him in the light of day.

Alec saw her embarrassment and was enchanted. He wanted nothing more than to carry her back into the room and make love to her until they were both too weak to move, but unfortunately that would have to wait. He allowed himself one final kiss before taking a determined step back.

"That was work," he said regretfully, brushing a blond curl over her shoulder. "I have to go in right away."

Miranda did her best to swallow her disappointment. "That's all right," she said, keeping her gaze fixed firmly on his bare chest. "I understand you must do your duty."

Her old-fashioned reply and the way she resolutely refused to look at him brought a grin to his face. He wondered if she realized she was standing before him without a stitch on, and then decided he was damned if he would tell her.

"Would you mind putting the coffee on while I hop in the shower?" he asked, turning toward the bathroom.

"Certainly," she agreed and began walking toward the stairs. He waited until she'd started down them before calling out.

"Miranda?"

"Yes?" She glanced over her shoulder at him.

He gave her a grin that was pure devil. "Don't you think it might be a good idea if you dressed first? Wouldn't want to give the postman any ideas, would we?"

Miranda was still burning with annoyance two hours later as she made her way up the steps of the British Library. The rogue! she thought, her fingers clutching her notepad to her chest. How dare he make sport of her? She could still hear his roar of laughter as she'd dashed back into her room, and even slamming the door had not alleviated her indignation. She'd been strongly tempted to remain there and let the arrogant beast see to his own coffee, but in the end she'd decided not to give him the satisfaction of knowing he had overset her.

She'd been chillingly polite at the breakfast table, and he countered by being as charming and diffident as a fortune hunter at Almacks. It was only as he was taking his leave of her that he reverted back to his usual autocratic self, ordering her sternly to remain in the house until he returned. He'd even kissed her before going, much to her fury. Well, she decided with a proud lift of her chin, he would soon learn she was not his to order about as he pleased.

Armed now with the title of the book destroyed in the explosion, she approached the Information Desk with a martial gleam in her eyes. She was fully prepared to do battle, only to discover the unhelpful clerk had been replaced by a middle-aged woman who could not have been kinder. Within less than half an hour, she had a stack of books dealing with the Regency period, and she sat down at one of the wide oak tables to study them.

The next hour passed quickly, as Miranda immersed herself in the world that was once all she knew. It felt odd to read of people she knew from a prospective of almost two hundred years, and she was surprised at how kind history was to those her society had dismissed as fools. All except Prinny, she thought, chuckling over one particularly acerbic description of him; it seemed he fared no better in this time than he had in hers. She was reading a biography of a wonderfully gossipy marchioness she recalled meeting at a hunting party, when she saw her name.

*"Of course, I never believed in that rot about her being murdered on her wedding night. What fustian! Doubtlessly the chit ran off with her lover. She was always TOO nice to my way of thinking, and such creatures are inevitably discovered to have dozens of cicisbeos tucked away. Not unlike the late Lady Jersey, who so ill served our prince's second wife . . ."*

"Of all the nerve, the hateful creature!" Miranda exclaimed indignantly, and then lowered her voice when several pairs of censorious eyes flashed in her direction. She dutifully jotted the notation down, muttering beneath her breath at the slur to her reputation. Mayhap *she* should write a book and tell her story, she thought sourly, flipping the book closed and reaching for another. If some foolish publisher had seen fit to print Lady Dexton's pack of moonshine, surely she could find someone willing to print hers. Heaven knew she couldn't do a worse—

*Murdered.*

She froze, her face paling as the significance of the word struck her full force. She had been murdered! She retrieved the book from the pile, thumbing through it until she found the page again. She reread it twice, just to be certain she had not misunderstood, and then she set the book down with trembling hands. She remembered wondering if it was assumed she died when she disappeared, but now she wondered if an even worse fate would have befallen her, had she remained in the past.

But who would have wished to murder her? she wondered, her heart beating with terror. And when would the crime have occurred? The night she disappeared? That is what the marchioness said, but could her veracity be trusted? She tried to think clearly and logically, as she was certain Alec would do, but she couldn't get past the horrifying possibility of her own murder. And then an even more horrifying possibility struck her.

Major Fitzburgh's journals had talked about "poor Harrington," and one of the books dealing with Stephen had been titled *Aristocracy on Trial*. Dear God! she thought, her stomach plunging to her toes, had Stephen killed her?

But even as the terrifying thought occurred, she was rejecting it. No, not Stephen. He would never have done anything so dishonorable. It was simply not in his nature. Blast it all! she thought furiously, her fists clenching in rage. What had happened? And had what happened been destined, or had she caused it by her unwilling trip through time? She had to find the answers, she decided, blinking back tears as she reached for another book. Until she solved the mystery of her past, there was no way she could hope to find happiness in her future.

* * *

"Can't let you out of my sight for five minutes, can I?" Deverham's voice was mocking as Alec walked into his office. "How are you feeling?"

"Like I almost got my bleeding bum blown off," Alec replied, seeing no reason why he should be polite. In truth, his burns and the injury to his back and ribs had all faded to a dull, bearable ache. And God knew they hadn't slowed him down last night, he thought, a wolfish smile touching his lips at the passionate memories.

"Glad you find this so humorous." Deverham's sharp retort made it obvious he did not share Alec's amusement. "I've been on the phone all morning with everyone from the Home Office to M-l, and I'm getting tired of having my backside roasted. As of now, you are out of service, and don't give me any backchat," he warned when Alec opened his mouth in protest, "or I'll have you assigned to the dullest job I can find!"

Alec's jaw snapped shut, fury narrowing his eyes to slits as he glared at the taciturn man behind the metal desk. "What the hell are you on my arse for?" he demanded crudely. *"I'm* the bloody victim here, in case you've forgotten!"

"A bloody victim who rejected protection when it was offered," Deverham reminded him icily, "but that's no longer an option. You're being placed under heavy watch, and that's the end of it."

Alec couldn't believe what he was hearing. He'd been fully prepared to have his ears pinned back, and he was even honest enough to admit he deserved it, for not taking the simplest of precautions. Hell, two of his best friends in the SAS had been taken out by a car bomb in Derrytown; he should have been aware of the possibility and searched the car before entering it. Instead he'd put Miranda inside a death trap.

"Look," he began, forcing himself to swallow his anger, "I'll own I was damned careless, but you can rest assured it won't happen again. Now that I know I'm a genuine target, I'll—"

"Do you know who called me at 8:15 this morning?" Deverham interrupted silkily. "Buckingham Palace, that's who."

"Buckingham Palace?" Alec was stunned.

"Yes, it seems her majesty was listening to the BBC, and was most distressed to learn one of 'her' police officers was almost blown to bits by a terrorist. I had to explain myself to the queen's minister!" Deverham's voice rose to a muted roar. "Have you ever tried explaining anything to a queen's minister?"

"No."

"You won't want to try, believe me. His lordship—or whatever the devil I'm supposed to call him—was quite polite, as he put my balls through a sausage grinder. When he was finished doing that, he informed me that her majesty wanted firm assurances you were receiving the best protection possible, and you'll get that protection, Inspector Bramwell, if it means I have to lock you in a room and sit on you myself. Is that clear?"

Alec made another grab at patience. "I don't want to be watched," he said, his thoughts turning to Miranda. If he was placed under watch, it would mean not only officers outside the house, but an officer inside as well. An officer who would find a woman without documentation decidedly interesting.

"That's too damned bad," Deverham said, his eyes icy with resolve, "because someone's already watching you, and that someone seems damned determined to get you. Read this," he tossed a report he'd been studying at Alec.

Alec picked up the report, flipping it open and scanning the neatly typed pages. The chemical report was just a preliminary, but it was obvious a plastique had been used. And as for the detonation device . . . "Remote controlled?" he exclaimed, his eyes widening in horror. "Good God, are they certain?"

"Of course they're certain!" Deverham glared at him. "Your precious SAS was in on the analysis, if you're so lacking in faith in this department. A small microchip was found in the wreckage, and it's been identified as the type commonly used to control those little motorized cars all the kids have. That means—"

"That means he was there," Alec interrupted, his fists clenching around the paper as he stared at Deverham. "The bastard was right there when it happened."

Deverham nodded, his expression solemn. "We estimate he was in the upper carpark. It has a good view of where you were parked, as well as a direct exit on to the road, so he could have been driving off innocent as a nun, while your car was going up in flames. He was *that* close to you, Bramwell. Think about it."

Alec had already thought of that and he leapt to his feet, his eyes filled with panic. "Miranda!"

"Who?"

Without answering, Alec snatched the phone off the desk, punching out his phone number and waiting with increasing anxiety as he listened to it ringing. "Pick up, pick up," he said, his palms sweating, "damn it, Miranda, pick up the goddamned phone!"

"She's not there, Bramwell."

Alec gave Deverham a stunned look, a deadly rage washing over him as the other man's words slowly sank in. He slammed the phone down and leaned across the desk, his murderous intent obvious in his feral expression. "If you've hurt her, you bloody son-of-a-bitch, I'll tear you apart with my own hands!"

Deverham didn't so much as flinch, his expression unreadable as he met Alec's burning gaze. "She's fine, Inspector. In fact, she's currently at the British Library, where two of our best operatives have her under close observation."

Alec sat back down on his chair, his hand still shaking as he thrust it through his hair. "The little devil," he muttered angrily. "I told her to stay in the house until I got back."

Deverham gave him a cool look. "Apparently her sense of hearing is as poor as yours," he said sardonically. "Or weren't you listening when I asked if you had a girlfriend?"

Alec raised his chin pugnaciously. "She's not my girlfriend," he denied through clenched teeth.

"Then what is she?"

Alec hesitated before deciding to go with the same story he'd told Rye. "A friend of Cara's," he said, knowing his sister would back him no matter what he claimed. "Her husband is fond of knocking her about, and she needs a place to hide." He allowed a self-deprecatory look to cross his face. "Poor kid; she'd have been better off staying with the sot."

Deverham picked up his pen and waited expectantly. "What's her name?" he asked when Alec remained silent.

"Miranda Winthrop," he supplied, knowing when to cooperate and when to stall. "But I don't want her name mentioned in any reports. Her husband is a brutal bastard, and he has a very long reach."

Deverham looked indignant. "I sincerely doubt his reach is long enough to reach A Squad's reports," he said, his tone as starchy as an old maid's. "At least, it had better not be."

Alec shook his head. "I won't take the chance it does," he said, knowing he now had a powerful bargaining chip. He waited a few moments and then leaned forward, his fist resting on the desk as he met Deverham's gaze.

"I'll do what you ask, Deverham," he told the security officer in a soft voice. "I'll take emergency leave, I won't leave the house without a whole bloody squad on my back, but I don't want Miranda's name mentioned. Have we a deal?"

There was a charged silence as Deverham kept staring at Alec. "You seem rather ardently determined to protect the lady," he said, leaning back in his chair. "Certain she's not your girlfriend?"

Alec thought so pallid a word a poor description for the feelings Miranda invoked in him. "Positive," he said firmly.

Deverham steepled his fingers and looked thoughtful. "It could be done, I suppose," he murmured, as if to himself. "So long as you give us full cooperation. Naturally we'll need to interview her and verify her story."

"No."

His blunt refusal brought Deverham snapping forward again. "Blast it, Bramwell, will you listen to me—"

"No," Alec prepared to play his trump card, "it's you who'll listen to me, if you have the slightest hope of winning my cooperation. Miranda is not to be interviewed, not to be treated like a damned suspect in any manner. You have no idea of the living hell she's gone through, I won't have her feeling like a prisoner again. It would destroy her."

There was another long silence, and then a sympathetic look flashed across Deverham's face. "Her husband must be a proper animal," he said, disgust plain in his voice.

"You don't know the half of it," Alec mumbled, hoping his lordship's ghost wasn't hanging about to take offense.

There was a long silence, and then Deverham gave a decisive nod. "All right, I'll do what I can."

"And I don't want an officer in the house," Alec added, deciding he had nothing to lose by going for broke.

*"What?"*

"I'll put up with the rest of it, if I must," Alec met Deverham's outraged scowl with steely determination, "but I'll be damned if I'll have some snot-nosed constable making a report of how many times I piss a night. The house is already as secured as a damned fortress, and I can take care of anyone who might manage to get past the alarms and the bars."

Deverham gave him a scornful look. "Like you took care of the man who planted the bomb in your car?"

Alec took the hit in stoic silence, telling himself it was no less than he deserved. "I'll take care of anyone I have to."

"All right," Deverham said at last, "we have a deal. But," he added when Alec rose to go, "there's a few other details we need to work out, before you go tearing off to the British Library to rescue your . . . houseguest."

Alec sat back down in his seat. "Such as?" he asked suspiciously.

"My plans to catch Talbot, of course." The smile Deverham sent him was pure steel. "How do you feel about being bait, Bramwell?"

Alec hoped he managed to hide his shock. "I suppose I might be interested," he said at last, intrigued despite himself.

"I rather thought you'd say that," Deverham took another report from his desk and opened it up. "Listen carefully, Inspector, this is what I have in mind . . ."

*Fourteen*

Miranda continued her search through the afternoon, meticulously recording every scrap of information she could find on either herself, Stephen, or—after careful consideration—her step-papa. She found several references to "the tragedy," "the unfortunate affair," or even "the recent unpleasantness," as one writer called it, but she was unable to find one substantial bit of proof to guide her. She was going over her notes and trying to make some sense of them, when someone sat down at the table opposite her. She glanced up curiously, her eyes widening when she saw Alec sitting there.

"Alec!" she exclaimed in delight, her earlier petulance forgotten in light of her discovery. "What are you doing here?"

"Gather your things together," he said, his voice low and tight with obvious anger. "We're leaving."

Miranda opened her mouth to protest, but shut it again at the expression on his face. Discretion, as Shakespeare had so wisely put it, was the better part of valor. Later, she promised herself, gathering her notes and papers together as she stood.

She was about to return the books to the librarian, when she suddenly thought of something. She turned to Alec, and was surprised to see him flanked by two men, one of whom she remembered seeing while she had been in the reference department.

"What is it?" Alec's voice was still pitched low, but she doubted he was speaking quietly in deference to the other patrons. Likely he was only waiting until they were alone before ringing a peal over her head, she thought, her spine stiffening in outraged pride.

"I was wondering, sir, if you have a library card I might borrow, so that I may have the use of these books," she said, her manner as coolly formal as she could manage.

His brows descended in the black scowl she recalled from their first days together, and she braced herself for the explosion she was sure would come. Instead, he dug out his wallet, muttering beneath his breath as he removed a square piece of plastic which he handed to her. "Here, just mind you don't lose the book," he said, his expression of impatience growing more pronounced. "And hurry up, we haven't all bleeding day."

Miranda was disappointed that the queue at the lending desk was so short, as nothing would have given her greater pleasure than to keep Alec and his two silent shadows cooling their heels the rest of the afternoon. Unfortunately, such was not the case, and a few minutes later she and Alec, followed by the two men, were walking down the steps of the library, his fingers closed tightly about her elbow.

"Will you kindly remove your hand from my arm?" she demanded in a furious whisper, trying discreetly to tear her arm free from his bruising grip. "You're breaking it."

"I'd like to break your damned neck!" he retorted, his voice equally as low and furious. "I thought I told you to stay home!"

"And I thought I told you I do not follow orders like a simpering child!" she shot back, wishing now she'd heeded his words and taken those lessons from Cara. The notion of knocking him on his arrogant backside was sweetly tempting.

Another surprise in the form of a black car was waiting for her at the curb, and Alec shoved her roughly inside, before she could utter a word of protest. The moment the door slammed shut behind them, the driver took off in a squeal of tires, merging smoothly with the traffic streaming down Great Russell Street. Miranda turned in her seat, her eyes flashing with fury as she prepared to do battle with her abductor.

"How dare you—" she began hotly, only to be silenced by a cutting glance from him.

"Put a sock in it," he warned softly, flicking the driver's head a meaningful look. "We'll talk when we're home."

Miranda cast him a baleful glare of her own before flinging herself in the corner of the car. Arms folded across her chest, she stared at the window. Pompous, imperious, self-righteous beast, she fumed silently, her temper simmering as they made their way through the heavy traffic. She'd expected him to be furious at her for disobeying him, and given yesterday's events she was even willing to concede that such fury was not without warrant. However, she added with an unconscious lift of her chin, that didn't grant him leave to treat her like a servant caught filching the silver. He might be her lover, but she was hanged if she would allow him to act as her husband.

Her temper was still decidedly piqued when they arrived at the house on Curzon Street. A second car pulled in behind them, and when Alec helped her from the car, she saw a uniformed bobby standing on the doorstep. The sight brought her to an abrupt halt, and then she was whirling around to grab Alec's arm.

"What's happened?" she demanded, her anxious gaze scouring his face. "Has there been another bombing?"

Her concern only partially eased the anger coiled inside him, but he wasn't so cruel as to keep her in unnecessary suspense. "Everything is fine," he said, taking her arm in a gentle grip and guiding her forward. "These officers are just here to make sure it remains that way. They'll be with us for the next few weeks, so you might as well grow used to them."

She cast the two stolid-faced men a quick glance over her shoulder, certain she would never become accustomed to their omnipresence. Although she'd grown up surrounded by servants, she'd never been comfortable with them always hanging about, and in the weeks she'd been in the future, she'd enjoyed the freedom of being truly alone. Now it seemed she would have to become inured to them all over again.

After a whispered conversation with the officer at the door, Alec led her inside, closing and locking the door carefully behind them. The moment they were alone, he turned to Miranda, his eyes glittering like topazes as he studied her. "Well, your ladyship," he drawled in a deceptively mild voice, "I'm waiting."

The presence of the police officer on the doorstep and those following them in the other car had effectively doused Miranda's temper. Understanding now the terrible danger Alec was facing, made her defiance evaporate, and her tone was quiet as she responded to his belligerent demand.

"You're right," she said, her tone solemn as she met his gaze. "It was very wrong of me to have left the house, after you told me not to do so. I'm sorry."

Alec blinked at her, disarmed by her quiet response. "What?"

His stunned expression brought an amused gleam to her eyes, and she stepped forward to lay a hand on his cheek. "I said I was sorry," she repeated, her fingers stroking the tense line of his jaw. "Had I been thinking properly, I should never have disobeyed you out of sheer pique. Unfortunately, you seem to have a most regrettable effect upon my reasoning abilities," she added, tilting her head back and sending him a provocative smile.

Alec glared down at her another moment, before his arms closed about her in a desperate embrace. "Damn it, Miranda, what the hell am I to do with you?" he asked, holding her against his wildly pounding heart. He couldn't believe she was being so cooperative when he'd been expecting a full-scale battle, but he wasn't about to question his luck. He simply held her closer, his eyes closing as he savored the sweet warmth of her body.

They stood like that for several minutes, until Alec drew back and smiled down at her. "You are a menace," he said softly, his hands lingering to stroke her neck. "I thought women of your era were supposed to be sweet and biddable."

Miranda's eyes sparkled with mock anger, as she tossed back her head. "I believe you are confusing us with sheep, sir," she said tartly, albeit with a smile. "Women of my day are like women of any other period, and we have a profound distaste for tyrants." Then she remembered what she had uncovered prior to his arrival, and her smile abruptly faded.

Alec saw the laughter die in her eyes, and he tightened her hold about her neck. "What is it?" he asked worriedly.

She hesitated for a moment and then gave a troubled sigh. "I fear I may have learned something about what happened after I disappeared," she said, her gaze holding his. "I was murdered."

*"What?"* He exclaimed in horror.

She repeated the pitiful amount of information she had managed to uncover, and he released her so that she could retrieve her notes. They moved into the parlor, sitting side by side on the low-slung divan, as she showed him all she had discovered. All that she feared. When she'd finished speaking, he was frowning with thought.

"Perhaps Stephen did murder you," he said at last, working out the puzzle in his head as he spoke. "I mean," he gestured as he fought to untangle his tenses, *"would* have murdered you, had you stayed. Perhaps that was why the room brought you forward in time. It was trying to save you."

"No, I am certain that is not true," Miranda rejected the notion with a firm shake of her head. "Not only because I know Stephen would never bring disgrace on himself, but because of the room. Such an act as you described would imply a certain degree of benevolence, and that room is not benevolent, Alec. It is evil, pure evil. I think I must have felt it from the start, and that was why I feared it. The first time we opened it, I remember the feeling of power inside waiting to be unleashed . . ." She shivered, clasping her hands about her arms. "No, I will not believe the room acted out of any sense of goodness."

"All right," he was willing to concede the point, considering Cara's negative response to the room, "but are you so certain Stephen wouldn't kill you? He married you for your money, didn't he? Greed is one of the most classic motives for murder."

"Perhaps," now it was she who had to concede, "but I know

Stephen, and he was a just and honorable man. He would never have killed for money."

Her defense of her husband was beginning to wear on Alex's nerves. "You can't know that," he insisted stoutly. "I'm a cop, remember, and I've seen people shot down for a few lousy quid!"

"But those men weren't Stephen!" Miranda exclaimed, furious with his determination to view Stephen as the villain. "Damn it, Alec, I am not some green girl fresh from the country! Do you think Stephen was the first man to seek my hand?" She broke off when she saw him staring at her in wide-eyed shock. "What?"

"You said damn," he said faintly.

"And do not think I mean to beg your pardon," she retorted, feelingly gloriously free as she glared at him. "I vow you would try the patience of a saint! Now, may I please continue?"

"Feel free."

She gave him a suspicious scowl at the stilted reply, and then continued. "As I said, Stephen was not the first to make an offer for me. He wasn't even the first man of rank to propose. I've been courted for my fortune since I was fifteen, and you may be very sure I was wide-awake to all accounts. When Stephen asked me to marry him, I took special pains to learn all I could of him, and it was only when I discovered him to be a man of impeccable character that I agreed to accept him."

"What do you mean 'impeccable character'?"

Miranda remembered all she had learned as if it had been yesterday. "To begin, his debts were not his own, but rather had been inherited along with his title, and he was doing his best to pay them. Also, he was a landlord who genuinely cared about his people and the land, and he saw to what improvements he could without ever once raising rents. I have seen other lords who proudly called themselves gentlemen, even as they bled their estate and tenants dry. But not Stephen. He would never seek to advance himself at the pain of others."

She sounded so ardent, so certain, that Alec felt the sharp lash of jealousy on his soul. He remembered Miranda insisting that she hadn't loved her husband, but how could he know? She certainly sounded like a woman in love, he thought, casting her a considering look beneath his lashes.

"Let's assume you're right," he said carefully, willing to play her game for the moment, "and Stephen's not the killer, then who is? Who would benefit most from your death?"

Miranda shifted uneasily. "Stephen. By law all I had became his the moment we signed our marriage lines."

He raised his eyebrows, but managed to refrain from making any further comments. Instead he forced himself to concentrate on the other facts of the case, such as he knew them. "On the night you disappeared, you said Stephen had a visitor; do you know who it was?"

She remembered the mocking, hateful drawl and shook her head. "No, I had never met him before, I am sure of it."

Alec fell silent again, discovering that if he put his own emotions on ice, he could actually enjoy himself as he worked to solve the puzzle. "It seems to me that a man wouldn't be likely to invite a complete stranger into his bedroom, especially on his wedding night. That means this gentleman must have been well acquainted with your husband. Did you know many of his friends?"

"All of them, I thought," she answered at once. "Ours was a small, insular world, and most of us knew each other by reputation, if nothing else. In the five months we were engaged, I'd met several of Stephen's friends. He was quite popular."

"Hmmm," a sudden thought occurred to him, and he gave her a speculative look. "Miranda, do you think there was any chance that Stephen was gay?"

"Gay?" She looked much struck by the notion. "Well, he'd always struck me as being rather the serious sort, to be truthful. Although he did have a rather dry sense of humor, and I noted toward the end that he had the ability to laugh at himself, which is more than can be said of others." Here she cast him a pointed look.

"I'll ignore that," he said, chuckling at her confusion, "but that's not what I meant by his being gay. I meant, was he queer? Homosexual," he added bluntly, when she continued looking blank.

Her face flamed bright red. "Certainly not!" she denied furiously. "How can you dare accuse him of anything so bestial! He was a gentleman!"

"He was a man," Alec said coldly, deciding that if she didn't stop waving Stephen's banner, he bloody well wouldn't be held responsible for his actions. "I'm sure that even back in your time there were plenty of opportunities for him to get you alone and make a move on you, and yet he never did. Why?"

Her blush deepened at what she considered an affront to her charms. "How do you know he did not?" she challenged with an angry toss of her head.

"How . . ." He gave her an incredulous stare. "Christ, Miranda, you were a *virgin* last night! You're a passionate, beautiful woman, and the only reason I can think of why any man could be engaged to you for five months and not make love to you is because he can't get it hard for a woman!"

She was torn between fury at his crude speech and a shiver of pride that he'd described her as passionate and beautiful. In the end vanity cooled her outrage, but she was still determined to defend Stephen against Alec's vile accusations. "That is not how it was in my day," she said stiffly, her gaze shifting away from his. "I am not saying couples didn't sometimes anticipate their vows, but those were love matches. Stephen did not love me nor I him, and so it was easy for us to wait."

Alec reached out a hand and turned her face until their lips were almost touching. "You keep saying that you don't love Stephen," he said softly, his fingers burying themselves in her soft hair as he held her gaze, "and yet you keep defending him. Maybe you love him, but you're not willing to admit it, because he's lost to you."

Miranda saw the doubt and the fear in his gold-flecked eyes and swallowed uneasily. She had vowed to keep her love to herself, fearing he was not yet ready to hear of it. Now she feared losing him, if she did not speak. Taking her courage firmly in both hands, she reached up and caressed his face with gentle fingers.

"Do you honestly believe that if I truly loved Stephen, I would have lain with you last night?" she asked, her heart pounding at the risk she was about to take. "I keep saying I don't love him, because it is the truth; I don't." She drew a deep breath and then said the words she had been longing to say. "I love you."

He closed his eyes as an agonized expression flashed across his face. "Miranda . . ."

"No," she interrupted, blinking back tears, "don't say anything. I know you don't love me, and I'm not asking that you do. I'm only asking that you accept my feelings without censure, without dismissing them as nerves or mere propinquity. I love you, Alec Bramwell, and now I would ask one other thing of you."

Alec opened his eyes and met her gaze, his own heart pounding with a terrifying blend of emotions, each more potent than the last. "What is that?" he asked, his voice hoarse

She leaned forward and pressed her mouth to his. "Make love to me."

Cara arrived shortly before dinner, and after pinning her brother's ears back with a blistering lecture, she threw herself into his arms and burst into tears. "You miserable lout, don't you ever do that to me again!" she sniffed, rubbing her hand across her eyes and scowling like a cross child. "How do you think I felt when I thought you'd been vaporized?"

"Doubtlessly like I felt when I heard you've volunteered for the Fraiser Task Force," he said, tilting her chin up until he could gaze into her eyes. "They don't promote corpses, Cara."

She flushed, but didn't bother to deny the danger. "No, and they don't promote women to Homicide, either," she said instead, her jaw clenching in determination. "But they will. When I hand them that madman on a silver platter, they will."

All this talk of madmen and corpses made Miranda decidedly uneasy. "What are the two of you talking about?" she asked, sliding her arm about Alec's waist and leaning her head against his shoulder as she studied Cara worriedly.

Cara raised an eyebrow at the telling gesture. "Nothing," she said sweetly, her gaze darting between them. "How did the pair of you pass the day? Or should I ask?"

Miranda's cheeks turned a bright red as she remembered the passionate afternoon she and Alec had shared. The thought that Cara knew what had passed between them was most disconcerting, and she hastened to distract the lively brunette before she could ask any more embarrassing questions. "I went to the library," she began in an eager voice, and then went on to tell Cara the very same things she had already told Alec.

"My money's on your stepfather, the greedy sot," Cara said as she helped Miranda add the finishing touches to the meal.

Miranda stopped chopping vegetables long enough to send Cara an incredulous look. "My step-papa?"

"Of course," Cara popped a slice of mushroom in her mouth. "Think about it; if you're dead, and Stephen's convicted of your murder, who else would have inherited the money?"

Miranda frowned as she considered the matter. "I do not know. Most of it would be used to settle the estate, I assume, and if there was anything left, I suppose Elias might petition the court for it, but that sounds rather chancy."

Cara added more chicken to what was already sizzling in the pan. "You'll have to research him as well, then, and learn if he ended up with any of it. If he did, he goes to the top of my list." She gave Alec an inquisitive look. "What do you think?"

Alec, who had been assigned the duty of setting the table, paused in his labors to ponder her question. "It's possible," he agreed, and was annoyed he had not considered the man himself. He was the next viable suspect, he admitted, and then he remembered something Miranda had told him a few weeks ago.

"Didn't you say you heard Stephen tell the other man your stepfather wanted him to sign the papers giving him control over your money after the ceremony, but that he refused?"

"Yes, that was my impression," Miranda said, struggling to recall Stephen's exact words on that long ago night.

Cara squirted more Hunan sauce in the pan. "Let's assume he did," she said, enjoying the task of deducing far more than she enjoyed the more prosaic chore of cooking. "Your stepfather may have thought Stephen was going to double-cross him, and so he got desperate. Maybe he decided to make sure your husband didn't get anything, period. Yeah," she gave a sudden grin, pleased at her own cleverness, "I like the way that plays. I'll wager that's precisely how it happened."

They continued the discussion over dinner, and after awhile, Miranda found herself caught up in the cool, logical way brother and sister solved a problem. They would approach it from several different angles, eliminating possibilities one by one until only one conclusion remained. If this was what being a police officer was like, she could understand why both found it so fascinating.

"What I don't understand is what happened to your body," Alec said, settling back in his chair with his glass of lager. "I'll admit I never understood Einstein's theory of relativity, but it seems to me a physical body couldn't exist in two different times concurrently. We *know* you didn't die, because you're here. So, how could Stephen have been charged with your murder, if there was no body to show you had died?"

"You're right," Cara agreed excitedly, her own glass of lager clasped in her hands as she leaned forward. "The writ of habeas corpus was in use even back then, and without a corpse the authorities couldn't possibly have put Stephen on trial for murder. If that's even what happened," she added, frowning as she remembered their appalling lack of information.

Miranda gave a disheartened sigh, thinking of the hours she'd spent pouring over books and journals. "I know, it's all so confusing. If I knew what *really* happened, then I should know what to do, but as it is, we've nothing but hints and innuendoes."

The three fell into a brooding silence until Alec thought of something. "When I was in training, I used to go to the law library at London University," he said slowly. "They had these piles of books dealing with every murder case since Peel formed the MPF. But if some of those books dated back before then . . ."

"Then they might have the transcripts from the trial," Cara concluded, sending Alec an approving smile. "Brilliant, brother dearest, perhaps there might be hope for you after all."

Miranda stirred uneasily, thinking of Professor Kingston. "I . . . I know a professor at the university," she admitted in a soft voice, hoping Alec wouldn't be too upset with her. "Perhaps if I were to contact him, he would be kind enough to get us permission to use their facilities."

Alec glanced up, his brows gathering in a disapproving scowl. "How do you know this professor?" he asked suspiciously.

"I met him at the Library my first day there," she said, deciding that was close enough to the truth to suffice. "He was very helpful in showing me the library's cataloging system."

Alec's disgruntled mutter did not need to be heard to be understood. "What's Sir Galahad's name?" he asked caustically.

"Professor Geoffrey Kingston," she provided, doing her best not to smirk at his predictable ill temper. "I believe he teaches Economics there."

Alec tucked the name away for future use. "Well, until the Yard decides to let me do something more strenuous than standing about playing with my toes, I suppose I could help you look into it," he said, deciding going with her was his best bet for keeping her safe. He'd already learned that beneath her prim and proper exterior, she was every bit as stubborn as his willful sister, and he knew better than to believe she'd actually heed his advice and stay put until Talbot was dealt with.

Cara suddenly snapped her fingers. "Oh, that reminds me! Flemming waylaid me in the corridor, and began pestering me about those damned symbols you showed him. He says they're associated with some sort of satanic cult that dates back to the

Middle Ages. He's all hot to learn more, so I daresay you can expect a visit from him any day now."

Alec rolled his eyes. "Thanks for the warning," he grumbled, clearly not looking forward to the experience.

Cara smiled sympathetically, thinking of the ghoulish forensic expert with his pale hair and eyes and even paler skin. "Yes, he is a bit much; isn't he?" she said, shaking her head. "Looks rather like an anemic vampire, or so I've always thought." She turned to Miranda, who had fallen into a thoughtful silence and was staring off into space.

"I've been meaning to ask why you're so keen on all this," she said, her manner as blunt and straightforward as always. "I can understand why you'd want to know what happened to *you,* and if what happened effected history, but why care about the rest of it? The trial, and what happened to Stephen? What good can it do? What's done cannot be undone, as someone once said."

"Shakespeare, Lady Macbeth, to be precise," Alec supplied distractedly, realizing he'd never thought to question Miranda's motives for her search. He'd considered her curiosity only natural, given the circumstances. Now he could not help but wonder, and what he wondered made his blood run cold.

Cara took another sip of her lager. "Trust you to know that," she grumbled, looking annoyed.

Alec ignored her, his attention focused on Miranda and the oddly determined light in her silvery green eyes. "Cara has a point," he said quietly, his heart pounding with an emotion that was uncomfortably close to fear. "What could you do, even if you did discover that Stephen was tried for your murder? It's already happened, and nothing you learn here can change that."

Miranda considered his choice of words oddly ironic, considering the conclusion she'd reluctantly reached. "I do not know," she admitted, her eyes not meeting his as she struggled with the dictates of her heart and the demands of her conscience. "I only know I must try."

# Fifteen

London University was located in a part of London Miranda had yet to visit. The presence of a large college in the heart of the congested city amazed her, as did the foresight of her successors in setting aside land for such an institution. It was a relief to know that the people who would be called Victorians had given thought to erecting something other than hideous statues, she thought, shuddering at the memory of the ghastly edifice Cara had identified as the Albert Memorial.

With their guards trailing at their heels, she and Alec went first to the Administration Building, hoping to contact Professor Kingston. Those hopes were quickly dashed when the gray-haired lady at the Information Desk informed them he was on sabbatical, and had not yet returned.

"I'd forgotten that!" Miranda exclaimed, remembering he had indeed mentioned the matter. "Do you have a number where I might contact him?" she added, giving the dour-faced woman her most cajoling smile. "When I last spoke with him, he told me he had just moved, and that his phone hadn't been connected."

"He has *moved?*" The elderly woman repeated, her nose twitching in disapproval. "Staff is never supposed to change residences without first consulting this office! No wonder he hasn't returned our new term rosters; I thought he was being difficult. The man's a Maoist, you know," she added confidingly, as if that explained the professor's obstreperous conduct.

"Indeed?" Miranda wondered what a Maoist might be. "Well, thank you for your assistance. You have been most kind."

Her impeccable manners must have met with the older woman's approval, for she unbent enough to give her a frosty smile. "You're most welcome," she said, turning to the switchboard that had begun to buzz and beep in back of her. "Oh, and if you should see the professor again, would you please tell him to ring his mother? He hasn't contacted her since going to Lyons, and the woman has been driving us to distraction, calling every other day to demand information."

Miranda agreed to pass the message along, and she and Alec took their leave. They were walking in the direction of the Law Library, when Alec gave a low chuckle.

"What is so amusing?" she asked, wishing they were alone so that they might hold hands. She knew public displays of affection were commonplace in the present, but she doubted Alec would wish to engage in such conduct with his colleagues looking on.

As if sensing her thoughts and wishing to prove her wrong, he suddenly reached out and caught her hand in his. "I was just laughing at the way that old dragon made Kingston sound like a prissy mama's boy and a wild-eyed anarchist all in the same breath," he said, swinging her hand in a carefree arc. "Her abilities are quite wasted here, if you want my opinion. We ought to have her on the Public Desk at the Yard. I daresay there's not a terrorist alive who would make it past her!"

The Law Library was located in a square glass building on the far end of the campus, and after dealing with a team of security officers, who were understandably nervous at the prospect of having three armed men in their midst, they went down to the basement where the archives were located. Here, too, they were disappointed, as the earliest murder case dated back to 1821.

"This is beginning to feel suspiciously like a conspiracy. For every step we take forward, we take another three back," Alec complained, his eyes filled with compassion as he studied her.

"We may never learn the truth, you know," he added, reaching out to take her hand in his. "Have you accepted that?"

Miranda nodded, having already faced that possibility in the early hours of the morning, when she'd lain in Alec's arms wondering what she was going to do if her worst fears were confirmed. "Yes," she said quietly, her eyes meeting his as she leaned over and brushed a strand of hair from his forehead. "But my answer is the same as it was last night. I have to try."

Alec stared at her, aware that he had never felt quite so helpless. On the one hand, he understood entirely her desire to learn the truth, and he admired her dedication. On the other hand, he was terrified that what she learned would take her from him, and that there would be nothing he could do to stop her. The thought brought a swift stab of pain, and he turned back to the books piled on the desk in front of him.

"Well, we've a few hours before lunch, yet," he said, ignoring the hovering guards with lordly indifference. "We might as well have a look through this lot. Sometimes one case will refer back to another, and if nothing else, we may be able to establish whether or not he was even brought to trial."

They spent the next three hours poring over the thick tomes, searching for the slightest bit of information. Alec dragooned the other two officers into helping, telling them Miranda was a writer doing research on a book she hoped to write. But even with three seasoned investigators examining the dusty records, they came up empty-handed. It was a crushing disappointment, and Miranda was hard-pressed not to burst into discouraged tears as they walked back to the carpark where they'd left the car.

They'd almost reached their destination, when Miranda saw a man standing beside a crowded doorway. Her gaze drifted past him and then snapped back, as something about him struck a familiar chord. She slowed her step, casting a curious look over her shoulder.

"What are you looking at?" Alec asked, having noticed the direction of her stare.

The man had disappeared, and Miranda was beginning to feel decidedly foolish indeed. "It's nothing," she said, her cheeks blooming with embarrassment. "For a moment I thought I saw Professor Kingston, but I must have been mistaken."

Alec stiffened visibly, his eyes taking on a dangerous sheen. "Where?" he demanded curtly, thrusting her behind him, his hand closing about the butt of his weapon.

"Over there," she replied, nodding in the direction of the doorway. "But I only caught a glimpse of him, and as I said, I'm sure I must have been mistaken."

Alec hesitated; it might be a coincidence, but he was a man who was damned suspicious of coincidences. Perhaps it was time they learned more of this mysterious professor of hers, he decided, nodding at the two guards. The men separated, one walking in front of them, and the other closing behind them as they resumed walking.

"What does this professor look like?" he asked, keeping his voice cool, even as his eyes never stopped scanning for danger.

Miranda frowned as she tried to describe the man she had just seen. "He is about your age, I suppose," she said slowly, realizing only then that she hadn't the slightest idea how old Alec might be. "He has light brown hair, thinning a bit on top, and blue eyes. Rather ordinary-looking, really," she added with a self-conscious laugh, more certain than ever that she had made a simple mistake.

Alec said nothing, thinking the description she'd given could fit a considerable portion of the male population of London. Including, he realized with a start of fury, Talbot. The thought made up his mind, and he decided that agreement or not, he was going to his office. He turned to the officer behind them.

"We need to report in," he said, his voice clipped with the edge of command. "Drive us to the Yard."

The officer, a younger man named Gifford, gave a curt nod of approval. "I was about to suggest the same thing, Inspector," he said, keying in the microphone clipped to his collar. "But first I'll have units sweep the area, just in case."

"Good idea," Alec agreed, making a quick note of the officer's name. CT was always looking for men with the brains to match their brawn, and he wasn't above pinching the man from A Squad if given the chance.

A quick check of the car revealed no trace of a bomb, and they were soon driving in the direction of Victoria Station, where the Yard was located. Alec rode in the front seat with the other officer, his fingers drumming out an impatient tattoo on his thigh as he tried to decide what to do with Miranda.

He was fairly certain the professor was exactly who and what he pretended to be, but on the off chance he wasn't, he didn't want Miranda learning the truth until he was ready to tell her. Knowing now how seriously she took what she regarded as her responsibilities, he didn't want her blaming herself for those injured in the car bombing. There was only one person who was to blame, and if Kingston was Talbot, Alec was determined to see he paid dearly for his actions.

New Scotland Yard was located in an uninspiring glass block, with only the revolving sign in front to differentiate it from any of the other modern office blocks in the area. There were other distinctions as well, but one would require a discerning eye to spot all the security cameras and motion-detection devices set up in the building's outer perimeters. The patrolling officers, some of whom were armed, were another difference, and Alec nodded to several of the men as he and the others entered the glass tunnel leading into the lobby area.

The problem of what to do with Miranda was solved when the officer at the desk steadfastly refused to give her a pass granting her access to the upper floors. Alec argued with the man for effect, but when the officer remained adamant, he turned to Miranda with an apologetic shrug.

"Sorry, love," he said, brushing a quick kiss over her cheek. "But I'm afraid you'll have to wait here until I get back."

Miranda eyed him suspiciously, thinking he'd given in rather easily. She was tempted to tell him she wasn't in the slightest bit deceived by his performance, but in the end she decided she didn't wish to embarrass him in front of the others. Pinning a sweet smile to her lips, she stood on tiptoe and returned his kiss.

"Of course, darling, I quite understand," she said, the sparkle in her eyes sending him another message entirely. "Will you be very long? You know I hate to be away from you," and she fluttered her lashes in imitation of an actress she had seen on the television last night.

Alec heard someone snicker in back of him, and the tips of his ears turned bright red. "I'll be back when I can," he muttered, surrendering the field to the little devil. "See that you're here when I do."

It took some talking, but he was able to convince both officers to remain with Miranda, while he made his way to the floor where SO 13 kept its offices. This was the most secure area in the complex, and so it took him several minutes before he managed to make it to his unit. He walked inside, acknowledging his mate's greeting with a wave of his hand. He'd just sat behind his desk when Deverham walked up to him, his face tight with fury.

"Conference Room Three," he said through clenched teeth, stepping back to let Alec pass. "Now."

Alec raised a mocking eyebrow at the Security Officer's preemptive actions. He'd just been about to ring him, but now it looked like he could make his request in person. He rose lazily to his feet, his manner just this side of insolent as he trailed Deverham into the office.

"Bramwell!" One of the other inspectors called out his name, and when Alec turned, the man was giving him a cheeky grin. "That's a record, mate!" the man said with a laugh. "Five seconds since you walked through the door, and you're already in for it!"

Alec flashed the man a thumbs-up sign, his cocky smile still in place when he turned around and saw Deverham glowering at him from the other side of the long oak table.

"What the devil are you doing here?" Deverham demanded

in a low growl, his palms resting on the table as he leaned forward. "I thought I put you on enforced holiday?"

"You did," Alec held up a placating hand. "I only came in to make a report, and ask a favor of you."

Deverham straightened, his expression frankly suspicious as he studied Alec. "What sort of favor?"

"A background check on a Prof. Geoffrey Kingston," Alec answered, settling on one of the plastic chairs lining the table. "He teaches Economics at London University."

"Any particular reason why you want him run?" Deverham asked.

"He met Miranda at the British Library the day before the bombing in Brighton," Alec explained coolly, his eyes narrowing as he studied Deverham's face. "Also, his physical description matches Talbot's."

As he expected, the other man stiffened at his words. "You don't think it's him?" he asked, and Alec swore he could hear his brain clicking like a computer processing data.

"Probably not," Alec admitted with a cautious shrug, "but I'm not willing to chance it. Another thing, Kingston's reported to have been in Lyons in the past few weeks. He apparently hasn't contacted his mother since returning, so there's a possibility he's gone missing. You'll want to interview the mother; see if a report's been filed, get some pictures, if you can."

Deverham had taken a chair and was busily making notes. "How do you know he's been to Lyons?" he asked, frowning at Alec. "Have you broken our agreement?"

"Not at all," Alec was able to assure him, telling himself that picking up random bits of information could hardly be called investigating. He then went on to explain their visit to London University, knowing the other man would doubtlessly read the details in his men's reports soon enough. He repeated everything the receptionist had told him; even adding the fact that Miranda had thought she'd seen Kingston on campus.

"It's probably nothing," he concluded with another shrug, "but I'd feel better if it was checked out. Just to be certain."

"I'll get on it straight away," Deverham promised, jotting down more notes. "Anything else?"

Alec hesitated only a moment before saying, "Yes, I want to see copies of the Interpol report on the ambush in Lyons."

Deverham lifted his head. "You're wanting to know if Talbot's really dead, aren't you?"

"You hinted there was some question," Alec agreed cautiously.

"There were several questions, and precious few answers," Deverham agreed, shifting back in his chair with a heavy sigh. "Oh, a body was found, burnt beyond recognition, naturally, but Forensics was able to establish that the victim was a white male in his thirties to forties."

"What about dental records?" Alec asked, after digesting the information he'd been given. "Didn't they compare Talbot's charts to the remains?"

A ghost of a smile touched Deverham's mouth. "There aren't any dental records for Talbot," he said, a note of grudging respect creeping into his voice. "Shortly after Talbot joined the RC— they were calling themselves the People's Coalition then—his dentist's office in Norwich went up in flames. The same thing happened to his doctor's office two days later."

Alec's eyebrows raised a notch, and like Deverham, he was willing to grant his enemy reluctant admiration for his ingenuity. "Thorough bugger, isn't he?" he said, his mind working rapidly. "What about DNA? Are any of Talbot's near relations alive, so we could do a comparison to the body?"

"Already being done," Deverham told him. "The FBI lab in Washington is cooperating with us. He's linked to two bombings over there, and we've promised them a crack at him when we get our hands on him. They've a state-of-the-art gene splicer I'd kill my sainted aunt for, and I'm hoping that if this makes our case, I can talk those bleeders in Purchasing to spring for one. They think we should be able to solve crimes using nothing but a magnifying glass and a deerstalker's hat!"

Alec smiled, and the conversation switched to the two bombings. Once the connections between the previous two targets was established, security had been tightened on Blackpool's other businesses and the drug lord was said to be so frightened for his life, he was talking a deal with a magistrate.

As they chatted, the Security Officer forgot his own edict, sharing new information with Alec and soliciting his opinion as they scoured the reports. They were reviewing a chemical analysis of the explosive compound used to destroy his car, when Alec happened to glance down at his watch. He swore softly, pushing away from the desk as he rose to his feet.

"I have to go; Miranda's waiting below," he said, casting a wistful look at the report. "I don't suppose . . ."

Deverham studied Alec's face, and then tossed him the sheaf of papers. "Here," he said, looking both resigned and amused, "I ought to have known you'd never be able to keep your nose out of it. And the lamentable fact is, we need you here. No one's quite so devious as you."

This last remark was both a compliment and a complaint, and Alec recognized it as such. More importantly, he also recognized what it portended. "Then I can come back?" he asked, not daring to hope he would be reinstated so quickly.

Deverham rubbed his hand across his jaw, but wasn't quite successful in hiding his grin. "Officially you're still on holiday," he reminded Alec sternly.

"And unofficially?"

"Unofficially you're to have your bum in here no later than nine o'clock," Deverham gave up trying to hide his wide smile. "And you needn't worry about your houseguest, while you're not there to guard her. I'll keep an officer on her at all times."

A lascivious quip occurred to Alec, but he bit it back. "I want Gifford assigned as her principal protection officer," he said, recalling his favorable impression of the younger man. "He seems to know pretty much what he's about."

"Hands off, Bramwell," Deverham cast him, a threatening scowl. "Gifford's one of my best men."

"It won't be my fault if the lad decides going face-to-face

with terrorists is more exciting than acting as baby minder to some target politician," Alec replied, contriving to look his most innocent. "It's a free country, after all."

Deverham said something exceedingly rude, and Alec was still chuckling as he hurried toward the elevator. He almost made it.

"Bramwell! Hold up, there!"

Alec turned at the sound of his name, his eyes closing in annoyance as he recognized the thin man hurrying toward him. He waited until the other man had reached him, before opening his eyes with a weary sigh. "Hello, Flemming."

"I heard you were in the building." Flemming either didn't recognize or chose to ignore the complete lack of welcome in Alec's voice. "Have you any more information on those pentagrams you gave me?"

"Well, actually—"

"I faxed them to a friend of mine at Oxford," Flemming ignored Alec's hesitation, his pale blue eyes shining with enthusiasm. "He's an expert on ancient cults, and he became quite excited when he recognized the symbols. They're apparently the sign of a group calling themselves The Brotherhood of Watchers. The sect dates back to the Tudor period, and several members were burnt as witches in the late 1600's."

Alec remembered the magic wand he'd found. "I thought it must have something to do with satanism," he murmured, thinking Miranda had been right when she'd said the room was evil.

"Oh, it was more than black magic," Flemming continued eagerly. "They were devil worshipers to be sure, but they were far more than *that!* They were alchemists and scientists whose progressive theories challenged the established order; which was doubtlessly why they were so ruthlessly persecuted once the Roundheads came to power. Of course," he gave a soft chuckle, "they were also a bit balmy. They believed they'd perfected a spell for time-travel, if you can imagine."

Alec couldn't have been more stunned if the thin, pale-faced man had whipped out a Hockler and started blasting away. "Time-travel?" he repeated incredulously.

Flemming nodded. "I had the same reaction, but Charles assured me they were quite serious about it. It was even rumored they had some sort of formula, but unfortunately all records were burned when they were arrested. More's the pity. Only imagine what we might have learned from them."

Alec managed a sickly smile. "Yes, imagine."

While she was waiting for Alec to rejoin them, Miranda entertained herself jotting down some ideas that had been teasing her for the past few days. Alec's telling the officers she was a writer wasn't so very far off the mark, as she had been toying with that very notion for some time now. She'd read many modern novels since coming forward in time, and she rather fancied trying her hand at writing one herself.

Not those terrifying books Cara had lent her, filled with vampires and murderous creatures that lived in sewers. Nor was she interested in the types of books Alec favored, with their cynical spy-heroes and a dazzling array of puzzling devices. No, what she had in mind was the sort of book written by Sir Arthur Conan Doyle. She'd been captivated by Mr. Holmes's brilliance, and the picture he painted of London one hundred years in the past 'twas an intriguing one.

She knew next to nothing of Holmes's London, but of *her* London she knew a great deal. The idea of writing a book set in the London of her day and featuring a character similar to Holmes had occurred to her, and the more she thought of it, the more excited she became. Only her Holmes would be a woman, not a man. A companion, perhaps, or better still, a governess. Yes, a young woman of gentle birth blessed with a sharp eye and a sharp mind, who helped solve mysteries for those who employed her. Perhaps she might be possessed of an equally sharp tongue, and that would explain why she was forever changing positions.

She was trying to decide on a name for her acerbic lady detective, when Alec reappeared, and the strained expression on his face pushed all thoughts of her plot from her mind. She tucked her notebook into her purse, and was rising to her feet as Alec walked up to her.

"Are you ready to go?" he asked, his voice so stiff and formal that it was all she could do not to wince. Something was clearly amiss, but she knew Alec too well to think he would tell her what that something was as long as they were in public.

"Of course," she said, refraining from adding that she had been ready to leave for the past two hours.

The ride home was as silent and uncomfortable as she'd feared it would be, and she could only wonder what the officer driving the car must think of them. As soon as they were in the house and the door securely shut behind them, she turned to face Alec, her eyes filled with concern as she studied his face.

"What is it?" she asked gently, stepping forward to lay her hand on his arm. "Has something terrible happened, and you are trying to think of some way to tell me?"

For a moment she thought he was going to refuse to answer her, and then a reluctant smile touched his mouth. "Nothing has happened," he assured her, bending down to brush a kiss over her soft lips. "You're becoming paranoid, darling."

Miranda had read enough to know what paranoid meant, and she gave him a stern look. "What I am becoming is well acquainted with the way your mind works," she informed him loftily, ignoring the way her heart beat faster at his nearness. "And I know that when you are being this evasive, it means you are trying to hide something from me. Now, what is it?"

He looked for a moment as if he meant to argue the point, and then he gave a heavy sigh. The last thing she expected, was the quiet answer he gave her. "I have decided to reopen the room."

She drew back slowly, her eyes never leaving his face. "May I ask why?"

He led her into the parlor, joining her on the divan as he told her of his conversation with Flemming. "I keep remembering those journals," he concluded, resting his cheek against the top of her head as he stared thoughtfully off into space. "They were filled with writing, gibberish, I thought, but now I'm not so certain. As I said, all magic has its explanations, and those journals may hold the key we've been seeking."

Miranda could not answer, as her head was reeling with a myriad of possibilities. Part of her wanted the room closed off forever, so that she would never have to leave Alec, but the other part of her knew she might have no choice. Both sides engaged in a fierce struggle, but in the end she decided it was best to have the room kept in readiness, should she have need of its special powers.

"You are right," she agreed, her heart overflowing with love as she gazed up at him. "And if it will make you feel better, I give you my most solemn pledge that I shall never enter the room without your permission."

His eyes darkened with an emotion she could not name. "Are you certain?" he asked, his voice husky as his hand slipped beneath her hair to massage the fragile skin on the back of her head. "I don't want you to think I'm trying to control you; I'm not. I'm only trying to keep you safe."

She felt tears gather in her eyes at the familiar words. "I know," she said, a sweet yearning filling her soul. "I want to keep you safe as well. I love you, Alec."

This time there was no denial on his part, no flash of pity in his golden eyes. Instead she saw a reflection of her own desire, and she gave a soft sigh as she pulled his head down to hers.

His mouth was hard and demanding as it met hers, his tongue flicking against her lips until she parted them to grant him entry. She lost herself in the passionate kiss, a wild need to make love to him destroying her usual shyness. Her fingers tangled deeply in his thick hair, her hips arching up until she could feel his masculine hardness rubbing against her.

"Make love to me, Alec," she begged, undulating against him

as she brushed frantic kisses down his neck. "Make love to me now!"

He lifted his head, his narrowed eyes searching her flushed face a moment, before a devilish smile stole across his own features. "Here?" he asked, clearly delighted at the prospect. She gave a jerky nod and his hands flew to her blouse, his clever fingers dispensing quickly of her buttons and the front closure of her brassiere.

She moaned in helpless pleasure at his teasing touch, and her hands slid up to his broad shoulders. The heat of his flesh burned through the knitted material, but she wanted more. She wanted the feel of his hard, smooth skin beneath her palms as he moved over her, and she began tugging at his sweater until she managed to get it over his head.

They kissed and teased each other to the point of madness, tearing at each other's clothes with more passion than finesse. In the hot struggle their positions were somehow reversed, and Miranda was gazing down at his tanned body with a hunger that would have once horrified the prim virgin she had been. She saw his masculine nipple peeking through his cloud of chest hair, and feeling daringly decadent, she bent her head and lightly bit it.

"God!" He arched his hips, almost lifting them from the divan. "Where did you learn to do that!" he demanded hoarsely, an expression of exquisite agony flashing across his face as he squeezed his eyes shut.

"From a video," she said, and because she was so pleased with the results, she repeated the caress. "Cara showed it to me."

His eyes flew open at that. "Cara?" There was suspicion as well as passion in his husky voice.

"Mmm," her mouth skimmed over his quivering stomach even as her fingers danced lower. *"Naughty Ladies Night Out."*

"It sounds like a porno flick!" he protested, his hands clenching around her hips as she kept teasing him.

Her tongue flicked over his navel. "I believe it was," she said, smiling in memory of the shocking images she had watched with wide eyes. "I found it . . . edifying," and then she kissed him in a way that had him moaning in ecstasy.

They continued their passionate play until they were both breathless, their hearts racing with the need for completion. Alec moved over her, his powerful arms shaking as they supported his full weight. She could feel his hardness nudging against her, and was waiting in quivering anticipation of his thrust, when he suddenly gave a lurid curse.

"What . . . what is it?" she asked, barely able to get the words past her trembling lips. She was hovering on the edge of the precipice, and knew she was only seconds from tumbling over.

"I didn't plan on this," Alec's tone was full of agony as he shifted away. "I'm not prepared to protect you."

She understood his meaning this time, and even though she knew she should be grateful for his thoughtfulness, she could not bear the thought of his leaving her. She lifted her hips, her legs wrapping around his muscular thighs. "Don't go," she implored, her eyes glowing as she gazed up at him.

He swallowed visibly, his brow beading with sweat. "Miranda, sweetest, you don't know what you're asking," he said, his body shaking. "I could make you pregnant."

The thought thrilled her more than she believed could be possible. "I don't care!" she insisted fervently, her fingers seeking him and guiding him to her aching softness. "I don't want to stop, I never want to stop!"

Her words shattered his fragile control and he thrust strongly into her, his hands sliding down to cup her buttocks as he moved urgently against her. Miranda cried out sharply as her climax erupted inside her, and then cried out again as a second explosion claimed her seconds afterward. Alec gave a hoarse shout, and then he was following her into ecstasy.

The sweet aftermath had barely passed before he began making love to her again, more wildly and completely than he had ever done before. She lost count of the times he drove her to the peak, sometimes pushing her right over, and other times keeping her hovering there until it was all she could do not to scream in frustration and wild satisfaction. It was as if he was possessed of the same demons driving her, and that he was determined to bind her to him by a magic as real and powerful as that inside the secret room.

She understood his desperation, shared it, for she longed to bind him with the same magic. The one magic she knew would be strong enough to counter the evil power of the secret room. Love.

# *Sixteen*

Miranda awoke the following morning to the feel of Alec's mouth brushing softly down her neck. The tender kiss made her lips curve in pleasure, and she reached up to curl her arms about his shoulders.

"Good morning, Inspector," she sighed, not bothering to open her eyes. His touch was making her body grow warm, and she delighted in the sweet pleasure of it.

"Countess," his voice was low and husky as he tucked her beneath him, sliding into her welcoming body with a boldness that brought her eyes flying open.

He was bent over her, his dark hair tousled from sleep and loving, and a look in his gold-colored eyes that was almost as arousing as what he was doing to her. Her hands tightened on his upper arms, and she bit her lip to keep from crying out.

"Wh-what are you doing?" she stammered, gasping as he began to thrust slowly inside her.

A piratical grin slashed across his face. "If you don't know, love," he drawled, bending to nip lightly at her breast, "it's obvious I haven't been doing it often enough!"

The teasing loving was as wildly erotic as the frantic passion that had consumed them last night, and when it was over, Miranda was dazed with happiness. Afterward Alec carried her into the bathroom, where they shared a shower and more love play before dressing and going downstairs for a hurried breakfast.

While Miranda prepared eggs and bacon, Alec sat at the table and made several calls. Although she tried not to eavesdrop, she would have had to be deaf not to hear his heated words as he argued with the person on the other end of the line.

"Listen, Deverham, I don't give a tinker's damn what I agreed to yesterday," he said, his voice taking on that belligerent tone she knew all to well. "You're the one who put me on holiday, so you're hardly in a position to complain if I don't jump at your command. I'm taking the morning off, and that's final!" He slammed the phone down with decided violence, his brows meeting in a scowl as he glared off into space. "Bloody bureaucrat," he muttered, taking a sip of his steaming coffee.

"You sound in a pleasant mood," she teased, unable to resist brushing a kiss over his cheek as she set his plate in front of him. He had told her he didn't expect her to cater to him, but she'd found the task of cooking surprisingly enjoyable. It gave her an odd sense of accomplishment, and she thought it a pity she'd never been given the opportunity in the past. Of course, she mused, turning back toward the pan, preparing a meal over an electric cooker was doubtlessly far easier than preparing a meal over one of those monstrous wood stoves she'd seen in the museums.

Alec's arm snagged about her waist and he dragged her down on his lap, ignoring her startled squeal as he took her mouth in a quick, passionate kiss. When he lifted his head, she was clinging to him. "I *was* in a pleasant mood," he said, eyes twinkling as he grinned down at her. "Care to help me recapture it?"

She was tempted, more tempted than she thought possible, but the smell of burning eggs recalled her to the present. She wiggled off his lap and hurried over to rescue her breakfast.

"Why did Mr. Deverham want you to come in this morning?" she asked, settling on the chair across from his. "Has there been a new development in the case?"

Alec paused with his fork halfway to his mouth. "Development in the case?" he repeated, looking amused.

" 'Hawaii Five-O,' " she explained, taking a delicate bite of her eggs. " 'Book 'em, Danno.' "

He shook his head and resumed eating. "I've got to start

monitoring what you watch," he muttered. "God knows what other tripe you've been watching. That reminds me," he added suddenly, "did Cara really show you a porn video?"

Miranda smiled sweetly. "What do you think?"

Alec's expression grew wolfish. "I think I may owe my little sister a very big thank you," he said sardonically. "But if you want to see any more of those things, let me know. We'll watch them together. How does that sound?"

Miranda thought it sounded delightful, although she doubted she would be watching any more of the daring films. One viewing had struck her as being more than sufficient. Then she realized that he hadn't answered her question, and she sent him a stern frown.

"You're trying to distract me," she said, pointing her fork at him accusingly. "Have there been any new developments in the case, or haven't there? Answer me honestly, now."

Alec hesitated, and then shrugged his shoulders. "We're trying to determine how Talbot got back into England," he said, deciding that was honest enough for the moment. "Deverham has some information from Customs he wants to discuss, but it will have to wait. I want to take the wall down this morning."

Miranda strongly suspected there was much more he wasn't saying, but she also knew he would tell her only when he was ready. Sighing, she turned her attention back to her plate. "You'll be wanting me to leave the house, I assume?" she asked, scooping up a bite of eggs with her fork.

"With proper escort, yes," he agreed slowly, eyeing her with curiosity. "Will you be going to the library?"

Miranda paused as she considered the question. "I hadn't thought of it, but I suppose I might as well," she said, brightening as a sudden thought struck her. "Perhaps they'll have that book I've been looking for. That would be wonderful."

"I don't want you talking to anyone," Alec warned, and she gave him a look of patient long-suffering.

"It's a library," she reminded him with a sigh. "You're not supposed to talk to anyone, or they toss you out."

He bent a forbidding look on her. "You know what I mean," he told her sternly. "Gifford will be on you for most of the day, and I don't want you making his life a misery."

It was a reasonable request, even if the way he phrased it made her want to dash a blunt object over his head, and after a moment, Miranda nodded in agreement. "I shall endeavor not to send him screaming for the door," she said coolly. "And in return, I want a look at what you find. I have the right, you know," she added when he did not reply.

As much as Alec agreed with her, he was still reluctant to expose her to whatever power the room possessed. "If I think it's safe," he temporized, deciding he would decide for himself when the time came.

Miranda accepted his reply with a resigned sigh. It was a good thing she loved him, she thought, giving her eggs an angry poke with her fork, otherwise his tendency to wrap her in cotton wool would have driven her mad by now. They would have to work on controlling his tendencies, if they hoped to have what the people on the television called "a meaningful relationship."

Gifford and the other officer arrived as they were washing up, and while Miranda ran up to get her things, Alec filled them in on their duties.

"Since I'm staying home most of today, I want you both to go with Miss Winthrop," he said, giving both men a threatening scowl. "You've studied the report of yesterday's incident?"

"Yes, Inspector Bramwell," Gifford answered for both men. "I've also requested officers in the area be given Kingston's description, should he attempt to contact her."

"Good," Alec said, his confidence in the young officer soaring. Still, he couldn't refrain from issuing a final word of warning. "Just remember I'm holding the two of you responsible for her safety. If there's any problem, it's me you'll be answering to, and not some bloody review board."

Miranda heard the last of this conversation as she walked into the parlor. "Oh, stop threatening the poor men," she said sternly, sliding her books from one arm to the other as she shrugged into her coat. "I'm certain they'll do an excellent job without your blustering admonishments."

Alec stared at her a long moment, thinking she looked like an angel standing there in the doorway. The sunlight was streaming through the window in back of her, surrounding her with a misty, golden light and making her blond hair shine like a halo.

He remembered the first time he'd seen her, when he'd thought her the product of his deranged mind, and his heart gave a sudden lurch. It was all he could do not to snatch her up in his arms and carry her off to the safety of their bedroom, and for a moment he almost did just that. Only the knowledge they weren't alone kept him from acting on the impulse, and he gave himself a few seconds to get himself firmly in line before walking over to where she was waiting.

"Mind you do what these officers tell you," he ordered gruffly, his hands not quite steady as he lifted the hair caught beneath her coat's collar and spread it over her shoulders. "You're not to go anywhere by yourself, not even the loo."

"That ought to make the ladies using the facilities quite happy," Miranda muttered, sliding an embarrassed look in the officers' directions. To her annoyance they actually looked as if they approved of his preemptory commands.

"Just do it," Alec ordered, making a mental note to have a female officer assigned her as well. His hands tightened in her hair, and the need to taste her was more than he could bear. He bent his head and pressed a quick, desperate kiss to her lips. When he lifted his mouth from hers, both officers were staring politely off into space.

"Any . . . any other instructions?" Miranda stammered, her heart racing as passion zipped through her veins.

Her breathless question recalled Alec to the present, and he shook his head as if to clear it. "Only that I meant what I said about talking to other people," he said, making the decision to at least partially warn her about Kingston. "That includes that professor of yours, should you happen to encounter him."

"Dr. Kingston?" she asked, frowning slightly. "But why shouldn't I talk to him?"

He treated himself to another kiss before stepping back. "Because any man who won't call his poor mother is not to be trusted," he said, and then, to her fury, gave her bottom a distracted pat. "I'll see you tonight, love."

After they'd gone, Alec rooted around his bookcase until he found the Bible his grandmother had given him. He felt slightly foolish carrying it, but he carried it nonetheless. It was his habit never to go into any situation without being as well armed as possible, and in the face of ultimate evil, he wanted to be carrying the power of ultimate good. And, he conceded as he climbed up the staircase, he'd sooner face torture than admit as much. His grandmother had insisted his Anglican upbringing would stand him in good stead, and he hated to prove her right. His father was right as well, he added ruefully, remembering how he'd once remarked that there were no atheists in foxholes.

Picking up the sledgehammer he'd borrowed from Cara, he made his way down the hall to where the hidden room was located. He paused long enough to admire his patchwork on the hole, and then began smashing away at the wall. In less than half the time it had taken him to repair the original damage, he'd knocked out an opening big enough for a man to walk through. In the event the situation soured and he had to beat a hasty retreat, he didn't want to have to wriggle through the damned thing like a badger popping into its burrow.

Once the opening was large enough to suit him, he picked up his torch and Bible and cautiously stepped into the room. It was just as he remembered it, and he quickly made his way to where the secret compartment was located. He'd opened it and was retrieving the items from inside, when the radio clipped to his belt crackled to life. Swearing in irritation, he keyed it before lifting it to his lips.

"Bramwell!" he snapped impatiently, thinking if it was Deverham pestering him, he'd take a great deal of pleasure in telling the Security Officer where he could stuff it.

"This is Constable Sangee," came the tinny voice on the other end of the line. "You have a gentleman out here who is insisting he be allowed to speak with you."

Alec's free hand began reaching for his weapon before he stopped himself. It was unlikely Talbot would walk up and politely request an audience, he realized, and relaxed slightly. "Who is it?" he asked, several possibilities leaping to mind.

"A Lt. Major Keller, sir."

Rye! Alec's lips thinned as he mentally bit back a string of furious oaths. He'd almost have preferred it was Talbot.

"Inspector?" The constable's voice sounded slightly frantic, and Alec could imagine the sweet hell Rye was doubtlessly giving him. He sighed and lifted the radio again.

"I'll be right down," he said, wondering how in the world he was going to explain all of this to someone like his former commander. He might find himself in that padded room yet, he thought, and went down to rescue Sangee before Rye decided to come looking for him himself.

Rye was standing on the doorstep, looking more dangerous than a dozen armed terrorists, and the constable turned to Alec in visible relief. "I wasn't sure if I should contact you, sir," he said, flicking Rye a nervous look. "The lieutenant's name wasn't on your list of approved visitors, and—"

"It's all right, Constable Sangee," Alec interrupted, giving him a reassuring smile. "Keller is a former colleague of mine, and it's my fault for not putting his name on the list. Sorry," and he stepped back to let Rye through the door.

"What the hell did you do to him?" Alec demanded, scowling as he secured the door and reset the alarm. "The poor bloke was shaking in his boots!"

Rye shrugged negligently, looking bored. "I simply told him I was going to see you," he said, his mouth curling derisively. "If that's the best the MPF can do for you, Bramwell, then you're in worse trouble than I thought."

"That's what you think," Alec said, thinking of the surveillance van parked half a block down on Clarges Street. "If you'd displayed any kind of weapon, you'd have been cut in half before you were halfway inside the door."

"And if I'd been carrying a bomb, you'd be holding this discussion with St. Peter," Rye's dark blue eyes glinted with humor. "And knowing you, you sorry bastard, you'd probably be arguing with him as well."

Alec's lips curved in a slight smile as he reached a swift decision. "It's interesting you should mention heaven," he said starting up the staircase. "I've something I want to show you."

Ten minutes later Rye stood in the center of the room, his face wearing an expression of complete disbelief as he glanced slowly about him. "And you're saying Miranda appeared in this pentagram?" he said, gesturing at the yellow and red star painted on the floor. "Just like that?"

"Just like that," Alec agreed, reaching into the hidden compartment in the wall and pulling out more artifacts. "I was drunk at the time, so you can well imagine what my response was; I thought I'd gone as balmy as you all thought I was."

"I never thought you were balmy," Rye denied, looking decidedly green about the gills. "But I'm beginning to feel as I may well be. A time-traveller," he shook his head again, and then sent Alec a wry smile. "Well, at least this explains why I couldn't find a single trace of either her or that alleged husband of hers. I was starting to think you'd been had."

Alec shot him an accusing look. "So you did run a check on her," he said, although in truth, he'd expected no less. Rye was nothing if not tenacious and appallingly thorough.

"I even checked with our mutual friends in Witness Relocation, in case she'd been through their program once before, but they'd never heard of her either," Rye said with an apologetic shrug. "Which reminds me, Jackson Broughmore has agreed to lend us whatever help we may need. He remembers you're the one who pulled his brother out of Armagh after he'd been taken prisoner by the IRA, and he's happy to be of service. By the time he's done, Miranda will have more documentation than she can use."

This came as welcome news, and Alec breathed a silent sigh of relief. If she stayed, at least he wouldn't need to worry about explaining her to the authorities, he thought, picking up a scrolled ring and holding it up to the light. The moment he did, Rye gave a vicious oath.

"What?" Alec glanced at him worriedly.

Rye's eyes had narrowed, and the Beretta he'd worn beneath his coat was now in his hand. "I don't know," he admitted, swinging about in a low crouch. "But it felt as if something just touched me."

Alec pocketed the ring, and began grabbing at the few objects that remained in the vault. "If the room starts glowing, I want you to get the hell out of here," he advised, moving as fast as he could. "I may have triggered something again."

Ignoring the order, Rye made his way to Alec's side, and together they gathered up the tokens of a force older and more powerful than either could ever have imagined. They fled for the safety of Alec's study, and it was only after they had closed the door behind them, that Alec allowed himself to relax. He settled at his desk and flashed Rye a mocking grin.

"I'm starting to feel rather slighted," he drawled, leaning back in his chair. "Everyone but me seems to have been affected by that room in one way or another."

Rye's lips thinned at the memory of the otherworldly touch he had experienced. "You wouldn't have wanted to feel that, I can promise you," he said grimly. "It's worse than being hit by a blast from a Tazer."

Alec had been downed by a charge from a stun gun while undergoing riot training, and he grimaced at the memory. "In that case, I think I'll pass," he muttered.

"Smart lad," Rye replied, then slanted him a curious look. "What now? You went to a great deal of trouble and apparent risk to retrieve this lot. What do you intend to do with it?"

Alec glanced down on the items spread out on the desk. "Study them," he said, picking up the mirror and turning it over in his hand. "Find out how the time spell works, and perhaps learn how to control it, if I can."

Rye leaned forward, his blue eyes narrowing. "You're not thinking of time-travelling, are you?" he demanded incredulously.

Alec abandoned the mirror for the deadly-looking dagger. "If I must," he said, thinking of Miranda. Should the room snatch her away, or, as he feared would be the case, she should elect to return to the past on her own, he wanted the option of being able to go after her and bring her back.

"That's absurd!" Rye snapped, pushing himself away from the desk and leaping to his feet. "Don't you understand there's no undoing what's already been done?" he demanded in a harsh voice. "I know you loved Jane, but that doesn't give you the right to go back and try to alter the past!"

"Jane?" Alec gave him a confused scowl. "What's she to do with any of this?"

Rye tilted his head to one side as he studied Alec's expression. "Isn't that why you want to go back?" he asked slowly. "To prevent her from being killed in that explosion?"

Alec felt as if Rye had plunged the curved blade of the dagger deep in his chest. He stared up at him, the blood draining from his face as he realized such a possibility hadn't even crossed his mind. But it should be easy, shouldn't it? he thought, thrusting a shaking hand through his hair. Once he'd mastered the time spell, he could travel back to that November afternoon and stop Jane from going out. He'd just tell her to go to another store, or wait for the January sales, or . . .

"Alec!" Rye's urgent voice made Alec jerk, and he glanced up to find his friend regarding him worriedly.

"Are you all right?" Rye demanded harshly.

Alec shook off the numbness caused by his stunning revelation, and managed a half-smile for Rye's benefit. "I'm fine," he said, releasing his breath in a heavy sigh. "And you're right, I can't change what's been done."

"Then why do you want to learn how to control the spell?"

Rye asked, frowning as he returned to his chair. "Why would you want to go to all that trouble, if you don't intend using it?"

Alec thought again of Miranda. "Miranda didn't come forward in time by choice," he began, picking his words as carefully as he picked over the items spread on his desk. "She was brought here by some sort of bizarre accident, and we have no way of knowing if anything was altered when she disappeared. Is what followed history as it was meant to be, or is it a history that should never have existed? We just don't know."

Rye digested Alec's anguished words in silence before giving a low whistle. "So that's it," he said, his eyes filled with a mixture of compassion and horrified comprehension as he studied Alec's face. "That's why you went into that damned room, even when you knew it was dangerous. You're going to send her back, aren't you?"

"Good god, what the devil is wrong with you?" Deverham demanded when Alec walked into his office shortly after noon. "You look bloody awful!"

"Headache," Alec replied tersely, giving the same explanation he'd been offering to everyone since entering the building. Even Flemming had emerged from his euphoria over the artifacts long enough to ask if he was contagious, so Alec could only conclude that he looked even worse than he felt, if such a thing was possible.

"Well, take something for it, then," Deverham responded unsympathetically, rummaging around in his desk and tossing Alec a bottle of tablets. "We've made a tentative ID on the body in Lyons, and we've good reason to believe it's not Talbot."

Alec's heart kicked into gear, but he forced himself to remain cool. "So? We've suspected as much from the start," he said calmly, uncapping the bottle and shaking out two aspirin into his palm. He swallowed them, using the dregs in the cup of coffee sitting on Deverham's desk.

"Ah, but now we've proof," Deverham sounded gleeful as he slid a report across the desk surface. "Read that."

Alec did as ordered, his eyebrow climbing as he read the high-lighted area. "That's why you're crowing? Because you've learned the victim's blood type?" he asked, flipping the report over and scanning for more information.

"Oh, we've learned more than that. I did as you suggested, and had Kingston's mother brought 'round for questioning. The poor darling was worried witless about her dear Geoffie, and she was more than willing to cooperate with us. She told us that not only has he not rung in over six weeks, but he hasn't been to his flat in almost as long. And he hasn't moved by the by, he's been living in the same flat he's had since she allowed him to move out some five years ago."

"What has any of this to do with the victim's blood type?" Alec demanded, not giving a damn about Kingston's relationship with his mother. He sensed where Deverham was heading and wished the other man would just get on with it.

Deverham tossed him a color photograph he'd extracted from a file. "In addition to this recent photo of Geoffie-boy, she gave us access to his dental and medical records, so it won't be but a matter of days until we have positive confirmation. But we're certain the victim was Kingston; both had the same blood type."

"B negative," Alec said softly, eyes narrowing as he studied the picture of Kingston. The photo showed a rather diffident young man with thinning brown hair and watery, pale-colored eyes, just as Miranda had described. But this Kingston also had a neatly trimmed beard and thick, dark-framed spectacles, and even as Alec reminded himself of razors and contacts, the skin on the back of his head began to prickle in alarm.

"One of the few facts I uncovered about Talbot in the last twenty-four hours, is that prior to discovering terrorism, he used to be a regular blood donor," Deverham continued, ignoring Alec's tense silence. "I found records from an old blood drive, and the bastard's O positive."

Deverham's words verified Alec's worse fears. "So," he said, putting a firm rein on his emotions, "we have to presume Talbot met Kingston, killed him, and then assumed his identity. All we have to learn is the where and the when, and we'll be one step closer to having him."

"We already know the where and when," Deverham said. "French Intelligence interviewed the owners of the hostel where Kingston was staying, and they said he'd become quite chummy with a fellow Englishman a few days after his arrival. So chummy, in fact, that he checked out of the hostel and went off with this man to explore the glories of the French countryside. You know the French," he added with an expressive roll of his eyes, "they're an open-minded lot."

Alec cared even less about Kingston's sexual orientation than he did his home life. All he cared about was how best to protect Miranda. His first inclination was to take her and Cara as far from London and Kingston/Talbot as possible, and the hell with any objections. But tempting as that was, he knew it was a temporary remedy at best. So long as Talbot lived, he was a threat, which meant he had to be taken out. Now.

"What about your plan to use me as bait?" he asked, meeting Deverham's speculative gaze. "Shall we put it into play?"

"We could," Deverham said slowly, his eyes measuring Alec's every move. "Or we could offer him an alternative target. He's already contacted Miss Winthrop, and—"

"Don't even think about it," Alec interrupted, his jaw clenching in deadly fury.

Deverham held up both hands. "Just a suggestion," he said quietly. "In the meanwhile, I want you to go over that file and see if you can come up with any fresh ideas. I've spoken with your Chief Inspector, and he's given you permission to use your old desk. Contact me the moment you have anything."

Alec accepted his dismissal silently, scooping up the file as he made his way out the door. His office was located in another wing from SO 8, and after pausing to chat with his teammates, he settled in to review the file in his hand.

He spent the next two hours working out a contingency plan

he felt comfortable with. It would mean hanging his arse in the breeze and hoping Talbot was crazy enough to try to blow it off, but it was a risk he was more than willing to take. Naturally this would mean shedding his protection, and that involved a series of complicated phone calls where he spent more time on hold than he did convincing skeptical officials to back his plan.

While he was waiting for yet another faceless bureaucrat to get back to him, Alec opened his desk's top drawer and began to idly fiddle with its contents. There were several pens, some twisted paper clips, and a rubber squeeze ball Jane had given him to help relieve stress. There was also an answering machine tape, and Alec's fingers trembled as he picked it up.

He turned it over in his hand, his mind racing almost as fast as his heart as he thought of what it contained. He'd told himself a dozen times he was going to tape over it, that it was pathetic, sick, even, to hang on to it. He couldn't bring himself to play it, but neither, he realized, could he bring himself to destroy it. It was his last link with Jane, and he knew when he erased it, she would be lost to him forever.

He rang off the call without even being aware of having done so, sweat breaking out on his brow as he stared down at the tape. The tape slid easily into the answering machine on his desk, and after drawing a deep breath for courage, he hit the play button.

"Hello, ducks!" Jane's voice flowed sweet and clear from the machine. "Sorry I'm not there to greet you . . ." and he listened to the rest of the message before hitting the stop button.

His eyes burned and his throat was unbearably tight, as the memory of her words hung in the air. He'd loved Jane, he acknowledged, the last remnants of pain sliding away. He had loved her more than life itself, but she was gone. Now there was Miranda . . . the woman he loved. He took another breath, and hit the erase button.

He had no sooner done that when the phone at his elbow gave an impatient ring, and he quickly scooped it up. "Inspector Bramwell," he said, expecting a blistering lecture from the man he had disconnected.

"This is the Red Coalition," a feminine voice with a slight German accent sounded in his ear. "Our mutual friend has your lover. If you wish to keep her alive, you must do exactly as I tell you . . ."

# Seventeen

"I do not understand," Miranda's voice was clipped with impatience as she glared at the clerk at the Information Desk. "You are saying the book I want is in, but that I can not have it. May I ask why?"

The clerk was the same young man she'd encountered on her first visit to the library, and it was obvious his skills hadn't undergone any marked improvement. "It's as I've already said, miss," he answered, sighing and rolling his eyes, "the book *is* here, but a member of staff has signed it out for the moment. As soon as it's returned, I'll have you paged. Is that acceptable?"

It was not, but Miranda could see it would be useless to continue arguing with the little mushroom. Instead she gave him her name, reminding him rather forcefully that she would be in the Reference Section in the rear of the room, should he need to contact her. That done, she stalked back to where Gifford and the other officer were waiting for her.

"Is everything all right, Miss Winthrop?" Gifford enquired, his eyes twinkling as she joined them. He had witnessed the exchange between her and the clerk, and it was obvious he found it amusing.

"I don't suppose I could convince you to take that wretch into custody?" she asked in reply. "He's the most vexing creature."

"Sorry," Gifford's mouth quirked in a half-smile. "But I'm afraid being vexing isn't a chargeable offense."

She shot the clerk a final glare. "More's the pity," she muttered, gathering up her things and leading them to the back of the spacious reading room.

Both officers sat beside her, their vigilant attitude drawing several uneasy glances from nervous patrons. They sat with their backs to the wall, their hands close to their sides, and their eyes continually sweeping the room for the slightest sign of danger. If anyone, especially a man, allowed his gaze to linger in their direction overly long, he quickly found himself the object of cold-eyed scrutiny. This usually had the effect of sending the person scurrying away, and after the third man beat a hasty retreat, Miranda turned to Gifford with a chiding frown.

"Far be it from me to tell you your job, Mr. Gifford," she began, her voice pitched low. "But do you think you and Mr. Dunlap might strive for a little discretion? I feel as if I'm being guarded by a pair of particularly threatening basilisks."

"Sorry, Miss Winthrop, but we've our orders," Gifford replied, unbending enough to flash her a smile. "We want whoever might be watching to know that you're under heavy watch. Believe me," he added, the wolfish glint in his eyes reminding her of Alec, "if we wanted it otherwise, he'd never know we were here."

By "he" Miranda assumed Gifford meant Talbot, and she gave an apprehensive shiver. It occurred to her that she didn't even know what the terrorist looked like, and she decided to demand Alec tell her when she saw him that night. Thinking of Alec brought a soft smile to her lips, and she wondered if it was possible to love anyone more than she loved Alec. And he loved *her,* she told herself fiercely. He may not be ready to admit it yet, perhaps not even to himself, but he loved her.

She spent a peaceful hour poring over more research books and making careful notations. She was reading a description of Carlton House that was woefully inaccurate, when she heard her name being paged. She turned to Gifford.

"That must be my book," she said, indicating the front of the room. "Do you wish to accompany me, while I go get it?"

He nodded, his hand slipping beneath her elbow as he helped her to her feet. They hurried to the desk, where they found a thin man with a thick black beard and a white work coat waiting for them. She noted that he held a book carefully in his hands.

"Are you the young lady who requested the book?" he asked, blue eyes studying her over a pair of badly smudged spectacles.

"Yes, I am, is there some problem?" Miranda answered, frowning slightly. Beneath his thick Scottish burr, there was something about his voice that was vaguely familiar, but she couldn't quite place it.

"I'm afraid I can not allow the book to be lent out," he apologized, his voice filled with obvious regret. "It's a rare edition, and should never have been put into circulation in the first place. Someone," here he flicked an accusing look at the clerk, "has made an error."

The action warmed him to Miranda's heart, even as his apology distressed her. "But I have been waiting for that book for weeks!" she protested, casting it a longing look. "It is vital to my research, and I really must have it. Please? I assure you, I will be ever so careful."

"Well," he hesitated, cradling the book in his hands as if it were a well-loved child, "I suppose you might borrow it for a *little* while. But it's not to leave the building; you do understand that?" He gave her another anxious look.

She bobbed her head anxiously. "I understand," she said, all but dancing from one foot to the other in impatience. "And again, I promise I shall be as careful as can be."

"All right," he surrendered the book with visible reluctance. "Where are you sitting?"

Miranda indicated the back of the room, her attention already focused on the slender volume. It was bound in red leather that was cracked and faded, the gilded lettering almost obliterated by age and use. But there was still enough left for her to read the title stamped deep into the front cover.

## "ARISTOCRACY ON TRIAL:
## THE TRAIL AND EXECUTION
## OF LORD STEPHEN HALLFORTH"

She gave a strangled gasp, sinking her teeth into her bottom lip to keep from crying out.

"Miss?" The man gave her an anxious stare, looking as if he was getting ready to snatch back the book. "Is something wrong?"

She held the book tighter. "I . . . it's just I can't believe I'm finally holding this book," she stammered, thinking quickly as she gazed down at the title. "I just can't believe it," she repeated, her voice breaking despite her best efforts.

The man looked unconvinced, and Miranda hurried away before he could change his mind. She reached her table just as her legs collapsed beneath her, and her hands were shaking as she opened the book and began reading. Inside, her worst fears were confirmed in conscientious detail.

Lord Stephen Hallforth, the earl of Harrington, was executed on the afternoon of April 26, 1812, after being convicted of the brutal murder of his young bride on the night of their wedding. The woman's remains were found in the Thames and were identified by her grief-stricken stepfather, who, the author added, had been instrumental in bringing the murderer to the king's justice. The earl had proclaimed his innocence to the very end, and his last words had been a heated denial of any wrongdoing.

Miranda's stomach gave a sickening lurch, and she clapped a hand over her mouth in horror.

"Miss Winthrop?" Gifford lay a solicitous hand on her arm, his expression anxious as he studied her pale face. "Are you ill?"

"I . . ." she couldn't seem to breathe. "I need a drink of water," she said, her voice trembling with shock as she pushed herself to her feet. "If you'll excuse me," and she stumbled toward the door, her promise to Alec forgotten.

She hadn't taken but a few steps, when she felt Gifford's arm slipping about her to steady her. They rushed to the Information Desk, and this time the clerk didn't hesitate in offering them help. Whether he was terrified of Gifford's menacing glare or the possibility of Miranda being ill in front of him, he quickly directed them to the nearest rest room.

"Idiot!" The man who had given her the book rushed forward with a worried scowl, "Let them use the employee's facilities! This way," and he guided them around the desk and through a swinging door. There was a narrow hallway in front of them, and he stood solicitously to one side to allow them to pass.

Suddenly Miranda heard an odd puff of sound, and Gifford's body jerked against her before he slid to the ground, pulling her with him. She levered herself up against him, confusion turning to horror at the bright crimson stain spreading across his side.

"What on earth—" she began, and then felt something cold and metallic touching her temple.

"Now, Miss Winthrop," the man's voice was silky as he slid his other arm around her neck, lifting her from the floor with a cruel jerk. "You'll do exactly as I tell you, or I will blow this officer's brains all over the wall. Is that quite clear?"

Miranda nodded her head cautiously, her eyes meeting her captor's malicious gaze with horror. He must have realized she recognized him, because he peeled off his beard, revealing the face of the man she knew as Professor Kingston. When he saw her look of amazement, he actually smiled.

"So, Miss Winthrop," he said calmly, tossing the black glasses on to the floor beside Gifford, "we meet again."


Alec sat as if turned to stone, the phone clutched in his hand. "What?" he said, certain he couldn't have heard correctly.

"You heard me," the woman's voice sounded impatient. "Talbot has your girlfriend. Do you want her back or not?"

Numbness turned to deadly anger. "I want her back," he said through gritted teeth, snapping his fingers to get the attention of the man at the desk next to him. The man glanced up and

Alec pointed at his phone, indicating he needed a trace. Even as the other man was snatching up his phone and placing the call, Alec was turning his attention back to the caller.

"How do I know you're telling the truth?" he asked, listening to her every word, even as he pictured himself killing her if she had anything to do with this.

There was a frustrated sigh. "She was taken from the British Library approximately five minutes ago, and the officer guarding her was shot," the woman said frigidly. "We believe he is taking her to a warehouse in East London, where he has been hiding. The name of the business owning the warehouse is Anglo-Canadian Enterprises. Be very careful; he will doubtlessly have placed several bombs in the area. He thinks he is very clever." The contempt in her voice was palpable.

"Why are you telling me this?" Alec demanded, sweat soaking through his shirt as he struggled to remain calm. He had to be calm, he kept reminding himself, his knuckles turning white as he clutched the phone. If he lost it, Miranda was as good as dead.

"Talbot is a liability the People's Revolution can no longer afford," the woman said, sounding surprisingly prissy. "We have given you information regarding him in the hopes you would rectify the situation for us, but you imperialist pigs are as ineffective as always. Therefore we have elected to deal with the problem ourselves."

"What is that supposed to mean?" Deverham had come dashing into the room and was plugging a handset into the open link on Alec's phone.

"It means you need no longer concern yourselves with Talbot. He will be dealt with." And the line went dead before Alec could ask any more questions.

He slammed the phone down and glanced up at the man he had asked for the trace. "Well?" he demanded.

"A phone booth in East London," the man said, tearing off a sheet of paper and handing it to Alec. "They're sealing the area off now."

Alec grabbed the piece of paper and raced for the door. "I'll need a car and the address for a warehouse belonging to Anglo-Canadian Enterprises," he called out over his shoulder, not bothering to wait for the reply.

With Deverham hot on his heels, Alec and the rest of the CT squad raced down to where their vehicles were parked. Alec climbed into the back of the first available unit, accepting without being told that he was in no condition to drive. Deverham climbed in after him, and they took off with sirens wailing. It was only when they were weaving their way through the thick knot of traffic that Alec managed to speak.

"What happened?" he demanded as they raced up Victoria Embankment toward Blackfriars Bridge. Information placed the warehouse in Southwark, and units were already responding.

"We can't tell just yet," Deverham admitted, a cellular phone held to his ear as he was fed reports from officers on scene at the library. "Details are still coming in, but apparently Talbot killed a binder at the library this morning and took his ID and work clothes. He was also wearing a disguise, so he was able to slip right past our noses. I'm sorry."

Alec gave a curt nod, not trusting himself to speak just then. "Gifford?" He asked after a few moments, a fresh pain slicing through him at the thought of the younger man being hurt.

"Alive, but critical," Deverham said, looking grim. "They were taking him to hospital as of three minutes ago. Dunlap, his partner, wasn't hurt. He was a few steps behind them, but by the time he found Gifford, there was no sign of Miss Winthrop or Talbot. We think they went down the freight elevator."

Alec nodded again, his throat still too tight for speech. She had to be all right, he told himself, turning his head to gaze out the window. He couldn't survive if he lost her as well.

As if aware of his thoughts, Deverham pocketed the cell phone and gave Alec a sympathetic look. "He'll want her alive, Alec," he said awkwardly, realizing empty words of comfort would be worse than useless. "She's no good to him dead."

Alec turned his head and met Deverham's gaze. "I know that," he said in a strained voice. It was all that was keeping him from turning into a raving lunatic, he thought, his breath hitching painfully in his chest. "But I also know Talbot's killed two, possibly three people to get to her."

"To get to *you*," Deverham corrected, giving him a stern look. "You mustn't lose sight of that fact. Talbot's using her to flush you out into the open so he can kill *you*."

Alec accepted that prospect with a roll of his shoulders. If anything happened to Miranda, he was dead anyway. "Looks like he'll get his wish, then," he said, his voice devoid of emotion. "Whatever he wants, we're playing this his way."

"Bramwell—"

Alec cut off the protest with an impatient movement of his hand. "I know what you're going to say, and to hell with you and your bloody procedure," he said, enjoying the hot rush of fury that was coursing through his veins. "Nothing else matters to me except keeping her safe. I'll trade my life for hers, if that's what he wants, and I'll kill anyone who tries to stop me."

The warehouse was old and smelled of wet paper and rot, and the more unpleasant stench of rodents. Miranda lay on the damp, rocklike floor, doing her best not to panic as she watched her captor hook wires to a complicated-looking device.

"Why?" she asked, forcing her voice to remain steady. "Why are you doing this?"

Professor Kingston—Talbot, she corrected herself, gave a surprisingly high-pitched giggle. "A silly question, Miss Winthrop," he said, clipping wires and attaching them to a digital clock. "Because I want to, of course. And because I can. Your lover has presented an interesting challenge, but in the end, it will all be very easy. It's always easy," he added, blue eyes shining as he raised his head and smiled at her.

That smile chilled Miranda to the very bone, for it was the very stuff of madness. "But why do you wish to hurt Alec? What did he ever do to you?" she persisted, praying that if she just kept talking, she might be able to convince him to let her go.

"Other than proving a general nuisance? Nothing really," he said with a one-shoulder shrug. "There was that awful stink when that first fiancée of his was killed by one of my little surprise packages, but to be perfectly fair, I suppose that wasn't *his* fault. Ursula was furious with me because of the negative publicity, and she wouldn't let me claim any credit for the bombing. It was one of my best jobs, too," he added, sounding appallingly like a sulky child.

Fear made Miranda's pulses jump, but she was too proud to let him see it. Instead she kept after him, clinging to the rapidly dying hope that she could make him see reason. "But why go after Alec?" she repeated, wriggling into a more comfortable position. "You said yourself he never hurt you."

Talbot looked up at that, his mouth thinning in anger. "He got all my press, didn't he?" he demanded indignantly. "The dailies were just full of stories about the SAS-trained hero, who'd lost his great love to a madman's bomb. It should have been my greatest triumph, and instead I was put in the same category as some stupid psychopath with a knife!"

"You want to kill him because he got his name in the paper?" Miranda demanded incredulously, scarce believing her own ears.

He gave her a querulous look. "Don't be absurd," he sniffed, pausing in his deadly task. "That's part of it, certainly, but all the publicity the papers gave him made me realize that taking out one man might prove as advantageous to one's career as taking down an entire building, so long as it was the *right* man. The police here think themselves so superior, so untouchable, that it convinces others they can't be harmed. I knew that if I were to kill one of their elite men, my reputation in the international community would be made.

"A reputation is everything in business you know," he added with that cool reasonableness she found so terrifying. "If I mean to sell my abilities to the highest bidder, I need something spectacular to make the rest of the world take notice. You would be amazed the amount of money some people would be willing to pay for a man with my special touch," he added, self-importance making him preen with delight.

"There's only one thing I don't understand," he added, frowning in sudden thought. "I'd had Bramwell's house under observation for days, but you seemed to appear out of nowhere. Wherever did you come from?"

Miranda toyed with telling him the truth, but in the end she simply shrugged. "I was beamed down from the Starship Enterprise," she muttered, borrowing a phrase from one of Cara's favorite shows. She was beginning to accept that she might not make it out of the warehouse alive, and a curious calm settled over her. Whatever happened, she vowed silently, she would never give her captor the satisfaction of seeing her cower.

In that moment, as she faced her own death, she knew there was but one thing in her life she would regret, and that was that she hadn't more time to spend with Alec. She believed now that she had been brought forward in time to find him, to fall in love with him, and she prayed that losing her as well as Jane wouldn't destroy his ability to love. And he deserved to be loved, she thought, blinking back scalding tears. He deserved it so much.

Another regret was that she hadn't been able to save Stephen. She grieved to think he died for a crime he had not committed, and she wished with all her heart that she might have set it right. How she would have done that, she did not know, she only knew that however much she loved Alec, she would never have been happy with him, knowing the awful price an innocent man had to pay.

"Very clever, I'm sure," Talbot said in response to her flip reply, "but we'll see just how clever you are in a few seconds." He pulled her up roughly, turning her around and wiring the bomb to the ropes cutting into her flesh.

"There," he said, sounding thoroughly satisfied with himself. "Let's see your lover get you out of this. If he attempts to cut the ropes off, he'll trigger the bomb, and you'll both be blown apart. And if he tries to take you out of here with the bomb still attached, the infra-red device above the door will activate, and *voilá,* I shall have the same results. Fiendishly ingenious of me, don't you agree?"

She refused to pander to his ego. "You won't get away with this, you know," she told him, facing him proudly. "Even if you do succeed in killing me and Alec, it will do you no good. His friends will come after you with everything they've got."

"Oh please, no tired cliches," Talbot said with a sigh, rising to his feet and fastidiously dusting off his hands. "I rather expected better of you. Now, if you'll excuse me, I believe I shall give Inspector Bramwell a ring. He'll have heard you've been taken by now, and I'm certain he'll be frantic.

"Oh, and Miss Winthrop," he paused by the door, "if you're thinking of making a dash for it, don't. The bomb I wired to you will only kill you and your lover, but the one I've attached to the outer door will take out this entire block. There's a school on the corner, you know," he added sweetly, "with dozens of little kiddies, who'll die if you trigger that bomb. Think about that, won't you?" And he disappeared, shutting and locking the door firmly behind him.

The moment she was alone the tears she had managed to keep at bay began streaming down her cheeks, and her body shook with the force of her sobs. She would die, she realized, and the most horrifying thing of all was knowing that Alec would die with her. She had to think, but she couldn't think as sorrow and terror robbed Miranda of her ability to reason.

She was trying to draw a deep breath, when through the open window above her head, she heard the sound of a car engine starting. Seconds later a deafening explosion shattered the window, showering her with glass and blocking out the sounds of her terrified screams.

*Eighteen*

The car Alec was in pulled up to the Command Post just as
the sound of an explosion rocked the area. He leapt from the
car, gazing up at the column of angry black smoke boiling up
into the pale gray sky, and literally felt his heart stop. Deverham
got out of the car with him, and Alec felt his hand on his arm,
heard him say words that made no sense. He shrugged off the
hand and began running, shoving police and other rescue personnel aside in his desperate bid to reach the source of the oily
smoke. He hadn't gone more than a few yards, when a flying
tackle from behind sent him sprawling into the dust.

"It wasn't Miranda!" Deverham shouted, fighting to hold
Alec down. "Damn it, Bramwell, will you listen? It wasn't Miranda!"

Alec went instantly still as Deverham's words penetrated the
thick fog filling his mind. He searched the other man's face,
deciding in some cold, remote part of his soul that he would kill
him if he discovered he was lying.

Deverham watched him warily, aware of the damage Alec
could inflict if he lost control. "It was Talbot," he said slowly,
lifting himself from Alec and taking a cautious step back. "He
just got taken out by a car bomb."

Alec rose to his feet, his gaze never leaving Deverham's face.
Behind him he could hear sirens and shouts as the others raced
toward the site of the bombing, but he paid them no attention.
Everything in him was centered on Deverham, as he struggled

to control the wild panic clawing at him. "Are you certain?" he asked, his voice unsteady with emotion.

Deverham gave a quick nod. "We were putting forward observers into position, and they saw Talbot leave the warehouse and start the car." He glanced at the smoke and back at Alec. "Looks as if the RC found themselves another cooker," he observed dryly.

Alec closed his eyes, understanding now the last part of Ursula Massendorf's remarks. The Red Coalition had indeed dealt with Talbot, he thought, and savored the sweet irony that a man who had killed as many people as Talbot had, should die the very same way. As far as justice went, he decided, it was perfect.

"What about Miranda?" he asked, opening his eyes to meet Deverham's gaze. "Has anyone confirmed whether she's inside?"

"Not as yet," Deverham admitted reluctantly. "One of the observers saw Talbot doing something to the front door, so we have to assume he has the whole place wired. We're waiting for the bomb doctor to get here before attempting entry."

The lover in Alec wanted to say to hell with that and rush in to check on Miranda himself, but the cop in him knew that such actions would only get them and a whole lot of other people killed. It was tearing him apart, but he knew the sensible thing to do was wait.

They began walking toward the warehouse, stepping over fire hoses, while discussing possible strategies. The area closer to the bombing was already sealed off, and ahead of them the still-burning remains of a car could be seen. The fire brigade was pouring water on it, but it was obvious that whoever had been inside was beyond any aid. Alec wondered if Talbot had felt anything, and hoped he had. It was only fitting.

While they were waiting for the Explosives Officer, Alec tried to remain objective, but he kept glancing at the warehouse, wondering if Miranda was inside and whether she was conscious or unconscious. He prayed it was the latter, because if she was awake and aware of what was happening, she was probably terrified out of her mind.

One of the constables had a bullhorn, and Alec gave it a wistful look. He would have liked nothing more than to call out to her, to reassure her that he was there and would get her out. But until they knew precisely what sort of device Talbot had left behind, he didn't dare attempt it. Bullhorns didn't broadcast signals as radios and cell phones did, but in Northern Ireland he had seen two bombs set off by the amplified sound of a bullhorn, and he wasn't about to take any chances.

The black ordinance van arrived a few minutes later, and Alec was relieved when he recognized the bomb doctor from his days in the SAS. Hames had nerves of steel, the pickiness of an old woman, and the talented fingers of a surgeon. As soon as Hames was out of the van and setting up his equipment, Alec hurried over to his side.

"Bramwell," Hames spared him a curt nod. "I heard you were involved. That your lady inside?"

This time Alec didn't hesitate to claim Miranda as his own. "Yes," he said, his eyes burning as he met Hames' black-eyed gaze. "That's my lady."

Hames nodded. "Then let's go get her, shall we?" he said, picking up a small black box and moving toward the building's large double doors.

Alec followed, and to his relief, no one bothered trying to stop him. He knelt beside Hames, watching curiously as he flipped up the lid of what looked like a laptop computer, and began punching a series of buttons. "What's that?"

"A new little toy from our friends in America," Hames said, his eyes never leaving the screen. "Remember the Gulf War, when they jammed radio frequencies in Baghdad? This is a portable version; it can block radio signals from any controlled device within a specified area. If this bomb is radio or remote-controlled, we can stop the detonation signal from getting through. All we need to do is . . . damn!"

"What?" Alec's blood ran cold at the disgust on Hames's face.

"The bomb wired to the door isn't electronic," he said, punching more buttons. "Looks like we'll have to do this the old-fashioned way." He trained a teasing look on Alec. "Your balls still where they belong?"

Alec smiled for the first time since receiving Massendorf's call. "Last time I checked," he drawled.

"Good." A rare smile lit Hames's eyes. "Then let's go blow this little darling."

After donning the specially designed bomb suit and gloves, Hames pulled on his helmet and set to work. Although Alec had some training in detonation, he was no expert, and he could only stand back and watch as Hames and his assistant dismantled the timing device that had been wired to several cans of petrol with wads of Semtex stuck to them. The bomb wasn't up to Talbot's usual sophistication, but it would have demolished buildings for several blocks, had it detonated. The moment it was discovered, the police had expanded the area of evacuation.

It took several agonizing minutes to defuse the deadly bomb, and even then Hames' job was far from over. They sent the robot in first, and a sweep of the building turned up three other devices. They were dealt with in a similar manner, and finally they were standing outside a wired door on the second floor. Alec was shaking with impatience, feeling as jittery as he had the first time he'd done a high altitude jump. Miranda was on the other side of the door; he knew it, and it was killing him not to be able to reach her.

"What about this one?" he asked, kneeling beside Hames. "Is it the same as the others?"

"No, this one's a ticker," Hames replied, picking up a small device that looked like a calculator. "Apparently our boy wanted to save the best for last. Lucky for us, he didn't know about our little friend here." He gave the black box a fond pat. "This will be as easy as playing a bit of Nintendo."

Alec sat back on his haunches as Hames worked his magic. Sweat was pouring down his back and face from the pressure of keeping himself under tight control. He hadn't called out to

Miranda, because he didn't want to distract Hames, but the strain was beginning to take its toll. If he could just talk to her, he thought, he would be all right.

Hames must have sensed his desperation, because he paused in his work long enough to send him an understanding glance. "Why don't you see if your girlfriend's in there?" he asked gently. "Let her know we're out here."

Alec gave him a grateful look and then carefully raised his voice. "Miranda?" he called out, praying she would answer. "Are you in there?"

Inside the room Miranda gave a convulsive start. She'd heard the arrival of the fire brigade and the other officers, but she'd been praying that somehow Alec had not come. She knew his tenacity, and knew he would die trying to save her. She also knew she would do whatever it took to save him.

"Miranda!" His voice was edged with desperation.

"Alec?" Her voice was thick with tears, but there was nothing she could do about that. "Go back, there's a bomb!"

Alec closed his eyes at the terror in her voice. "I know," he said, sick with helpless rage. "We're taking care of it now. We should reach you in just a few minutes. Hang on, darling."

"No!" She called out, choking on a sob. "I—I mean in here. He—he has me tied to it. Go back, Alec, please!"

Alec started to leap to his feet, but Hames' warning had him freezing in place. "Hold it in," he advised, his fingers flying over the box's keyboard. "You've enough experience to have expected he would likely booby-trap her. Don't go off half-cocked, or she's dead."

The blunt warning kept Alec under control, his mind racing with fear and anger. Hate welled up inside him, and he wished Talbot back from the dead, so that he could have the pleasure of sending him to hell again. Time passed with agonizing slowness, and just as Alec was certain he would go mad, Hames said, "Ask her if Talbot said anything about the bomb being on some kind of timer."

Alec tried not to think about a clock ticking Miranda's life away. "Miranda?" He concentrated on making his voice sound firm and in control. "Did Talbot say anything about a timer?"

There was another long silence as Miranda tried to remember the insane man's last words to her. "N-no," she said at last, tears streaming down her cheeks at the hopelessness of her situation. "He only said you couldn't disconnect it from me without being killed. Go away, Alec," she added in a broken voice, her head dipping toward her chest. "I love you."

Alec's eyes smarted with tears, and he didn't give a damn if anyone saw him crying or not. "I love you, too," he said, placing his hand against the door, his fingers spread wide. "I swear to God, I love you."

"Got it!" Hames exclaimed, and then clamped a warning hand on Alec's arm. "Wait," he said, his dark eyes meeting Alec's. "I know this is hard, but you have to approach her as you would any active bomb. Any sudden moves are out, do you understand?"

Alec wanted to scream and curse that this was Miranda and not some bloody stick of dynamite, but because it *was* Miranda he reined himself in. "No sudden moves," he agreed, and then he carefully opened the heavy metal door.

Miranda saw the door swinging open, and braced herself for the explosion. Other than the first one, she hadn't heard any others, but she couldn't forget Talbot's mocking warning. The thought of others dying because of her was even more terrifying than facing her own death, and she called out a warning the moment Alec and the others rushed into the room.

"Stay away!" She pleaded, eyes wet, "The bomb may go off!"

"Not if I can prevent it," a heavy-set man with a fatherly smile on his face said, kneeling in front of her. "You just sit quietly and let me do my job. I'll have you free of this little trinket before you know it."

Miranda leaned back against the wall, too exhausted to keep arguing. She kept her eyes fixed on Alec, drawing courage from his beloved features. When she felt stronger, she asked the question that had been torturing her for the past hour.

"I—I heard a bomb go off earlier. Was anyone hurt?"

Alec hesitated, then decided to tell her the truth. "Talbot was killed by a car bomb," he said coolly. "His own people must have planted it."

Miranda closed her eyes. " 'All they that take the sword shall perish with the sword,' " she quoted softly, and then opened her eyes to meet Alec's gaze. "I suppose I should be sorry for him, but I can not be. He was mad, you know."

"I know." Despite his promise to Hames, Alec couldn't resist moving closer to Miranda. If he didn't touch her, he would die. He lay his hand on her cheek, the tight knot of tension coiled inside of him slowly unraveling at the feel of her warm flesh beneath his fingertips. "I love you," he said, unable to keep the words inside now that he'd spoken them. "Will you marry me?"

"I'd think twice before answering, if I was you," Hames advised, bending closer to study the intricately woven wires. "I've known this lout a good ten years, and he's a handful, I can tell you. Devil's own temper, stubborn as a bloody block of wood, and proud as a peacock in the bargain. Certain you care to take him on?"

Miranda gave a shaky laugh at the other officer's teasing description of Alec. "You do know him, don't you?" she said, and then smiled mistily at Alec. "I would love to marry you," she said, pushing all thoughts of Stephen and what she had learned from her mind. In the event she survived, she would deal with what she must do, but for now all that mattered was letting Alec know how very much she loved him.

"Well, kiss the girl, binnie," Hames commanded, using the derogatory term for those men who failed SAS's rigorous training. "We haven't got all bloody day."

Alec grinned, feeling surprisingly light-hearted, given their grim circumstances. "Aye, Sergeant!" he said, and then leaned forward to take Miranda's mouth in a kiss that was rife with the love burgeoning in his heart.

Behind him the other officers broke out into applause and wolf whistles, and there were tears in Alec's eyes as he raised his mouth from hers. "You have to marry me now," he told her, reaching up to caress her cheek. "You've compromised my good name, and I demand you make an honest man of me."

Miranda shook back her hair and gave another soft laugh. "I shall endeavor to do what I can, sir," she said, eyes bright with love as she smiled at him. "But it seems to me your reputation was beyond repair long before we met."

The next fifteen minutes passed slowly as Hames carefully unwound each strand of wire from the ropes. His jamming device provided a dampening field that kept the primary detonation device from functioning, but there were still back-up points to be dealt with. While Miranda and Alec kissed and exchanged soft words of love, Hames kept up a running commentary, alternately praising and cursing Talbot's skill. At last he unwound the final strand of wire and cut the ropes binding Miranda's hands, and she tumbled forward into Alec's waiting arms.

He held her close, his eyes squeezing shut as he sent a prayer of heartfelt gratitude winging heavenward. Finally he drew back, cupping her face with shaking hands. "Let's go home, darling," he whispered, sweeping her up in his arms and carrying her outside where the ambulance was standing by.

"I was so afraid," Miranda said softly, as she lay in Alec's arms, her head pillowed on his hair-dusted chest. "Not just for me, but for you. He wanted you dead."

"I know." Alec's fingers tangled in her hair, stroking the golden strands as he savored the sweet feel of her safe in his arms. If he lived to be one hundred, he knew he'd never forget the sight of her crouched on the floor of the abandoned warehouse with a bomb wired to her body.

After he'd taken her outside, he'd used his shoulders as a shield to prevent her from seeing the bombed-out car that still contained Talbot's remains. The forensic teams were swarming over the wreckage, and he didn't want her to have to deal with the horrifying images. God knew she already had enough to deal with, he'd thought bitterly.

Overriding her protests, he'd insisted she be transported to hospital, not relaxing his vigilance until the doctor assured him she was unhurt. An intense interrogation followed, as Miranda was grilled by officers from several departments. He was also questioned, and in the end it was decided that with Talbot dead the threat against him had been minimized. His protection status was downgraded to its usual level, and he and Miranda were allowed to go. In the hallway they were reunited with a tearful Cara, who brought the welcome news that Gifford had survived surgery and was expected to make a full recovery.

Miranda had wanted to go visit him herself, but he and Cara were able to dissuade her. They returned to their house, and the door had scarce closed behind Cara, before he and Miranda were in each other's arms. He'd kissed her frantically, passion exploding in a fireball of desperate necessity. He'd needed to know she was truly alive, and there was only one proof his heart and his body would accept. He carried her up the stairs to his room, laying her gently on the bed and making love to her until they were both too exhausted to move.

Similar memories were flitting through Miranda's mind, and she remembered how Alec had kissed her, whispering of his love again and again as he'd moved ardently against her. It was as if he was sealing his vows with his body, and the eternal pledge he made—only made her love him more. Her arms tightened protectively about him before she spoke.

"I have to go back."

Alec stiffened beneath her, his hands clenching about her arms as he lifted her until he could gaze into her eyes. What he saw reflected there sent a shaft of pain tearing into his heart.

"You learned what happened to Stephen," he said, his rough voice lacking the smallest trace of emotion.

Miranda gave a miserable nod, and quietly told him about the book she'd discovered. The entire time she was speaking, she kept touching him, stroking his warm, resilient flesh as if she somehow drew strength from the feel of him.

"And you're positive he wouldn't have killed you, if you'd stayed?" Alec asked when she'd finished speaking. "How can you be so certain?"

"Because he did not," she replied, recalling their earlier conversation on the subject. "Stephen may not have loved me, but he would never have killed me. I would stake my life on that."

"If you go back, that's precisely what you'll be doing," Alec said grimly, trying to see past the pain that was eating him alive. He wanted to forbid her to even think of leaving him, but tempting as that thought might be, he knew it would never answer. If they solved the riddle of the hidden room, the decision to go or to stay was hers. It had to be.

Miranda saw those anguished thoughts reflected on his face and pressed a frantic kiss against his pursed mouth. "I'll come back," she promised recklessly, tears filling her eyes as she gazed at him. "I swear by all that is holy, that if it is at all possible, I will come back to you!"

"But what if it's not possible?" he demanded rawly, unable to keep the terror out of his voice. "This isn't a bloody flight to Paris we're talking about here, this is time-travel! How do you know where you'll end up, or if you'll ever be able to come back again? And even if you do manage to come back to me, how will we know how much time will have passed? It could be a moment, or even a lifetime. We just don't know."

Miranda accepted his words with a soft sigh. "You're right," she said slowly, searching for the words that would convince him. "We don't know. But then, we didn't know I'd survive this afternoon, did we?"

Alec's eyes narrowed in pain. "Damn it, Miranda, I—"

"No, listen," she interrupted, laying a gentle hand over his mouth. "I didn't say that to attach blame, or to make you feel guilty. I am stating a simple fact. We *didn't* know. All we could do was pray and believe that I would survive.

"When Talbot first took me, I remember thinking that fate

had brought me forward to find the one man in all eternity I was destined to love. That man is you, and I believe with all my heart that we were meant to be together. If I do succeed in returning to the past, I have to believe that the powers that control time will bring me back to you. I need to believe that, Alec," she added brokenly, her eyes never leaving his, "and I need you to believe it as well."

At first Alec couldn't speak, emotion leaving him bereft of words. He loved her so much, feared losing her above all else, and yet he knew he would have to let her go. He touched his hand to her cheek. "I love you," he whispered, unable to think of anything else.

"And I love you," she returned, blinking back tears. She pressed a kiss to his chest, the need to make love with him awakening the passion in her. Her hand sought him, her gaze holding his as she began stroking him. "Let me show you how much," she said, her touch taking them both to paradise.

Alec went to the library the following morning and retrieved the book for Miranda. While she was studying it for clues as to what had happened, he went into work and cornered a flustered Flemming in his lab.

"Really, Inspector, I'm not a computer, you know!" the smaller man protested, bristling as Alec loomed over him. "You only left the journals off yesterday. You can hardly expect me to have deciphered them already!"

"Why the devil not?" Alec demanded, being deliberately intimidating. "You claimed to have an expert working with you; how much of an expert can he be if he can't even translate Latin?" The brief glimpse he'd caught of the books showed him the entries had been made in that ancient language.

"Because the journals also contain ancient Hebrew, Greek, and a language I've never seen before!" Flemming huffed, defending his friend vehemently. "Also, the books are extremely fragile, so I can hardly fax them to Charles, can I?"

"What do you intend doing, then?" Alec snapped, reluctantly deciding the annoying scientist had a valid point. "I need to know what those journals contain."

"They appear to be a list of spells and incantations!" Flemming provided, eyes gleaming with excitement. "I know enough Latin to translate that much, and it's quite fascinating. Where did you say you found them?" He gave Alec a curious look.

"I didn't," Alec retorted. "Did the bit you read mention anything about time-travel?"

"As a matter of fact, it did!" Flemming said quickly. "The author's final entry mentioned casting such a spell to escape the witch-hunters. He also said something about a talisman being the key to unlocking the spell. Did you find anything like that?"

Alec thought of the pendant Miranda had been wearing when he'd first seen her. "I may have," he admitted cautiously. "Do you know what it looked like?"

Flemming dug some notes out of his desk. "A pentagram of some kind," he said, frowning over his own handwriting. "Rather like the first drawing you showed me, I believe. Perhaps it is the key to a code, like the Rosetta Stone. That is what helped break the hieroglyphics, you know."

Actually Alec did know, recalling the bit of information from a long-ago visit to the British Museum. "Is there anything else you can tell me?" he asked abruptly, deciding he'd wasted enough time on this nonsense. He was anxious to return home and see if Miranda had discovered anything helpful. Hopefully she'd been more successful in her search than he had, he thought sourly.

"Only that these journals and other items are valuable and ought to be in a museum," Flemming said, bending a reproachful frown on him. "In fact, I believe keeping them is a violation of the Antiquities Act, especially if they can be authenticated."

"Then we just won't tell the bleeding authorities about them, will we?" Alec replied silkily, giving him his most threatening smile. "If those entries are spells, who knows what I might be tempted to do if I find out you've been telling tales out of school, hmm?" His smile widened when the other man paled. "I see we understand each other. Goodbye, Flemming. I'll be in touch."

At the house on Curzon Street, Miranda vacillated between grief and outrage as she read the account of her husband's trial.

"What a packet of lies and moonshine!" she raged to Cara, who had stopped by for a visit. "How could anyone in their right mind believe my stepfather over Stephen? It is ridiculous!"

"Well, you have to admit Stephen's defense is rather shaky," Cara said reluctantly, frowning over excerpts from the trial. "Refusing to give evidence in his own defense seems a foolish thing to have done. How could he have been so pigheaded? He must have realized it made him look guilty as hell!"

"That is because you do not understand Stephen's concept of honor," Miranda replied with a sigh, drumming her fingers on the desktop. "Asking him to take the stand and give evidence would have been an insult. He was a gentleman, and to him, giving his word that he was innocent was evidence enough."

"He was an idiot, and his solicitor must have flunked the most basic tenants of cross-examination!" Cara retorted unfeelingly. "Look at the statements given by this mysterious Lord Q," she added, waving the book for emphasis. "He contradicts himself half a dozen times or more!

"He did see you, he didn't see you. He didn't see you, but he saw Stephen's hands covered with blood! Any halfway decent barrister would have made mincemeat of him! Other than hinting that 'his lordship seemed a trifle confused as to the sequence of events,' the dolt didn't say a word! He ought to have been calling him a bloody liar and threatening him with perjury!"

"I hadn't noticed that," Miranda said with a frown, taking the book from Cara and re-reading the passage, "but you are right." She set the book down and gave Cara a curious look. "I never knew you were so familiar with the law," she said, not wishing to trespass into Cara's private life. For all the other woman had always been quite friendly toward her, she realized there was very little she actually knew about her.

Cara shrugged and took a sip of cola. "Paul was a Queen's Counsel, and I used to help him with his briefs," she said, looking so uncomfortable Miranda hastened to change the subject.

"Well, you're right about Stephen's solicitor," she said, pinning a smile to her lips. "He does seem to have been most incompetent. Of course, to be fair, it didn't help matters that stepfather lied incessantly."

"Did he?" Cara look intrigued. "About what?"

"About everything," Miranda said with disgust. "But most especially about the necklace he claims I always wore, the necklace that was about the poor woman's neck when he allegedly identified her as me. I never wore such a necklace in my life!"

"Interesting," Cara murmured, cupping her chin in her hand and looking thoughtful. "But, of course, he would have needed a body, wouldn't he, to have Stephen charged?"

"I suppose," Miranda agreed, trying not to think of it. "But I still do not understand who this Lord Q person is, or why he should have lied in the witness box. The man I overheard in Stephen's room was his friend, or so I thought. But why would a friend tell such dreadful lies, when he knew it would lead to an innocent man's conviction?"

"That's something we may never learn, at least not from here," Cara said after considering the matter. "Perhaps when you go back, you'll be able to sort it all out. Speaking of which, what are you going to do once you do get back?

Miranda paused before answering. This was a matter she had already considered at great length, and she'd finally arrived at what seemed to her the only possible solution. "If I arrive in time to prevent Stephen's execution, I shall do whatever I can to have him released from jail," she said quietly, meeting Cara's curious gaze. "Once he is free, I shall then ask him for an annulment, so that I can return and marry Alec."

Cara raised her dark eyebrow in surprise. "Then you're coming back?"

"Of course," Miranda frowned at her. "Why would I wish to remain in the past, when Alec is here?"

"No reason," Cara said, but a relieved smile crossed her face. It faded just as quickly, replaced by a sullen scowl. "What if he doesn't let you?" she asked, sounding belligerent. "Stephen, I mean? I've read about that period, and women were treated like property! If he refuses to grant you an annulment, what will you do?"

Miranda had already considered that as well, and her cheeks grew pink as she said, "He will grant me one. When I tell him I have taken a lover and may be with child, he will not be able to be shed of me quickly enough. No man in his position would trust his title and the succession to soiled goods."

"You're pregnant?" Cara gave a delighted squeal.

"I may be," Miranda said, smiling as she touched her stomach. "I haven't had my monthly flow, and Alec and I have not been as . . . er . . . careful as we should," she added, blushing furiously.

"Say no more," Cara held up her hand. "But I can't believe you would refer to yourself as soiled goods. You really don't think of yourself like that, do you?" She looked so outraged that Miranda quickly reassured her.

"*I* do not, certainly, but that is how a man like Stephen would see it," she said gently. "That is why I know he won't hesitate to give me my annulment. Our marriage was never consummated, and so an annulment is the best for all concerned; and, of course, it will leave him free to marry without the slightest question of impropriety. Even for a man, a divorce would have caused a dreadful scandal in those days."

Cara gave a loud snort. "I'll say it yet again, luv, thank God I was not born in your time! I'd have gone mad!" She sighed and then asked, "How will you explain where you've been? People are bound to ask, especially if you've been gone for months."

"I've thought of that as well, and I intend telling the court and the others that I've been in Ireland with my lover, and that I've only returned to prevent a grave miscarriage of justice."

"Mmm." Cara gave an approving nod. "But why Ireland? Why not France or something?"

"Because we are—were at war with France," Miranda reminded her. "I chose Ireland because that is where my father's family was from. Elias knows I have always longed to go there, and he, at least, will accept what I say."

Cara tapped her hand on the desk. "What about Stephen?" she asked. "What do you intend telling him?"

"The truth."

Cara blinked as if she couldn't have heard correctly. "The *truth?*" she echoed in disbelief. "Have you lost your bloody mind? You can't tell him the truth! He'll have you clapped in Bedlam or some equally godforsaken place!"

"No, he won't," Miranda said with a smile, feeling a wave of confidence settling over her. "Because I intend bringing him proof that everything I tell him is the truth. And you, dear Cara, are going to help me get that proof."

# Nineteen

Alec arrived home to find Miranda and his sister huddled over their plans. After getting a cup of coffee he joined them, listening to Cara's suggestions with a mixture of amusement and exasperation. After one particularly intriguing suggestion, he leaned over and gently cuffed his sister under the chin.

"Don't be absurd, darling," he said, eyes sparkling with laughter as he drew back. "Of course, she's not bringing a copy of *The Daily Mail* with her. She wants to convince Stephen she's been to the future, not the bleeding planet of Mars."

"Very funny, brother, dearest!" Cara sent him a burning glare. "I don't see *you* offering any brilliant suggestions. I only meant that she should bring something with her that couldn't possibly have existed back then."

"Yes, stories about two-headed cows in crop circles and the Princess of Wales going topless do tend to be late twentieth-century phenomenon, I grant you," Alec conceded, deciding the only way he could survive this discussion was to make as much fun of it as possible. "But I think she should bring back something of historical importance. Something about the moon landing, perhaps, or even a book about the Blitz. Stephen is bound to find that far more convincing than the latest gossip on Michael Jackson."

"I do not know about that," Miranda felt honor-bound to intercede. "And as for Stephen not believing stories about the Princess going topless, I can only assume you've never heard of *our* Princess of Wales. She would have provided enough fodder to keep the dailies going for years, believe me."

"And she can't bring back books about the future," Cara said, looking surprisingly solemn. "If she does that, she could change everything. No, it will have to be something else, something that will convince him absolutely, but won't give him specific knowledge about the future . . ."

"I have it!" Alec exclaimed, clapping his hand on the desk. "I'll be right back," and he dashed from the room, returning a few minutes later with a video camera tucked under his arms.

"Alec, you're brilliant!" Cara said, clapping her hands in approval. "It's the perfect answer!"

"What is it?" Miranda leaned closer to examine the object.

"It's a camcorder," Alec replied, handing it to her. "Like what they use to shoot television programs. We'll film some video of present-day London; show him cars, airplanes, that sort of thing, but nothing specific, like Waterloo Bridge," he added before Cara could speak, "and then when you get back, you can show it to him. That ought to convince him soon enough."

"But how will I be able to show it?" Miranda asked, turning the camera over with a frown. "There aren't any television sets back then."

Alec took the camera from her and upended it. "You just pop the video cassette in here," he indicated a slot, "hit play, and you can review whatever you've shot. As Cara said, it's the perfect solution."

"Yes, it is," Miranda agreed, beginning to warm to the notion. One of the few personal things she did know about Stephen was that he was fascinated by mechanical objects, and doubtlessly he would be intrigued by the camcorder's function. She set it aside and turned back to Alec. "What else should I bring?"

"The book," Cara said, and when Alec opened his mouth in protest, she added, "I know, I know, but in this case it's not the future we'll be unveiling, it's the past. Besides," she gave a thoughtful frown, "I've been thinking, and it's my belief your Stephen was set up. Someone besides your stepfather was out to get him, and I think he has the right to know that. Anyway, if you do manage to get him acquitted, the book wouldn't have been written in the first place. Right?"

That made a twisted sort of sense, and so the book was chosen as the second object to accompany her through time. They debated for another hour before Alec decided upon the last item she would take with her.

"A sledgehammer?" Cara looked at him as if he'd taken leave of his senses. "Why in the world would she want to lug one of those things about with her? They must weigh a bloody ton!"

"They weigh a few pounds, and if she gets zapped back to a time when the room is enclosed and the house abandoned, it will be her only chance of getting out again," Alec said bluntly, the look on his face daring Cara to disagree any further. "She's taking it with her."

Cara gave a loud sigh and turned to Miranda. "Well, at least he's not suggesting you take an Uzi back with you," she said. "A fine impression *that* would have made. You'd look like Rambo."

Since Miranda hadn't a clue who Rambo might be, she thought it wisest to change the subject. "Well, all of this may be for naught, if we can't figure out how to access the time-travel device," she said, giving Alec a curious glance. "Were you able to learn anything from this Sergeant Flemming?"

Alec didn't reply at first, thinking that he had only to remain silent, and let them believe Miranda was stranded here with him, that there was no hope of her ever returning to her time. It was sweetly tempting, and for a moment he allowed himself to believe he could do it, and then he gave a heavy sigh.

"He's working on it," he said, his gaze fixed on his clenched hands. "The journals are in some sort of code which they're attempting to decipher, but he was able to learn enough to know that this is the key." He extracted the pentagram from his pocket and handed it to Miranda. "I think you should start wearing it from now on."

Miranda stared at the pentagram, feeling its power vibrating in the palm of her hand. The ancient symbol terrified her even more than it had in the past, because now she understood it had the power to take her away from Alec.

"Put it on," he said, sensing her reluctance. "You said it was only after you'd put it over your head that you were transported here. Evidently it focuses the room's power, or perhaps acts as some sort of tracking device, like on 'Star Trek.' "

"But I am a Christian," Miranda said, her skin crawling at the thought of donning the evil thing. "I can not wear the mark of the Devil."

"You must, if you mean to help Stephen," Alec said firmly, determined that she do what she felt she needed to do. "Remember what you said about needing to believe the room would bring you back again? Well, perhaps you need to believe that God will understand, and that His power is even greater than the room's. He'll keep you safe. I know He will."

Miranda's reluctance faded under his gentle words, and she slipped the medallion over her neck. "Very well," she said, studying his face wistfully, her heart overflowing with love. "What do we do now?"

"Tomorrow we'll start filming," Cara said, gathering up her purse and coat. She'd seen the look on Miranda's face and was feeling decidedly *de trop*. "We'll shoot some of the tourist-type places like Picadilly Circus and Trafalgar Square, and perhaps take the tube out to Heathrow. I daresay the sight of a jumbo jet ought to prove pretty convincing, hmm? Bye, luvs!" She kissed them both on the cheeks and dashed out of the house before either Miranda or Alec could stop her.

An uneasy silence descended between them, as they each wrestled with the enormity of their feelings. Miranda capitulated first, holding out her hand to him in mute supplication. He hesitated but a moment before reaching out to accept it, his fingers closing protectively around hers.

"I want to thank you for bringing me the pentagram," she said, her gaze holding his. "I know it can't have been easy for you."

"Not easy?" he repeated, his lips twisting in a bitter smile. "It was one of the hardest things I've ever done." He lifted their linked hands to his lips and brushed his mouth over her soft flesh. "Why does it seem as if all I do is put you in danger?" he asked in a raw voice.

Her fingers tightened around his. "You're not putting me in any danger!" she protested, horrified that he was blaming himself for her decision.

"Aren't I?" he asked, rejecting her offer of comfort with a derisive laugh. "First Talbot, and now this. If I had a particle of sense, I'd plaster up that room and say to hell with it. Of course," a reluctant grin touched his lips, "if I had a particle of sense, I wouldn't be involved with anything so farfetched as time-travel to begin with."

She smiled in response, her eyes soft with love as she gazed at him. She still hadn't told him of the babe, and had won a promise from a reluctant Cara that she would also remain silent. In the event their efforts failed and she remained trapped in the past, she didn't want him to suffer the anguish of knowing their child had been lost to him as well.

"I've also had moments when I've doubted my sanity," she told him, her lips curving in an answering smile. "But the one thing I have never doubted is that I love you, and that we were destined to be together."

Her simple declaration made Alec's pulse race, and using their linked hands, he pulled her to her feet and into his arms. He carried her to his room, his mouth already feasting greedily on hers as he set her down beside the wide bed. His lips skimmed down her neck, tasting and tormenting her even as his hands were disposing of their clothes.

"You are so beautiful," he groaned, his hands gentle as he caressed her bared breasts. "I love you so much!"

Miranda's fingers tightened in his hair, as she tilted her head back and bit her lip to hold back an answering groan. His mouth had replaced his fingers, and his tongue was swirling over her nipple in the playful manner that never failed to drive her wild.

When his fingers began teasing her as well, she gave in to the passion building inside of her with a soft cry of delight.

Hearing her soft sigh of surrender sent Alec over an invisible edge, and he pushed her gently on to the bed. Kissing and caressing each other they rolled across the sheets, their limbs entwining as he thrust deep inside her. She met his powerful movements eagerly, wanting nothing more than to give him as much pleasure as he was giving her.

The sun poured through the partially opened drapes, enveloping them both in soft, golden light as they drove each other to the peak over and over again. The more they touched, the more they wanted, both driven by fears neither would acknowledge. They were afraid it was the last time they would feel each other, and the sun was low in the sky before the fear was laid temporarily to rest.

At Miranda's insistence they took the tube to Picadilly Circus, and once she learned how to look through the view finder without getting dizzy, she insisted upon being allowed to do most of the taping.

"I know what shocked me," she told Cara and Alec as she posed them in front of the flashing Coca Cola sign on Regent Street. "Now stop complaining and wave to Stephen."

"Lord, we have another Spielberg on our hands," Alec muttered to his sister, refusing to smile and mug for the man he considered his rival.

"More like another mother," Cara returned through gritted teeth. "Remember how she used to take those bloody awful home movies of us when we were kids? 'Smile for Auntie Bette!' Hell. I thought I'd outgrown this."

Once Miranda was satisfied she had filmed enough of Picadilly, they went to Trafalgar Square, where she shot video of the snarled traffic and the tourists who had come from all over the world. She'd wanted to film the changing of the guard at Buckingham Palace, but Cara sternly vetoed the idea, insisting it was among the specific details Stephen could not be told. She also refused to let her film anything involving Queen Victoria, as she felt Stephen's learning that Princess Charlotte did not accede to the title could change history as they knew it.

They took the hour-long tube ride out to Heathrow, where Miranda was awestruck at the sight of the jets. This was the closest she had ever been to one of the huge crafts she had occasionally glimpsed overhead, and she was terrified at the very thought of riding in one. She handed the cam corder to Cara, content to let her film the jets landing and taking off and provide a running commentary for Stephen's benefit.

The next day she and Cara went out again, filming more sights and each other. Miranda felt decidedly odd in her modern clothes, as she explained her new life to the husband she'd left so many years in the past, and she was grateful when Cara lowered the camera and announced a break for lunch. They returned home afterward, and spent the next few hours going over the published account of Stephen's trial.

Cara's knowledge of law stood them in good stead, as she pointed out bits of testimony she thought would help in Stephen's defense, should the authorities question Miranda's identity. Miranda was writing the information down, when Cara suddenly clapped her hand on her forehead and swore colorfully.

"Your clothes!" She exclaimed, gazing at Miranda in horror. "You can't go back dressed like that!"

Miranda glanced down at her sweatshirt and jeans, and flushed in agreement. "You are right," she said, feeling foolish for not having thought of it herself. "Such attire would cause a most dreadful scandal, and it certainly would not aid my cause in the slightest. What do you think we should do? I fear I have never been overly gifted with needle and thread."

"Me either," Cara admitted, frowning as she considered the matter. "I have it! I've a friend who does theatre in the West End; I could give her a ring, tell her I'm going to a costume party as one of Jane Austen's characters and need her advice. She's a nut on costumes, so I'm sure she'll be happy to help.

I'll go ring her right now," and she hurried into the kitchen to use the phone.

While she was gone Alec returned from work, the expression on his face so grim Miranda's heart sank to her toes. Before she could ask what had gone wrong, he sat beside her and took her hand in his.

"Flemming and his chum think they may have solved part of the riddle," he began without preamble, his jaw clenched as if he were in the greatest of pain. "Apparently once the spell's been cast, the room functions on a sort of autopilot. Travel through time can only be accomplished when the room is glowing, and we can't figure out how to make that happen. Which means that until the damned thing starts to glow of its own accord, there's not a bloody thing we can do."

"Except wait," Miranda said slowly, ashamed to realize she was secretly relieved by his news. It meant she was being given even more time with Alec, and that was something she could never bring herself to regret.

"Except wait," Alec agreed, wondering what was going on beneath the remote expression on her face. Was she disappointed? he wondered, trying not to be hurt. He knew how much saving Stephen meant to her, and he felt like an utter failure for not giving her the one thing she desired above all else.

They were sitting in strained silence, each lost in their own dark thoughts, when a smiling Cara rejoined them.

"Done!" she exclaimed, throwing herself onto the divan beside Miranda. "A company on Sloane Street just finished a run of *The Rivals,* and Jennie gave me the name of the supply house that furnished their costumes. We'll have you rigged out like Lydia Languish in no time!" she added, her smile fading at the look on her brother and Miranda's faces. "Now what?"

Alec repeated what he had just told Miranda and, as he expected, Cara was all for trooping up to the room and having a go at recasting the spell herself. "How hard can it be?" she argued when he curtly refused. "You said it began glowing when you started removing things from the vault, so there must be some kind of triggering device inside. All we have to do is find it, and *zap!* Problem solved."

Alec opened his mouth to repeat his refusal, when he abruptly closed it again. "You're right," he said slowly, frowning as he tried to remember his actions on that day, and the day he had shown Rye the room. It hadn't glowed then, but he must have triggered something, because Rye had definitely responded. He couldn't recall touching any sort of switch, but he supposed he must have. He surged to his feet as he reached his decision.

"Let's go," he said to Cara, and then turned a threatening glare on Miranda when she also stood. "Where do you think *you're* going?" he asked in a voice of silky menace.

"With you, of course." She frowned at his tone.

"The hell you are," he retorted, his brows lowering in a scowl. "You're not stepping foot in that room, until you've been properly prepared. We're not risking having you beamed back until we're ready."

It was a valid point, and arrogant as she found his behavior, she knew it would be foolish to argue the point. She contended herself with a haughty look, resuming her seat with a toss of her head as she folded her arms across her chest.

"As you wish, sir," she said, her voice as cold and rigid as the first time she'd clapped eyes on him. "I suppose as I shall be returning to an era of female subjugation, it is best I accustom myself to masculine brutality. I shall remain here dutifully, until my lord and master returns to fetch me."

"I wish you'd stop laughing," Alec complained as he and Cara climbed through the hole and into the secret room a few minutes later. "It wasn't that bloody funny."

"Yes, it was," Cara assured him, trying to ignore the frisson of uneasiness she felt almost immediately upon entering the room. "You should have seen the expression on your face; you looked as if you'd just swallowed a live eel."

Alec grimaced at the thought. "I was only thinking of her," he muttered, defending himself against the charge of despotism.

"After all the preparation we've gone through, it doesn't make sense to take foolish chances."

"I know."

The subdued reply made him glance over his shoulder in surprise. Cara was standing at the far end of the room, rubbing her arms as she glanced apprehensively about her. "Are you all right?" he asked, taking a concerned step toward her. "If the room bothers you, you can wait outside."

She gave a small shudder before dropping her hands to her sides. "I'm fine," she said curtly, refusing to give in to the way her senses were screaming a warning to get as far from the room as humanly possible. "Let's get on with it, shall we?"

Alec was tempted to override her, but knowing Cara's stubborn nature, it would have been a colossal waste of time. And time, he was beginning to realize, was a commodity of which they had but a short supply.

Making a mental note to keep a sharp eye on his sister, he made his way over to the hidden cabinet and began poking about. He'd removed most of the items when he and Rye had been there before, but a few small pieces remained. He was pleasantly surprised to find a sack of some coins, gold or silver, he was certain, and there was another leather sack containing a dazzling assortment of jewels. He held one up to the light coming from his electric torch, and Cara gave a sharp cry.

"Alec! Something's happening!"

He glanced up immediately, but he could see nothing unusual. The room was as murky as ever, lit only by his torch and the faint light poking in from the hallway. He hesitated, trying to hold himself open for any vibrations, but to his disappointment, he felt nothing. "Are you certain?" he asked Cara, making another try. "I can't feel a thing."

"Well, I can, and I don't like it!" Cara retorted, not caring if she was behaving like a typical female or not. Facing a drugged-out rapist in an alley was one thing, she thought, edging back toward the opening. Facing the humming power of whatever dark force the room contained was another. She was all for getting the hell out of there, and to devil with her pride!

"Describe it!" Alec demanded, feeling a surge of annoyance that he was excluded from the room's influence. "Is it electrical? Rye said it felt like a Tazer."

Cara took another step back, forcing herself to concentrate on the sensations she was experiencing. It *was* electrical, she decided, closing her eyes and focusing her mind on the power she could feel sizzling about her.

"It is electrical in a way," she said at last, her heart hammering so hard she thought it would burst from her chest. "But it also feels a bit like sound vibrations, like from a loud stereo. When you raised that thing to the light, it felt as if someone had turned the woofers up full blast."

Alec filed away the description, so that he could see if it compared in any way to Miranda's experience of the room. Maybe once the power was tripped, he thought, it could be activated with the pentagram. "Anything else?" he asked Cara.

"No, and I want to get out of here," Cara responded, deciding she'd been brave enough to earn two Queen's Crosses. "I'll be waiting downstairs with Miranda," she said, then turned and fled as quickly as she could.

The next week flew past as they finalized preparations for the bizarre journey. Miranda and Cara went to the theatrical warehouse, and were able to piece together an ensemble that, while not in the first crack of fashion, would allow Miranda to present an acceptable appearance. Cara hooted over the styles, especially the Lavinia bonnet, but when she put it on her dark hair, Miranda thought she made a most fetching picture.

Miranda continued her research, and the more she learned of Stephen's trial, the more she was certain that Cara was right, and that an unknown and powerful enemy was conspiring against him. But who? she wondered fearfully, and what could they possibly hope to gain by his demise? They couldn't have been after his title, for according to Debretts, that had died with him. Her other research had also proven that her villainous stepfather had managed to abscond with her money. So what was their motive? It was a bewildering and frightening puzzle, and she could think of no way to solve it.

She was still worrying over the matter a few nights later, when something roused her from her sleep. She reached out automatically for Alec, and found him tense and awake beside her. "Alec?" she asked, her voice quaking with fear as she recognized the sensations washing over her.

"I know," Alec replied quietly, his voice strained with emotion. "I feel it, too." And it was just as Cara had described it, he thought, feeling the wash of humming power brushing over his bare flesh.

"Is it . . . is it the room?" She moved closer to his back, as if seeking protection. Faced now with the chance to return to her own time, she realized she did not want to go. She loved Alec, she thought, fighting weak tears. How could she leave? Then she thought of Stephen, dying brutally for a crime he did not commit. How could she possibly stay?

Alec hesitated, his heart tight in his chest as he acknowledged his greatest fear was about to come true. "I'll check, you stay here," he ordered, and then climbed from their bed and padded to the door. He was back in less than a minute, flicking on the light in their room.

"You'd better get ready," he said, his strained face showing the terrible toll the words cost him. "It's time."

Miranda had never felt such pain in her life, and it was all she could do not to scream from the agony of it. What she was asking of herself was a price no one should have to pay, she thought, wiping a shaking hand over her tearstained cheeks. To be forced to chose between honor and love was almost more than she could bear, and for a brief moment she wondered if she had the fortitude to do what must be done.

"Miranda," she felt Alec's hands on her shoulders, and she glanced up to find him kneeling in front of her.

"I love you," he whispered, his eyes bright with tears as he leaned forward to tenderly kiss her forehead. "I want you with me for a hundred lifetimes, and for whatever comes after that. But I want you to be certain that is what you want as well."

She swiped at the tears streaming down her face. "It is what I want," she said, her voice breaking as she reached out to caress his face. "I love you, Alec."

"And I love you," he repeated, still touching her. "All of you, Miranda, and that includes your stubborn pride and your wonderful, exasperating sense of honor. If you don't at least try to go back and rescue Stephen, it will eat away at you until the woman I love no longer exists. You know it would."

She dipped her head in mute acknowledgement of his gentle words. He slipped his hand beneath her chin, raising her head until once more he was gazing into her eyes.

"Remember what you said about needing me to believe you'd come back?" he asked, ignoring his own pain in his determination to convince her. "Well, I *do* believe it, Miranda. I have to believe it, or I'd never let you out of my sight."

"Alec, I—"

"Shhh," he lay a trembling finger against her lip. "You get dressed, and I'll go get the other things."

While he was gone, Miranda wasted a few precious moments engaging in heart-wrenching sobs, and then she got up and began donning the costume that had been hanging in the wardrobe in anticipation of this moment. She picked up a reticule she had fashioned from a square of fringed silk, and inside she tucked the gold coins Alec had acquired for her. He'd traded several of the coins he'd found in the room for them, telling her teasingly that it was only fitting that the warlock who'd originally cast the spell should help to pay some of her costs.

She'd just finished fastening her lace mitts, when Alec returned carrying the book and the camcorder. The sledgehammer was already in the room, and she'd promised to carry it with her. The camcorder was in its carrying case, and he hung it over her shoulder as he handed her the book.

"Is this how you dressed back then?" he asked, studying her thin gown of sprigged muslin with admiration.

She nodded, pulling her shawl closer about her bared shoulders. "I've forgotten how dreadfully drafty these things were," she said in a weak attempt at humor. "I fear I have become too accustomed to fleece and cotton."

His smile was equally as strained as he gazed down at her. "Are you wearing the pentagram?"

She reached beneath her fichu and raised the pendant to show to him. It felt surprisingly hot, and she wondered if it was tuning itself to the room.

He touched it briefly. "I don't know if it's proper to pray to God this hellish thing works," he said, his voice cracking despite his best efforts, "but that's precisely what I intend doing every day, until you come back."

They walked down the hall, and she could see the greenish light spilling out from the entryway Alec had knocked in the wall. She could hear the humming, and for the briefest of moments, her resolution wavered.

"Miranda?" He was regarding her worriedly.

"I don't want you to come in there with me," she said, raising her gaze to his face.

"But—"

"No," she shook her head. "I couldn't bear to have you see me disappear. I want to say goodbye here."

Everything in Alec screamed a frantic denial, but he knew she was right. It was best to end it here. He drew her into his arms, holding her against his heart. "I'll wait for you," he vowed rawly. "I don't care if it takes a thousand years; I'll wait for you."

"And I'll come back," she vowed, holding him tight. "If I have to track down another warlock to recast the spell, I will come back to you."

They kissed deeply, passionately, pouring every bit of the love they bore each other in that final, desperate caress. Then they drew back reluctantly, their lips clinging as if loath to part, and she took a stumbling step back.

"I love you," she whispered brokenly, her gaze never leaving his face. "Wait for me."

She stepped into the hole, and Alec watched the light spilling from the room grow brighter. Suddenly there was a brilliant explosion of light, and he thought he heard Miranda's scream. The sound had him running toward the opening, his heart in his throat as he called out for her. He stumbled through the opening, prepared to fight the very forces of hell if need be, but the room was empty. Miranda had vanished.

# Twenty

It was the sound of screaming that awakened Miranda this time. The voice was piercingly shrill, and had she possessed the energy, she would have cheerfully consigned its owner to the devil. But even that simple act was beyond her meager store of strength. She could only lie there, her body shaking as she fought off the painful effects of passing through time. She was about to attempt opening her eyes, when she was suddenly struck squarely across her back.

"Be gone, foul spirit!" the voice cried out, striking her a second time. "Depart this Christian house at once!"

Several more blows were landed before Miranda managed to roll to one side, her head spinning as she opened her eyes to glare at her attacker. "Will you cease that caterwauling!" she snapped impatiently, studying the young woman whose starched mobcap and white apron proclaimed her position as a maid. "And stop striking me. I am the Countess of Harrington."

The maid's mouth dropped open, and her blue eyes went even wider before they rolled up in her head and she collapsed on the floor in a dramatic swoon.

"Oh, bloody hell," the oath slid easily from Miranda's lips as she pushed herself up on one elbow. She was about to crawl over and see if the silly chit was all right when several other maids came dashing in. At the sight of Miranda and their fallen comrade, they set up a cacophony of shrieks that had Miranda putting her hands to her head in agony.

The room was soon filled with screeching servants, and it

wasn't long before the noise attracted the attention of the butler
and the housekeeper. Miranda recognized the pink-cheeked
woman at once, and it was all she could do not to cry with
delight. She had done it!

"My—my lady?" The housekeeper was staring at Miranda in
horror, her hands clutched to her bosom. "Is . . . is it truly you?"

"Indeed it is, Mrs. Finch," she replied, relieved that she had
remembered the woman's name. She felt awkward lying there
on the floor, and knew it was time to assume her role as countess.
"Would you please assist me to my feet?" she requested, holding
out her hand in imperious demand. "I am growing weary of
lying in the dust."

Her cool tones broke the paralysis holding the other gawking
servants, and she was soon pulled to her feet, a dozen pairs of
hands swatting at the dust clinging to the skirts of her gown.
The young maid had recovered her senses and was wailing loud
enough to wake the dead.

"There were a flash, and there she were!" she was sobbing
into a handkerchief the butler had given her. "I told you this
room was haunted, didn't I?" And she began sobbing even
louder.

There was an uneasy stir among the servants, and even the
dignified butler looked a little apprehensive as he cleared his
throat. "I beg pardon, my lady, but might one ask how you came
to be in this room?" he questioned, his tone anxious.

Miranda thought of Alec, imagining how he would have han-
dled the butler. At once her head snapped back, and her eyes
narrowed in mock fury. "And might one ask, Mr. Mansfield,
how it came I was able to walk into this house unmolested? Why
was there no footman at the door? If I were of a criminal bent,
I could have walked off with half the family silver, and no one
the wiser."

"But—but, my lady, I am certain there was a footman on
duty!" he protested, wringing his thin hands in a manner that
assured her he was more concerned with protecting his position
than with dunning her for the truth.

*"I* saw no evidence of one," Miranda retorted, her voice chillingly polite. "When no one responded to my knock, I had no choice but to let myself in. I came upstairs looking for someone, when I saw this child," she nodded at the young maid who had been helped to her feet and was staring at her as if she were a Medusa. "I walked up to speak with her, but before I could utter a word, she started shrieking and attacking me with that broom."

The butler swallowed uncertainly. "But my lady—"

She raised an eyebrow coldly. "Are you doubting my word, Mr. Mansfield?" she asked, every word dripping with haughty disdain. "Or mayhap you choose to believe this chit and think that I appeared in this room like some sort of apparition?"

The butler's face turned a dull red. "No, my lady, indeed not!" he stammered. "And allow me to apologize for any discomfort you may have suffered. This is a very well-managed household, I assure you!"

"I am sure it is." Now that she had skated past that uncomfortable moment, Miranda was anxious to get to the reason for her harrowing journey. "Where is his lordship?" she asked, struggling for a calm demeanor. "Is he at home?"

"Oh, my lady, they think he killed you!" Mrs. Finch exclaimed, shoving Mr. Mansfield aside as she hurried forward. "He is on trial before Parliament, and they say he will hang!"

Miranda closed her eyes for a brief moment, savoring the satisfaction that she had arrived in time. "Then I must go there at once," she said, opening her eyes to meet the upper servants gaze. "Please have a carriage summoned."

Her words sent the servants scrambling, the footmen knocking each other aside as they fought to be the one to carry out her instructions. Mrs. Finch tutted and fluttered around her, and when she suggested Miranda might wish to change her clothing, Miranda hesitated only a moment before agreeing. The clothes she had brought back with her from the future might do well enough to fool a handful of servants, she thought, but if she meant to convince a room filled with suspicious lords, she would need all the defenses she could muster.

She was relieved to find her belongings just as she had left them. Most of her jewelry was gone, and she wasn't the least surprised to learn her stepfather had shown up on the doorstep a few days after "her" body had been discovered to demand them. There were still some jewels belonging to Stephen's family left in the vault, and Miranda donned them with only a slight twinge of guilt. The more she looked like a countess, she reasoned, the more she would be granted credibility.

She gazed into her cheval glass, turning her head to one side as she studied her reflection. Her hair was arranged in a smooth chignon, and with the rubies and diamonds dripping from her ears and throat, she looked every inch the imperious lady. She lifted her chin higher, her green eyes glimmering with a mixture of fear and fury as she thought of what lay ahead of her. It would be hard, she knew, but having already accomplished the impossible, she refused to contemplate even the possibility of failure. She would do what she had come to do, she told herself pulling on her gloves, and then she would go back to Alec.

After leaving instructions that the items she'd brought with her were to be put in her room and guarded, she hurried down to the waiting carriage. The trip to the House of Parliament seemed to take forever, and glancing out the window at the passing traffic, she couldn't help but compare this London to the one she had left one hundred and eighty-four years in the future. It was odd, she mused, that while she had grown up in this London and had lived there all of her life, it was that future London she now regarded as home.

Getting into the chamber where the trial was being conducted proved almost impossible, but Miranda had not come this far to be turned away at the door. She argued her way past several guards and numerous flunkies, before being brought to a halt by a stolid sergeant-at-arms who would not be swayed by threats or tears. She was contemplating using some of the tricks Cara had taught her, when she heard a stunned gasp behind her.

She whirled around, to find herself confronting one of her old beaus. He was staring at her with that mixture of horror and incredulity she was coming to recognize, before taking a hesitant step toward her. "My God . . . Miranda! Is . . . is that you?" he asked, his voice quavering with disbelief.

"Indeed it is, Lord Danburton," she said, recalling he was one of the few suitors she had contemplated marrying before meeting Stephen. "Would you please tell this . . . person . . ." she gave the guard a fulminating glare, "to grant me passage? I must stop these fools, before they send an innocent man to the gibbet."

The marquis bustled forward at once, all aristocratic outrage as he took her arm. "Get out of the way, you lack-wit!" He ordered the still-suspicious soldier. "This lady bears important evidence in this trial! Stand aside, I say!"

The sergeant reluctantly did as ordered, and then Miranda was inside the massive chamber, walking calmly down the aisle as pandemonium erupted around her. She could hear screams and shouts, but her attention was all for Stephen, standing stiff and silent at the bar. His blue eyes also widened, but he didn't so much as blink as she walked up to the bench where the lords in their wigs and robes were sitting.

"I am Lady Miranda Hallforth, the Countess of Harrington," she said, pitching her voice loud enough to be heard over the din. "I understand there has been a slight misunderstanding."

"And you say, my lady, that you have been living in Ireland these past eleven months, and knew not that your husband had been charged with your murder?" one of the bewigged officials demanded, his eyes dark with suspicion as he studied Miranda down the length of his nose. "I find that difficult to believe."

"As would I, your honor, had I been residing in Ireland the entire length of my disappearance," Miranda replied with the cool control she had displayed for the past hour. Her hopes that Stephen would be released once she was identified had faded the moment her stepfather, recovering quickly from his amazement, had set up a stream of sputtering protests.

His insistence that she was an impostor was quickly dis-

missed, as there were too many present more than willing to
identify her, including one member on the bench who had known
her since she was in leading strings. But he refused to let the
matter drop, and so Miranda was forced to stand at the bar,
answering increasingly pointed questions with as much pride as
she could muster.

"But did you not just say that was the case?" another lord
demanded, showing more than a little skepticism.

"No, my lord," she answered quietly, accepting philosophically that she was blackening her reputation for all times. "What
I said was that I was residing in Ireland when I heard of his
lordship's arrest, and that I came here from there. Prior to that
I had been living in Scotland, where I fled on the night I ran
away. It was all in the note I left for Stephen."

"A note which conveniently disappeared!" her stepfather
sneered, winning a reprimand from the judges, who were showing increasing impatience with the blustering man.

Miranda gave him a cool look. "I have noted that many things
have a tendency to disappear when it is in *your* best interests,
sir. Like the five thousand pounds from my dowry and the other
ten thousand you allegedly invested on my behalf, and yet of
which I knew nothing. Perhaps you would care to explain that,
Mr. Proctor?" she added with a goading smile.

She'd learned of the missing money from her research, recalling that Stephen had been accused of taking it on one of the last
days of the trial. If she had arrived before that information was
offered in evidence, she could use it to plant seeds of doubt
against her stepfather's testimony.

"How dare you accuse me of thievery, you little witch!" As
she expected, the veiled accusation brought her stepfather to his
feet, his hands clenching in fists as he glared at her. "I'll teach
you to tell tales about me!"

Stephen made an abortive movement toward Elias, but was
hampered by the shackles that remained about his wrists and
ankles. The sight of the manacles tore at Miranda's heart, and
convinced her more than ever that the loss of her virtuous name

was small recompense for what Stephen had suffered because of her. She waited until the judges had reprimanded her furious stepparent before continuing.

"My lords, if I may say something for the official record?" she said, following Cara's instructions as best as she was able.

"You may." Permission was granted by the first judge.

She paused, gathering her courage before turning to the bench, her chin held high as she met their hostile gazes. "When I ran away that night, it never occurred to me that things could come to such an impasse, that a man as good and honorable as his lordship would be charged with so vile a crime as murder.

"I wish to say, for the official record, that Stephen had naught to do with my disappearance. I wish to state that I left him because I did not love him. I loved another man, and I left my husband to be with him. I was not murdered, your lordships, I ran away to join my lover. That is *my* crime, my sin, and I freely confess it before you all. His lordship is guilty of no crime, and I ask that you release him at once."


"What lover?" They were scarce in the carriage before the words were forced from between Stephen's clenched teeth. They were sitting in the carriage she had acquired, his back stiff, and waves of cold anger fairly radiating from his lean body. He'd lost a great deal of weight since she had last seen him, and this visible reminder of all he had endured made her writhe with shame. She had to make it up to him, she thought, blinking back hot tears. She'd thought saving his life would be enough, but now she wondered if anything she could do would be enough to pay him for all he had lost.

Her impassioned plea to the judges had the desired effect, and Stephen was released amidst jubilant cries from the packed galleries. She had to listen to her stepfather's vile curses and cries of "Whore!" and "Jezebel!" from the spectators, but she'd accepted them as her due. The important thing was that she had accomplished at least part of her goal. Now she had to convince

him to accept the truth from a woman he now had every reason
to hate and distrust.

"Madam!" His sharp voice recalled Miranda to the present,
and she turned to find him studying her through narrowed eyes.
"What is the name of your lover?" he repeated, his jaw clenched
with fury. "I demand to be told his name."

Because she felt she owed him nothing but the truth from this
point forward, she said, "His name is Alec Bramwell, and I believe I am carrying his child."

He flinched, his mouth growing even tighter. For a moment
a deadly anger glimmered in his dark blue eyes, and his hands
formed angry fists. "Why?" he asked at last, his voice raw with
emotion. "Why did you do this to me? Can you hate me so
much?"

Miranda's lips quivered slightly, but she would not look away
from him. "I do not hate you at all," she said with as much
dignity as she could muster. "And it was as I said, I had no way
of knowing you would be charged with my death. But the moment I learned what had happened, I came back to do what I
could to exonerate you. No matter the cost, I knew it was not
right that you should pay the price of Alec and I being together."

Stephen muttered a harsh expletive beneath his breath, his
eyes going past her to stare out the window. They drove another
few blocks before he spoke again.

"What do you mean 'no matter the cost'?" he asked, his tone
still stiff, but without the cutting anger of a few seconds earlier.
"Are you referring to the way you publicly confessed to being
an adulteress?"

She did pale then, but her voice was steady as she answered.
"That's part of it, yes."

"What is the other part?" he persisted, surprising her by his
tenacity. Evidently he was more like Alec than she would have
supposed, she thought with a sudden flash of irreverence.

"That is difficult to explain, my lord," she said, noting with
relief that they were on Picadilly. "With your permission, I

should like to wait until we are at home before answering any more questions. I—I have something to show you."

He didn't reply at first, and she took his sullen silence for acquiescence. He leaned back against the cushions of the carriage, his expression hard and remote as he stared out the window. She studied him curiously, comparing the Stephen she recalled to the man sitting opposite her. This one seemed older, somehow. Paler and thinner, with a hard, naked edge that had been absent before. Or perhaps it had always been there, hidden beneath the veneers of society, and the experiences of the past few months had torn it away. The true man, with all his strengths, was exposed for all the world to see.

"What is it you wish to show me?" Stephen's deep voice cut into her reverie, and she glanced up to find him regarding her with marked suspicion. "I warn you, madam, if your lover is waiting at the house, I will doubtlessly kill him."

At first Miranda was uncertain how to answer him. Alec was at the house, but certainly not in the way Stephen meant. "No, he is not waiting for us," she said, her voice firm. "I left him behind when I decided to return to London."

"And he let you go?" Stephen's lips curled in an ugly sneer. "It would seem your lover is not so noble a figure, my dear. No man who counts himself such would allow the woman he loves to take such a risk. How does he know I will allow you to leave again? I *am* still your husband, you know," he added on a note of silky menace.

She ignored that, deciding he was more than entitled to get a little of his own back. However, that didn't mean she intended allowing him to slander Alec. She raised her chin proudly as she met his narrowed gaze. "Alec knew and accepted the dangers I would face when we decided I should return," she said in a cool tone. "And I will thank you not to sneer at him. You have no idea what allowing me to return cost him."

She knew by the way his head jerked back that she had said precisely the wrong thing. She opened her mouth to recant, but before she could managed to utter a word, Stephen was grabbing her and shaking her roughly. "Cost *him?*" he roared, his eyes glittering with rage. "Do you know what I went through when you disappeared? I'm not talking about the damned trial, or even the weeks I spent in that pestilent cell, I am talking about *me!* About the hell I went through not knowing what had happened to you, not knowing if you were dead or alive!"

"Stephen, I—"

"What did you expect I would do when you ran off and left, hm?" He gave her another shake. "Did you think I would simply shrug my shoulders and go have a cup of tea? I looked for you, damn it! I searched night after night through parts of the city you would swoon with horror should you see them. Every time the body of a young woman was found, I would go to the hospital to see if it was you. In the beginning I always prayed it would not be you, but toward the end I prayed it would, so that at least I would know what had happened to you."

He shook his head, his hands tightening on her arms as a particularly horrifying memory rose to taunt him. "I remember one girl, blond, like you, but so young . . . so young. She looked as if she had been torn to pieces by a wild animal . . ." he shuddered visibly. "I went home and drank two bottles of brandy, before I could get the memory of her face out of my mind."

Tears burned Miranda's eyes as she managed to free herself from his grip. But instead of moving away, she simply lay her hand on his cheek. "I am sorry," she said in a soft voice, her heart breaking for what he had suffered. "I know how weak those words are, but I am sorry. I never, never knew you would be the one to pay the price for what happened to me."

His eyes were almost black with pain as he studied her. "Why did you leave me, Miranda?" he asked, his voice so low she could scarce hear the words. "I know you did not love me, but why did you marry me only to leave on our wedding night?"

The carriage had turned on Clarges Street, and Miranda knew they were almost home. She gave Stephen's cheek another gentle pat. "When we are alone, I will tell you everything," she promised, moving back to her own seat. "All I ask is that you be patient until then, and when I do tell you all that has happened, I ask one more thing from you."

"And what is that?" His voice was wary.

"I ask that you keep an open mind," she said evenly. "You may not wish to believe me at first, but I want you to listen before deciding that I am insane."

At first Stephen could not believe the evidence of his own ears. He wanted to believe Miranda was lying, that she was spinning the most fantastical story she could concoct, in hopes of winning his cooperation. But the expression on her face, the certainty in her voice as she described where she had been for the past eleven months, put paid to that faint hope. However nonsensical her tale, it was evident she believed every word of it, and that meant but one thing. In addition to being no better than a strumpet, his bride was a madwoman. The realization rocked him, and he took a moment to allow it to sink in before attempting a reply.

"And you say it was the hidden chamber that allowed you to make this journey to the land of the future?" he asked, wondering bleakly how much more scandal his name could endure. He would have her taken out of the country, he decided, planning carefully. Some place quiet and peaceful where, perhaps with time, her sense would one day return. He was beginning to doubt her wild tale of a lover, who was something called a policeman, and if such a person did not exist, it meant she was still his responsibility. And despite all the havoc she had caused, it was a responsibility he had no intention of shirking.

His cool manner and deliberate tone of voice reminded Miranda of how Alec had reacted when she'd claimed to come from the past. Both men had acted as if she was a madwoman who was to be humored at all costs, and she was surprised to find their condescending behavior made her long to break something over both their stubborn heads.

"We believe some sort of black magic was involved," she said coolly, deciding that if he patted her hand, she would kick him in the shins. "As I said, there is much about the power of the room we do not understand, but that is neither here nor there. What is important is that I was able to return in time to prevent your death. Now I shall be free to return to the future and Alec."

Stephen glanced down at the book she had given him, and had to admit he was unnerved by the title. "You have to agree it is all rather implausible," he said carefully, his thumb brushing over the letters stamped into the leather. "One can not hop about in time as if going from one room to another."

Miranda realized the time had come to show him the video, something she had been reluctant to do for fear of frightening him. He had already been through so much that she hated the realization she was about to shatter his concept of the world as he knew it. Unfortunately she had no choice. If she wished his agreement to grant her the annulment, he had to be convinced.

She hesitated a moment and then moved away to retrieve the camcorder from the wardrobe. After extracting it from its cloth carrying case, she checked to make sure the batteries were functioning, and then carried it back to where Stephen was waiting. He was eyeing her warily, his body tense as if he were waiting for her to do something violent.

"One of the things I first admired about you was your intelligence," she said quietly, shocking him more than a little. "Unlike most men in the *ton,* you are possessed of a keen mind and an inquiring nature, and I am relying upon that to help you accept what I am about to show you." She turned the camera over, flicked the play button, and handed it to Stephen.

He accepted it gingerly, his brows meeting in a curious frown as the small window in the box suddenly flickered to life. When Miranda's face appeared, it was all he could do not to cry out in alarm. Even as he was telling himself this could not be, her image began speaking to him.

"Hello, Stephen," she said, her voice calm as she gazed at him. "If you are watching this, it means that we've succeeded, and that I was able to reach you in time. This is where I have been; it is the future, and I want to share it with you so that you will understand why I must return. This is *my* time, now, Stephen. It is where I belong."

Stephen continued watching the flickering images in the small window, the hair on the back of his head standing up in a mixture of terror and astonishment. He gave up telling himself that he could not see what he was seeing, and simply watched as an astonishing new world was unveiled before his eyes.

He saw buildings taller than anything he could have imagined, as well as buildings that were as familiar to him as his own home. He saw streets packed with things Miranda called cars, and held his breath as they boarded an impossibly long carriage she referred to as a tube. He saw people, too. People of every description and hue, moving about a city he recognized and yet had never seen. And just as he thought he couldn't take another shock, he saw a huge object take to the sky, making a screaming noise that made his ears ring.

"That is called a jet," Miranda said, seeing the incredulity on his face. "In one of these, it is said you can travel to America in less than six hours."

Stephen shook his head weakly. " 'Tis impossible," he said, but even as he watched, another of the objects came roaring down from the sky to touch on the ground with the grace of a bird.

Other images filled the screen, including a man with curly black hair and brown eyes. Stephen had seen him in the earlier images, but he had always seemed stiff and uneasy, as if he wanted no part of the little box. He still seemed uncomfortable, but his manner was resolute as he stared out at Stephen.

"This is damned awkward," he said, shifting to one side and stuffing his hands in the pockets of his jacket. "Miranda left the camera with me and asked that I leave a message for you, although I have no idea of what I'm supposed to say. How the bloody hell is one man supposed to tell another man that he's in love with his wife? But I am, you know. I love Miranda with all my heart, and I give you my word I will do everything in my power to keep her safe and happy. I—I just wanted you to know that. Goodbye, my lord." And the window went white with a crackle of light and noise.

Stephen was struggling to comprehend all he had heard and seen, when the window blinked and the image of a woman came into view. He recognized her from other scenes. She had curly black hair, and her eyes, lavishly trimmed with thick lashes, were the color of the most costly brandy. Her face was more exotic than beautiful, and Stephen was wondering who she might be, when she spoke.

"Hello, your lordship," she said, her voice cool and edged with a note of mockery Stephen could not like. "I'm Cara Marsdale, Alec's sister. Miranda doesn't know I've taped this, but I wanted the chance to have a private chat with you. Sorry, luv," her full lips lifted in a wry grin as if in anticipation of Miranda's stunned gasp, "but you should have known I wouldn't be able to resist putting a little of my own in."

The woman's expression hardened, and Stephen had the impression she was standing directly in front of him. "Everything Miranda has told you is the truth," she said in a voice that was almost masculine in its certainty. "Every bloody word of it. And that includes the fact that she is in love with my brother, and he with her. Knowing Miranda, I'm certain she didn't tell you she risked death to return to the past to save your aristocratic neck, but she did.

"So, my lord, if you're half so noble and fine a gentleman as Miranda says you are, you'll grant her the annulment she wants and send her back home straight away. If you don't, I swear to God, I'll find some way of coming after her, and when I do, you can be very sure I'll make your life a sweet hell." And the image vanished in a crackle of sound.

Stephen turned to Miranda, his shock turning to annoyance at the woman's parting words. "What a thoroughly forward creature!" he exclaimed, his lips thinning with annoyance. "Are all women of the future so bold as she?"

Miranda smiled at his reaction. "Not really, but Cara is a police officer, like Alec, and she is used to looking after herself."

"With a tongue like that, I shouldn't be surprised. I daresay there would be few men willing to perform that task for her," he grumbled, and then shook his head again. "My God," he said slowly, turning dazed blue eyes on her, "it's true then? You've been to the future?"

"Yes, I have," she said, relief making her weak as she realized he had finally accepted her story.

He studied her another long moment. "And you truly wish an annulment?" he said, laying a gentle hand on her arm. "You do not think there is any hope for us?"

She shook her head, her eyes bright as she thought of Alec. "No, my lord, there is no hope."

He closed his eyes for a brief moment, intellect and reason waging a pitched battle with his pride. In the end he knew there was only one answer he could give, and his expression was somber as he opened his eyes again to meet her gaze. "Very well, then," he said, inclining his head with stiff formality. "Then that is what we shall do."

In the end it took six long and painful weeks to sort everything out. Stephen took rooms at the Albany, while she remained in the house, and not a day went by but that she didn't enter the room. She no longer feared its power, and being in it made her feel somehow closer to Alec. It was almost as if she knew that one hundred and eighty-four years into the future, he was standing in that same room waiting for her to return.

As the weeks passed it became increasingly obvious that she was indeed with child, and once that was confirmed, the courts were quick to grant the annulment. With that settled, she infuriated her stepfather by signing her entire fortune over to Stephen. Stephen protested, naturally, but she was finally able to convince him it was the only way she would be truly happy. Once that was done, she began making preparations for her return journey, anxious to return to Alec and the life she had grown to love.

She waited, her anxiety becoming stark terror when, despite all her efforts, the room refused to function. She even opened the hidden vault, taking out the objects Alec would later find and playing with them, but nothing she did seemed to have the slightest effect. She had now been in the past for ten weeks, and she greatly feared she would remain there.

One evening, after having spent the entire day in the room trying with all her might to summon the room's power, she collapsed in the center of the pentagram, sobbing with frustration and pain. "Alec," she cried, her hand clenched around the pendant, "Alec, I love you. I love you."

At first she thought the voice she heard was a hallucination, a product of exhaustion and wishful thinking. But when she heard it a second time, her head came up in alarm.

"Alec?"

There was nothing, and she was about to start crying again, when she heard his voice echoing eerily in the small room.

"Miranda? Miranda, where the hell are you?"

"Alec!" She leapt to her feet, staggering slightly. "Alec, I'm here! I'm here!"

"I can't see you, blast you! Come home!"

She gave a hysterical laugh at how cross he sounded, like a petulant little boy demanding his mama's immediate attention. "I'm trying!" she called, laughing and crying all at the same time. She was so emotional she wasn't aware of what was happening, until she felt the brush of energy against her flesh. The room was glowing with the light she had been praying for, and she stumbled out of the pentagram long enough to grab the book, the camcorder, and sledgehammer and drag them back.

She could feel the currents of time crackling around her, and as the sound and light intensified, Alec's voice grew more distinct. The power hummed ever louder, and she hurled herself into the heart of it, embracing it with all of her heart.

"I'm coming, Alec! I'm coming!" she cried out, then cried out again as she was sucked into the powerful maw of the time storm.

"Miranda! Miranda, where are you?" Alec was standing in the center of the pentagram, enveloped by the brilliant light. He'd been coming into the damned room every day for the past four weeks, calling out to Miranda until his voice was barely more than a croak. He had nightmares about what might have happened to her, but those nightmares were tempered with the great love he bore her. He kept remembering her promise to return to him, and it was that promise that kept him sane.

His superiors took his demand for a month's holiday as understandable, but he knew he would have to report back to duty soon. He had all but given up hope, when something had drawn him into the room, and when he'd first heard her voice, he was afraid to believe he had really heard it. But he believed now, and his heart was racing as the room glowed with the light of a thousand suns.

There was the brilliant, white explosion he remembered from before, and when he could see again, he was almost afraid to look down. If she wasn't there, he didn't think he could survive. He took a deep breath, and slowly opened his eyes.

"Miranda!"

The sound of her name being cried out in joy brought Miranda out of the fog, and she blinked her eyes sleepily. She could feel the hot splash of tears falling on her cheeks, as kiss after kiss was pressed to her mouth. She recognized Alec's touch, and she opened her eyes to find him bending over her.

"Alec?" Her voice quivered as she raised trembling hands to his face. "Alec, is it you?"

"Miranda!" He could only murmur her name, holding her against his heart as he rocked her. "I love you," he kept repeating, brushing kisses over her face. "Never leave me again, damn it! I can't bear it without you."

"And I can't bear to be without you," she replied, her heart breaking with happiness. "I'm home, my darling, I'm home, and I give you my word I shall never leave you."

They kissed each other wildly, making promises and pledges to each other as he gathered her in his arms and carried her from the room. They were already making love when the glow in the room began fading. Somewhere faraway a door was closed, but not locked, and the power that had been unleashed dulled to a distant hum as it waited . . .

Dear Reader,

When the idea for *The Door Ajar* first came to me, I intended having Miranda and Cara switch places via the secret room. But as I began fleshing out the book, I realized Miranda's story was too big, and to do it justice I'd have to concentrate on her, and leave Cara where and when she was. Still, the image of Cara, salty-tongued and belligerent, struggling to adapt to a society where women were regarded as merely decorative, wouldn't go away.

How would she cope with the rules and restrictions, to say nothing of being deprived of her beloved junk food and the modern conveniences she'd always taken for granted? And what of the lack of an organized police force? Cara is a police officer first and foremost. Would she be able to sit idly by while a vicious murderer cuts a bloody swath across the city? Of course not, and that's the impetus behind *Time's Tapestry*.

In *Time's Tapestry* Cara runs afoul of the room's awesome power, and is transported back to 1812, and into the arms of Miranda's former husband, Stephen Hallforth, the earl of Harrington. Stephen has already suffered greatly because of the room's magic, but he is finally getting his life under control. The last thing he needs is another time-traveller; especially one as beautiful and annoying as Cara Marsdale. Her independent ways and blunt manner of speaking horrify him, even as he finds himself helplessly drawn to her exotic beauty and proud spirit.

In the following scene Cara is determined to investigate a series of brutal murders that have been terrifying the city, and

Stephen is equally as determined to stop her. Both have been struggling to adjust to each other, but the strain is beginning to tell on them both.

I hope you've enjoyed *The Door Ajar,* and that this teaser scene will convince you to buy *Time's Tapestry,* due for release in August 1996.

Sincerely,

*Joan Overfield*

# *Time's Tapestry*

"Forbid?" Cara repeated incredulously. "You *forbid* me to go to Covent Garden?"

Too late Stephen realized the error of his ways, and hastily attempted to make amends. "Perhaps forbid is too strong a word," he said, silently cursing himself for forgetting Cara was unlike the females of his time. The chit was too stubborn by half, and he knew he would have to tread carefully, if he had any hopes of winning her cooperation now.

"What I meant to say," he added, struggling to keep his own temper in check, "is that it would be best if you kept out of this unpleasant business, and allow the proper authorities to deal with it. That is their duty, after all."

Cara remained silent for several seconds, her hands curling into fists as she resisted the urge to toss Stephen out of the nearest window. "For your information, you condescending pig, I *am* the proper authorities! And as for duty, I took an oath to serve and protect the citizens of London, and the fact I'm trapped in the past doesn't change a bloody thing! You've a damned serial killer on the prowl, and the only thing standing between him and his next victim is *me!*"

"That is precisely my point." Stephen abandoned any attempt to reason with her. "What you propose is dangerous, and I can not allow it. Whether you accept it or nay, your safety is my responsibility, and I will not have you taking foolish risks. You are not going to Covent Garden, and that is the end of it."

Cara glared at him for several seconds, words she had learned working two terms in narcotics burning on her tongue. It was sweetly tempting to say them, but she managed to control herself. Stephen's paternalistic attitude was nothing she hadn't encountered before, and she knew there was but one thing she could do. She drew a deep breath and raised her head to meet his wary gaze.

"Are you quite finished, your lordship?" she asked, her sweet tone at odds with the anger sparkling in her eyes.

"I am," he replied, his attitude clearly distrustful.

"Good," she turned and walked to the door. She pushed it open, her hand resting on the doorknob as she turned to face him.

"Lord Harrington?"

"Yes?" His tone was even more wary.

She gave him a beatific smile. "Sod off," she said, and then slammed the door closed behind her.